THE GIRL
from
LONDON

OLIVIA SPOONER

THE GIRL
from
LONDON

MOA
PRESS

MOA
P R E S S
Published in New Zealand and Australia in 2023
by Moa Press
(an imprint of Hachette Aotearoa New Zealand Limited)
Level 2, 23 O'Connell Street, Auckland, New Zealand
www.moapress.co.nz
www.hachette.co.nz

A catalogue record for this book is available from the National Library of New Zealand.

ISBN: 978 1 8697 1512 0 (paperback)

Cover design by Christa Moffitt
Cover images © Mark Owen / Trevillion Images and Kira Volkov / Shutterstock
Author photo by Samantha Donaldson Photography
Typeset in 13.5/18.2 pt Centaur MT Std by Bookhouse, Sydney
Printed and bound in Australia by McPherson's Printing Group

MIX
Paper from
responsible sources
FSC® C001695

The paper this book is printed on is certified against the Forest Stewardship Council® Standards. McPherson's Printing Group holds FSC® chain of custody certification SA-COC-005379. FSC® promotes environmentally responsible, socially beneficial and economically viable management of the world's forests.

To Grace, Sophie and George

With love xxx

I

HAZEL

It was too late to change her mind. Hazel hadn't truly believed she'd be brave enough – or was it foolish? – to go through with it, but here she was at the Auckland Airport drop-off zone, about to board a plane to London.

London, England, where instead of being midday on a warm spring Thursday, it was currently midnight on a chilly autumn Wednesday. Incredulity ballooned in Hazel's chest, and she had a sudden recollection from almost two decades ago, when she'd scattered carrots on the back lawn for Santa's reindeer and on Christmas morning had run from one half-eaten carrot to the next, exclaiming in wonder, 'They've taken a bite out of this one too, Gramps, look!'

Gramps turned the key now and the engine fell silent. He stared intently at the windscreen, and Hazel could hear the faint whistle in his chest – an insidious new frailty they both chose to ignore. 'No turning back now,' he said, eyes still fixed ahead.

His wrinkled left hand shook as he reached up to tap the top of his tartan cheesecutter — a habit so familiar to Hazel it made her heart contract. Her grandfather lived in that hat.

'Before you go, I . . . I want to give you something,' he said gruffly.

'You've already given me so much, Gramps. I don't –'

Gramps turned to look at her and she stopped mid-sentence. It wasn't often she bore the brunt of that fierce expression, which had earned him a reputation as a curmudgeon, though Hazel knew that beneath his grim demeanour was a kind and thoughtful soul.

He reached awkwardly behind him and dug about in the footwell, pulling out a small, faded green book. It was the kind of thing Hazel's eyes would have passed over and dismissed at a garage sale. As her grandfather thrust it at her, she wrinkled her nose at the musty, mildewy smell. 'Thanks, Gramps, but I've already got a book for the flight.'

'It's about me,' he told her. 'How I ended up here in New Zealand.'

'Your evacuation as a child during the war?' Hazel asked, surprised. She had long given up asking Gramps about his early childhood in Glasgow and his journey to New Zealand. He'd made it clear any talk of his life before or during the war was forbidden territory. 'It's in the past for a reason,' he would say curtly.

Hazel read the title — *Oceans Apart* — then glanced up at her grandfather.

'With you heading off to London, it feels only fitting you should' – his breathing seemed a little laboured now – 'you should know her story.'

'*Her* story? I thought you said the book was about you.'

'I never told you about Ruth, but I should have. In fact, you often remind me of her. Only it was hard . . . to mention her would have . . . she was . . .' Gramps stared at the book in Hazel's hand, suddenly seeming very far away. 'She was important to me,' he finished. He drew a breath and then erupted into a hacking cough that brought tears to his eyes. 'Damn body,' he muttered, pulling a handkerchief from his pocket.

Hazel threw her arms around his neck and rested a cheek against his old maroon cardigan. 'I'll miss you,' she said softly. 'And I promise I'll read the book on the plane.'

She felt his arms go around her and was reassured by the strength with which he hugged her back. She was even more reassured when he muttered, 'It's bound to be better than most of the trash you like to read.'

She smiled and released him. 'You don't need to get out of the car,' she said, kissing him quickly on the cheek. 'I'll call you as soon as I can.'

Tucking the book into her shoulder bag, Hazel climbed out of the car and hurried around to heave her suitcase from the boot. It took her two attempts to slam the boot of the rusty old Escort closed.

She wheeled her suitcase to his open window and leant down. 'Bye, Gramps,' she said, a lump forming in her throat. 'Don't forget to use the new inhaler every day.'

'I'll be right as rain, my girl – now go have an adventure or two.'

He started the engine, obviously eager to make a hasty exit, and Hazel smiled. She knew how much he disliked goodbyes.

Only when he'd disappeared from view did she let the smile slip from her face. She turned towards the departure terminal. 'Let's do this,' she said to herself, straightening her shoulders and striding towards the doors.

⌒

'I'm so sorry,' Hazel gasped, watching as a brown splotch bloomed on the stranger's pale blue t-shirt.

'Bugger,' he muttered, staring at the offending stain.

The past two hours had been one stressful episode after another. First, Hazel had waited over an hour to check in (she'd never stood in a queue for so long in her life), then she'd been taken aside at the security screening because she'd forgotten to take out the small pocketknife she always carried in the small zipper compartment inside her bag. Then she'd got lost trying to find her gate, and ended up running for what felt like several kilometres, only to arrive hot and flustered to discover the flight had been delayed. She'd been so desperately thirsty she'd backtracked to the nearest vending machine and had taken a couple of desperate gulps of her drink as she'd walked briskly back to the gate, worried they might have started boarding. She wasn't watching as she turned the corner, and smacked straight into the poor guy who now had a Coke stain the shape of Africa on his front.

He lifted his head, and Hazel waited for him to let rip. He was quite pale, she noticed; surely she hadn't given him that much of a shock. His hair was a shaggy mess and his stubbly beard was dark blond with flecks of ginger. In his tracksuit pants and

Nikes he could have been a student straight from Dunedin, but surely he was too old; he looked at least thirty.

'I really am sorry,' Hazel told him.

He shrugged. 'It's no bother.'

He gave her a half-smile, half-grimace, then turned and walked over to a row of plastic seats. He sat, dropping a tatty bag onto the floor by his feet. Leaning back, he shut his eyes.

The guy had a whopping great stain down his front. Wasn't he even going to attempt to rinse it out?

Hazel drank the rest of her Coke – wishing she hadn't wasted so much of it ruining a stranger's t-shirt – then dropped the can in a rubbish bin and walked over to the windows. Soon that giant plane outside would be lifting her up, up and away.

⁓

'Excuse me, ma'am.'

Hazel glanced up at the flight attendant. 'Yes?' she said nervously. She'd only been sitting for a couple of minutes. Had she done something wrong already?

'There's been a little mix-up, and I'm afraid Mrs Jenkins there' – the flight attendant dipped her head towards the elderly woman sitting next to Hazel – 'has been seated on her own. Her husband is further down the back and he wondered if you might consider switching seats so they can sit together?'

There was only one correct answer, and Hazel gave it.

'Yes, of course,' she said, smiling. She pulled her book from the pocket of the seat in front, picked up her shoulder bag and stood up.

The flight attendant led her to her new seat. It was on the aisle, at least, she noted – and then her eyes widened in dismay as she realised who she would be sitting next to. He had his head tipped back against his seat, his eyes closed yet again and a large brown stain down his front.

'Thanks,' Hazel muttered. She edged into her seat, careful not to disturb her neighbour. Unfortunately, as she lifted her shoulder bag off her lap, her book slipped out and landed directly in his crotch.

He sat up with a start.

'Hi,' said Hazel. 'Sorry again.'

He just stared at her for several long seconds, then held out her book. 'I'm assuming this is yours.'

Hazel thought she detected a hint of a smile on his face but she couldn't be sure.

'Believe it or not, that was actually an accident,' she said. 'And contrary to how it might appear, I've not been put on this earth to make your life a misery.'

'How can you be so certain?' he asked. His accent was English, she thought.

Hazel wrinkled her nose. 'I guess I can't. We'll just have to hope.'

He nodded once, then closed his eyes again, dismissing her.

What a jerk! Hazel thought. He could have introduced himself, at least.

'I'm Hazel,' she said loudly.

'Joe,' he murmured, without opening his eyes.

'Are you British?' she asked, refusing to be defeated.

'Yes.'

When he didn't offer anything more, Hazel gave up. 'That explains it,' she said, more to herself than him, as she extracted the safety card from the seat pocket and began to examine it. Was she supposed to be reassured by the picture of a person leaning forward with their hands on top of their head? How was that going to help if the plane crashed headlong into the Pacific Ocean?

'Explains what?'

Hazel looked up. The guy – Joe – was staring at her. 'Nothing.'

He studied her a little longer, his dark blue eyes unreadable, then shrugged. 'Okay.'

'You're reserved,' Hazel blurted.

'And you've bought into the stereotype. I'm British, therefore I must be repressed.'

'I said reserved, not repressed.'

'You're Kiwi, which means you think it's perfectly acceptable to be overly friendly towards anyone, even when they're trying hard to signal they want to be left alone.'

Hazel wished she could tell the flight attendant she'd changed her mind and return to her original seat. She wanted to get as far away from this asshole as possible.

He must have read something in her expression because he sat up straighter. 'I'm sorry – I meant that as a joke, but I can see you didn't take it that way.'

'You think?' Hazel hoped he could detect her sarcasm.

His smile appeared so suddenly it caught Hazel by surprise. It was as if his whole face lit up.

'Perhaps we should start again.' Joe held out his hand. 'Hi, I'm Joe, I'm a reserved Londoner, and I had no sleep last night or the night before that.'

As they shook, Hazel was pleased to note that his grip was firm but not overconfident.

'I'm Hazel, a Kiwi who has never travelled out of her home country before and who has an unfortunate habit of spilling drinks on unsuspecting strangers.'

Joe laughed. 'So I'm not your first then?'

Hazel raised her eyebrows. 'No, Joe, you're not my first.' Oh God, she'd gone and flirted with him. What was wrong with her? It was his stupid big smile that had done it. Also, she was nervous, and when she was nervous, she flirted. It was a bad habit she needed to break.

Joe shifted back in his seat. 'So, are you going through to London or stopping at LA?'

'I'm going all the way.' Oh God, why had she said that? She hadn't even registered the double entendre until too late.

'Right.' The smile was gone now, his face once again pale and strained. 'Are you going for a holiday or work?'

'It's a working holiday, I guess,' said Hazel. 'I have a job lined up.'

'Brilliant.'

Hazel shrugged. 'I hope so.'

The stilted exchange was interrupted when an immaculately made-up woman tapped Hazel on the shoulder. 'That's my seat,' she said, indicating the window.

Hazel shuffled into the aisle and Joe did the same. They waited in silence as the woman took an inordinately long time to put her expensive-looking carry-on in the overhead locker, remove her leather jacket and inch her way into her seat.

Avoiding eye contact with Joe, Hazel pretended to be interested in a comic the small boy sitting opposite was reading. She sighed with relief when Joe returned to his seat, tilted his head back and once again closed his eyes.

Hazel turned her attention to the book Gramps had pressed on her. It was strange, she thought; all these years of silence on the subject of his past, and now this. But how had there come to be a book about her grandfather's journey from Glasgow to New Zealand? she wondered. And who was this Ruth he'd mentioned?

She opened to the first page and began to read.

2

London, 1940

Propped against the pillows, Ruth was struggling to keep her eyes open as she read *The Times*; the mid-afternoon heat was making her drowsy. Still, knowing how important it was to keep up to date with the war news, she resisted the pull of sleep.

She turned the page and her eyes immediately moved to the bottom right-hand corner of page four. The headline glowed, as if printed with luminescent ink. She quickly scanned the article then sat up. 'Peter, listen to this.'

Her fiancé glanced up from his seat at the small table beside the window. He'd been polishing his recently issued boots for the last half-hour. 'Hm?'

Ruth swung her legs over the side of the bed and began to read aloud. '*The Children's Overseas Reception Board, otherwise known as CORB, are calling on volunteers to act as escorts for children being transported to the dominions as part of the overseas evacuation scheme. We ask for those with experience working with children to apply to the below address. Knowledge of the dominions would be useful though not essential.*' Ruth looked up at Peter, her eyes wide with excitement. 'Well, what do you think?'

He frowned and shook his head. 'I can't believe any parent would contemplate sending their child to the other side of the world. Or that Churchill would let them go. Hardly a great show of confidence.'

'Whatever do you mean?'

'One minute he's saying we'll stand firm against the enemy, the next he's telling us to abandon ship.'

'He's putting poor, innocent children out of harm's way,' Ruth objected. 'And what mother wouldn't want her child to be sent somewhere safe? I haven't been able to get the looks on the faces of Mrs Hamble's little ones out of my head all day. Imagine how you would have felt as a young boy, being woken in the middle of the night by screaming sirens, rushing to a shelter while clutching a gasmask and wondering if your house would still be standing in the morning or would be blown to smithereens.' Ruth's breath caught in her throat as an image leapt into her head of Brenda trapped in rubble calling for help. She forced the image away, her chest tight. 'You would have been terrified.'

Peter smiled and shook his head again. 'Dearest, you have permanent blinkers on where children are involved. Most young lads find all this thrilling. I expect I would have been the same. It's exciting, Ruth. Invigorating.'

'War is *invigorating*?' Ruth frowned at him. 'That's an awful thing to say.'

Peter shrugged. 'London is buzzing. You said so yourself. It's like we've been jolted into life.'

Ruth threw the paper onto the bed and stood up. The strap of her satin slip had fallen off her shoulder, and she yanked it back up. 'I said it was chaotic, Peter. Barbed wire going up everywhere, drilling all day and night, sandbagging, these constant ghastly air raids. It's nervous energy out there, not — not what you're implying.'

'And what would that be?'

'That somehow this is a good thing.'

Pushing back his chair abruptly, Peter took four short paces across Ruth's bedsit to the tiny kitchen tucked into one corner. He threw a wad of screwed-up newspaper stained with black shoe polish into the rubbish bin, then washed his hands in the sink.

'I'm sorry,' Ruth said. 'That wasn't fair.' She went to stand behind him, slipping her arms around his waist and resting her head between his shoulder blades. 'I simply can't bear the thought of you going. And I . . . well, I want to go somewhere too. Be useful. I don't want to stay here and simply wait.'

Peter turned and placed his wet hands lightly on Ruth's arms. She shivered at the sudden cold on her hot skin. He kissed her on the top of her thick dark curls. 'I thought you were going to stay with your aunt in the country,' he said. 'Away from danger.'

Ruth narrowed her eyes. 'I never said any such thing.'

'Your mother told me last night at dinner.'

Scowling, Ruth retrieved the newspaper from the bed and took it to the table, pressing it flat to read the article again. 'Mother believes if she wants something, it happens,' she muttered. 'That's another reason to apply. I need to get away from her meddling in my life.'

'Wait.' Peter strode over, took Ruth's elbow and turned her towards him. 'You're not seriously contemplating applying to be an escort? That's ludicrous, Ruth.'

'I'm a teacher, I've spent time in New Zealand – I'm exactly the type of person they're looking for.'

'But we're to be married. And there is so much you could be doing *here* for the war effort.'

'Such as?'

'Oh, Ruth, you could volunteer for all sorts of things. You're needed here in England, not on some boat entertaining children.'

'It's important work, Peter.'

'It's running away from the war, Ruth – and me.'

Ruth crossed her arms. 'You're the one who's disappearing off to France or some other dreadful place.'

Peter dropped his hand from Ruth's arm and stared at her till she averted her eyes. 'I'm going to fight for the freedom of our country,' he said quietly. 'I would have hoped you would be proud of me.'

Ruth looked back at him, her eyes filling with tears of frustration. 'I am. And I thought you'd be proud of me applying for this.' She jabbed a finger at the newspaper. 'Instead, you want me to go and hide away with my mother, of all people.'

'That's ridiculous. You know, you have a habit of doing this, Ruth.'

'What?'

'Rushing into things without thinking it through. I love that you're impulsive, but sometimes you need to recognise the compulsion within yourself. Take time to consider the wider picture.'

'When have I ever done something without thinking?'

'This bedsit?' Peter asked, raising his eyebrows.

Ruth put her hands on her hips. 'How was I to know it was above a butcher shop when my cousin mentioned it? Besides, I rented this for both of us. You were complaining about how little time we got alone. And we've got used to the smell, you said so yourself. Plus, it's handy having the bus stop right outside.'

'Those buses run all night long, Ruth. One day the glass is going to fall out of your window from all the rattling. And you never even thought to come and have a look first. You just said you'd take it, sight unseen. Would you honestly have taken this place if you had seen the size of it? It's smaller than my office. Anyway, this is just one example – I could come up with more.'

Ruth stormed over to her tiny wardrobe and pulled a summer frock off its hanger. She stepped into the dress, and slipped her feet into her favourite pumps. 'I trust you're quite done finding fault with your soon-to-be wife.' She took her handbag off the doorhandle and opened the door.

Peter sighed. 'Ruth, stay and let's talk this through. If you'd calm down, you would see –'

'Stop.' Ruth held up her palm. 'I can't bear to hear any more.'

'What about the German U-boats? Have you even thought of them? They're swarming all over the Atlantic right now.'

'Yes, I know.'

'They'll attack anything.'

Ruth stared at her fiancé: at his newly cropped reddish-brown hair; his shockingly pale blue eyes; the moustache above his soft, familiar lips; his broad shoulders beneath the impeccably ironed white shirt. She loved every inch of this man and had done from the moment she'd laid eyes on him two years earlier. But sometimes she found it difficult to like him. Walking up to Peter, she kissed him lightly on the cheek. Then she picked up the paper and slipped it into her handbag. 'I'm going to see Florrie,' she said, turning back to the door.

'Ruth, please, this isn't the time to go running off to your friend.'

'It's exactly the time,' she said, without turning around, 'to visit a friend who understands what you don't.'

She opened the door, stepped out, and shut it firmly behind her.

On the pavement outside, Ruth paused. The afternoon sun was attempting to melt the streets of London, and her skin prickled in the heat. She knew the right thing would be to go back upstairs. Peter was worried about her safety and he was right; she should be focusing her efforts here at home rather than sailing to the other side of the world. But there had to be a reason she'd spied the article on the exact same day she received a rare letter from her father. He'd been full of his usual enthusiasm for life in New Zealand, and surely his comment that 'you'd be safer out here' meant he wished she would visit him again. She had enjoyed her trip to New Zealand – had it really been three years ago? – and she'd been desperate for him to invite her back. Of course, her mother would have a conniption if he did. While Ruth could never condone her father's decision to abandon his wife and children – the scandal had followed her like a ghost since he'd disappeared the day after her twelfth birthday – she could understand how he'd been driven to it. The urge he'd had to change the course of his life. To escape.

'Afternoon, Ruth,' Mr Hamble yelled from his shop doorway. He wore a bloodied apron, and his black hair stuck to his forehead. The smell wafting from the open door of his shop was enough to turn Ruth's stomach. Warm air did not mix well with animal blood. 'Another rough night, eh?'

Ruth smiled. 'How are Fred and Annie?'

'Fine, fine. Bored, actually. I don't know what to do with 'em now school's finished. My brother's offered to take 'em, but I'm not packing 'em off to the countryside just yet. No point in running scared before you need to, eh? You must be pleased, though, to have a break?'

Another image of Brenda rushed into Ruth's head. This time the little girl was sitting in her usual seat in the front row of the classroom, her hair in ribbons, her face turned to Ruth as she listened. Brenda had been a quiet student. She had also been intelligent, thoughtful, sensitive and inquisitive.

A fist closed around Ruth's heart and she forced herself to smile. 'To tell the truth, I miss teaching already.'

Mr Hamble laughed and his large belly jiggled. 'I thought you'd be enjoying some quality time with Peter before he leaves.' He gave her a knowing wink.

Feeling a change of subject was in order, Ruth wiped her forehead and said, 'Looks like it's going to be another scorcher.'

'Indeed, indeed. Might as well shut up shop. The queue was round the corner this morning; I got nothin' left now but a couple of pig's heads.'

Ruth thought of her rations book stashed in the top drawer of the kitchen dresser. She should have brought it with her. Peter had been most put out having to eat his toast and marmalade without butter, while Ruth had barely noticed the difference. Sometimes she wondered if she wasn't quite British enough.

'Well, better get on.' Ruth straightened her shoulders, hoping she looked more grown-up and in control than she felt. 'Good day, Mr Hamble.'

She hurried past the greengrocer and a long row of matching white Georgian houses. She would walk through the park, she decided. The underground was bound to be stifling, and the buses were dreadfully unreliable these days.

Crossing the road, Ruth entered Regent's Park. She followed a trio of ducks as they waddled along the path in front of her, slowing her pace to enjoy the simple distraction they provided. Veering off the path, the ducks quacked towards the pond. An abandoned model boat bobbed about in the murky water. Normally the park would be teeming with excited children on a day like today, but Ruth doubted she would bump into a single child now that so many had been evacuated to safer areas. London had never felt so empty.

Passing through the rose garden, Ruth found it hard to believe her country was at war. On this perfect summer's day, as she inhaled the warm, sweetly perfumed air, young men were fighting, shooting at one another, dying. And the enemy drew nearer.

Ruth recalled crossing the Channel a year earlier with her mother on their annual trip to Paris. It had been one of their more successful trips away together. Ruth had been in a relaxed, forgiving mood, having recently become engaged, and her mother had been in a rare state of calm; she'd barely mentioned Ruth's father and the family he'd left in disgrace and ruin. Paris had been beautiful as always – London's more fashionable twin.

But now Paris had fallen into enemy hands. England was so close, she thought with a shiver; so vulnerable.

⁓

Ruth had pressed the buzzer several times and was on the verge of giving up when Florrie's blonde head suddenly appeared at the window above. 'What time do you call this?' she demanded.

'Three o'clock,' Ruth shouted back. 'You can't honestly be in bed.'

'I was up half the night and I've had a frightfully busy morning. Besides, what else is there to do in this heat? Come up.'

The door buzzed, and Ruth entered the cool foyer. The parquet floor smelt of polish, and the banister of the wide sweeping staircase gleamed. 'Your mother coming over then?' Ruth asked, entering Florrie's apartment on the first floor.

Florrie walked out of her kitchen holding a glass of water, wearing nothing but a petticoat and a brassiere. 'She's coming for tea tomorrow – I've been cleaning since I got back from the shelter early this morning.' Florrie sighed dramatically. 'Lord help me.'

Ruth and Florrie had bonded in their first year at teacher training college over their mutual sufferance of their domineering mothers. It was surprising and somewhat embarrassing how many of their conversations through the years had revolved around the topic.

'I have news,' Ruth said, pulling the newspaper from her bag. She unfolded it and pointed to the article.

Florrie gave her glass to Ruth, took the paper and scanned the page. When she finished, she raised her eyebrows. 'You're going to apply,' she stated.

'Peter doesn't want me to.'

'Of course he doesn't. But you're still going to.' Another statement.

'Yes. I think so.'

Florrie shook her head. 'No thinking about it. This is exactly what you need, Ruth. I haven't seen this much colour and life in your face since Brenda died.' Florrie held up her hand. 'I know, I know, you don't like to talk about it and you're very good at pretending you're fine, but I can read you as easily as this newspaper.'

Ruth was annoyed at Florrie for bringing up Brenda's name, but she repressed her irritation. Tipping her head to one side, she gave her friend an imploring look.

'What?' Florrie asked, suspicious.

'There's a certain someone I need your help with,' Ruth said.

Florrie's eyes widened. 'Oh no – no way.' She thrust the newspaper at Ruth and disappeared into her bedroom.

Ruth followed, watching as Florrie pulled on a pale blue blouse and black skirt. Florrie had the narrowest waist Ruth had even seen. Unfortunately – according to Florrie – this only accentuated the ampleness of her bottom and breasts.

'Please, Florrie. I can't do it without you.'

'No.' Florrie stood at her dresser and began to brush her long straight hair. 'I value my life too much.'

'Mother likes you. She'll be calmer with you there.'

'She'll be beside herself, and you know it. Ask Frank – he'll hold your hand. Or Peter. Your mother will behave for him.'

Ruth flopped onto the bed. 'Peter is likely to side with Mother; he's convinced it's just another reckless, impulsive idea.' She lay on her back and stared at the glinting chandelier above her. 'He accused me of not thinking things through. I would never criticise his character in such a way. It's . . . it's demeaning, that's what it is. And I can't ask Frank; he just enlisted and –'

Ruth jolted upright at the sound of breaking glass. Florrie was glowering at her, brandishing her hairbrush like a weapon, a bottle of perfume in pieces at her feet. 'What do you mean Frank joined up?' Two perfectly round red splotches had appeared on her cheeks.

'Oh, Florrie, what choice did he have?'

'He said he wouldn't. He said it would be better for everyone if he stayed in England and helped by doing what he did best. He's not cut out for war, Ruth. You *know* he isn't.'

Ruth looked at Florrie's shaking hand. 'He's entitled to his decision.'

'You're simply saying that so you can tell people your brother is going and they'll stop asking questions.'

'That's not true.' Ruth sprang from the bed and placed her hands on her hips. 'I hate the thought of Frank going. He never told me he planned to enlist, and if he had I would have tried to talk him out of it. But he's made his decision, Florrie, and I have to support him. We all do.'

Florrie threw her hairbrush on the bed. 'Now you sound like Peter,' she muttered. 'He talked Frank into it; I bet he did. Doing your duty and all that rubbish.'

'Florrie, listen to yourself. Peter would never do such a thing. Anyway, I thought you and Frank were over. David is the new love of your life.'

Florrie crossed her arms. Her body was tight, rigid.

'Florrie?' Ruth said softly. 'Are you okay?'

With a wail, Florrie collapsed on the bed. 'I can't get over him, Ruth. Heaven knows I've tried. But there's no-one else like him.' Tears streamed down her face. 'If he goes to fight, it will change him, Ruth. All that savagery. He's not meant for war. He's meant to invent, to research; to write boring articles about things no-one but him has a hope of understanding.'

Ruth sat on the bed and stroked Florrie's hair. 'It's going to be okay. He'll survive this. We have to have faith.'

Florrie sniffed. 'It's not about having faith. He's not strong enough, Ruthie.'

Looking towards the tall sash window, Ruth thought of her brother. How different they were from one another. Frank would never do something impulsive. He would examine all the facts, look at every angle, study the details, talk to experts. If Ruth was the thoughtless one, then Frank was the one who thought too much. His decision to enlist would have been long and considered. 'Did I ever tell you about my missing hairpin?'

Florrie raised her tear-stained face to stare at her friend. 'You seriously want to tell me a story about a hairpin?'

'Well, it's not about my hairpin as such. It's more about Frank. Surely I've told you the hairpin story. It's legendary.'

'Enlighten me.'

'When I was ten, there was this horrid boy who lived across the road. It was before my father left, when we still lived in that glamorous house in Hampstead.'

'The one with ten bedrooms and three maids.'

'That's the one. Anyway, this boy, Terence, hated me. I have no idea why; the only time I ever spoke to him was when I told him his shirt was missing a button. But he used to tease me, call me names. He constantly had me in tears. His parents had sent him out from America to live with his aunt. She was a mean old lady, always stopping my father in the street to complain about things. I was completely terrified of her.'

'I'm not grasping the connection to Frank so far.'

'Give me a chance,' Ruth said, tugging Florrie's hair gently. 'For my tenth birthday, Dad gave me a beautiful hairpin with little pearls on it. Mother thought it was far too grown up for me, but Dad insisted it was perfect. I was really proud of it, and I wore it every chance I could – anything to make my awful, unruly hair more attractive. But, one day I couldn't find the hairpin anywhere. I was distraught.'

'Don't tell me – Terence had it.'

Ruth nodded. 'Yes, he did. But this is where it gets interesting. Frank had seen Terence pick up the pin from the footpath – it must have fallen out of my hair when I was walking home – and put it in his pocket.'

'The rotter.'

'My brother confronted Terence, but he denied he had my pin, so Frank came up with another plan to get it back.'

'Did the plan have twenty-two steps and involve a manual to implement?' Florrie asked, raising her eyebrows.

They both laughed. 'Not quite,' Ruth said. 'He was only eight at the time. Anyway, he figured out the window above the conservatory at the back of the dreadful aunt's house led to Terence's bedroom, and that night he dragged a ladder out of Dad's shed, carried it across the road, climbed onto the roof of the conservatory, and placed a dead rat he'd trapped that day on Terence's windowsill. He'd designed and built some complicated trap and set it every morning down the back of our garden by the stream. Called it his Rat Exterminator.'

''Course he did,' Florrie murmured fondly.

'So, after three more nights of leaving a dead rat on the windowsill, Frank left a rock with a note under it stating that if Terence didn't give me back my hairpin, the next rat would be in his bed.'

Florrie whistled. 'Impressive.'

'But Terence must have shown his aunt the note, because when Frank carried over the ladder the following night, she was waiting for him.'

Florrie gasped. 'She wasn't!'

'Oh yes she was. She marched him into her house and up the stairs to Terence's room to apologise. Frank told me later Terence looked dreadfully embarrassed.'

'What happened then?'

'Frank pulled a rat from his pocket and demanded the hairpin.'

'He didn't.'

'He said he'd put the rat in Terence's bed unless the hairpin was returned.'

'Oh, I love him, I really do,' Florrie said, tears filling her eyes once more.

'The aunt was in complete hysterics, screaming at Frank to get the disgusting thing out of her house before she had him arrested, but Terence got out of bed, lifted up his mattress and handed Frank my hairpin. Frank walked out of the house, threw the rat in the gutter, retrieved the ladder and left the hairpin on my pillow.'

'Did he get in trouble?'

'Oh, mountains of it. He had to beg the aunt's forgiveness and do extra chores. Mother was so mortified by his behaviour she took to her bed for a week.'

'That doesn't surprise me.'

'Father thought it was hilarious. Said he was proud of Frank for taking a stand.'

Florrie was silent.

Ruth patted her cheek, then dropped to her knees to collect up the bits of broken glass. 'He's brave, Florrie,' she said. 'That's my point. And that's what counts in this war. When you're brave, you can take whatever is thrown at you and pick your-self up again.'

Florrie slid off the bed and knelt next to Ruth to help. 'I'll go with you,' she said. 'To tell your mother.'

Ruth met Florrie's eye. 'Will you talk to Frank before he goes? Maybe there's a chance . . .'

'I don't know,' Florrie said, her voice catching. 'I cheated on him, Ruth.'

'You had too many martinis, got into a fight with Frank and kissed another man. I'd hardly call it cheating.'

'It was to Frank. He's black and white, remember? Grey areas don't exist for him. I was guilty and that was the end.'

'Well, perhaps he needs to accept human beings aren't flawless. I seem to recall he wasn't above flirting with that silly secretary at his office.'

Florrie bit her lip, and Ruth's heart sank. When Florrie did that, bad news inevitably followed. 'What is it?' Ruth said. 'Tell me.'

'David asked me to marry him.'

Ruth swore silently. 'You said yes, didn't you?'

Florrie nodded, avoiding Ruth's eye. 'It seemed like a good idea. Move to the Scottish Highlands, breed sheep and children.'

'You hate the countryside!' Ruth exclaimed.

'I've never lived there before – I might love it. Plus, my mother would never dream of visiting. Far too removed from civilisation . . . and Harrods.'

'You can't marry the man to get away from your mother.'

Florrie raised her eyebrows at Ruth meaningfully.

'What?' Ruth said.

'You want to go to New Zealand. It'd be impossible to get further away from your mother if you tried.'

'That's not the reason I'm applying. Well, not the only reason, at least.' Ruth stood and walked to the window. Across the road, a group of men were filling sacks with sand and piling them against a building. They were drenched in sweat, yet they were laughing, joking with each other as they worked.

On the other side of the world, across vast stretches of ocean, lay a country beset by winter. Beautiful islands of beaches and mountains; a haven where children would be safe. Ruth had failed to save one little girl, but now she had a chance to save other children. It would never make up for the loss of Brenda, but Ruth hoped it might alleviate some of her guilt.

'I want to help children escape this terrible war,' murmured Ruth. 'I want their parents to rest easy, knowing I'll do my very best to deliver their children safely into the arms of caring New Zealanders.'

'That's quite a speech,' Florrie said.

Ruth turned to look at her. 'You think I'm being impulsive too?'

Florrie sighed. 'I think you're convinced you're missing out on something.'

'What?'

'I'm not sure, but you've been looking for it for a long time.'

'You don't think I should apply?'

'On the contrary. You should go. Carry on the search.'

'Why don't you apply too? You've done some teaching, and you've volunteered for the Salvation Army for years.'

Florrie shook her head. 'I belong in this beautiful, bruised old city.'

'What about David? Breeding in the Highlands?'

'I don't know what to do about him anymore, but I *have* made one decision.' Florrie stood straighter. 'I'm going to sign up to be an ambulance driver. It's something I've been considering for a while now. Time for me to do my bit for the war, too.'

'Your mother will forbid it.'

'Of course she will.'

Ruth smiled and threw an arm around her friend's shoulder. 'We were meant to be friends, you and I. And I guarantee you will be the most formidable ambulance driver this city has ever witnessed.'

She let Florrie go and sank into the armchair by the window. 'I'm not running away from the war, am I, Florrie?' she asked quietly.

Florrie picked up Ruth's hand and squeezed. 'Honey, you don't have to be living in your country to be fighting for it.'

3

JOE

Joe heard Hazel sigh loudly. He opened one eye, tilted his head sideways and watched her slap her boarding pass down to mark her page, slam her book closed and lean out to peer down the aisle. Accepting sleep was officially off the table, Joe lifted his head. 'Are you all right?' he asked.

Hazel glanced at him, and he was struck once more by her eyes — they seemed to change from green to hazel, depending on the light. Right now they reminded him of the moss in the alpine streams he'd been hiking past five days ago, when he'd been feeling good, happy even. Before he'd received a phone call from his wife.

'We haven't even left the ground yet,' she said.

They were in a queue of planes waiting to take off. Joe was used to queues — queuing was practically a British pastime — and it hadn't occurred to him to find this one frustrating. 'I think it's fairly standard.'

Hazel sighed again.

'So what's the job you have lined up in London?' Joe asked, wondering if she was always this on edge. Maybe if he got her talking for a bit she'd start to chill out. It seemed unlikely, based on his experience with her to date. Joe tugged at his t-shirt, his skin sticky where the Coke had dried.

'I'm a pharmacist. I'm going to work in a private hospital.'

Joe whistled. 'Impressive.'

Hazel looked bewildered; he suspected she was surprised that he was making conversation. Admittedly he hadn't been particularly nice to her so far, but he was aware that if he encouraged her early on there was the risk she'd want to talk for the next twenty-five hours.

'I'm not sure what to expect,' said Hazel. She tucked her short black hair behind her ears, revealing small, silver, butterfly-shaped earrings. 'It actually sounds unbelievable when I say it out loud. I'm the first one in my family to ever go to university, let alone overseas.'

'They must be proud.' Joe couldn't keep the edge of bitterness from his voice.

Hazel tipped her head sideways. 'I think more confused than proud.'

'How so?'

'Dad didn't really understand why I wanted to go to university in the first place, or why I applied for the job in London. My two older brothers and I were born and raised on the family farm. Farming is in our blood, apparently.'

'You're the black sheep.'

Hazel rolled her eyes.

'Sorry, bad pun.'

'Farming never interested me. Neither did working in the local pub or being a courier driver, which were Dad's other suggestions.'

Joe suppressed a smile. 'Not that there's anything wrong with those professions.'

'I'd hardly call them professions. Anyway, the only person who encouraged me to get the hell out was Gramps.'

'Your grandfather? He said that?'

'Those exact words.'

'Sounds like a top bloke.'

'He is,' she murmured, patting the book on her lap. 'He gave me this book. Told me I had to read it on the plane. Apparently it's about his experience during the war.'

Joe leant over to read the title on the cover, his arm brushing against hers. 'Let's hope it's more interesting than it looks.'

Hazel laughed, and Joe instantly wished he could make her laugh again. Realising he needed to put some more space between them, he rested back in his seat. 'What about your mum?' he asked, keeping his voice even.

'What about her?'

'How does she feel about you heading off overseas?'

'Mum and Dad divorced when I was eleven and she fairly quickly shacked up with some guy down in Christchurch, so I only see her maybe twice a year. She rang me last night to wish me luck, which was a surprise.'

Hazel's hand gripped the armrest as she spoke, and for one wild second Joe contemplated putting his hand on top of hers. 'I'm sorry.'

'Oh, it's fine. Mum hated living on the farm and she fought with Dad constantly, so it was actually a relief when she left. Anyway, one big positive of the whole mess was that I could move into town and live with Gramps, 'cause Dad got fed up with driving me back and forth from the farm to school.'

'How long did you live with him?'

'About six years. Until I finished school. I was much happier. He left me to do my own thing, but at the same time he was always there for me. I'd get home from school soaking wet from the rain and he'd have got the fire going and heated up some soup. And on Sundays we always had a roast for lunch and played cards afterwards. In the summer we went to the beach most weekends for a swim, even though it was an hour's drive away. I think he liked the company. His wife died before I was born from some kind of heart problem. To be honest, Gramps can be a bit of a grump, but that's just on the surface.' Hazel's voice cracked. 'It's going to be strange not having him around.' She glanced at Joe and grinned sheepishly. 'Sorry, I ramble when I'm nervous.'

Joe smiled and shook his head. 'It's fine. Good, actually. Stops my own thoughts doing laps in my head.'

Hazel nodded. 'I know what that's like.'

The plane began to pick up speed as it roared down the runway.

Hazel's eyes travelled past Joe to the window. Shadows whipped across her frightened face.

'What about you?' she squeaked, her wide eyes moving back to Joe. 'What do you do? Why were you in New Zealand?'

The plane lifted into the air, and Hazel sucked in her breath. Her hands pressed down onto the book in her lap as if trying to crush it.

'I help run the family pub in West Hampstead,' Joe said. 'It's been in our family for seven generations.'

'Oh.'

'I dropped out of college when I was nineteen, much to my mother's disappointment. She was sure I would become a doctor, or a lawyer . . . or a pharmacist would have been nice. Anything other than a pint-pourer like my dad.'

He waited for her to register his words. 'Oh God,' she said. 'I'm sorry.'

Joe smiled, pleased he'd managed to distract her. She no longer looked as if she was about to throw up. 'I'm just teasing you. I like working in the pub.'

Suddenly the plane jolted, dropped, and jolted again.

'Oh God,' whispered Hazel, the colour draining from her face.

'It's turbulence, Hazel. We'll be above it soon.' Joe rested his hand on the armrest, palm up. 'If you want to squeeze the life out of my hand, I promise I won't yell.'

Immediately, Hazel's clammy hand latched onto his. 'I've only been on a plane twice before, and the planes were so much smaller than this one.' Hazel sat ramrod straight and stared at the seat in front. 'I mean, look at the *size* of this thing, Joe. How on earth does it stay in the air? It's too big and . . . and *heavy*.'

'Big engines, I suppose.'

'It defies logic.'

'All sorts of things in life defy logic,' said Joe, staring at their intertwined fingers. He had been alarmed earlier when he'd thought Hazel was flirting with him, but maybe she was just being a typical Kiwi. Joe had lost count of the number of people he'd met during his time in New Zealand who had slapped him on the back, or pulled him into a hug, kissed him on the cheek, or sat on his knee — okay, that had only happened once, and the drunken girl had definitely been flirting.

Joe was surprised to realise he was glad Hazel was sitting beside him. She'd be a welcome distraction until he arrived home in London and had to face the music.

The plane levelled off, and Hazel let go of his hand. She smiled awkwardly, her cheeks red. Then, without another word, she opened her odd-looking book and resumed reading.

4

London, 1940

'You cannot be serious, Ruth. What is Peter's view?' The infamous Mrs Victoria Best — Ruth's mother — sat in her velvet chair in the parlour holding her teacup. She wore a chiffon blouse, tartan skirt and lemon yellow cardigan with pearl buttons. Her grey hair was swept into a dignified bun and her face was thick with make-up. Since her husband's departure, Mrs Best had vowed that no matter what the situation, however dire her financial affairs, no-one in Hampstead or beyond would ever accuse her of having lowered her standards. Ruth was sure the reason her mother refused to use the public shelter during air raids — instead setting up a bed in the cellar — was for fear of not presenting at one hundred per cent her best. Pun intended.

'Peter doesn't know yet, Mother. He's training at Braunton Burrows.'

'Well, then, you must contact him immediately. Tell him what you have done and let him talk some sense into you. Fancy thinking about leaving now; it's disgraceful.' Mrs Best looked down and brushed her hands along her skirt, smoothing away invisible wrinkles. 'This is simply another one of your foolish ideas, Ruth. It's the war, darling. It makes people restless. You should volunteer, find something to keep you busy till school starts up again. I expect teachers would be useful anywhere. Audrey is helping at the train station now. Imagine it! Your aunt serving tea and toast to soldiers.' Victoria Best shook her head.

The rivalry between Mrs Best and her sister Audrey had existed for as long as Ruth could remember. For years, the two had treated Christmas as an opportunity to upstage the other. A few years earlier Mrs Best had taken great pleasure in showing off her new vacuum cleaner, giving a long and noisy demonstration to Audrey and her three children. Audrey had topped this the following year, when she'd insisted on taking everyone for a ride in her new Bentley. She spoke loudly and repeatedly about obtaining her driver's licence and how easy it was to travel to Bath to visit friends. Mrs Best only rode in the car once, her lips pursed, and complained afterwards of the noise and fumes, declaring she would much rather catch a train.

Ruth placed her teacup carefully on her saucer and tried to look relaxed. 'They were impressed with my application.' She hesitated, glanced at Florrie, then looked back at her mother. 'I have an interview with the CORB office tomorrow. If selected, I need to be ready at a moment's notice.' She breathed faster, unable to hide her excitement. 'It's highly secretive.'

Mrs Best narrowed her eyes. 'You are engaged to be married, Ruth. This is not something you do.'

'But, Mother, the country has turned on its head – you said so yourself. Women are doing all sorts of things they wouldn't have dreamt of doing before the war. There isn't a male taxi driver left in London, and last week I recognised the fire warden as the mother of a boy who was in my class last year. I can tell you, she was the last person in the *world* I would have expected to volunteer for such a role.'

'They are admirable women stepping up to help our country. You cannot suggest taking children on a ship to the dominions is in any way comparable.'

'For goodness sake, escorts have been taking children to reception zones in all manner of far-flung places in Wales and Scotland. You've been very complimentary of their efforts.'

'And many of those children are returning home. Children should be with their parents at times like these. It's unnatural to send them miles away.'

Ruth felt a sharp pang at these words. But she hadn't told her mother about Brenda, and she couldn't let her see how much her words stung.

After a long silence, her mother sighed heavily. 'Let us hear no more about this, Ruth. It's hard enough to think of Frank leaving soon.'

Florrie's cup rattled against her saucer at this, drawing Mrs Best's gaze to her.

'You've been very quiet, Florrie,' Mrs Best observed. 'I suppose you are here to help soften the blow?'

Ruth had been wondering when her friend was going to jump in with a show of support.

Florrie took a sip of tea before speaking. 'I understand your reservations, Mrs Best, but I do believe Ruth would be a wonderful representative of Great Britain. Don't you agree?'

Ruth stifled a smile. Oh, Florrie was good.

'In what way?' Mrs Best asked, leaning forward.

'There is a great deal of interest in the overseas evacuation scheme. It has been written about in the newspapers in Canada, South Africa, Australia and New Zealand. I'm sure you've heard about the overwhelming number of families offering to take one, two, even three children. The dominions are eager to do all they can to help us.'

Mrs Best sniffed. '*I* wouldn't consider handing over my children to some complete stranger. It's bad enough they're being shipped into the countryside, but to the *dominions*. Heaven knows how they do things over there. They're very behind the times, you know.'

Florrie nodded. 'So I've heard, Mrs Best.' She paused. 'It would be so important for escorts to ensure their young charges upheld proper English principles.'

'Yes, absolutely crucial,' Mrs Best agreed, nodding vigorously. 'Without principles, we might as well be heathens, like those Germans.'

'Well, now, Mother, I'm not sure —'

Florrie flicked Ruth a warning look and Ruth closed her mouth.

'Of course, I would miss Ruth dreadfully,' said Florrie. 'But everyone must do their duty.' Ruth had never seen her friend with such a serious look on her face. Florrie should have been an actress.

'It would be dangerous,' Mrs Best objected. 'There's news of ships being sunk, you know.'

'Yes, it's dreadful,' said Florrie. 'Though reassuring to know the children will be accompanied by a naval convoy until they reach safer waters.'

'Is that so?'

Ruth leapt off her chair and knelt at her mother's feet, gripping her soft, wrinkled hands. 'Oh, Mother, please let me do this. I'll be back in a few months – six at the most.'

Mrs Best regarded Ruth for several seconds, her eyebrows arched in thought. 'Perhaps the war will be over by then,' she murmured.

'Let us hope,' Ruth whispered, though she had grave doubts.

'Fancy *both* my children leaving me to deal with the Hun on my own.' There was a wobble in Mrs Best's voice. Tears welled in Ruth's eyes and she tried to blink them away. How could she even contemplate leaving her mother at a time like this?

'You won't be alone, Mrs Best.' Florrie stood. 'I will be here. Besides, I understand you plan to move out of London.'

Mrs Best's face softened when she noticed her daughter's tears, and she reached out to gently pat Ruth's cheek. 'None of that now, Ruth. Florrie's right. We must all do our duty. If mine is to put up with my sister's hospitality for the remainder of this blasted war, then that is the burden I will bear.'

'I haven't been accepted yet, Mother.'

'Yes, well, they'd be fools not to take you.' Mrs Best sat back and briskly smoothed her skirt again, pushing Ruth's hands off her lap in the process. As she resumed her seat, Ruth caught Florrie's wink.

'I imagine Aunt Audrey will be pleased if you go alone,' said Ruth, wiping her eyes. 'With food rations becoming scarcer, it's getting harder and harder to feed everyone.'

Mrs Best gave a loud harrumph. 'That sister of mine has been hoarding food in her cellar for months. It's all she talks about. Makes my humble stockpile look meagre.'

'Perhaps I can send you some things from New Zealand. I believe they have hardly any rationing at all. Aunt Audrey would be –'

Mrs Best's voice rose. 'You're going to New Zealand?'

Ruth winced at her own thoughtlessness. 'I don't know where I'll be sent if I'm accepted,' she said hastily. 'But New Zealand would be the most likely place because I've been there before. I can prepare the children for what to expect. But there's no guarantee. I might go to Australia, South Africa, maybe Canada.'

'Your father put you up to this,' Mrs Best hissed.

Ruth felt the hairs rise on the back of her neck. 'He knows nothing about it, Mother. *I* saw the advertisement in *The Times*. This is all my idea.'

'You would do this to me. After everything I have done for you.' Mrs Best rose to her feet, and Ruth quickly stood too. They glowered at one another.

'I'm not doing this to hurt you, Mother.'

Mrs Best strode to the window overlooking the garden. With her back to Ruth, she said in a low voice, 'Promise me you will come back. If you stay there with your . . . if you stay, I will never forgive you.'

Ruth blinked back tears once again. She was a terrible daughter. 'I'll come back, Mother. I promise.'

Mrs Best's shoulders sagged. 'That's that then,' she said. 'My son is leaving for the front line any day, my daughter is planning to sail across dangerous waters, and my country is under attack.' Her eyes were glistening. 'Everything in the world is wrong, Ruthie. Not a thing is right or just, anywhere.'

'Oh, Mother.' Ruth stepped forward and hugged her mother tightly, something she hadn't attempted to do in years. 'I'm sorry,' she murmured, breathing in her mother's familiar lily-of-the-valley scent. 'I'm sorry for everything.'

Her mother returned the hug hesitantly.

'Well, now I've seen everything,' said a deep voice from the doorway.

Ruth and Mrs Best released each other and turned.

'Frank! I didn't know you were home.' Ruth hurried over to hug her brother.

'Arrived just this minute. Mother is kindly taking me in until I head to France in a couple of weeks.'

Frank smelt of cigarettes and had the shadow of a moustache on his upper lip which Ruth resisted the urge to poke fun at.

'What happened to your flat?' she asked.

'I gave it up. No point in paying rent when I'll hardly be there.' He looked across the room. 'Hello, Florrie,' he said, his expression neutral.

'Hello, Frank,' croaked Florrie, her face so ashen Ruth worried she might pass out.

Ruth felt awful. If she'd known Frank was going to be here, she would have forewarned her friend.

'Well,' said Ruth. 'I was telling Mother my news and now you can hear it too.'

Frank glanced at his mother and back to Ruth, his face a picture of consternation. 'Oh, Ruth, you're not bringing the wedding forward, are you? All the girls in Britain seem to think they must get married before their fiancés leave.'

Ruth laughed. 'No, Frank. We plan to marry when this blasted war is over and not before.'

Mrs Best sniffed loudly. 'Well, I believe girls *should* have the security of marriage before their men abandon them. Plus, you would be entitled to allowances.'

Both Ruth and Frank knew better than to argue.

'Well,' said Frank, 'if an early wedding isn't on the cards, I must confess I have an inkling of your news already.'

'You have?' Ruth frowned at her brother's teasing smile.

Frank nodded. 'When I spoke to Florrie last week, she may have let slip about your application to be an escort on one of those ships heading to the dominions. I'm assuming you were successful.'

Ruth's eyes widened. Florrie hadn't mentioned that she and Frank had been in touch. Ruth immediately wondered what else they had spoken about. 'I have an interview tomorrow,' she said. 'I haven't been accepted yet.'

'I'll be honest,' Frank said. 'I don't fully agree with this notion of sending children overseas. And I understand Churchill has his misgivings, as it creates an unpleasant air of defeatism. I saw those queues of parents at the CORB office last week – they stretched for miles – and I have a friend working there who says they've had to take on more than six hundred staff in order to deal with all the applications.'

'Parents are scared for their children,' said Ruth. 'Can you really blame them for wanting to try to keep them safe?'

'It must be a very difficult decision – one I'm relieved I don't have to make.'

'So you don't think I should have applied?' said Ruth.

'I think it's brave of you to volunteer, and I know how much you love an adventure.'

'That's not why –'

Frank held up his hand. 'I know that's not the main reason, but it can't be denied that only the more adventurous types would contemplate going. I will say they would be lucky to have you, the children especially.'

'Thank you.'

Frank crossed the room, bending down to kiss his mother on the cheek. Then he sat in the chair Ruth had recently vacated, leant back and folded his arms, crossing his legs at the ankles. 'Well, I have some interesting news of my own.' Rather than look at Ruth or Mrs Best, he stared at Florrie, who had moved to stand by the window. They looked at each other without speaking for several moments, and Ruth had a strange sensation of vertigo.

'You've decided not to go,' Mother said in a quavering voice.

'No . . .' Frank faltered, his voice cracking. 'That decision won't change.'

'What then?' Ruth asked, her pulse racing.

Frank looked from their mother to Ruth. 'I've decided to get married.'

Ruth froze.

'It seems I'm one of those lads who wants to get things sorted before I leave. Of course, I haven't asked the young lady to marry me yet, so I might be getting ahead of myself. But I think the war serves to focus the mind . . . and the heart . . . on what's important.'

Ruth struggled to find her voice. 'But . . . but you can't. You can't marry someone we've never met.'

Florrie fell backwards against the window frame with a thud.

'Frank!' Ruth shouted. 'You can't do this to Florrie.'

Frank stood, his face red. 'It's her I mean to ask, silly,' he said softly.

Florrie crumpled onto her knees, and Frank strode over to pull her to her feet. She placed a hand over his mouth. 'Don't,' she whispered.

He pulled her hand away. 'Florrie, I'm sorry, I needed a little time to think, you know how I am, but –'

Florrie's hand clamped over his mouth again. 'I refuse to accept your proposal in front of your *mother*, Frank. At least have the decency to take me to another room.'

A tiny squeal escaped from Ruth's lips as she hurried over to throw her arms around her brother and best friend. 'I can't believe it!'

'I haven't asked her yet,' Frank said gruffly.

Ruth glanced over his shoulder. 'Mother, are you okay?'

Tears were flowing freely down her mother's face. 'Ask her now, Frank,' Mrs Best choked out. 'Take her into the garden and ask her right this minute.'

Frank glanced at Ruth and raised his eyebrows. 'Very well, Mother, if you insist.'

Florrie smiled tremulously as he took her hand and led her from the room.

Pulling a handkerchief from her pocket, Ruth handed it to her mother and sat down heavily in the chair next to her. They were silent, but for the odd sniff from Mother as they listened to the faint low rumble of Frank's voice.

'I thought their romance had ended,' Mrs Best said.

'So did I.'

Minutes later, Frank and Florrie re-entered the room, holding hands and beaming.

'Florrie has agreed to marry me,' Frank said, 'on one condition.'

'What's that?' Ruth asked.

'That when the war is over, we have a glorious wedding with all the trimmings.'

Ruth laughed. 'That would be right.'

Mrs Best cleared her throat loudly. Frank approached and, taking her outstretched hand, helped her to her feet. 'Mother, I apologise for springing this on you.'

'Nonsense, my boy.' Mrs Best tossed her head and patted Frank awkwardly on the arm. 'You know I think very highly of that girl.' She glanced at Florrie. 'Lord knows, I've seen enough of you over the years.'

Florrie stepped forward and gave Mrs Best an awkward hug. 'I'll take good care of him, Mrs Best.'

Ruth jumped as an air-raid siren began its familiar wail. 'Drat,' she said loudly.

'Right, everyone down to the cellar,' Mrs Best ordered. 'We can toast your good health and fortune down there.'

'We can?' Frank asked.

'I put aside a bottle of champagne the day this dreadful war started,' Mother said over her shoulder as she led them towards the cellar stairs. 'I was saving it till victory, but we will open it now instead.'

Ruth stared at her brother, stunned.

'The wonders of war,' he said, smiling broadly at his sister before gently kissing his fiancée's hand.

'Wonders indeed,' Ruth said, following them from the room.

⁓

Lying on her bed a few weeks later, Ruth tried to ignore the fact her bedsit felt like a furnace. She couldn't possibly open her window to let in cooler air as the smell wafting up from the butcher below was so abhorrent. If Peter were beside her he'd be chuckling, telling her, 'I told you so,' and reminding her once again how impulsive she could be.

Was volunteering to transport children to the other side of the world simply another impulsive act? One she might live to regret as much as she currently regretted renting this small, stuffy room? Neither Ruth nor Peter had mentioned the article in the paper again before he'd left for training, though Ruth suspected Peter knew she hadn't dismissed the idea. Now she would have to tell him that she'd received the official letter of acceptance from CORB. But what if he demanded she stay? What would she do then? Would she really be willing to defy him?

She'd just have to break the news gently, she decided. First she'd tell him about Florrie and Frank's engagement, then . . . then she would tell him that she'd applied to CORB and been accepted. She'd tell him she'd given it a great deal of thought and it was important to her. She'd say his support meant everything to her, but she was going regardless.

Sighing loudly, Ruth rolled onto her side. What was she thinking, leaving England? Leaving her family, her friends, her fiancé? It was a ridiculous notion, and yet every time she thought about boarding a ship and heading across the sea with those poor, scared children, her heart would thump and she'd be over-whelmed with the complete and utter conviction that this was the one thing she was called to do. Ruth hoped CORB would be in touch soon with a departure date. The longer she stayed, the harder it would be to leave.

⌒

A telegram finally arrived from the CORB office one week later. The following day, Ruth was to take the morning train to Liverpool, where she would be met by CORB personnel. Further information would be given on arrival.

'You don't even know where you're going?' Florrie exclaimed. She had stopped by Ruth's bedsit on the way home from her night shift and was still in her ambulance uniform. She smelt strongly of antiseptic and petrol fumes.

'I'm sure it will be New Zealand.'

Florrie pushed open the window, lit a cigarette, inhaled deeply and closed her eyes. 'What a night,' she said, blowing smoke outside. 'Just as well you're going now, Ruthie – though I shall miss you terribly.'

Ruth sat heavily on her bed. 'All of a sudden I'm not sure.'

'About what?'

'About going. What am I doing leaving London at a time like this?'

'Oh, Ruth, it's too late to have doubts now. You'll be fine once you're on the boat. It's the leaving that's hard.' From the stricken look on Florrie's face, Ruth knew she was thinking of Frank. They'd heard nothing from him since he'd left for France, and Florrie refused to listen to the radio or read the paper, insisting it was easier not to know.

'I hate leaving you and Mother,' said Ruth. 'I sent a telegram to Peter this morning, but I could be gone before he reads it. I'm sure he believes I'll change my mind and stay. He said as much when I spoke to him last week.' The conversation had been strained, but after a prolonged silence Peter had finally said that, while he was disappointed, if it meant so much to her he'd support her decision.

Florrie studied Ruth for a moment. 'You have to do what's right for you, honey. It's the only way to stay sane in all this madness.'

'I'll regret it if I don't go,' Ruth said quietly.

'Well, there's your answer.' Florrie stubbed out her cigarette. 'I'm going to head home for a bath and a rest. I'll be back this afternoon to help you pack.'

Florrie walked over to Ruth and laid her hand on Ruth's head. 'Just make sure you come back, okay?'

Ruth nodded. 'And you be sure to stay safe,' she whispered.

Florrie sighed. 'I'll do my best. Just like everyone else.'

5

HAZEL

'Where do you plan to stay in London?' Joe asked.

Hazel finished chewing her mouthful of chicken and pumpkin. She couldn't decide if she liked her meal or not. 'I'm staying with a friend until I can find a room to rent.'

Joe nudged his leftover food around on his tray with his fork. 'Where does the friend live?'

There was an unpleasant aftertaste in Hazel's mouth and she put down her flimsy plastic knife and fork. 'Camden,' she said, wiping her mouth. 'Is it just me, or does this chicken taste like something that isn't chicken?'

Joe laughed. 'I was thinking the same thing. The only reason I'm eating it is because I'm worried I'll get hungry later.'

Hazel watched Joe take a gulp of his beer as she sipped on her water. 'I'm regretting my decision to pass on a beer,' she said.

'It's not too late.'

'I'd be embarrassed to ask.'

'Why?'

'I should have got one before.'

Miraculously, a flight attendant paused at their row moments later. 'Yes, ma'am?' she said to the woman seated on Joe's other side.

Glancing up, Hazel noticed the call light above the woman's head was on.

'Another glass of champagne, please,' the woman said briskly. 'And you can take my tray away.' She gestured to her untouched meal. 'It was inedible.'

Seeming unfazed, the flight attendant took the tray. 'I'm sorry you didn't enjoy your meal. Would you like a packet of crisps?'

The woman looked at Joe, then Hazel. 'Would we?' she asked.

'Uh, sure,' stammered Joe.

'That would be great,' Hazel said quickly.

The woman continued to gaze at Hazel and lifted her eyebrows as if to say, 'And . . .'

'And could I please trouble you for a beer?' blurted Hazel.

The attendant smiled. 'Of course. I'll be right back.'

The woman by the window winked at Hazel. 'Well done,' she said. Then she put her giant headphones back on, the gold bracelets on her arm chinking, and pressed a button on her screen to restart her movie.

Catching Joe's eye, Hazel grinned. 'Lawyer?' she mouthed.

'Probably,' Joe mouthed back.

Picking up her bread roll, Hazel started to nibble the edge.

'I hope Camden is close to where you'll be working,' said Joe. 'Commuting can be a nightmare.'

Hazel was surprised at the change in him. When they first met he seemed determined to have nothing to do with her. Now he was positively chatty.

'The hospital is in Marylebone, near Baker Street. It doesn't look too far on the map, but I'll need to figure out a bus or the tube or something.'

'Marylebone, eh? Fancy.'

'Is it?'

'Oh yeah.'

Hazel frowned. 'I'm not too comfortable with fancy.'

'A good thing in my book. Speaking of books . . .' Joe nodded towards Hazel's book, tucked in the seat pocket in front of her. 'How's it going?'

'Interesting.'

'That bad, huh?'

'No! Just different from the kind of thing I usually read. Plus I haven't worked out where Gramps comes into it yet.' Hazel remembered Joe talking about the pub that had been in his family for generations. 'Was your family affected by the bombings in London during the war?'

Joe nodded. 'The pub managed to escape damage but my grandparents' house was destroyed.'

'Were they all right?'

'Yes, luckily they were in a shelter at the time.'

'I can't even imagine what it must be like to suddenly lose your home.' Truth was, she didn't know what it was like to have a home to lose in the first place. She'd never felt like she belonged on the farm, and while living with Gramps had come close, it had never felt like a permanent arrangement. For the past few years she'd moved from one flat to another, sharing with a motley assortment of people, some good, some awful.

'You right?' Joe asked, his cobalt eyes searching her face.

'Fine.' Hazel needed to change the subject. 'So far the book's about a young woman who's volunteered to take children overseas as part of an evacuation scheme. She's about my age. A teacher.'

'Why'd she do it?'

'For the adventure, as far as I can tell. Plus I think she was having cold feet about marrying her fiancé and wanted a break from her disapproving mother.'

'Sounds like you could relate.'

'How so?'

Joe held up one finger. 'First, you're off on your own adventure.'

'Hardly the same!'

He held up another finger. 'Second, your family don't approve.'

'They don't understand — I never said they didn't approve.'

Joe waved a third finger and raised his eyebrows. 'Any broken-hearted man you've left behind?'

Hazel looked away quickly.

'There is!' said Joe. 'Tell.'

Hazel stared fixedly at the black screen on the back of the seat in front of her. 'He's not broken-hearted and we are definitely not engaged.'

'But there's someone, right?'

She shrugged. 'Matt's been my boyfriend for about two years.'

'What's the plan? He going to join you in London?'

'There's no plan.'

'You must have talked about it?'

'Not really.' Hazel paused. 'I told him I was going and he just accepted it like that.' Hazel clicked her fingers.

'You didn't ask him to go with you?'

'No.'

'So it's a clean break.'

'I said I'd call him after I landed.'

Matt hadn't been bursting with enthusiasm when she'd announced she was going overseas, but he hadn't been upset either. Not that he was the kind of guy to get emotional over anything, except maybe the Mustang he was restoring in his mate's garage.

Hazel frowned at her tray. If they'd only clear it away, she could get up and walk down the aisle for a bit. 'How long have we been flying?' she asked, glancing in Joe's direction but not quite meeting his eye. 'I feel like I've been stuck on this plane forever.'

'I'd say we've been in the air for less than two hours.'

'Great.'

'I get the impression you don't like to sit still for very long.'

'It feels really claustrophobic.'

The flight attendant returned with their drinks. The woman by the window barely glanced up from her movie as she took her glass of champagne; Hazel immediately took three long gulps of her beer. To her relief, the attendant also cleared away her and Joe's trays.

Joe smiled. 'Better?'

'Much.'

Hazel envied Joe. He seemed quite content sitting in his cramped seat, drinking his beer and watching a Jason Bourne movie – a movie he'd confessed to having seen twice already. It was as if he wasn't in any rush to get to London at all.

'What were you doing in New Zealand?' she asked, deciding it was time for her to ask *him* some questions for a change. 'Holiday?'

'Something like that.'

'Well, since I'm not going anywhere for many tedious hours, maybe you could elaborate?'

Joe shifted his legs around. 'I'm not used to being the one doing the talking. Working in a pub, it's always punters wanting to tell me their life story, not the other way around.'

Hazel held up her hands. 'No offence – I'm sure your life story is absolutely fascinating – but how about you just stick to what you've been up to for the past few weeks?'

Joe hesitated. 'I guess you could say I was running away.'

'Excellent!' Hazel leant forward. 'Now I'm intrigued.'

Joe opened his mouth to speak then closed it again. 'Actually, I don't mean to be rude, but would you mind if I didn't talk about it?'

Hazel felt her cheeks grow hot. What was with this guy? He was quite happy to ask her a whole lot of personal questions but the second she asked him anything, he went all aloof and British. 'Sure. Whatever. I didn't mean to pry.'

'No, you weren't.' Joe touched Hazel's arm. 'Please, I'm enjoying talking to you, I just . . .' He paused as if unsure of what to say.

'It's fine, Joe. Really.' Hazel snatched up her book and opened it to the bookmarked page.

From the corner of her eye she saw Joe restart his movie, but when she flicked a glance at his face, he was staring out of the window.

6

Liverpool, 1940

The train was packed with servicemen. Several of them stared at Ruth for longer than she considered polite, and she kept her gaze fixed on the passing landscape outside her window. She had no idea how far they had travelled – all the signs with place names having been removed – and the journey had taken far longer than expected.

When they finally neared the station in Liverpool, she stared in horror at the battered city. While the radio and papers had mentioned a recent spate of heavy bombing in the north, Ruth was still shocked by the damage the enemy had inflicted. Walls had been torn off buildings, revealing a tableaux of lives inter-rupted: dining tables, fallen chairs, broken picture frames and beds dangling precariously from upper floors. Mounds of bricks lay at the foot of many buildings, and Ruth shuddered to think of what or who may have been crushed beneath.

'You'll be looking forward to escaping all this, eh, lovey?' An older man sitting opposite nodded at Ruth's armband. He'd watched her pull the strip of cloth printed with CORB from her suitcase moments earlier. She'd felt self-conscious – guilty, even – as she'd quietly slipped it on.

'It's only for a few months,' she said, her cheeks hot.

'Oh, it's a grand thing you're doing, miss,' said a boy with a broad Welsh accent. He was standing in the aisle, his uniform starched and spotless. He couldn't possibly be eighteen, Ruth thought, staring at his rounded cheeks. 'My brother and sister are hoping to get on a boat. I'd be right thrilled if they could get away from all this.'

'Thank you.'

'Taking responsibility for the crown jewels,' said the older man. 'That's what they say, you know.'

The middle-aged man in a suit sitting next to Ruth snorted. 'Harebrained idea, if you ask me,' he stated.

'Well no-one did,' retorted the older man. He gave Ruth a wink and she returned her attention to the scene out the window. Her armband felt tight and uncomfortable. She wished she could take it off, turn the train around and return home.

The train lurched to a stop.

'Ladies first,' said the Welsh boy, helping to lift her suitcase down from the overhead rack.

Ruth had hoped she could wait for everyone else to get off and then follow. 'Oh, thank you, that's very kind.' She squeezed past the other men in the carriage, conscious of her hot face, and stepped down to the platform.

There were men in uniform everywhere. Naval men mostly, but plenty of army and Home Guard too. Some looked serious, but most were gathered in groups talking, smoking, laughing and showing little concern for where they were going or what they were about to face.

Looking around, Ruth spied an older woman with a clipboard and the distinctive CORB armband. She hurried towards her.

'Hello, I'm Ruth Best. I'm to be an escort. A CORB escort.'

The woman's eyes were pale blue and appeared unusually small behind her glasses. 'Well, I can see that very well myself, can't I?' she said, gesturing at Ruth's own armband. She scanned the list on her clipboard. 'Best, Ruth. There you are. From London, are we?' She looked Ruth up and down. 'Thought as much.'

Ruth gripped the handle of her suitcase with both hands. She hadn't a clue what to say to that.

'I'm Mrs Shearing. Stand there while I gather up the rest.' The woman pointed towards the wall behind her.

'Yes, ma'am.' Ruth did as she was told and watched as Mrs Shearing ticked off the names of two more women who arrived together. They looked a similar age to Ruth and appeared more interested in staring at the men nearby than listening to anything the matronly CORB coordinator had to say.

Soon the girls came to stand with Ruth.

'Hello there, I'm Betty, and this is Una,' said one. 'We're from Hammersmith. You from London too?'

'Yes, I'm Ruth, a teacher in North London.'

'We're both nurses. It's quite an adventure we've signed up for, in't?'

Betty and Una giggled and glanced around.

'Right then.' Mrs Shearing approached, a grey-haired clergyman wearing a CORB armband by her side. 'That's everyone. Girls, this is Reverend Kelly from Oxfordshire.'

The three young women repeated their names to the clergyman then followed Mrs Shearing out of the station and into a waiting car.

The trip was slow and bumpy, with a number of detours due to closed roads. During the drive, Mrs Shearing explained how CORB had commandeered a school at which the evacuating children and their escorts would stay until their departure. They would likely be boarding their ship in a couple of days, however the information would be given only at the last minute for security reasons. Ruth wasn't sure if it was the erratic driving or nerves making her stomach lurch.

By the time they arrived it was late afternoon, and Ruth was surprised at how deserted and empty the school appeared. There wasn't a soul in sight. The dark grey building appeared stark and ominous. Ruth thought of how the children would feel seeing it for the first time and wished someone had tried to find a way to make the place look brighter.

As if sensing her doubts, Mrs Shearing smiled for the first time, transforming her face from unpleasant to kindly. 'Enjoy this moment. The children arrive first thing in the morning, and there'll be no peace then.'

She showed Ruth and the two nurses to a classroom with a set of bunk beds. Most of the beds had already been claimed, suitcases and coats laid on top.

'Find a spare bed then head down to the hall. Everyone else is there already. Facilities are at the end of the corridor.'

The girls each chose a bed, freshened up and then, after a number of wrong turns, found their way to the school hall. Waiting at the doorway to greet them stood a serious, soft-spoken man who introduced himself as the chief escort, Mr Callihan. He ushered them inside the hall where around forty people, wearing the obligatory armbands, stood chatting. They seemed so relaxed, Ruth thought, as they each stepped forward to introduce themselves. Ruth shook their hands and hoped they didn't notice how much her own hands were shaking.

Then Mrs Shearing called for their attention and gestured to a sombre-faced, suited gentleman at her side.

'Welcome,' said the man, his voice echoing loudly. 'My name is Mr Hungerford and I am a member of the Children's Overseas Reception Board Advisory Council. I first must take a moment to thank you for your service to our country. This is a most worthy cause and you should take great pride in being a part of it. I trust you will take care of our precious children and deliver them to their destination safe and well. Now, let's get down to business, shall we?'

Ruth clasped her clammy hands together and tried to focus as Mr Hungerford spoke about air-raid shelters, mealtimes and procedures for settling in the children, but she was distracted by a small voice in her head saying, *This is it, I'm really doing this. Am I really doing this? What am I doing?*

Betty, standing by Ruth's side, whispered 'All right, love?' She pressed her shoulder against Ruth's while keeping her eyes on Mr Hungerford.

'I'm not sure,' Ruth whispered back, also fixing her gaze ahead. 'It seemed like a jolly good idea at the time.'

Betty snorted and several people glanced their way. 'We're in for the time of our lives, Ruth,' Betty murmured. 'Make no mistake.'

Ruth felt comforted by the other woman's kind, conspiratorial tone and hoped this marked the start of a friendship. Ruth needed a friend right now. Thinking of Florrie, her legs felt so weak she was worried she might collapse to the floor. Pushing thoughts of her best friend away, she pressed her fingernails into her palms and concentrated on the rise and fall of Mr Hungerford's thick grey moustache. It would be fine, she told herself. *She* would be fine. This was what she had wanted, wasn't it?

⁓

The evening and night continued in a fog. Unable to fall asleep in her bunk bed with all the strange noises and smells around her, Ruth was almost relieved when the air-raid siren sounded a little after midnight. Silently the escorts made their way to the brick shelter, and once they'd settled onto the narrow bench seats, they began to talk. There were a few teachers like Ruth, more nurses, a couple of doctors, a chaplain and several members of the Salvation Army. People had come from all over Great Britain, judging by the array of accents, and Ruth was conscious of her plummy London accent and fashionable brown coat. She observed how friendly and open these complete strangers were with one another – quick to laugh and joke together, despite the fact they were sitting in a gloomy bunker in nightshirts and coats, planes passing overhead and the sound of explosions filling the air. Or perhaps it was because of the war that the usual British reserve had disappeared.

When the all clear sounded at four o'clock and they returned to their bunks, Ruth managed to fall into a deep – if brief – sleep. By eight o'clock she had showered and breakfasted, and was standing before Mrs Shearing in a small office being handed a sheet of paper with a list of names. Ruth was to be responsible for fifteen boys, all from the same area of Glasgow. 'We have selected children whose parents would otherwise not have been able to afford to send their children overseas,' the coordinator informed her. 'They are, I expect, much poorer than the children you have taught. They will come with their own unique problems, but the most significant one will be homesickness. This is not something we have a treatment for; we must simply do our best to take their minds off what they have left behind, and focus on the exciting adventure that lies ahead.'

'I see,' Ruth said, trying to hide her unease. She had assumed she would be asked to care for girls. Boys would require a different mindset entirely.

'While I am not at liberty to give you the name of the ship you will be sailing on, I can tell you that your destination is Sydney, Australia.'

Ruth looked at her in surprise. 'Australia? But, well, I haven't been there. I thought . . . well, I *have* been to New Zealand.'

'I understand. However, Australia is where you will be going, Miss Best. There are many similarities between the two countries, no doubt.'

Ruth nodded. She knew if she opened her mouth again, it would be to let out a sob.

Mrs Shearing rose to her feet. 'Thank you, Miss Best, for taking on this important role. I trust you will keep a close eye on your charges.'

Forcing a polite smile, Ruth joined the other escorts waiting in the schoolyard. Australia. She knew nothing about the country. She knew no-one there. Her heart beat faster and louder as a bus pulled up by the school gate.

'Here we go,' Reverend Kelly murmured, coming to stand beside Ruth.

She felt nauseous. Any moment, she was going to be sick.

The Reverend took her hand in his and she glanced at him in shock. He smiled gently, and his twinkling eyes and wrinkled face reminded Ruth briefly of her father.

'If you want to squeeze the life out of my hand, I promise I won't yell,' he said in a low voice.

Ruth took a deep breath, straightened her back and, as the children began to file off the bus, she took up his offer and squeezed.

7

JOE

Hazel sucked in her breath so sharply Joe could hear it through his earplugs. He pulled them out, opened his eyes and turned towards her. He was sick of trying to sleep anyway.

'You right?' he whispered.

The plane was dark and silent, but for the monotonous hum of engines. Beyond the circle of light cast by the small bulb above Hazel's head, everything was in shadow.

Hazel lifted her eyes from the page. 'It's nothing. I got a surprise, that's all.'

'Did something exciting happen?'

'Not exactly.' Her voice was quiet. 'More like déjà vu.'

'Look I'm sorry about earlier,' he whispered.

'That's okay.' She was looking forward rather than at him, her face impassive.

'The thing is, I was really enjoying chatting with you and I'm sorry if I spoilt it.'

'If there's stuff you don't want to discuss, I get it,' she said.

'Thanks.' He was acting like an idiot. It was no big deal. Why hadn't he simply told her why he'd ended up in New Zealand? It wasn't because they'd only just met and he was reluctant to discuss his personal issues with an almost stranger, he realised; it was because he could be a different person in her eyes. A better person. That was the main reason he didn't tell her — but not the only one.

'I can't sleep,' Joe whispered. 'Wanna fill me in?' He dipped his head at the book.

Hazel shook her head as if she was about to tell him to piss off, but then she seemed to change her mind and dropped her head back on the headrest, turning it so her face was near his. 'Did you know parents sent their kids overseas during World War II?'

Joe wished she wasn't so close. He only needed to lean forward a few inches and his lips would touch hers. 'I learnt a bit about it in school,' he murmured, avoiding her eyes and lips and focusing on her chin. 'The big displacement experiment.'

'Sorry?'

She smelt like a lime milkshake. Joe shifted his head back a fraction. What was wrong with him? 'Lots of kids never returned,' he croaked. 'Or if they did, they couldn't settle. Their parents were like strangers to them. Or they were strangers to their parents more like.'

Hazel seemed to be oblivious to Joe's discomfort at their closeness. 'Were they gone a long time?' she asked.

'The duration. Up to six years, some of them.'

'God, that's awful. How could the parents send their children away like that? To the other side of the *world*.'

'It must have been hard. I guess they wanted their kids to be safe. Also, no-one could have known at the time how long the war would go on for.'

'I guess.' Hazel's eyes dropped to Joe's lips, then she abruptly reached above her head to turn the light off. 'I'm going to try to get some sleep,' she said, rolling to the other side, pulling up her knees and curling into a ball.

Joe watched the gentle rise and fall of Hazel's back and thought of when the plane had taken off and he'd offered her his hand to squeeze because she'd looked so terrified. It was ridiculous, but his hand had felt strange ever since. He kept having to flex it to stop the tingling. Maybe she'd squeezed so hard she'd bruised a bone or damaged a tendon or something. A thin line of skin was showing between Hazel's t-shirt and her jeans. Joe wanted to reach across and gently tug her t-shirt down to cover it up, but he didn't.

8

Leaving Liverpool, 1940

'There he is.' Mr Vernon pointed to a scrawny boy holding a little girl's hand. They wore satchels on their backs and held gasmasks in their free hands. The girl was crying silently, her red face screwed up tight. As Ruth approached, the girl let go of the boy's hand, rubbed her runny nose, then gripped the boy's hand again. He grimaced and tried to pull his soiled hand free.

'Stop your snivelling, will you, Rosie?' Ruth heard the boy mutter. 'It ain't no good. We're here now. We ain't going back.'

'Fergus, my boy.' Mr Vernon clamped a hand on the boy's shoulder. 'This is your escort, Miss Best.'

Fergus gave Ruth a fleeting glance then stared defiantly into the distance. He wore a coat at least two sizes too big and so threadbare around the shoulders and buttonholes she could see his shirt underneath. There was a large brown stain near the coat's bottom hem. If it weren't for the stiff new brown woollen flat cap on his head, Ruth would have taken Fergus for an orphaned street urchin.

She bent to lift up the CORB disc hanging from a shoelace around his neck. 'Fergus McKenzie,' she read. 'It's lovely to meet you.'

He continued to look past her.

The tag fell from her fingers and landed back on his chest. She crouched before him, blocking his view, and he lowered his gaze to her shoes.

'Fergus, it is polite to look someone in the face when they are trying to speak with you,' Ruth said softly. 'No matter how terrifying.' She contorted her face into a dramatic grimace. Rosie giggled and Fergus squeezed her hand till she yelped. He gave Ruth a hard stare. 'It's not polite to make faces either, miss.'

Ruth forced a laugh. 'Quite right, Fergus,' she said. 'Now, I'm going to hazard a guess that this young lady, by the name of Rosemary McKenzie, is your sister. Am I right?'

'Aye, miss,' hiccupped the girl.

Ruth sorely wished she could pull out her handkerchief and clean the girl's face. At least the tears had ceased.

'Well, Rosemary, I expect Fergus has been taking very good care of you, but I'm afraid you are not on my list. I understand you will be with another escort and a lovely group of little girls.'

'She sticks with me,' Fergus blurted. 'Ma said I'm to watch out for her the whole time.'

'Yes, I understand, but now you are both to be looked after by adults like myself. I will be taking care of you, Fergus, and another escort will take care of Rosemary.'

'But —'

Ruth held up a hand. 'There will be plenty of opportunities to spend time with your sister on board the boat, Fergus. We will be a long time at sea.'

'We've never been on the sea before,' Rosemary said.

'Well, then, this will be quite an adventure, won't it? I've been on a boat to New Zealand once and it was a wonderful experience. The sunrises and sunsets knocked me right off my feet — or maybe it was the waves.' She gave Rosemary a wink and was rewarded with a small smile from the girl. Fergus raised his eyes briefly to the sky and turned his head away.

Mr Vernon cleared his throat. 'Fergus,' he growled. 'Manners, please.'

Ruth had forgotten Fergus's teacher was there. He was a tiny slip of a man, and could have passed for a child if not for the thin moustache above his top lip. It had been Mr Vernon's job to bring a group of six boys and ten girls down from Glasgow and hand them over to the escorts with any relevant information. He'd informed Ruth that Fergus had an older brother staying behind to help his mother in the munitions factory, and a baby sister being taken care of by an aunt in the countryside. The father was a coalminer. While academically able, Fergus had a short attention span, according to Mr Vernon. The boy was happiest and least disruptive when he was outdoors.

'How old are you, Fergus?' Ruth asked.

'Nine, miss.'

'And Rosemary?'

'She's six,' Mr Vernon answered for the girl. He consulted the clipboard in his hand. 'According to my list, her escort's name is Mrs Ellis.'

'Oh, yes.' Ruth stood on tiptoes and scanned the crowd of children and escorts; she had chatted to Mrs Ellis earlier that morning. Eventually she spotted the other woman's head of thick grey hair. She caught Mrs Ellis's attention and waved her over.

'Is that a Rosemary McKenzie you've found there, Ruth?'

'Indeed it is.'

'Ach now, that's grand. Hello there, Rosemary darling, I'm your escort for this mighty voyage. My name's Mrs Ellis and I've got a niece about your age, to be sure.'

Rosemary let go of Fergus's hand and stared at Mrs Ellis's ample chest.

'How about you come with me, Rosie, dear? I've got a lovely group of girls who can't wait to meet you.'

Rosemary didn't so much as look at Fergus as, trance-like, she took Mrs Ellis's hand and they walked away. Fergus stared after his sister while wiping his hand on his tattered shorts.

Ruth touched his arm gently. 'Why don't you come and meet the other boys in our group? They're all from Scotland. In fact, I believe one or two of them are from your school.' She smiled as he finally looked at her. 'We have done our best to make sure you're grouped with friends, or other children from a similar . . . area to yours.'

'I don't have to, miss,' Fergus said. 'I can go with others – from someplace else, I mean.'

Ruth's smile faltered. 'The next few weeks are not always going to be easy. It can be comforting to have people you know around.'

Fergus looked down. 'Aye, miss,' he mumbled, and he followed Ruth to the group of boys she had left standing by the flagpole.

'Right, boys,' Ruth said. 'I understand some of you know Fergus here. Callum and Will are from your school, isn't that right?'

Fergus acted as if he hadn't heard her.

'Aye, miss,' said Callum, grinning at Fergus with misshapen yellow teeth.

From the scowl on Fergus's face, Ruth wondered if knowing one another wasn't necessarily a good thing.

'And the rest of the boys are also from Glasgow, or thereabouts,' she said brightly. 'Now then, we're going to head into the hall over there, where some kind senior students have given up their holidays to help prepare a meal for everyone, and then we'll get you settled. You must be very hungry after that long train ride.'

'We've not eaten a thing since we left,' said Will loudly.

Ruth stared at him. 'But that was almost eight hours ago.'

'Yes, miss.'

'Didn't your mothers pack something for the journey?'

There was a light shuffling of feet as the boys all looked in different directions. 'It was something small,' a tall boy standing next to Fergus said. 'We ate it for breakfast.'

The boys nodded and murmured in agreement.

'I see,' said Ruth, wondering if food rations were worse in Glasgow or if she was dealing with something else. 'Well, we'd better make our way to the hall right away – beat the queues,' she said with a wink.

'Aye, miss,' the boys chorused.

Ruth watched as Fergus scanned the crowd of children milling around the yard till he spied his sister. Rosemary stood slightly behind a group of girls and was staring straight at her brother, tears pouring down her face. He frowned and shook his head, and she wiped at her eyes, her lips quivering.

Fergus took a deep breath, dropped his head, and followed the other boys.

Excited chatter filled the hall as the boys queued for their meal. Having been shown where to sit, they picked up their knives and forks and started eating. Within minutes, their plates were scraped clean.

'Well, you *are* enthusiastic eaters,' said Ruth, sitting at one end of the table. 'I hope you've had enough.'

'Aye, miss,' they mumbled, staring at her half-eaten meal.

Ruth's appetite had deserted her since leaving London, but she forced down a few more mouthfuls before standing up. 'Now, we have quite a busy schedule ahead of us, so let's go gather your things and I'll show you where you'll be sleeping tonight.'

For a split second, Fergus's eyes met hers, and she smiled encouragingly. His flat expression didn't alter as he looked away, and Ruth couldn't help but wish she was older and more capable. Teaching in a classroom was far removed from her current situation.

They returned to the main foyer, and the few boys who had arrived with suitcases retrieved them from the rows lined up against the wall. The rest of her group picked up their small satchels and slung them onto their backs. Ruth's heart ached seeing how few possessions they owned.

She led them towards the classroom where they would be sleeping. Straw mattresses were laid out on the floor in an otherwise barren space, all the desks and chairs having been removed. The boys regarded their beds forlornly, and Ruth couldn't blame them. Even the hairy grey blanket folded up on the end of each mattress appeared thin, scratchy and uninviting. 'I'm afraid you'll need to use a bundle of your clothes as a pillow,' she said with as much enthusiasm as she could muster. 'Remember, boys, our big adventure hasn't really started yet. I'm sure you will have a proper bed once we are on board the ship.'

In silence, the boys selected a straw mattress each and placed their possessions on top. Then they removed their coats, placed them next to their belongings and put their gasmasks at the foot of their beds.

'Right, let's go and see the air-raid shelter. Hopefully we'll have a quiet night but best to be prepared.' Ruth ushered them out of the building, across the schoolyard and into the concrete bunker.

'Is this it, miss?' asked Will.

'Yes, Will. Is something wrong?' All the boys were looking about, frowning, she realised.

'We're used to Anderson shelters, miss,' said Callum.

'I see. Well this should be a lot more comfortable, don't you think? And quite likely even safer.'

'Aye, this is grand, miss,' Will said.

The other boys nodded – except Fergus, who was at the entrance staring out. Looking for his sister again, Ruth surmised.

The next hour was spent standing in a queue with her boys as they waited to be seen by a doctor. She stood nearby as the doctor looked in the boys' ears, listened to their chests, examined their skin and then sent them on their way.

Afterwards, Ruth let the boys play in the yard until her group were called to a classroom, where nurses deloused the boys' hair, gave them each a bar of soap and sent them to have cold showers. Next, nurses tended to any sores or scratches in the treatment room, where Ruth was relieved to see Betty's friendly face.

'You all right there, Ruthie?' asked Betty as she applied a salve to a nasty grazed knee.

Ruth nodded; she suspected if she tried to speak, she would likely start to weep with exhaustion and with sorrow for these poor boys so far from home.

'Today was always going to be challenging,' Betty said loudly, 'but we British are made of stern stuff, are we not?' She was addressing everyone in the room. Ruth immediately felt bolstered by her words and hoped the boys did too. It was surprising to observe Betty in her nursing role. Her professional, caring, no-nonsense approach as she ministered to the boys was a far cry from the giggling girl at the train station. As Betty applied antiseptic to a cut on Fergus's foot, she told Ruth firmly that it was important to ensure injuries were seen to as soon as they occurred and to send a child straight to the hospital on board if he contracted any illness or showed signs of distress. While Ruth was sure the advice was meant to help, it did nothing to ease her growing fear she was out of her depth.

As daylight faded, the children helped volunteers and escorts to put blackouts over the windows, then all the children gathered again in the hall, where they were given a mug of warm cocoa and a biscuit.

Mr Hungerford, who had been absent all day, strode into the room and blew a whistle, causing the hall to fall silent. 'A very warm welcome to you children,' he shouted. 'Shortly you will be boarding a boat to go on a great adventure across the oceans, where our kind friends in the dominions are waiting eagerly to meet you.'

He sounded like a circus ringleader, Ruth thought. She wasn't sure that was quite the right note to strike.

'This is a time of difficulty and change for everyone here in Britain,' he continued, 'but your parents have chosen to send you somewhere safe from the dangers of war. They are to be commended for their decision, and your job, young children, is to prove to them how brave you can be and to show us how well you will represent this country abroad.'

Ruth noticed Fergus was watching his sister as Mr Hungerford spoke. Rosemary was crying again. If she kept it up much longer, Ruth knew there was a risk the girl would be sent home, as severely homesick children would not be allowed to leave. Ruth wondered if Fergus knew this too. The way he frowned and shook his head at his sister suggested he did.

The moment Mr Hungerford finished his speech, the escorts conducted their charges back to their makeshift beds, and Ruth, numb with exhaustion, collapsed onto her own. She hoped she would fall quickly into a heavy sleep and wake refreshed and full of confidence that she could face whatever lay ahead.

Unfortunately, the Germans had other ideas. It seemed only seconds after she'd finally dropped off to sleep that Ruth was woken by the shrill of an air-raid siren. Sitting bolt upright, it took her a moment to remember where she was. As the other escorts in her room leapt from their beds and threw on their coats, Ruth hurried to do the same.

When she reached the classroom, her boys were calmly and quietly pulling on their shoes and coats. Ruth stood, torch in hand, and watched their small, dim shapes reach for their gasmasks and line up at the door. To think this was already something so commonplace. The children could have been getting ready for a school trip to the museum.

With her torch casting a faint ghostly light, Ruth led them down the stairs and across the yard to the bunker, where they filed inside and sat on the narrow benches without a word. Ruth tried to think of words of comfort or a joke she could share, but her mind was blank.

Mrs Ellis, who was sitting opposite, leant forward and gave Ruth's knee a squeeze. 'How 'bout a wee song, eh?' she said, then started to sing softly. Slowly, the children joined in.

Eventually, Ruth was able to do the same.

9

HAZEL

Hazel examined the contents of her breakfast keenly.

'Appealing, isn't it?' said Joe.

'I thought they said it was scrambled eggs,' she said. 'This is something else entirely.'

'And it bounces, look.' Joe tapped his fork on the offending egg and grinned as it wobbled. He seemed to be in a good mood, and Hazel felt similarly buoyant, even though she'd only managed to snatch a couple of hours sleep. Once the lights had come on and the window shades were lifted, it was as if everyone was silently congratulating themselves for overcoming a painful hurdle. Returning their seats to an upright position was cause for celebration.

Hazel delicately placed a forkful of what she hoped were baked beans in her mouth, chewed thoughtfully, and swallowed. 'They're edible. Just.'

Bolstered, she ate some egg and grimaced. 'It's like rubber.'

'Yeah, I'd leave the rest if you want to make it to London unscathed.'

'Thanks for the heads-up.' She pushed her tray aside and looked at the cover of the book she'd been reading on and off throughout the night.

'I don't know why Ruth, the character I was telling you about, wants to put herself through it. I'd rather stay in London and risk being bombed.'

Joe whistled. 'That bad?'

'So far, the kids are miserable, scared and homesick, and the ship hasn't even left England yet.'

'Who do you think wrote the book? Is it a true story?'

'I'm not sure. I assume it's based on actual events at least. It's written by a Mrs Florence Wright and June Sullivan,' she said, reading the names printed on the spine. 'Ruth's good friend is called Florrie, which might be short for Florence.'

Suddenly Hazel gasped and jerked in her seat, knocking her tray. She only just managed to grab it before it tipped all over Joe. 'I can't believe it.' Hazel was astounded she hadn't joined the dots till now. 'The boy's name is Fergus, Joe! *Fergus!*'

Joe raised his eyebrows. 'Okay,' he said. 'Clearly this is important news.'

Hazel snatched up her book and waved it in front of Joe. 'Ruth is in charge of a group of boys from Glasgow, and one of the boys is called Fergus.' She banged herself on the head with the book. '*Gramps* is Fergus. Everyone calls him Mac, short for McKenzie, his surname, so I didn't make the connection at first. But he said this story would help explain how he ended up in New Zealand.' Hazel shook the book. 'The Fergus in this book must be Gramps! He told me he was an evacuee but that's all; he never wanted to talk about the war or his childhood.' Hazel shook her head in wonder. 'Wow, this is amazing. Poor Gramps. How must he have felt, being sent off and –' Hazel stopped mid-sentence and frowned. 'He's never mentioned his sister, though. The Fergus in this story has a little sister, Rosie, but Gramps has never mentioned her.'

Joe pursed his lips in thought. 'Maybe she died when she was young and he couldn't bear to talk about it.'

'What a terrible thought! I can't believe that's where your mind went.'

'Well, hopefully it'll become clearer as you read on.'

Leaning back, Hazel held the book against her chest. 'Imagine how those children must have felt, Joe. Leaving their families, their country, boarding a ship with a bunch of strangers.'

'How old was Gramps? I mean, Fergus.'

'He was nine and his sister was even younger. I'm starting to wonder if they never made it back home to Glasgow. What if they never saw their parents again? And they're going to Australia. I don't know how Gramps ended up in New Zealand.' Hazel sighed. 'I wish I'd tried harder to get him to talk. I'm starting to think I don't know anything about him at all.'

Joe ate a mouthful of mushy cooked tomato and Hazel waited for his reaction. He swallowed and shrugged, as if to say 'not bad', so she decided to risk it too.

'I'd say it's quite common,' said Joe. 'Not knowing much about our grandparents. I used to spend two weeks of every summer holiday with Dad's parents down in Cornwall, and they'd come and stay with us pretty regularly, but I have to admit I barely know them. Just the surface stuff. Where they grew up, what they like to watch on TV, the fact they eat their main meal at midday and a piece of toast for supper. Nan is always complaining it's too cold and Pop that it's too hot.'

'It's sad, don't you think? They've lived through such an incredible time in history and had all these experiences, but we just see them as old people who go to bed early.'

'You're right. But at the same time, they seem quite content *not* to talk about it. Maybe it's a generational thing.'

'Hmm.' Hazel stared morosely at her tray of food, imagining Gramps as a scared, homesick young boy, then told herself to snap out of it. 'So, what can you tell me about London?' she said brightly. 'Anywhere I should go that's not in the Lonely Planet? What's the insider's scoop?'

Joe stared hard at Hazel. 'It's incredible how you can do that.'

'Do what?'

'It's like you can flick a switch and suddenly be all happy and excited.'

'I've been wanting to travel for as long as I can remember. It's all I've thought about for years and I'm finally doing it. Of course I'm excited! I'm also freaking out, which is why I can't stop talking. I'm actually quite a quiet person, you know.'

'Sure,' Joe said, not bothering to hide his grin.

'I am,' insisted Hazel, giving him a light punch on the arm and grinning back.

His grin immediately slipped away and his eyes became hooded. Hazel knew it must be because she'd accidentally started to flirt with him again. What was wrong with her? He clearly wasn't keen and neither was she. He was way older than her, for a start, and he had a massive stain down his front and didn't even care (which surely said something significant about him), and technically she still had a boyfriend. Maybe she should just come right out and tell him that he had no cause for concern.

They silently picked away at their food, and the moment the trays were cleared away Hazel stood up and stepped into the aisle. 'I'm going to stretch my legs for a bit,' she said, avoiding Joe's eye. She felt stiff and awkward as she moved away, almost as if she'd forgotten how to walk.

IO

Batory, 1940

At dawn, the sound of bombs tearing up the city finally ceased, and the all clear sounded. Everyone returned to their beds, the school thankfully unscathed, and Ruth managed to snatch an hour's sleep before Betty shook her awake.

The day was spent playing games in the schoolyard or listening to some of the escorts who had been to Australia talk about what to expect. One of them played a recording of a bird called a kookaburra, and many of the children spent the rest of the afternoon mimicking its astonishing call.

A couple of times during the day, Ruth took Fergus to check on his sister, hoping it would help to cheer him up. Unfortunately, as soon as Rosemary saw her brother, she began to cry and told him she wanted to go home.

Mrs Ellis pulled Ruth aside and suggested it was best if Fergus kept his distance, at least until they were underway.

In the late afternoon, the children were taken into a class-room where brand-new clothing, kindly donated by Mr Simon Marks of Marks and Spencer, was issued to those who had been unable to bring all the items on the recommended packing list. Fergus was given a sturdy coat, new shirts and socks. Ruth was pleased to see a brief smile on his face as he wrapped the coat tightly around his thin frame.

After supper, the children gathered in the hall and were told by a stern-faced Mrs Shearing that in the morning they would be boarding a ship that would take them to their kind friends in the dominions. The children became still and quiet, and Ruth found she had to look away from their tender, vulnerable faces.

All the children were given a piece of paper and told to write a letter to their parents, which would be sent once they had safely departed. Mrs Shearing encouraged the children to keep their letters positive. The last thing anyone needed was for parents to be unduly worried, and a cheery letter would help to put their minds at ease.

By breakfast time the following day, the mood had changed from fear and anxiety to nervous excitement. Ruth rounded up her group and led them to a bus that took them through the eerily quiet streets of Liverpool to the busy docks, thronged with men in uniform. Barely anyone glanced at the large group of chil-dren instructed to sit in neat rows on the wharf. Time dragged slowly, with much shuffling about as children's bottoms grew numb and legs started to cramp.

'We've been here ages, miss,' Callum complained. 'I'm starving.'

Ruth sighed and peered towards the end of the wharf. 'It has been a long time, Callum, I agree.' She wiped a strand of hair from her cheek. 'I'm sure we won't have to wait much longer, though.'

Observing her group of boys, she realised any excitement they'd felt on first arriving at the docks had dissipated. As the afternoon wore on, they grew quiet and withdrawn, barely talking at all.

'Look,' someone called, pointing. 'Food.'

With relief, Ruth watched as two ladies walked between the rows of children with a large tray, handing out sandwiches. The boys started to stir in anticipation, but before the ladies reached their group, they turned and walked away.

'What on earth?' Ruth said loudly.

'They've run out, apparently,' called another escort, rolling his eyes.

Those who had missed out began to protest.

'Have they indeed?' Ruth said, putting her hands on her hips. 'We shall see about that.' Though she had been given strict instructions to stay with her group, something had to be done. 'Right, boys,' she said. 'I trust you to be on your best behaviour while I go and sort this out.'

'Aye, miss,' they shouted as she strode towards the retreating sandwich ladies, who were accompanied by Mrs Shearing.

'Miss Best,' said Mrs Shearing sharply as Ruth approached, 'you are to stay with your charges.'

Ruth lifted her chin. 'My boys are hungry and they missed out on sandwiches.'

'That is no excuse for leaving your group unattended.'

83

'I believe it is an extremely valid excuse. They have eaten nothing since breakfast.' Ruth was determined to stand her ground, even with legs like jelly.

'Hmph.' Mrs Shearing sniffed as if there were something rotten in the air. 'Return to your group, Miss Best, and I will ask for more sandwiches.'

'Thank you,' Ruth replied.

On her way back to her boys, she caught sight of Betty, who waved and winked. 'Well done,' the nurse mouthed.

Suddenly, a loud whistle sounded, and sandwiches were forgotten as Mr Hungerford addressed the rows of children.

'You will shortly be boarding your ship. Please ensure you have your CORB tag visible. You no longer require your gasmasks. You must carry them as far as the ship, where you will be asked to hand them over before going aboard.'

Everyone clambered to their feet eagerly. As Ruth and her boys joined the mass of moving bodies, children started to point and shout. 'It's got to be that one,' said Arthur, a tall boy in Ruth's care.

'Oh no, we wouldn't all fit,' said the boy behind him.

'I hope it's *that* one,' Will said, pointing to an imposing grey ship with giant funnels and bristling with guns.

They veered right and Ruth stopped walking. Ahead of her, children were streaming up the steep gangway of a huge grey ship. It was so imposing she felt smaller and more out of her depth than ever. She could see hundreds of soldiers in uniform standing on the upper decks, staring down at the children as they boarded.

'What a beauty,' Callum said. 'Look at the size of her.'

'Her name's *Batory*,' screeched Arthur, pointing to the name on the hull. 'We're going on the *Batory*.'

Willing her legs to move, Ruth shuffled forward.

'Gasmasks here,' said a man in uniform standing near the gangway.

Ruth watched as the children placed their masks on the growing pile. When it was Fergus's turn, though, he held out his mask as if to drop it, then tucked it beneath his satchel before making his way onto the boat.

On deck, waiting stewards directed the escorts and their charges to their cabins. They spoke slowly with unusual accents, and it was clear English was not their first language. They appeared nervous about having so many children on board – not that Ruth could blame them.

'Well, boys,' Ruth said, as they gathered at the entrance to one of the three cabins the boys had been allocated. 'This will do just fine.'

She was relieved to see there were four proper bunks with mattresses and bedding. Though the cabins were very small and narrow – the only patch of daylight limited to a small, round porthole – they had a homey, comforting look. 'Select a bunk and leave your belongings. We are to make our way to the dining saloon for a well-deserved early dinner.'

They stared at her as if she hadn't spoken.

'Snap to it,' she said as brightly as she could. 'I'm sure you boys are hungry.'

Once they'd found their way through the confusing maze of passageways to the dining saloon, and the boys were seated with their meals, Ruth joined other escorts at a table nearby, glancing across at her group regularly to make sure they were behaving. She smiled as her boys once again ate with great gusto – except Fergus, Ruth noted. He pushed his food around his plate, but barely managed a mouthful.

Ruth ate a few more mouthfuls of her own meal before going over to him. 'You must eat, Fergus. Are you unwell?'

He shook his head. 'No, miss,' he muttered.

She surveyed his bowed head before addressing the table. 'Righto, boys. I trust you to make your way back to your cabins and start unpacking your things. I'm going to take Fergus for a quick visit to the nurse then I'll come back to check on you. When you're done, we'll have a proper explore of the ship.'

'Aye, miss!'

With one hand on his back, Ruth steered Fergus along the passageways – stopping now and then to ask directions of a passing sailor – to the hospital. Betty, dressed in a nurse's uniform, rushed over to greet them. 'Hello, Ruth, how are you getting on?'

Ruth smiled, relieved to see her familiar face. 'Hello, Betty. Sorry to bother you so early in the piece, but Fergus here appears to have lost his appetite.'

'No problem at all.' Betty turned to Fergus, her eyes taking in his wan face. 'Now, my boy, what seems to be ailing you?'

Fergus shrugged.

'Hmm.' Betty took Fergus's temperature and asked him a few questions, then she told him to lie on a bed. Bringing him a cup of hot cocoa, she said, 'I want you to take nice little sips, Fergus, and I guarantee you'll start to feel chipper.'

She then withdrew with Ruth to the other side of the room. 'He's just homesick, the poor soul.'

'Are you sure that's all it is?' Ruth asked.

Betty tipped her head to one side. 'Don't you think that's enough?'

Ruth bit her lip. 'Yes, of course. Sorry.'

'Have you ever been homesick?' asked Betty.

Ruth's trip to New Zealand was the only time she'd been out of England on her own. She'd been so pleased to get away and explore a new country she'd barely thought of home at all. 'No, I don't believe I have.'

'Wouldn't wish it on my worst enemy. I don't think I'll ever forgive my parents for sending me to boarding school.' Betty looked back at Fergus. 'Look at him. He's leaving everyone and everything he's ever known. Leaving his whole world behind in a war zone. Who knows what things will be like when he returns?'

Ruth knew from the expression on Betty's face her thoughts weren't only with Fergus. Ruth thought of Peter, Florrie, Frank and her mother. She found it difficult to conjure an image of their faces. It was as if they had begun to fade away. Ruth wondered if there was something wrong with her. She felt so distant from everything happening around her.

Pulling up a chair beside Fergus's bed, Ruth watched him focus intently on the contents of his mug rather than look at her.

'Your parents want you to go somewhere safe, Fergus. I know it's difficult but –'

'They didn't send my brother,' Fergus blurted.

'Sorry?'

He lifted his head and glared at her. 'Eddie got to stay, but I have to be the one to go and take care of Rosie. They sent us away, but not him or Lily.'

'Who's Lily?'

'My little sister,' Fergus said, taking another sip.

'That must be hard, leaving your siblings.'

Fergus shrugged.

'I'm sure your parents found the decision difficult.'

'I didn't even get a choice.'

'Sorry?'

A single tear rolled down his cheek as he shakily placed his mug on the bedside table and slowly removed the cap from his head. He gripped it in his hands and stared at it as if it might be about to speak. Ruth was surprised to see he had short tight curls much like her own and realised it was the first time he'd removed his hat since they'd met. 'They didn't ask me if I wanted to go,' he muttered. 'And they only told me I was going three days ago. I said I didn't want to leave, but they said I had to, for Rosie.'

'Three days!' Ruth exclaimed, before recovering herself. She willed herself to speak calmly. 'That must have come as a shock.'

'They gave me this cap and said I finally got to have a new hat because I was going on a special trip, but I don't even care about it now, not really, even though it was all I wanted before.' He squeezed the cap into a tight ball then let it drop onto his lap so he could swipe the tears from his cheek. 'Guess it was easier to send me than Eddie.'

'Why?'

'He's the smart one. And he gets on with everyone.'

'Oh, Fergus! I suspect you and Rosie mean so much to your parents they couldn't bear the thought of anything happening to you.'

Ruth had never seen a child look so alone and scared. She threw her arms around him and pulled him into her chest. 'You'll come back to your family, Fergus. I'm sure of it. And when you do, you'll have all sorts of wonderful stories to tell them about your big adventure overseas. Your brother and sister will be so envious, they'll wish they'd been chosen instead.' She wondered if trying to convince him their trip was going to be all fun and excitement was unfair to the boy. How could she possibly predict what lay ahead?

Fergus sniffed and leant against her heavily. 'I hope so, miss,' he whispered.

When he had finished his cocoa, they returned to their cabins, Ruth breathing a sigh of relief to discover her charges hadn't wandered.

'We have to go to the top deck, miss,' Will said the moment she arrived. 'A nice steward with a funny accent came looking for us. We need to get our lifebelts.'

Ruth wished she could go to her own cabin, lie in her bed, and pull the covers over her head. She was feeling increasingly dizzy and light-headed as the day wore relentlessly on. 'Right then,' she said gaily. 'Let's go.' And up they went to the top deck.

Once the boys were given their lifebelts, all the children were gathered together and given a lecture on what to do if they came under enemy fire. Drills were repeated again and again as the children lined up by their cabins and moved quickly to their designated stations by the lifeboats. It was a relief for them all,

Ruth included, when they were finally released to acquaint themselves with the layout of the boat.

'Can't we take these off at all?' groaned Callum, pulling at his lifebelt. 'What if we hold them in our hands, like?'

'You heard the captain, Callum,' Ruth said firmly. 'They are to be worn at all times.'

'They're right awkward,' muttered Will.

As they jostled their way among the other groups of children, they came across Mrs Ellis with her group of evacuees. Rosemary was gripping Mrs Ellis's hand, her eyes puffy and red.

Fergus rushed towards her. 'Rosie! You all right?'

The girl's eyes seemed out of focus as she turned to her brother. 'Yes, Fergus. I'm going back to look at the lifeboats with Mrs Ellis.'

Mrs Ellis smiled at Ruth. 'The drills were a tad overwhelming. We're running through everything again a little more slowly so Rosie here can remember.' She looked at Fergus. 'I've been reassuring your sister that the drills are just a precaution, Fergus. We are very unlikely to encounter any danger at all. Especially as we'll be accompanied by a flotilla of other ships.' She bent to whisper in Rosie's ear. 'Our own personal bodyguards.'

Rosie appeared not to hear as she continued to look at Fergus with that strange, blank expression. There was no colour to her lips and cheeks at all.

One of the girls standing beside Rosie asked if they could go back to their cabins, and Mrs Ellis nodded curtly. 'In a minute, girls.'

Fergus placed his hand on his sister's shoulder and she startled. 'How about I come see where your cabin is, eh, Rosie?

Has it got a funny round window like mine? I bet you picked a top bunk. You've always wanted to sleep in a top bunk.'

Rosie frowned. 'I have?' she asked, her voice flat.

'Aye, remember when we went to Aunty May's last year and you begged to be allowed in the top bunk, but Da said you were too young and might fall out?'

Rosie's bottom lip began to wobble and Fergus glanced at Ruth in panic.

'Why don't you show us your cabin, Rosie, so Fergus knows where to find you? Then he can show you where he's going to be sleeping.' Ruth willed the girl not to break down in tears.

'That's a grand idea,' said Mrs Ellis.

Callum sighed dramatically. 'Do we all have to go, miss?'

Ruth was wondering how best to respond when everyone was distracted by a loud clumping noise. They all moved to the rail and looked over the side of the ship to the wharf below. A long line of men were marching past, rifles hung across their shoulders. In the fading evening light, their faces were hidden in shadow beneath their helmets.

There was a loud thud nearby, quickly followed by a girl's scream. Ruth spun around to see Rosie had collapsed face down on the deck. Mrs Ellis dropped to a crouch beside her and Fergus knelt at her head.

A tall male steward appeared from nowhere and scooped Rosie into his arms. 'I'll take her to doctor,' he said in a lilting accent.

Rosie's eyes fluttered open. 'Am I going home now?' she asked hopefully.

Mrs Ellis locked eyes with the man and neither of them spoke.

'Rosie,' Fergus said grimly. 'Stop this nonsense.'

Rosie continued to stare at the steward. 'I didn't mean to fall down. And I am trying hard, truly. But there's this dreadful feeling all over me, and I can't get rid of it.'

Mrs Ellis stroked the hair from Rosie's cheek. 'It's okay, child, that's just a bit of homesickness. It'll pass.'

'It is?' Rosie turned her faraway gaze on her escort. 'But I've been trying not to think of Ma and Da at all. If they even so much as pop into my mind, I pinch myself on the arm – see?' The girl pulled up the sleeve of her blouse to show them the angry red marks.

'Oh, Rosie,' Mrs Ellis murmured.

Fergus blinked rapidly. 'She's fine, Mrs Ellis. It's just her being dramatic, like. She once held her breath till she went blue just because Da said she wasn't allowed to walk to school on her own.'

Rosie glared at Fergus. 'You hated having to take me to school anyway. That Callum was always following us and saying nasty things. I was doing it for you too, so he'd leave you alone.'

'Okay,' the steward said, lowering Rosie to the ground. 'You stand now and be brave and strong girl.'

Her cheeks flushed pink. 'I can be very strong, mister. I once had to carry my baby sister all the way home from the butcher when Ma hurt her back. She said I was stronger than my brothers.'

Fergus rolled his eyes and opened his mouth to say something, before wisely closing it again.

Rosie looked up at the steward. 'Where are you from, mister?'

'Rosie,' Fergus muttered.

'It is fine,' the man said. 'I'm from Poland,' he said proudly. 'This is a Polish ship.'

'You speak funny,' said Rosie.

Ruth wondered where this suddenly talkative little girl had come from.

'I don't know English so well,' said the steward. 'Maybe you teach me?'

Rosie smiled for the first time since Ruth had met her. 'That's a good idea,' she said firmly.

The man's laugh was deep and loud. 'I have daughter at home, same age maybe? She is seven.'

Rosie wrinkled her nose. 'I'm six,' she said, before adding quickly, 'but I'm *almost* seven.'

Mrs Ellis interjected. 'Right, come on, my girls — let's get settled in for a good night's sleep. There's been more than enough excitement for one day. Fergus, you can come and see your sister's cabin tomorrow.' Taking Rosie's hand and guiding the other girls in front of her, Mrs Ellis swept out of sight.

Ruth turned to face her own group of evacuees, their faces soft and glowing in the evening light. 'We should sleep well after this long and eventful day, boys.'

'Aye, miss,' the boys said, their voices wobbly with tiredness and emotion.

Before leading her young charges below deck, Ruth turned to stare at the dusky pink horizon. Tomorrow, they would be sailing towards it. The thought made her feel wobbly too.

II

JOE

'Can I have my book back?' Hazel asked, flopping into her seat.

Their fingers brushed as Joe handed over her book. He'd picked it up, looking for a distraction. 'Sorry.'

'You know, the general idea is to start a book from the beginning, not part way through.'

'Thanks for the tip.'

Hazel flipped through the pages. 'Don't give anything away,' she warned.

'Wouldn't dream of it. Besides I didn't get very far.' He hadn't been able to focus on Ruth's story, thinking instead about how to broach the topic of his wife. He needed to tell Hazel before . . . before his scrambled thoughts went any further.

'I'm working up to starting another movie,' he said lightly.

'Fair enough. It feels like we've been flying for an eternity.'

'Yep. Three long and painful hours to go till LA.'

'Have you ever been to Australia?' Hazel asked. 'It's where they're heading to in the story.'

Joe frowned. 'Once. After my twenty-fifth birthday I did a bit of travelling with my girlfriend at the time.'

'She's no longer the girlfriend I take it.'

'No.' Joe hesitated. This was his chance. 'She's my wife.'

Hazel blinked. 'You're married,' she said softly.

'Yes.'

Quickly averting her eyes, Hazel cleared her throat. 'I didn't pick it. You don't wear a wedding ring, and you're on your own, and . . .' Hazel stopped.

'She left me two months ago,' Joe said. 'I got back to our apartment after closing up on a Saturday night and all her stuff was gone.'

Hazel stared at him. 'That sucks.'

Joe attempted a smile. 'Yeah, it did a bit.'

'Is that why you came to New Zealand? To get away and recuperate or something?'

God, he wished he'd met Hazel in some alternative universe where he was single. A part of him wanted to sit beside her for days, and another wanted to get as far away from her as possible.

'I guess so. My parents insisted I take a break, so I booked a flight without really knowing what the hell I was doing. But I'm glad I did. I was having a fantastic time until a couple of days ago. I actually had no intention of going home. I was in Queenstown when my wife called. She'd been refusing to talk to me since she left, but now she says she wants to give us another go, whatever that means.'

'So you're heading back to her?'

'I guess.'

'Why did she move out?'

Joe ran a hand through his hair and shook his head. 'You aren't afraid to ask personal questions, are you?'

Hazel's eyes widened. 'Sorry,' she whispered. 'I'll leave you alone.' She opened her book and ducked her head as if to read.

'My wife – Klara – she's Swedish,' he said abruptly. 'She came to work in the pub for a holiday job and we ended up getting together. She was keen to return to Sweden but I didn't want to go, so she stayed in London. I promised we'd try living in Sweden once she got pregnant, but she . . . well, we tried for two years and nothing happened.'

There was a long silence. 'I'm sorry,' said Hazel finally.

Joe felt a pain expand within his chest. While he'd been in New Zealand, he'd let himself forget about the mess he'd made of his life, but it was returning to him vividly now. All the arguments and tears and frustration. The drawn-out silences. 'She left me to go back to her family. Maybe I should have followed her there, but the truth is . . .' He trailed off. He shouldn't say it.

'What?'

He closed his eyes. 'It was a relief,' he said quietly.

Hazel whistled. 'Harsh.'

Joe opened his eyes. 'It is, isn't it?'

'Yep.'

He couldn't figure out from her expression what she was thinking. Maybe it was no big deal to her that he was married. She was young and beautiful and off to have a big adventure overseas. It was ridiculous to think she might have feelings for him; they'd only just met, for crying out loud.

'Why was it a relief?' Hazel asked.

Joe realised his hands were shaking. 'Ever since Klara left, it's like I can breathe properly again. Everything has been hard between us for so long.'

Hazel didn't speak and Joe wanted the conversation to be over. He needed to move on and get through the rest of the flight. 'Anyway, I thought I'd better head home to see her and . . . I don't know . . . try again.'

'You don't sound convinced.'

'I was feeling pretty confident earlier. I was going to suggest we move to Sweden together. Give it one last try.'

'And now?'

He turned to look out the window. 'Now I don't know what to do,' he murmured.

12

East Coast, USA, 1940

'Looks like we won't be stopping in New York,' said Reverend Kelly, standing with Ruth at the deck railing. Having finally managed to get their charges into bed, a handful of escorts – Ruth and the Reverend among them – had retreated to the deck to catch a glimpse of the American coastline: a black smudge on the fading indigo horizon.

Rumours of a stop in America had swirled about the ship all afternoon, ever since land had been spotted in the distance. But a short time ago the convoy of ships that had accompanied the *Batory* across the Atlantic had split in two, the majority of the fleet turning towards the Middle East to deliver troops, while the *Batory* and her remaining escorts had headed south. On the one hand, Ruth felt breaking up the convoy was a positive sign, as it surely meant the risk of attack was deemed lower, yet on the other it left the *Batory* more exposed. Since leaving Liverpool a few days earlier, Ruth had tried hard to hide her anxiety at the possibility of being attacked. The high level of naval protection – including eight destroyers and a number of cruisers – should have been reassuring, yet Ruth couldn't help but be alarmed, especially when during the first twenty-four hours of their journey a number of depth charges had been dropped by the destroyers in case of submarines lurking nearby. Ruth had shuddered each time she heard the faint explosions, recalling how she had dismissed Peter's concerns about the German U-boats. She could almost hear him telling her she'd been too hasty in deciding to sign up with CORB, and how once again she had failed to think things through.

Ruth's shoulders were tight, and she made a conscious effort to relax them. Even though her boys were now safe in bed, she remained on edge, her senses alert for signs of distress.

'More's the pity,' she said, realising she should say something in response to the Reverend's observation. 'A break in New York would have been nice.'

The clergyman stroked his moustache. 'I'm not sure a stop so soon into our voyage would be a good idea. The children are only just starting to settle.'

Ruth shook her head. 'It is overly generous of you to describe the children as being settled, Reverend, but I admire your positive outlook.'

He laughed softly and she gave him a rueful smile.

'It may not seem to be the case, Ruth, but they are improving. Before you know it, the children will be running about on deck and we'll be wishing they had less energy.'

From the moment the *Batory* had started to pitch and roll as they drew away from the shelter of Liverpool harbour and into the heavy weather and mountainous seas, the children had been a mass of misery, a vicious combination of seasickness and homesickness lowering the spirits of everyone on board. Ruth had battled through her own nausea to help her group of boys, but there was little she could do except encourage sips of tea and provide a clean handkerchief to wipe their tears. Even brief spells of air on deck were few and far between, as passengers were often barred from the decks due to the huge curtains of spray sweeping across them.

Shivering, Ruth wrapped her arms about herself and breathed in the fresh, salty air. A stiff breeze, which had brought choppy seas all day, had finally died down and the *Batory* was on a nice even keel, yet Ruth still felt unsteady on her feet, her stomach delicate. 'I look forward to that moment,' she said. 'Though it seems a long way off right now.'

The Reverend placed a comforting hand on her shoulder. 'Come on, Ruth, let's head inside. I believe there is a whisky waiting for me.'

Together, they withdrew to the dining saloon, where the escorts had gathered to play cards, have a quiet drink and take a moment to relax.

As the Reverend headed to the bar, Ruth joined Betty, Una and a few others at a table in the corner.

'Ruthie! I was wondering where you'd got to.' Betty flashed a smile and dragged a chair in beside her, indicating for Ruth to sit. 'I thought you might have fallen asleep.'

'I was tempted,' Ruth said, collapsing into the chair.

Una giggled. 'I said you were probably pacing about outside your boys' cabins.'

Ruth stiffened. 'Why would you think that?'

'Well, you do take your role very seriously.'

'As we all do,' said Betty quickly.

Devan, a young male escort from the Midlands who was sitting opposite, leant forward. 'Quite right,' he said, gazing at Betty intently. Ruth had caught them casting surreptitious looks at one another on several occasions and wondered if they were aware of the CORB rule that stated there were to be no romantic liaisons between escorts. Perhaps they were aware and didn't care.

'It's a foolish idea, evacuating young children to the other side of the world,' said a tall man seated at the other end of the table. He spoke in a low, languid tone, his arms crossed as he leant casually back in his chair. A hint of a smile played about his lips as he caught Ruth's eye and raised his eyebrows. It was as if he were challenging her to react to his ludicrous statement, and she glared at him before looking away. Ruth couldn't remember meeting this man in Liverpool. No doubt she'd been so overwhelmed at dealing with the children, she had no memory of their introduction.

Una laughed and twirled a strand of hair around her finger. 'Oh, Bobby, why on earth did you sign up to be an escort if you don't agree with the scheme?'

Exactly, Ruth said to herself silently.

Bobby grinned. 'I wasn't going to pass up a free ticket home to New Zealand, now, was I?'

'We're going to Australia,' Ruth snapped.

Bobby continued to grin as if she'd made an amusing comment. 'True enough. But I'll be continuing on.'

Ruth wondered how CORB officials could have considered this Bobby character to be an appropriate escort, especially considering his lackadaisical attitude. She felt her cheeks grow hot. Did he think their voyage was one big joke?

'So you would rather the children stayed home to be bombed and possibly killed?' she asked sharply.

Bobby narrowed his brown eyes. 'Of course not,' he said. 'I'm simply saying this is a rather extreme reaction.'

Ruth's stomach clenched painfully; she wasn't sure if it was from remnants of her seasickness or from the anger pulsing through her chest and pounding in her head. 'An extreme reaction to war is taking children to safety?'

Bobby reached for his glass of beer. He took a long sip and eyed her calmly over the rim. She glowered back, determined not to lower her gaze.

'I want the children to be safe just as much as anyone, Ruth,' he said quietly.

Ruth had the sense that everyone at the table was holding their breath. With a jolt, she looked down and saw that Betty had placed a hand on top of hers. Ruth realised her whole body was shaking.

'You're all right,' whispered Betty, squeezing Ruth's hand. 'Take a deep breath.'

Glancing about, Ruth noticed more faces looking at her with concern. 'I'm fine,' she said, pushing back her chair. 'Just tired. I think I'll retire early.'

'Don't go just –'

Ruth cut Betty off. 'See you all in the morning.'

She heard Bobby call out to her as she stumbled to the door, her eyes blurry with tears. The past few days had been so terribly hard, and the truth was Ruth herself had sometimes questioned the wisdom of taking the children so far away from their homes and their families. But the alternative – leaving children at the mercy of the enemy – was so much worse. Ruth caught her breath as she pictured Brenda's animated face in the front row of the classroom. She may have failed to save Brenda, but she would do everything she could to save the children on this ship, no matter what – or who – she had to battle on the way.

A short while later, Betty appeared at her cabin door. 'Are you feeling a little better?' she asked, coming to sit beside Ruth on her bed. 'You weren't yourself just now.'

Ruth concentrated on the grey sea visible through her porthole rather than meeting Betty's eye. 'Much better, thank you.'

'Anything you'd like to talk about?'

Ruth shook her head. 'I'm tired, that's all.'

'Hmm.' Betty sounded unconvinced. 'You know, you are allowed to at least try to enjoy yourself on this trip, Ruth. It is a grand once-in-a-lifetime adventure, after all.'

'So I keep reminding myself.'

'Bobby was worried he might have upset you.'

Ruth snorted. 'I doubt the man worries about much at all. Anyway . . .' Ruth was determined to steer the conversation in another direction. 'What's going on between you and Devan?'

Betty's eyes widened and she leant forward to clasp Ruth's hand. 'Oh, Ruth, isn't he marvellous? I feel utterly ridiculous but I'm completely besotted. Though I'm worried Mrs Ellis might be on to us. She seems to be watching my every movement.'

Ruth smiled at her friend's glowing cheeks. 'Well of course she suspects something; you've hardly been subtle, Betty.'

Betty squeezed Ruth's hand, her expression turning serious. 'Ruth, we haven't known one another long, but I feel like we are friends already. So if you ever need someone to talk to — about anything — I'm here, all right?'

Ruth's throat ached. 'Thanks, Betty. I feel as if we're good friends too, and . . . well, perhaps there is something, but I'm not ready to talk about it. Not yet.'

'I understand.' Betty stood. 'I'll leave you to get some rest. Night, Ruthie.'

'Night, Betty. See you at breakfast.'

Ruth watched her friend leave, then turned to stare out of the porthole once more, her mind strangely calm and empty of thought.

⁓

That evening proved to be a turning point not just for Ruth, but for everyone on board. The seas grew calmer, the days warmer, and spirits rose as seasickness finally released its cruel hold. Most significantly, the children missed their homes and families far less as their energy and excitement returned.

A few days later, Ruth was chatting to Betty in the dining saloon when she sensed someone at her side. 'Good morning, Will. You're a tad late for breakfast.' She took in the wariness on the young boy's face. 'Oh, surely you're not feeling unwell again? The sea is so calm.'

'No, miss — it's Callum, I can't find him, miss.'

Ruth froze. She had only recently allowed the boys to make their own way to the dining saloon, though they were under strict instructions to go nowhere else. 'What do you mean?'

'He wasn't in his bed when we woke up, and no-one's seen him, miss.'

Panicked, Ruth leapt to her feet. She glanced over to the table where her boys usually sat. Except for Callum, they were all there. Fergus was even eating his cornflakes — something he hadn't been able to stomach in days.

'I'm sure he hasn't gone far,' said Betty, also getting to her feet. 'I'll get some of the crew to have a look around.'

Ruth gripped Will's shoulder. 'Thank you for letting me know, Will. I'm sure he's off somewhere causing mischief. How about you go and have some breakfast, and then you boys should tidy your cabins ready for the captain's inspection.'

'Aye, miss.'

Trying to look more confident and in control than she felt, Ruth strode towards the door. A couple of days earlier she had reprimanded Callum for climbing about on the lifeboats. She'd warned him he might topple into the water, and he'd laughed. He was such a wilful boy and Ruth had struggled to warm to him, especially as he seemed to enjoy picking on Fergus and finding new ways to challenge Ruth. But he was her responsibility, and right now he was missing.

For the next twenty minutes — though it felt infinitely longer — Ruth scoured the ship. She returned to the lifeboat where he had been caught climbing; she asked the first-class passengers if they had seen him, knowing how much he liked to spy on their movements; and she searched the main hall, in case he had snuck in to play on the piano. But he was nowhere to be found.

Finally, she heard Callum's distinct staccato laugh as she rounded a corner near the rear of the ship. She retraced her steps, following the sound, and peered in the half-open door to the exercise hall. There, standing in the centre of a makeshift boxing ring, was Callum, gloves on his hands and a wide grin on his face as he rapidly punched rectangular pads being held up by a tall, singlet-clad man standing with his back to her.

She shoved the door open so hard it banged against the wall, and both man and boy turned in surprise.

Marvellous, thought Ruth, recognising Bobby. Why was she not surprised to find he had been the cause of one of her boys being led astray?

'Oh, miss,' said Callum, tugging off his gloves and looking more genuinely contrite than he ever had before. 'I lost track of time. I'm sorry; I expect I've missed breakfast entirely.'

'Yes, you have.' Ruth marched towards them, trying to keep her voice even. Her head felt light with relief, her palms clammy. 'And you have half the crew out looking for you. Of all the irresponsible, heartless things to do. I thought I had made myself clear, Callum, but you have deliberately disobeyed me and I won't stand for it! You will —'

'Easy on there, Ruth,' said Bobby.

Till then, Ruth had avoided looking at the Kiwi escort. She was so angry with him she wanted to climb into the ring and swing a punch herself. 'I suppose you think this is funny then, Bobby?'

'No, actually, I don't.' Bobby threw the pads to the ground, his eyebrows drawing together. Beads of sweat glistened on his bare arms. 'Callum assured me he had spoken with you and that you had agreed to him having a boxing lesson this morning. I apologise if the lesson ran on; we both lost track of the time.'

Ruth put her hands on her hips and stared at Callum. 'I agreed to no such thing.'

Callum bit his lip as if he was about to cry, then he looked at the ground in silence.

'Well, Callum? What do you have to say for yourself?' Ruth demanded.

'You wouldn't have let me,' he muttered.

'I'm sorry?'

Callum lifted his head. 'You won't let us do anything, miss. I tried to ask you, honest I did, but you said boxing was for –' Callum stopped.

'For lower-class men with no work and nothing better to do,' Bobby said tersely. 'I believe those were the words you used.'

Ruth met Bobby's bristling gaze and realised he was just as angry as her. Had she really said such a thing? Perhaps she had, but she'd simply said the first thing that had come into her head when Callum had expressed his interest in the sport. Unfortunately, it happened to be what her mother had said upon discovering their cousin James had lost two front teeth in a boxing match in Bristol. The truth was, Ruth didn't care one way or another about boxing – she just knew there was far too high a chance of one of her boys getting hurt.

Ruth opened her mouth to speak, and closed it again. Why did she feel as if she was in suddenly in the wrong?

'I'm sorry you feel boxing is so lowly, Ruth,' growled Bobby. 'I've been teaching boxing to boys from all backgrounds, moneyed or not, for the past ten years, and I can assure you it is a brilliant way to get fit and strong. More importantly, it helps boys to overcome all manner of frustration and poor behaviour. I felt it would be a good outlet for Callum, as I'd heard he was giving you a hard time.'

Crossing her arms, Ruth blinked hard to stop her eyes from welling. 'I'm quite capable of managing my charges, thank you.'

Bobby sighed and shook his head. Turning away, he walked to the back of the ring and climbed out between the two ropes.

'Come, Callum,' said Ruth, annoyed at the wobble in her voice. 'We'd best let the others know you've been found.'

Callum tripped on the rope as he scrambled towards her. 'I'm right sorry, miss. I didn't mean to make anyone worry.'

Ruth held the door open as Callum passed through, then she followed him out, letting the door slam closed behind her.

13

North Atlantic Ocean, 1940

'Fancy seeing you again, Ruthie,' called Betty, leaning over a bed and draping a wet flannel over a small girl's forehead. The girl's face and neck were covered in a red rash Ruth had come to recognise well.

'Not another case,' Ruth said from the hospital doorway. 'You must be exhausted, Betty. It's stifling hot in here.' The *Batory* was drawing close to the equator and the air had grown warmer and more oppressive with each passing day.

'I wouldn't say no to cooler weather, that's for sure. These poor urchins are struggling something dreadful.' Betty washed her hands and came to the door. 'Morning, Fergus. Come to check on your sister again, like a good boy?'

Fergus nodded and removed his cap. 'Aye, miss.' Ruth watched him squeeze his cap in his hands and smiled ruefully. The hat was already looking well-worn and stained with sweat and salt spray. Most of the boys had abandoned their hats, but Fergus seemed reassured by its presence, tapping his head from time to time, as if to check the hat was still there. Perhaps it served as a small reminder of his parents and home.

'Well now,' said Betty. 'I believe wee Rosie is better today. Only I can't let you in, remember? I have enough sick ones as it is; I don't need any more.'

'Would you give her this for me?' Fergus held out a whistle he had spent most of the previous two days whittling from a piece of driftwood. The captain had given Reverend Kelly a pile of weathered sticks and Ruth's boys had spent many a happy hour making various toys.

'Well, that's a fine whistle,' said Betty. 'She'll be very pleased. Though I might not be if she starts blowing on it in here.' Winking, she took the whistle from the boy's hand. 'How's that seasickness now, Fergus?'

'Much better thanks, miss.'

'He's certainly got his appetite back,' said Ruth, smiling at Fergus's tanned face. Gone was the pallid, wretched boy of the early days of their journey.

'That's the story. Making up for lost time, eh, Fergus?' Betty said.

Fergus nodded, but his expression remained grave. 'Has Rosie eaten any breakfast?' he asked quietly.

Betty glanced at Ruth and then back at Fergus. 'She had a few sips of tea, and a couple of nibbles on a piece of toast.'

At this, Fergus grinned. 'That's grand!'

'It is,' Betty murmured.

Ruth put a hand on Fergus's arm. 'How about you head back to the cabin and get changed? I understand they'll be putting the hoses on shortly.'

'Aye, miss,' the boy said brightly.

'No running!' Ruth called after him as he took off up the stairs, his lifebelt banging against his leg. The children had given a cry of delight when the captain had announced they were no longer required to wear their lifebelts, but their joy was dampened when they learnt they would still be required to carry them whenever they moved about the ship. Ruth regularly had to send her boys back to their cabins when they turned up to breakfast without them.

Betty and Ruth watched Fergus disappear from view.

'That's a happy boy there, Ruth. You're doing well.'

Ruth pressed her lips together, remembering her confrontation with Callum and Bobby in the exercise room the week before. She hadn't told anyone about their heated conversation, or how often she had replayed the scene in her head – particularly Callum's accusation: *You won't let us do anything, miss.*

Ruth had come to realise she'd been so determined to ensure nothing happened to her boys, she'd lost track of the fact that her role was not just to keep them safe but to try to ensure they were happy too. As hard as it was, she was doing her best to loosen the reins and allow the boys – and herself – to have some fun.

Ruth had even – after a cooling-off period and a long frank conversation about respect – let Callum resume his boxing lessons, which had unfortunately necessitated a short, stilted exchange with Bobby. Thankfully, she'd been able to avoid the man completely since then.

'I'm keeping going, Betty, just as we all are. Not that I should be complaining. At least we can be up on deck; it doesn't seem fair you being stuck down here.'

'Ah, it's not all the time. I get breaks.'

'Why don't I bring you some ice?'

Betty brightened. 'Would you? That would make our day.'

Ruth smiled at her friend. If it hadn't been for Betty's unwavering positivity, Ruth doubted she would have survived the past few weeks at sea. 'See you at dinner?'

'With a bit of luck. So long as we don't have too many more measles cases coming in the door.'

Ruth glanced at the beds lining either side of the large room. Two nurses were helping a frail-looking boy down the aisle. 'Goodness, you're nearly full in there, Betty.' In the bed second from the end, Ruth spotted Rosie's familiar blonde head. 'Did she keep it down?' Ruth asked quietly.

Betty shook her head. 'Poor lamb. We started her back on a drip this morning.'

'Have you ever known seasickness to go on this long?'

'Never. There's nothing left of her, Ruthie. It's hard to watch the wee girl suffer.'

'You're doing a marvellous job, Betty, really you are.'

Her friend grimaced and wiped the hair from her sweaty forehead. 'Not quite the adventure I had in mind when I signed up.' She winked. 'But I've no regrets.'

Ruth guessed what — or more accurately *whom* — Betty was thinking of. Her romance with Devan had blossomed rapidly, and they'd made little attempt to hide their affection for each other.

'I'll be back with ice as soon as the hosing is done,' said Ruth. 'Give Rosie a kiss from me – and one from Fergus, of course.'

'Right you are, Ruthie. How about you have a cool off for me, eh?'

'You know, I might just do it this time, Betty.'

Betty raised her eyebrows in surprise. No other female escort had been brave enough to face the hose yet. Ruth suspected that, like her, the others were too embarrassed to strip down to their swimming costumes and leap about, especially with soldiers and crew looking on. Secretly, Ruth had been harbouring the notion that she would be the first bold woman to step up for a dousing. She'd hoped it would impress her boys and prove something to them *and* to herself: something she knew was important but was unable to put into words.

On the top deck, there were squeals and shouts as Reverend Kelly held the ship's hose and sprayed the children jumping about. With fresh water in short supply, this saltwater hosing was the closest thing to a bath the children would have all week. In the sticky heat so close to the equator, a rinse-off was a godsend.

Ruth led her boys forward as their turn approached. The unruly group ahead of her were hollering and hooting loudly to the raucous encouragement of their escort, whom Ruth discovered with a sickening thud in her chest was Bobby. He was right in the middle, jumping about, slapping his boys on the back, lifting them up and swinging them around, and generally making a right fool of himself. Water dripped from his hair and his drenched swimming trunks hung low, revealing a tan line around his waist. It was clear from his defined musculature the man was fit, and Ruth begrudgingly accepted he was attractive before she realised she was staring and quickly looked away.

Glancing about, she realised she wasn't the only one transfixed by the sight of a grown man acting like a buffoon. Every one of her boys had their eyes fixed on Bobby, their mouths agape, faces awestruck. Fergus looked as if he might drop to his knees and raise his arms in worship.

'Ridiculous,' Ruth muttered under her breath. She'd put on her swimming costume and wrapped herself in a towel, determined to join her boys under the hose, but now she was unsure. How could she hope to follow that sort of performance? All the children had eyes for only one escort on deck, and it most certainly wasn't her.

Reverend Kelly temporarily stopped the hose and there were loud groans from Bobby and the dripping bodies surrounding him. 'All right, you lot,' called the clergyman. 'Time for Ruth's boys to have a go.'

Bobby glanced in Ruth's direction briefly before he shouted to his group, 'Time's up, boys.' Reluctantly they moved to the side, nudging one another as they went. Passing close to Ruth, Bobby raised his eyebrows and gave her a laconic grin. 'Going to brave the hose, are you, Ruth?' he asked politely.

She didn't know how to respond. Was he trying to be nice or was he simply teasing her?

'Possibly,' she said crisply.

Bobby studied her for a second then, tipping his head forward, he gave it a rapid shake. Ruth gasped as water flew off his hair and sprayed her from top to bottom. How dare he! He'd clearly done it to test for her reaction.

Scowling, Ruth wiped the water from her face.

Turning away, she faced her boys and tugged off her towel. 'Let's go,' she yelled. Without waiting, she ran across the deck and directly into the middle of the spray. The cold stream hit her with such force it nearly knocked her off her feet. Shouting, the boys immediately surrounded her, wide grins on their faces.

'Look at you, miss!' shouted Callum.

'You're soaked!' yelled Will.

Ruth laughed. 'Yes, I am, Will.' She spun about on the spot, her skin prickling with the cold. It was glorious! Why hadn't she been doing this all along? Why had she cared what others might think? She was miles from England now. From her mother, from convention, from unspoken rules of conduct. She was free to be whomever she chose to be, and right now Ruth chose to stand dripping wet but blessedly cool on the deck of a ship in the middle of an endless blue ocean on a stifling hot afternoon. No wonder this was the highlight of the children's day.

Ruth felt a strange sensation of release, as if she'd been holding on to something tightly and was finally starting to let it go.

Fergus grabbed her hand, his face alight with joy, and she laughed again. Slick with water, she snatched at Will's hand as she and her boys formed a circle. They stretched the circle as wide as it would go, then, with a cheer, they ran into the middle and raised their joined hands into the air. Back and forth they went, their cheers becoming louder each time they surged forward into the spray.

Water streamed down her face and she could barely see, but Ruth refused to be the first to break the chain to wipe her face. Suddenly, Fergus's hand was wrenched from Ruth's as his feet slipped out from beneath him and he landed with a thump on the deck. 'Ow,' he said, a hand on his buttocks.

The group immediately dropped hands and erupted into gales of laughter.

'Are you all right?' Ruth asked, reaching to help him up.

'Aye, miss,' Fergus said, giggling and slipping back to the deck again. He lay flat on his back in a starfish shape and closed his eyes. 'I'm good as gold.'

Wiping strands of wet hair from her face, Ruth tasted salty water on her lips and felt the sting of salt in her eyes. She was reminded of her visit to New Zealand, when her father had taken her to the beach and they had spent the entire day going in and out of the water, the sea warm enough that you could stay in for long stretches but still exit feeling refreshed. Ruth had marvelled at the empty beach; the fine, white sand; the rare presence of her father by her side.

Glancing around, Ruth wondered if Bobby had left, and spied him with his towel draped around his shoulders, watching her, a small smile playing at the edges of his mouth. He raised his eyebrows and shouted, 'If the ladies of London could see you now, eh, Ruth?'

Flushing, Ruth raised her eyebrows briefly in reply before she turned back to her boys. It was strange to think that Bobby knew she came from London, when she had no idea about his background at all.

'Bobby?' said Una. 'Oh, Ruth, everyone knows he's been teaching in Edinburgh for the past two years.'

'Well, I can't be expected to remember where every escort hails from, surely?' Ruth concentrated on cutting into the boiled potato on her plate. She'd tried to be discreet, bringing Bobby into the conversation in an offhand manner, and here Una was practically shouting his name to the heavens. Ruth hoped he couldn't hear from his table near the door.

'When he's as devilishly handsome as young Bobby over there, how could you not?' Una pressed a hand to her forehead and swooned dramatically across the table.

Ruth resisted the urge to roll her eyes. While her friendship with Betty had been easy and rapid, her relationship with Una was far less agreeable.

'Sorry to burst your bubble, Una,' said Devan, seated opposite, 'but Bobby informed me yesterday he has a sweetheart back in New Zealand and he plans to propose to her once he gets home.'

'Drat,' said Una, slapping her hand on the table. 'It's always the handsome ones.'

Ruth sat up straighter. 'Has he already worked out a plan to get to New Zealand once we reach Australia?'

'He has,' said Devan. 'There's a handful of children on board who are carrying on to New Zealand to stay with relatives, two of Bobby's lot included. He'll be accompanying them.'

'Goodness,' Ruth breathed. 'Then I might have an opportunity to travel to New Zealand too.'

'I don't see why not.' Devan glanced behind Ruth and immediately leapt to his feet. 'Betty,' he exclaimed. 'You made it.'

Betty flopped into the seat next to Ruth. 'Thought I'd never get out of there,' she said. 'Another three cases of measles arrived this afternoon.'

'I'll get your meal,' said Devan. 'I asked them to put something aside for you.'

Betty blew him a kiss. 'Thank you, my darling.'

Ruth elbowed Betty in the ribs. 'Do you want to get into trouble?'

Betty's head dropped against the back of her seat and she closed her eyes. 'After the day I've had, I couldn't give two hoots about what is appropriate, Ruthie. I'd plant a giant kiss on that gorgeous man's lips in front of everyone here if I had any energy left.'

Ruth smiled. Betty reminded her so much of Florrie. Perhaps that was why they'd hit it off. Ruth had been thinking more and more of Florrie and was desperate for news of home. War reports received via the captain were so depressing Ruth had stopped wanting to hear them. Guilt washed over her. She'd left her best friend risking her life rescuing the injured in a London being hammered with bombs, her brother and fiancé were who knew where fighting for their country, and her mother had been left to fend for herself with her dreaded sister, of all people – and here Ruth was, cruising on an ocean liner to the other side of the world.

'Eat up,' said Devan, placing a plate of food in front of Betty. 'Gotta keep your strength up.'

'Thank you,' Betty mouthed.

'Honestly, Betty, you're going to get caught,' whispered Ruth. She'd been receiving regular updates from Betty about the couple's stolen kisses behind the lifeboats. Once, Mrs Ellis had asked Ruth where Betty had disappeared to and Ruth had muddled her way through an excuse about Betty needing some alone time on deck after the strains of dealing with sick children.

Ruth had to admit she was jealous of Betty. She'd never been as breathless and sparkly-eyed around Peter.

'What is it with the Poles and their perfect eyebrows?' Una asked, fluttering her eyelashes at the steward near the door.

Ruth tried not to let her irritation with Una show. All she seemed to do was flirt incessantly with men in uniform and complain about the lack of fresh water for washing. Betty, who had gone to school with Una, assured Ruth that Una was a wonderful person, and she was simply being a little over the top because she was nervous. 'Una's always worried about whether or not people like her. Give her a chance, Ruth.'

Ruth had tried, but Una's constant flirting and ridiculous giggles were just too hard to take, to the point that Ruth was now finding ways to avoid her.

'Rumour has it we're to stop over in Cape Town,' said Reverend Kelly, who up until then had barely spoken. He looked tired, thought Ruth, taking in the bags under his deep-set eyes. Older than his fifty-odd years too. Like Ruth, the Reverend seemed to be always concerned for his charges, checking where they were at all times. She imagined they shared a similar heavy burden of responsibility. It seemed to Ruth that few of the other escorts appeared weighed down to quite the same degree.

'Oh, wouldn't it be wonderful to set foot on land again?' said Elinor, another young escort. 'And to have a chance to deal with all the dirty laundry. I hope we'll have time for a bit of shopping for the children, too. My wee Cathy has barely an item of clothing left that is fit for purpose.'

Ruth nodded. Most of her boys were in a similar situation. The clothes they had brought with them were thin and worn to begin with; now, after a few of weeks of wear, they were in a sorry state.

'I hope we'll receive a warm reception,' said Una. 'Do you suppose the people of Cape Town are even expecting us?'

'Let's hope so. The children are doing well, but they could certainly do with a break from ship life,' said Devan.

'And the Polish food,' whispered Betty.

Everyone laughed. They had eaten extremely well since coming aboard, with ample supplies of butter and meat and other foodstuffs that had been in short supply in Britain, yet some of the food was a little different from what they were used to. Beetroot in particular seemed to be a favourite with the Poles, and both the children and escorts suppressed groans whenever the vegetable was served.

Ruth knew very little about South Africa – not that anyone could be sure that was where the *Batory* was headed. The captain was extremely tight-lipped when it came to their route, no matter how hard he was pressed for information. He could regularly be seen pacing back and forth on his deck or inspecting the lifeboats and watching the various drills. Ruth imagined her concern for the children was nothing compared to the immense responsibility the captain must feel with almost five hundred children under his care, not to mention the several hundred troops, crew and passengers.

Ruth tried her best to keep the children away from the paying passengers, who had no doubt been expecting a more relaxed, quiet journey. Many were friendly, smiling and chatting with the children, but several of the first-class passengers had made it clear they were less than pleased to be on a ship with so many children.

It was the Polish crew who had surprised everyone by immediately taking the children into their hearts. While many spoke little to no English, they found a way to communicate that brought tears to Ruth's eyes. The Polish stewards were the first to respond if they spotted a child crying in a corner, and would scoop them up, piggybacking them around the room, distracting them with a game or a toy. Or, if the child was in a very bad way, they would simply hold the child on their lap until the fit of sadness had passed. Sometimes the Poles were a little too soft-hearted, filling their pockets with treats and slipping them into a child's eager hand. Mrs Ellis had been forced to have a word with the chief steward, who smiled and nodded, but continued to be the worst culprit of all.

As kind and helpful as the crew had been, there was no denying it would be a relief to arrive in Cape Town – assuming that was to be their destination – for a brief respite before the next leg of their voyage. And, Ruth added mentally, thinking with a pang of her friends and family, there might even be letters waiting from the people she travelled further from with each passing day.

14

HAZEL

Returning to the plane after her short stopover in Los Angeles was both a relief and an effort. Hazel was glad to be out of the chaos of LAX, and she was one step closer to her destination, but she wished she didn't have to sit for hours more on a cramped plane with stale air and bad food. She wished she could snap her fingers and be in London, showered and confident and ready to face an unknown and exciting future.

Instead, Hazel was unwashed, irritable and still had a furry, bitter taste in her mouth, even though she'd brushed her teeth before boarding.

She glanced down the aisle, hoping she might be able to return to her original seat. Perhaps dear old Mrs Jenkins and her husband had disembarked in LA. Sadly, she spied them with their heads together, chatting to one another.

When she reached her seat, Joe was sitting by the window. He glanced at her and smiled hesitantly. 'Apparently no-one is in the window seat for this leg, so I thought I'd move over and give you some more room. Unless you'd rather we swap? Would you like to be by the window?' His voice was proper and polite.

'Thanks, but I'm good here.' Hazel had decided she would be friendly with Joe but limit the conversation. She'd blabbed on enough already. Having a seat between them would help.

First, though, she had to give him something.

'Here,' she said, throwing Joe a white plastic bag. 'I got you this to say sorry.'

Joe opened the bag and pulled out a pale blue t-shirt with *Los Angeles Lakers* printed across the front.

'I wanted to find you a plain t-shirt but everything had something written on it and –' Hazel stopped abruptly. Oh God, Joe no longer had a giant Coke stain down his front; he was wearing a clean grey t-shirt instead. 'You bought a new one already.'

Joe smiled as he folded up the t-shirt and put it back in the bag. 'Thanks, Hazel, you didn't need to do that.'

Hazel felt her cheeks grow hot. 'Keep it anyway', she mumbled. 'Consider it a replacement.'

Joe pinched his t-shirt. 'I had this in my bag all along, only I'd forgotten about it.'

Hazel laughed. 'You're joking.'

'I kid you not.' The glint in Joe's dark blue gaze caused Hazel's legs to wobble.

She busied herself getting settled into her seat and immediately pulled out her earbuds. For some reason she hadn't wanted to listen to music on the first leg of her journey, but now she couldn't wait to zone out and listen to some familiar tunes.

'What did you think of the famous LAX?' asked Joe.

Hazel pulled out her earbuds. 'Sorry?'

'Los Angeles airport. What did you think?'

So much for not engaging in conversation. Joe was a hard man to read.

'It was carnage,' she said. 'By the time I got through passport control, collected my bags and checked in again, it was time to board.'

'I lost sight of you when we got off.'

Hazel wasn't sure what to make of his expression. 'I dashed for the bathroom.'

Neither of them spoke for several seconds and Hazel reached for her earbuds. 'I was worried,' blurted Joe. 'Thought you might have got into trouble.'

'Trouble?'

Joe shrugged. 'An innocent young Kiwi girl on her first trip overseas . . .'

Hazel smiled. Joe really was a total enigma. 'I'm quite capable of taking care of myself, Joe. It's not like I've been living in a convent.'

'I guess when you've been mugged four times you tend to be a little more aware of the dangers that might be lurking around unsuspecting corners.'

'Four times?' Hazel squealed. 'In London?'

"Fraid so.'

'Well that's just great. I'm not at all worried about living there now.'

'You'll be fine. It was bad luck, that's all. Plus, I probably should be a little more careful about where I walk at three o'clock in the morning.'

Hazel couldn't work out why Joe was making such an effort – or was she the one who was feeling awkward and he was acting normally? Surely nothing had changed between them just because Joe had told her he was married.

'Do you make a habit of wandering around at that time of night?' Hazel asked.

Joe picked at something under his thumbnail. 'I don't sleep very well,' he admitted.

'Do you have insomnia?'

'I guess that's what you'd call it.'

'Same.'

'Really?'

'Oh yeah, I'm hopeless.' She paused. 'So when you can't sleep, you go out walking the dodgy streets of London?'

Joe laughed. 'I enjoy it, apart from the occasional mugging. There's something about the old buildings and shadowed gardens. I imagine all sorts of stories about people who've lived there in the past. It's odd, I know.' He cleared his throat. 'What about you? What do you do when you can't sleep?'

Hazel's cheeks grew warm. 'I make up songs.'

'In your head?'

'No. I get out my guitar and muck around with soppy lyrics until they become so nauseating I go back to bed. Or I go to the kitchen, make coffee and watch the sun come up.'

'I guess we've both seen a lot of sunrises over the years.'

Hazel grinned. 'You've likely seen more.'

'What's that supposed to mean?'

'Well, you're much older . . .'

Joe pretended to look horrified. 'How old do you think I am?'

Hazel frowned, examining his face. 'Forty?'

Joe's eyes widened. 'Forty!'

Hazel laughed. 'I'm joking!'

'I bloody well hope so.'

'So?'

'So what?'

'How old are you?'

Joe pursed his lips. 'Thirty-three. And you, oh young and innocent one?'

Hazel's heart skipped a beat at his playful tone. 'Twenty-five.'

'The prime of youth,' Joe said sagely.

Hazel picked up her book and threw it at Joe. He caught it easily and placed it on his lap. 'Thanks, I needed something to read.'

'I want that back after I've listened to some music,' Hazel warned him.

Joe smiled as he opened her book.

What the hell was going on? Hazel wondered. Joe was being friendlier than ever. Maybe now he'd told her he was married he could be more relaxed. Oh no! That was it. He'd picked up on the fact she liked him, and now that he'd told her he was married he could afford to be friendly because he'd made it clear he was unavailable. Hazel wanted to run back down the aisle and demand they open the door to let her off the plane. For the first time, Hazel admitted to herself she'd been attracted to Joe from the moment they'd met. Finding out he was married had affected her more than she wanted to admit. Hazel put her earbuds in and pressed play, determined to put this stupid infatuation behind her.

15

Crossing the line, 1940

Fergus slipped his hand into Ruth's and squeezed, a nervous grin on his face. He leant against her, while the other boys in her group pressed close, holding their breaths as they stared at the spectacle before them. The captain stood on a raised platform on the wide sundeck with a trident in his hand and a fierce expression on his face. He was no longer wearing the starched, crisp uniform they had always seen him in. Now he was dressed in a long, flowing white robe with a gold rope tied around the waist, and a crown adorning a long golden wig. Around him stood several members of his crew in similar robes, mischievous smiles on their faces.

'I am King Neptune, ruler of the seas, and these are my Tritons,' the captain shouted, his English far better than Ruth had anticipated. 'If you wish to cross the great equator, you must become initiated into the brotherhood of the great seas. Who among you will be brave enough?'

The children shuffled and whispered, excitement mingling with fear on their young faces.

Reverend Kelly raised his hand. 'I am ready, King Neptune,' he said solemnly, before turning and winking at the gathered children.

Everyone watched as Reverend Kelly removed his shirt and stepped forward. The Tritons grasped him by the arms, dragging him dramatically across the deck, and doing their best to keep straight faces as they demanded he crawl through the long barrel they had positioned in front of King Neptune. Once the Reverend had crawled through, he was doused with the saltwater hose and made to kneel briefly at Neptune's feet.

Realising they had nothing to fear from this unusual sea ritual, the children began to step forward one by one, the ensuing laughter and shouts of encouragement echoing across the still and listless seas. When it was the turn of Ruth's group, she was the first to crawl through the barrel as her boys cheered her on.

Eventually, everyone completed the initiation, some needing more coaxing than others, and the captain spoke again. 'You have been duly initiated and baptised into my court and shall henceforth be helped, assisted and protected from all pirates, devils and perils of the seven seas. As such, we present you each with a document that shall be valid forevermore, and which is signed and sealed in accordance with ancient tradition.' Then the children and escorts were handed certificates stamped with the red seal of Neptune.

'We're safe now,' Ruth heard a young girl say to her friend, both clutching their precious certificates to their chest. 'The enemy can't touch us.'

Ruth wished she had their confidence. She was aware the risk of attack had lessened as they travelled south, but they were still vulnerable. She was glad some of the children's anxieties were alleviated, though.

'Miss.' Fergus tugged at the towel she had draped around her shoulders. 'What about Rosie? She needs to be protected too.'

Ruth thought quickly. Rosie was improving slowly but was still unable to leave her sickbed. Thankfully, Reverend Kelly overheard and he knelt before Fergus. 'She has already undergone her own initiation. King Neptune visited all the children in the hospital before he came here.'

'He did?' asked Fergus hopefully.

'Indeed. Next time you visit Rosie, she can show you her certificate.'

Fergus's face brightened.

'Run along with the other boys and get ready for dinner,' said Ruth, smiling.

'Aye, miss.'

Ruth and the clergyman watched him race across the deck, his thin arms and legs tanned from the sun.

'Is that true?' Ruth asked. 'Did the captain visit the children in the hospital first?'

'Of course! Our dear Betty made sure of that.'

'Bless her heart,' murmured Ruth.

'Indeed.' Reverend Kelly cleared his throat. 'How is young Fergus doing?'

Ruth sighed. A few days earlier, she'd mentioned Fergus's inability to settle down to any of the activities being offered to the children on board. 'No improvement, I'm afraid. You've seen him wandering about, Reverend. He's always so restless. It's as if nothing piques his interest.'

While there were no school lessons per se, the escorts had made a concerted effort to ensure the children had a clear structure to their days. After breakfast, they tidied their cabins before engaging in drills and physical exercise – mostly dancing for the girls and ball games for the boys. Then talks were held for the older children, given by various escorts, soldiers or passengers on board who had special knowledge in areas ranging from geography, to Australian customs, to the mechanical workings of an engine. The younger children gathered in another area of the ship for games and activities more suited to their age.

After lunch and a short rest in their cabins, it was back to the decks and common rooms for further games, activities and the much-loved spray with the hose. Then it was dinner followed by a film, concerts put on by the children or board games, before the children were encouraged by their weary escorts to retire to their beds.

Most children were happy enough to participate in the activities offered, but Fergus struggled. He'd drift from one activity to another, and was most often found standing at the railings staring out to sea.

Ruth sympathised. She'd found it difficult to find a purposeful role herself. Without a proper curriculum to teach, she'd felt at a loss. She'd moved about assisting wherever she felt she could most be of service but never feeling particularly helpful, until one day she was taken firmly by the arm and dragged towards the piano by an older Australian escort called Meta Maclean. Meta was passionate about singing and had been rounding up larger and larger groups of children to join in with various songs. Already the children had performed three concerts for passengers and crew, with another big one planned for the following week. They would perform a song Meta had written especially for the young passengers of the *Batory* describing their experiences.

'Let me hear you sing, Ruth,' Meta had demanded.

'Oh no!' Ruth hadn't sung since she was fourteen years old, when her mother had forced her to join the church choir. As a self-conscious adolescent, Ruth had found standing before the congregation mortifying. 'I have a terrible voice.'

'Nonsense. Now let's hear it.'

Meta had sat at the piano and started to play and sing 'There'll Always Be an England', and Ruth had reluctantly joined in.

Initially, she was hesitant, but as the song continued Ruth had found her heart beating faster, her voice growing more confident. She sang the final note loudly, and as it faded away her lungs continued to fizz.

'Bravo,' shouted Meta. 'You're hired, Ruth.'

'For what exactly?'

'I need help organising the concert and rallying the children, teaching them their various harmonies. You, my lucky duck, can help me.' Meta stood and shook Ruth's hand. 'Please,' she added. 'I promise it will be fun.'

And, remarkably, it had proven to be just that. Ruth had surprised everyone, herself most of all, with her enthusiasm and commitment to her new role.

If only Fergus had found something to capture him in the same way.

'I notice Fergus has been rather taken by the young New Zealander,' said Reverend Kelly now, stroking his chin. 'Perhaps Bobby could encourage him into an activity, such as boxing?'

Ruth kept her expression neutral. Fergus had been seeking out Bobby's company more and more recently, sitting beside him during various performances and following him about on deck. Ruth didn't mind, of course, but nor did she want to encourage what she viewed as a mild infatuation. At least Fergus had shown no interest in boxing. In fact, he seemed to be doing his best to avoid the boxing sessions altogether.

'I'm not sure that would be Fergus's cup of tea,' Ruth said carefully. 'But perhaps I could have a word with Bobby, see if he has any other suggestions.'

Ruth didn't want to have a conversation with Bobby. Mostly because it was high time she thanked him and she could only imagine his look of smug satisfaction. Callum's behaviour had improved dramatically since he'd started his boxing lessons. He was calmer, more respectful and polite, and he'd even on occasion been friendly to Fergus. Ruth prided herself on being right about most things, but in her attitude towards boxing she knew she had been too rash.

~

The following morning, after yet another long, restless night with the blackouts over the portholes preventing any hint of a breeze from entering her stifling cabin, Ruth rose early and made her way to breakfast. She was on her third cup of tea when Bobby entered and she waved to get his attention. He looked at her in surprise before crossing the room to greet her. 'Good morning, Ruth,' he said.

'I wondered if you would join me for breakfast,' Ruth said. 'I was hoping to discuss something with you.'

He raised his eyebrows. 'All right,' he said, dropping into the chair opposite. 'This should be interesting.'

A steward arrived at his side to take his order, and Ruth waited until he had gone before she began.

Avoiding eye contact, she said, 'Well, first I have to thank you. Callum's behaviour is much improved and I' – Ruth took a deep breath – 'I believe it's a result of his boxing lessons with you.'

Bobby nodded. 'Quite possibly.'

'I was also, well, I was wondering if you had any advice regarding Fergus. He's taken rather a shine to you, as you're no doubt aware, and, well, he's struggling to settle.'

'Yes, I'd noticed.'

Ruth couldn't quite read his tone. Did he think she should be doing a better job with her charges? 'I have tried to engage him in various activities,' she said defensively.

'I'm sure you have.'

His laidback air bordered on dismissive and Ruth found herself growing angry. She wished she'd never called him over. 'I was going to ask for your advice, but I've changed my mind,' she said curtly.

Bobby bit his lip, evidently trying not to smile.

'I'm a joke to you, aren't I?' Ruth snapped.

His grin disappeared and he leant forward. 'No, Ruth, not at all – I'm sorry if I've made you feel that way. It's just that you appear so pained at the prospect of having to talk to me, let alone ask for my help, and it's . . . well, it's amusing.'

'You're laughing at me,' Ruth stated, snatching at her toast and taking a bite.

Bobby opened his mouth to respond but closed it again as the steward returned and took quite some time about pouring tea and placing a plate of toast with butter and bacon before him.

'Thanks, mate,' said Bobby, flashing the steward his laconic smile. 'I'm starving.' He picked up his knife, glancing at Ruth. 'Your determination to ensure that Fergus and all the other children in your care are happy, regardless of the situation, is charming.'

'Thank you,' said Ruth sarcastically.

'And unrealistic,' Bobby continued. 'I'm surprised most of the children have adapted as well as they have done. Although I suspect there are still plenty of secret tears at night. I agree Fergus is unsettled, but it's to be expected. He tells me he didn't want to leave home or his family, he feels responsible for his younger sister, and he lives in fear of Callum and his little gang of followers causing trouble. I'd feel out of sorts too in the circumstances. You can't wave a magic wand and make those concerns disappear.'

'So what do you suggest? I leave him to drift about aimlessly?'

Ruth waited while Bobby chewed his bacon. A part of her wanted to get up and leave because the man was so infuriating, but another part was interested in what he had to say. She'd never had a discussion with a man who spoke with such frankness.

Bobby took a sip of tea before speaking. 'I'd suggest that since Fergus doesn't like to sit still for long periods, he would benefit from more physical exertion.'

'I agree.'

'I'd like to give him some private boxing lessons to raise his confidence.'

'Fergus doesn't want to box.'

'Yes he does. He told me as much.'

'Really?'

'He knows you don't approve and so has done his best to hide his interest.'

'That's ridiculous.'

'He's very fond of you, Ruth. He wants your approval.'

'I never . . .' Ruth paused. Come to think of it, she might have told Fergus more than once how glad she was he hadn't taken up the sport. And maybe she'd been more negative about boxing than she should have been. 'Did he really say he wanted to learn to box?'

'He did.'

'And will . . . that is, would you be willing to teach him?'

'Of course,' said Bobby. 'If you'd be willing to let him participate in such a lowly pastime.' His expression told Ruth he was teasing her, and she was surprised to find herself smiling back.

'I suppose I could allow it,' she said, with a false primness.

Bobby laughed. 'That's more like it, Ruth.'

She was somewhat astonished to find herself laughing in return.

16

Cape Town, 1940

'There it is,' yelled Rosie, her face glowing as she pointed towards the distinctive outline of Table Mountain on the pale blue horizon. They had been gathered on deck for some time, waiting for a glimpse of land, and there were squeals of delight from the excited children. Rosie and Fergus stood side by side, gripping the handrail and gazing in wonder.

Mrs Ellis and Ruth smiled at one another, acknowledging what a relief it was to see some life and colour in the small girl at last.

Ruth was relieved, too, to have finally left the tropical heat behind them. It was the perfect temperature, neither too hot nor too cold, and the air was pleasantly crisp and dry.

'Can you believe this is winter?' said Mrs Ellis. 'It's like a decent summer day back home.'

'Certainly doesn't feel like any winter I've known,' agreed Ruth.

'Miss,' said Callum, pulling at Ruth's sleeve, 'I've not finished my letter to Ma.'

'Don't worry, Callum. We still have plenty of time.' The children had been frantically writing letters to their loved ones ever since the captain had announced they would be calling in at Cape Town. A mountain of letters sat in the office of Mr Callihan, the chief escort, waiting to be posted once they reached the port. There were also piles and piles of carefully labelled clothes, ready to be given a proper clean.

Ruth felt as excited as the children at the prospect of stepping off the boat. Almost as excited as she felt about putting on a freshly laundered outfit.

'Do they know we're coming?' asked one of Mrs Ellis's girls.

'Of course!' Mrs Ellis exclaimed. 'They can't wait to meet you.'

'What if they don't like us?' another girl asked.

'Ah now, Claire, how could they not? Especially because I know you will all be on your very best behaviour.'

'That's right,' said Betty, who'd taken a small break from hospital duties to join everyone on deck. 'They're going to fall in love with all of you, just like everybody on this ship has.'

Ruth hoped she was right. She feared that without gentle care and attention the children could become overwhelmed, and their homesickness — never far from the surface — would swamp them once more.

From the moment they pulled into port, Ruth knew she had nothing to worry about. Crowds of smiling faces waved and cheered as the *Batory* drew close. Some of the mothers holding babies in their arms had tears in their eyes as they shouted words of welcome. There was a diverse mix of people in an array of attire, from the golden-tanned men and women in shirts and dresses whom Ruth assumed must be Afrikaners to the locals in colourful robes and dresses.

'That man's selling oranges,' cried Rosie. 'Look, Fergus.' She pointed to a cart overflowing with fruit.

Children pressed against the railing, waving. 'No-one is wearing a coat, miss,' cried Callum. 'Can't we take ours off?'

'Soon,' said Ruth, the sun in the clearest of blue skies laughing in the face of winter.

'Look at those mountains,' Betty said. 'They're so green and tall and solid. Such a blessed change from flat and endless blue.'

As eager as they all were to go ashore, there was a long wait as authorities came on board and engaged in various discussions with the captain and Mr Callihan. Finally, after showing a great deal of patience, and helped by the novelty of being issued with a small amount of pocket money they were told they could spend while in Cape Town, the children were led down the gangway and onto waiting buses.

There was much pointing and shouting as they drove through the city to the nearby showground, where a group of smiling volunteers waited to greet them.

'Welcome, we are so happy to have you all,' cried a woman in a Salvation Army uniform. 'Come along and find a seat, and soon we'll have something delicious for you to eat.'

'We think you are so brave,' said another volunteer, taking a child's hand. 'We're very proud to meet you.'

Everywhere Ruth looked, there were smiling, friendly adults, and her tension began to ease.

The moment all the children were seated, a man strode onto the lawn before them and spoke into a microphone in a strange accent. 'Brave girls and boys of brave mothers and fathers of Great Britain, all of the people of South Africa say welcome. Are you ready to have some fun?'

Everyone cheered.

A glorious afternoon ensued, with a delicious packed lunch, races and other fun activities on the grass. Plus, with so many locals keen to entertain the children, the escorts were able to retire to the grandstand for a rest.

'I haven't felt this relaxed since we left Liverpool,' said Una, stretching out her legs. Ruth agreed, pleased she felt no irritation towards Una for a change. Now they were safe on land, Ruth felt lightness in her chest as a small measure of responsibility and care was temporarily lifted.

Catching sight of little Rosie with flushed cheeks giggling in the sack race, Fergus running alongside shouting encouragement, Ruth had to bite down on her cheek to stop herself from bursting into tears. She was so pleased to see them happy. Fergus had even removed his beloved cap and was running with it in his hand, a sure sign he was feeling relaxed too.

'The children won't want to leave,' murmured Bobby. He lay on his back across several chairs a few rows below Ruth, with his hat over his face. She'd assumed he'd fallen asleep, he had been still for so long. As unburdened as she felt right now, she couldn't imagine ever being as relaxed as Bobby. She still wanted to keep an eye on the children at all times. Studying Bobby's chest as it rose and fell, Ruth couldn't decide if she should be the one to relax more, or if she should tell Bobby to jolly well sit up.

'I understand we are to be entertained at the Governor-General's house tomorrow,' said Reverend Kelly, tipping his hat forward to shade his face from the blazing sun.

'Fancy that,' murmured Mrs Ellis, leaning back and closing her eyes.

Ruth immediately thought of her mother and how much she would enjoy informing her sister, and anyone else she came into contact with, that her daughter had been to the house of the Governor-General of South Africa. Just thinking of her mother's proud, superior air made Ruth cringe. Perhaps she wouldn't include the news in her next letter to her mother after all.

Ruth wondered what time it was in London. She imagined Florrie driving an ambulance through darkened, bomb-damaged streets. She thought of her fiancé, Peter, and her brother, Frank, possibly lying in a muddy trench somewhere while here she sat, miles and miles from home, with a half-peeled juicy orange in her hand.

'Do you suppose there will be mail for us?' she asked, licking at the juice dribbling down her wrist.

'I believe it is being sorted on the *Batory* as we speak,' replied the Reverend.

'Gosh, it will be good to finally have some news from home . . . won't it?' There was some hesitation in Betty's voice.

Ruth was looking forward to reading her mail but, like everyone else, she worried about what the letters might contain.

'Well,' she said, rising to her feet, 'I'm going to get another cup of tea.' Rather than sit and dwell, she would try to be more like the children and focus on this moment right here, with the laughter and the scent of cut grass in the air. They deserved a distraction from what they had left behind and, more importantly, from the unknown future ahead.

The next few days in Cape Town flew by, starting with an afternoon tea in the sprawling grounds of the Governor-General's house, where the children roamed freely and delighted in being served copious cakes, jellies and ice cream. Then there was a trip to a golden sand beach, an afternoon at the zoo, a frenetic morning at the shops – surprisingly the children spent the majority of their two precious shillings not on themselves, but on souvenirs such as postcards, paper knives and handkerchiefs to send to their parents – and picnics in parks surrounded by exotic plants and flowers the children and their escorts had never seen or heard of before.

It had been decided to withhold all mail until the *Batory* was once again at sea, mostly so the children could enjoy themselves and not be disturbed by possible unfortunate news from home. And so it was that a group of nearly five hundred tired yet happy children gathered on the decks to wave farewell to Cape Town as the *Batory* slowly pulled out of the harbour.

Fergus leant against Ruth's leg and she draped her arm around his shoulders.

'Everyone back in Glasgow would be right jealous,' Fergus said. 'Wouldn't they, miss?'

'Indeed they would, Fergus,' she replied.

On the way to tea, there was much excited chatter among the children as they talked about all they had seen and done, but as their ship drew away from the coast and the swell picked up, the dining saloon grew quiet. After their meal, mail was handed out, and the children became even more tremulous as their heads were filled with home once more.

Making her way from one child to another, Ruth discovered that most of the letters from their parents were deliberately light-hearted, but a few children became distressed as they learnt that their home had been destroyed or a family member was injured, missing or killed.

The crew, soldiers and passengers did their best to bolster their spirits, but it was painfully difficult, especially as the sight of one child in tears would often set off another.

By the time all of her boys were settled in their beds that night, Ruth retired to her cabin emotionally exhausted. She lay motionless on her bunk until eventually she was able to summon the energy to sit up and open the letters waiting on her desk. She started with the two from her mother and was relieved to discover they were mostly filled with grievances about her sister. Florrie's letters were far more entertaining, and Ruth was pleased her friend continued to be her usual determined, optimistic self. Neither Florrie nor her mother had heard from Frank since he'd gone to France, but as Florrie wrote more than once, no news was good news.

The last letter Ruth opened was from Peter. He was unable to say where he was, he wrote, but he was well and looking forward to being granted leave soon. Apart from mentioning that he missed her and hoped for her safe return, there was little in the way of affection in his words, and certainly no passionate declarations of love.

Sighing, Ruth placed the letters in the bottom of her suitcase and readied herself for bed. With thoughts of home racing around in her head, Ruth tried to focus on the engine's gentle hum, and eventually it sent her off to sleep.

17

Indian Ocean, 1940

When Ruth entered the dining saloon for breakfast none of her boys had appeared yet. None except Fergus, looking fresh-faced and eager.

She wandered over to say hello.

'Good morning, miss,' he said brightly, spreading butter on his toast.

'Hello, Fergus, what brings you to breakfast so chipper?'

He froze, the toast inches from his mouth. 'I've my boxing lesson, miss.'

'Oh, yes, of course.' Ruth suppressed a smile. How could she have forgotten? It was all Fergus talked about since Bobby had started sessions with him on Wednesday mornings.

Which reminded Ruth she needed to have a word with Bobby about another escapade the previous week. The problem was, she wasn't sure yet whether she wanted to thank or scold the Kiwi. Either way, Ruth secretly wished she could have witnessed the event, instead of receiving a second-hand account from Reverend Kelly.

After he'd caught Callum giving Fergus a shove, Bobby must have taken it on himself to try to resolve the ongoing tension between the two boys. According to the Reverend, Bobby put them both in the boxing ring and told them the first one to get their opponent on the ground would be the winner. Callum had strutted into the ring confident of victory. What he didn't know was that the previous day Bobby had taught Fergus a special manoeuvre guaranteed to drop his opponent to the floor.

Within seconds of Fergus and Callum facing off in the ring, Fergus had executed the move flawlessly, and Callum had found himself sprawled across the mat. The Reverend said Callum had surprised everyone, most of all Fergus, by getting to his feet and slapping Fergus on the back. 'Good move,' Callum had said, grinning. Fergus had grinned back, and from that moment on boxing was the most exciting pursuit Fergus had ever known, Callum was a friend rather than foe, and Bobby was a fully-fledged superhero.

'Mind you listen carefully and be sure to say thank you,' said Ruth sternly.

'Aye, Miss Ruth,' replied Fergus, giving a brief salute.

She smiled at his flushed face and returned to her table, where several other escorts were now seated.

'Morning, Ruth,' said Devan, sitting opposite. 'We're crossing the equator again shortly but there'll sadly be no crossing the line ceremony, now that we're seasoned sailors.'

'I'm glad,' said Una. 'Last thing I want is to crawl through that blasted barrel again.'

'It's unfortunate we need to cross the equator again at all,' said Devan. 'The journey is going to take a lot longer than expected if we have to keep zigzagging all over the show. Although I hear we're headed to a port somewhere in Asia, which should be interesting.'

'It's turning into a round-the-world cruise,' said Betty. 'I must say, I'm in no hurry.' She glanced at Devan and her cheeks flushed.

'Except,' said Reverend Kelly, leaning forward and speaking in a low, quiet voice, 'we're not extending this journey out of choice. I understand we have already had one or two close calls with the enemy.'

The mood at the table sobered immediately. Sometimes Ruth found it easier to pretend they were simply having a wonderful cruise rather than acknowledging the bleak and often terrifying reality.

'I've always wanted to go to Asia – all those exotic spices and flavours,' said Betty, clearly trying to raise their spirits.

'Yes,' said Ruth, determined to be positive too. 'It's wonderful for the children to be exposed to new and interesting cultures. Remember how much they enjoyed South Africa?'

Everyone nodded.

'Well' – Devan pushed back his chair and stood – 'I've promised some of the lads a game of football on deck.' He leant closer to Betty. 'Might see you later on?' he whispered.

Betty grinned. 'I'm counting on it.'

Devan had barely moved out of earshot before Una exclaimed, 'Oh, Betty, I do believe you are in love.'

'Shush,' said Betty, glancing over her shoulder at the adjacent table, where Mrs Ellis sat with Mr Callihan.

'Oh, come on, there's no point in trying to hide it anymore. Besides, they can't exactly tell you to pack your bags and go home now, can they?'

Ruth laughed and Una stared at her, surprised.

'What?' Ruth asked.

'Nothing – I just don't think I've made you laugh before.' Una's smile was hesitant as she got to her feet. 'Well, I'd better get back to the hospital. Have fun, Betty.' She winked at her friend and weaved her way among the tables to the exit.

After settling her boys into their beds that evening, Ruth headed up to the deck. It was still and balmy, the sun low and fat on the horizon. Standing at the railing, she watched flying fish soar over the water and dip below the surface, causing barely a ripple. The sea stretched in every direction, glinting and glorious. Sometimes Ruth panicked at the vastness: her heart would start to race and she'd feel light-headed, overwhelmed by how small and insignificant their ship seemed in comparison to the enormity of blue that enveloped them. Tonight, however, Ruth was filled with a calm, respectful awe.

'Hello, Ruth.'

Turning, Ruth smiled at Reverend Kelly. 'It's a beautiful evening.'

'Yes,' said the Reverend carefully.

Ruth knew from his grave expression that something was terribly wrong.

'What is it?' she asked.

The Reverend sighed, tears in his eyes. 'I'm sorry to have to tell you this, Ruth, but we've just heard on the wireless that the *City of Benares* has been sunk. It was bound for Canada with' – his voice cracked – 'with many young evacuees on board.'

Ruth's hand flew to her mouth. 'Oh no!' she exclaimed.

'I'm afraid there appear to be few survivors.'

Ruth's thoughts flew to Fergus and Rosie and all the other children sleeping peacefully in their beds below deck. What would their mothers and fathers be thinking after learning the fate of the *City of Benares*? As for the parents of the poor children who had lost their lives, it was simply too dreadful to imagine what they would be going through.

'They were brave to the end, the children apparently singing as the ship went down.'

'Don't,' gasped Ruth, turning back to look at the horizon so the Reverend wouldn't see her tears. The Indian Ocean was no longer glorious but dark and ominous, as if guarding terrible secrets within its depths.

'We must keep it from the children,' she said fiercely.

Reverend Kelly put a hand on her shoulder and squeezed. 'The escorts are meeting in the dining saloon now to discuss what to do.'

Taking a shuddering breath, Ruth turned her back on the sea.

The sombre mood of the dining saloon was in stark contrast to a few hours earlier, when it had been filled with the chatter and laughter of many children. It was as if Ruth had arrived at a funeral.

'Oh, Ruthie, I can't bear it.' Betty ran across the room and collapsed into Ruth's arms. Escorts were scattered about the room, crying and comforting one another.

'It isn't going to happen to us,' Ruth said firmly, her throat tight. 'I . . . I won't allow it, Betty. I *won't*.'

Mr Callihan called for everyone's attention and the room fell silent. 'Our prayers are with the families of the children who have lost their lives at sea.' The chief escort's quivering jaw betrayed the emotion behind his stern expression. 'Unfortunately, I have just been advised some of our older evacuees overheard some passengers discussing the tragedy, so I ask that you please go urgently and check on your charges, comfort them as best you can, and where possible please try to shield the younger ones from the news.'

Everyone filed out silently and Ruth went to find her boys.

The first cabin she entered was quiet and still, but for the faint and reassuring sound of steady breathing. Their innocent, peaceful faces brought an ache to Ruth's chest. She checked beside each bunk to ensure lifebelts were within easy reach, along with a coat, shoes, a sunhat and a mug.

Hearing shuffling noises from across the passageway, Ruth slipped out and hurried to the opposite cabin, where she found four of her boys huddling together on one bunk, their knees tucked up to their chins.

'Is it true, miss?' asked Callum, white-faced.

Ruth crouched before them. 'I'm afraid it is.'

'If . . . if it happens to us . . .' stammered Will.

'It won't,' Ruth broke in. She repeated what she'd said to Betty: 'I won't allow it.'

'But you can't stop the Germans, miss.'

It was true. She couldn't stop a torpedo and it was silly for her to pretend she could. 'Perhaps not. But I know this. You are brave British children and if – I don't believe it will happen – but if we are attacked, you will react quickly and calmly and we will make our way to the lifeboats and we will be safe.'

'We *are* brave,' said Will, sitting up straighter. 'And fast.'

'And we do like an adventure, miss,' said Callum, with a ghost of a smile.

'We do.' Ruth leant forward and gave each of the boys a hug. 'Now, you can chat for a little longer but then I want you to try to sleep. I have to check on the rest of my group and then I'll be back to see how my brave boys are getting on, all right?'

'Aye, miss,' they piped.

Ruth found all the inhabitants of the next cabin sound asleep. In the last cabin, three beds contained sleeping bodies, but the fourth was empty.

'Oh, Fergus,' Ruth murmured, looking at his empty bunk. She hurried to her own cabin to find him slumped in the chair at her desk. Leaping to his feet, Fergus said, 'Rosie can't know.' His voice was wobbling. 'Not till we reach Australia.' With a splutter he ran towards her and she held his trembling body tight.

'We'll try to keep the news from her, Fergus, but I can't make any promises.'

Sniffing, he sagged against her. 'I don't want to be at sea no more,' he whispered. 'I know we're not to say it, but I want to go home to me ma and da, miss. I want us all to go home.'

Ruth couldn't sleep that night. After calming Fergus, settling him into bed and ensuring all her boys were asleep, she paced around her small cabin. If she tried to lie down, even for a minute, thoughts of the children on the *City of Benares* flew into her head. She imagined their fear during the attack, the growing horror as their ship started to sink, the freezing cold of the ocean as it dragged them into its depths. Then her thoughts would turn to Brenda. Brenda, crushed beneath the rubble of her home, calling out to her parents lying silent and lost within the mountain of bricks.

As the dark night wore on, Ruth felt the *Batory* start to pitch and roll with ever-increasing surges, a howling wind causing the ropes and pulleys outside to jangle and smack against each other. Ruth peered through her porthole into a night so dark she could see nothing but blackness.

Finally Ruth could bear the confines of her cabin no longer. She dressed and staggered along the pitching passageway, desperate to escape her thoughts. Leaning her full weight on the door to force it open against the wind, Ruth burst onto the deck, gripping the railing for support. The sky and sea made a wall of angry grey as Ruth stumbled forward, rain lashing at her face and forming pools on the slippery deck. It was as if the raging storm matched the turmoil inside her head. She told herself she needed to stay strong, maintain a calm demeanour, a stiff British resolve.

'Ruth!' Bobby appeared as if from nowhere, his hair in disarray and his eyes wide and startled. 'What are you doing out here in this storm? Are you looking for Rosie?' He reached out as if to clasp her hand, then abruptly grabbed on to the railing instead as the ship lurched to one side.

'Why would I be looking for Rosie?' She had to shout above the roar of the wind and sea.

Bobby hesitated, his expression tense.

'Bobby, what's happened?' Ruth yelled.

'Mrs Ellis raised the alarm when she discovered Rosie wasn't in her bed. I've just checked with Fergus to see if perhaps Rosie had gone to visit him, but he hasn't seen her and now I've caused him to worry.' Bobby stepped closer to Ruth and placed a hand lightly on her arm. 'Fergus asked me to find you.'

Ruth stumbled back, turned away and clung to the handrail with both hands. She couldn't let Bobby see how close she was to coming apart. What if Rosie was injured or trapped somewhere, calling for help? Or, worse, she'd fallen overboard and been swallowed by the angry sea?

A warm hand pressed into her shoulder. 'We'll find her, Ruth. She'll be all right.' Bobby's mouth was close to her ear as he spoke, and suddenly she wanted to lean back against his body. She wanted him to put his arms around her. For him to squeeze her tightly and somehow banish the anguish and pain she was struggling to supress. Instead, she held herself rigid, determined to hide her vulnerability.

Bobby's hand dropped from her shoulder. 'Fergus is in the dining saloon,' he said. 'With some of the escorts and crew. They're arranging a search party.'

'Right,' said Ruth. 'We should go.'

They made their way back inside. Fergus was sitting at a table with Mrs Ellis. The moment he spotted Ruth he slipped from his chair and ran towards her. 'They won't let me look for Rosie,' he said, tears running down his face.

Ruth crouched down and pulled him into a hug. 'We're going to find her, Fergus. Can you think of where she might have gone? A secret hiding spot maybe?'

Fergus started to shake his head, then stopped. 'We found a storeroom beneath the captain's deck. Rosie loved it because she could hear the captain's voice above us. Mostly he spoke in Polish, but sometimes he used English words and she loved to try to figure out what he was saying. She –' he swallowed – 'she liked to imagine we were spies.'

'I'll take a look,' said Bobby, turning towards the door.

The ship pitched and rolled as Ruth led Fergus back to his seat.

'What if she fell overboard?' Fergus said, his voice high-pitched and shaking. 'What if she's in the sea?'

Taking a seat beside him, Ruth grasped his hand. 'This is a big ship, Fergus. Rosie could be in any number of places. We must stay positive and –' her voice broke off. She didn't know what to say or how to comfort him.

'That's right,' said Mrs Ellis, who was on Fergus's other side. 'Rosie is an adventurous wee girl; chances are she's –'

Suddenly Bobby burst through the door, his wet clothes stuck to his body. Tucked against his hip, with her arms tight around his neck, was a smiling, pale-faced Rosie. 'I got stuck in the storeroom,' she said, her eyes bright with excitement. 'Something must have slid in front of the door, and I tried to push it open but I couldn't get out.'

A cheer went about the room as Bobby lowered Rosie to the ground and Fergus dashed towards his sister. Ruth's vision blurred. Nausea swept through her and she lowered her head, waiting for it to pass.

'Ruth?' Bobby knelt beside her. 'Are you all right?'

'I'm fine,' Ruth snapped without lifting her head.

She needed him to leave her be until she could gather herself.

'Right,' muttered Bobby, standing. 'Of course you are.'

Ruth wished she could run from the room and hide in her cabin. But first she would have to encourage Fergus to return to his bed.

⁓

'Ruth, it's me, Betty, open up.'

On her narrow bed, Ruth rolled over to face the wall. Her clothes were still damp from being out in the storm, but she hadn't the energy to change. She hoped if she stayed silent Betty would go away.

The doorhandle rattled. 'You know you aren't supposed to lock your door,' Betty shouted. 'If you don't let me in, I'll go and tell the captain.'

Sighing, Ruth rolled back to face the door and got up. She walked to the door and opened it. 'I'm fine, Betty,' she said.

'So I've heard.' Betty pushed past Ruth and strode into the cabin.

Ruth closed the door and leant against it, her arms crossed.

Betty perched on the edge of Ruth's bed. 'Bobby told me about Rosie. He came to find me because he's worried about you.'

Ruth snorted. 'Bobby doesn't worry about anything.'

In the silence that followed, Ruth knew she had spoken unfairly.

'Everyone has been shaken by the news of the *Benares*,' said Betty quietly. 'Rosie going missing wouldn't have helped.'

'I'm fine.'

'In actual fact, you are not fine and I wish you would stop saying that, Ruth. What is going on with you? You're hiding something, something you carry around with you like a little storm cloud. I can practically see it hovering above your head, threatening to burst.'

'Don't be ridiculous,' muttered Ruth.

'Rosie is fine, Ruth.' Betty rose and walked slowly towards her. 'All the children are. You can't dwell on what might happen to them. Nothing bad has happened and it more than likely never will.'

'You're being naive,' said Ruth loudly. She wanted Betty to stop talking rubbish. 'Bad things happen to innocent children, Betty.' Ruth took a deep breath and clenched her hands to stop them from shaking. 'There's no sense to it. Brenda didn't deserve to die and neither did those children on the *Benares*.'

Ruth began to gasp for air, her chest tight.

'Who is Brenda?' Betty asked gently.

'Don't,' rasped Ruth. 'Don't mention her.'

'Why?'

'Because she's dead and . . . and it's my fault. I should have made her go with the other children in her class during the evacuations but she didn't want to leave her parents. She didn't want to live with strangers in the countryside. She was timid, shy, and the thought of leaving London terrified her, so I agreed with her parents that she should stay.' The words tumbled from Ruth's mouth in a torrent. 'But she shouldn't have stayed, Betty — it wasn't safe.'

'What happened?'

'She was killed in her own house. It collapsed around her, crushing her, but she was alive.' Ruth gasped, an agony of guilt crushing her chest. 'The rescuers heard her,' she whispered hoarsely. 'But they couldn't get to her in time.'

'Oh, Ruth. It's not your fault.'

'Of course it is. And if anything happens to my boys, to any of the children on board, that will be my fault too.'

'Listen to yourself, Ruth. You can't hold yourself responsible for random acts of God.'

'Yes I can. I can and I must.'

'Why?'

'Because otherwise their deaths are senseless. My guilt is part of the pain of their deaths: the part that keeps them alive within us.'

'No, Ruthie,' said Betty firmly. '*No.* I have seen people die in all sorts of ways, and they aren't kept alive through guilt — they're kept alive through *love.* Love for everything they were and the joy they brought to ourselves and others simply by existing.'

Ruth shook her head. She wanted to believe Betty's words, to remember Brenda with love and affection instead of guilt and pain. 'She was special,' murmured Ruth. 'Teachers aren't supposed to have favourites, I know, but Brenda was . . .'

Pressure built in Ruth's chest as she thought of Brenda's round, freckled face, her glasses slipping forward down her nose as she stared up at Ruth with her eager expression. 'She was the smartest in the class, even though she was the youngest.'

'I bet she loved having you as her teacher,' said Betty.

Doubling over, Ruth let out a sob that rocked her body, then she was gathered into Betty's arms.

18

JOE

Joe was doing his best not to cry. He'd never felt this way reading a book before.

'Why do you keep reading from where I got up to?' Hazel asked.

Joe glanced at her screen to see her movie had finished. 'Lazy, I guess.'

'Lazy?'

He closed the book, pleased to have a diversion. 'Can't be bothered going back to the start. This way I'm one step ahead of you.'

Hazel rolled her eyes. 'You're such a guy.'

'What do you mean?'

'Always wanting to have the upper hand. The male ego at work. You think you have to know more about everything — which you never will, by the way.'

'Because I'm a guy?'

'Precisely.'

'Don't you think that statement has a whiff of female ego about it?'

Hazel sniffed. 'There's no such thing.'

'Puh-lease,' groaned Joe. 'Why is it so important to you that I read this book from the start in an orderly page-by-page manner?'

'Because that's how you read a book.'

'Why? What's so wrong with reading from the middle, or even' – Joe flicked through the pages to the back, widening his eyes in mock horror – 'the end.'

'Don't you dare!' Hazel leant over and snatched the book from Joe's hand.

Joe laughed. Her openness and passion were like nothing he'd encountered before. It made his hands tingle.

'I'm glad you find it funny,' muttered Hazel, her cheeks reddening with the effort of trying to keep a straight face.

'I can't help it; I'm a funny guy.'

'Hilarious.'

'Seriously, though . . .' He dipped his head at the book on her lap. 'The story's pretty compelling. Sad, but interesting.'

'Let me guess: now you want to tell me all about it.'

'Saves you having to read the last chapter. I could give you a quick precis.'

'That's exactly what I want – for you to spoil the whole bloody book for me.'

'Wow, lack of sleep is starting to show.' Joe leant down to rummage in his backpack. 'I think I've got a sleeping pill in here somewhere if you'd like . . .'

A small white pillow hit Joe in the side of the head. 'I'm beginning to understand why your wife left you,' Hazel said, her smile letting him know she was joking.

Joe was amused rather than offended by her comment. He was glad she'd mentioned his wife freely. Perhaps when they got to London they could continue to catch up. As friends. 'Here I was thinking I was being charming.'

'You call this charming? That, my friend, is your ego telling you you're somehow much greater than you are.'

'And funnier,' Joe said. 'I'd be lost without my ego, Hazel. It's the one thing us males can rely on to get us through. Our egos think we're fantastic, even if no-one else does.'

'How am I supposed to survive another six hours sitting beside you and your ego?'

'I know: how about we read the book aloud to one another? A chapter each. I'll go first if you like.'

'No way.' Hazel shook her head. 'I'd rather eat aeroplane eggs.'

'Come on, it'll be very British of us. London is full of earnest types who sit around in circles reading alternate chapters of literary masterpieces and drinking tea.'

Hazel suddenly covered her face with her hands. 'Oh, Joe, what have I done?' she said, her voice muffled. 'I should never have taken this job.'

Hazel's shoulders began to shake. 'Gramps was always trying to get me to read Dickens and Austen, but I couldn't get into them. This is a disaster.' Her voice was choked, her face still hidden in her hands.

'Oh hell, Hazel, I was joking.' Joe scrambled into the middle seat and put a solicitous hand on her shoulder. 'I'm sorry, it was —'

Then he heard what sounded like a muffled snort. He pulled her hands from her face to reveal eyes shining with mirth. 'You little . . .'

Hazel's giggle turned into an outright belly laugh. 'You should see your face,' she spluttered.

Joe leant closer. 'That was low, Hazel,' he whispered, watching her lips.

Hazel stopped laughing and her gaze flitted to his lips, then up to his eyes.

'Joe,' Hazel murmured, her hands pressing into his chest. 'What are you doing?'

Pulling back, Joe blinked. What on earth *had* he been doing? 'Nothing,' he growled. 'Sorry.'

Silently, Joe returned to his seat. He could feel a vein pulsing at his throat like a flashing red light. Joe spent a long time rearranging his pillow and blanket and fiddling with his headphones. When he eventually glanced at Hazel, she was staring right at him.

'What?' snapped Joe. 'I said I was sorry.'

'I know.'

'So why are you looking at me like that?'

'Because I'm sorry too.' She paused. 'I'm sorry you're married,' she said, then immediately winced. 'Oops, that came out louder than I was expecting.' Her smile was tentative, nervous.

Joe wanted to hit something. Correction, he wanted someone to hit *him*. He'd been lying to himself. He liked Hazel way more than he should and he had wanted to kiss her so much he still ached.

Hazel's smile disappeared. Then she fumbled with her seatbelt, tumbled into the aisle, and hurried away.

'Hazel,' Joe called.

She continued on as if she hadn't heard him.

19

Sydney, 1940

'There she is, Fergus.' Ruth pointed to the Sydney Harbour Bridge. It looked even more impressive than in the pictures they had been shown during one of the shipboard talks. 'What a beauty.'

It was so sunny and bright that everyone had to squint as they lined up excitedly along the deck. Ruth had never seen such vivid colours. The glinting blue harbour was littered with small motorboats, yachts and cargo ships. From a sailing boat nearby a tanned older man wearing an unbuttoned white shirt and sunglasses waved in their direction, and Ruth's group of boys waved back enthusiastically.

'This is better than a Glasgow winter, eh, miss?'

'It certainly is, Will,' said Ruth. Ever since her outburst over Brenda, Ruth had felt calmer, yet more fragile. She still worried, but not to the point of having to know exactly where her boys were and what they were doing at all times. Looking about, Ruth smiled at her charges, so groomed and dapper in their Sunday suits, while the girls chattering excitedly nearby were arrayed in their best frocks and coats. She couldn't imagine waking up the following morning and not seeing them again. Fergus particularly had been such a constant presence that when she wasn't close to him she felt a loss, as if the sun had gone behind a cloud. She was surprised and a little alarmed by her affection for the boy. She wondered if parents experienced a similar mix of pride, joy and fear; a desperate need to keep their children safe at all costs.

As if reading her thoughts, Fergus slipped his hand into hers. 'I can't believe we're finally here, miss. It's like we're in a film.'

Rosie was standing on her tiptoes on the other side of Fergus, gripping the rail and jiggling with excitement. 'Look, Fergus, they're swimming,' she squealed, pointing to a small bay with golden sand and a handful of people in the water. 'Oh, I hope we get to go swimming, Miss Best. I've never been swimming in the ocean before.'

Ruth smiled. 'I'm sure you'll be doing plenty of swimming, Rosie.'

Fergus tightened his grip on Ruth's hand while his other hand reached up to tap his cap — a gesture Ruth now knew meant he was either nervous or worried, or both. 'What happens now, miss?'

'I understand many of the host families are here to greet you. I'm sure things have been well organised.'

'We don't have relatives like some of the others,' said Rosie. 'We have to go with a pretend family instead.'

Ruth frowned and crouched before Rosie. 'Most of the children who will be staying with an aunt or an uncle have never met them before. It won't be so very different from you and Fergus and the other children who are going to live with' – Ruth hesitated to use the word 'strangers' – 'foster parents.' Apparently the couple who had volunteered to take Fergus and Rosie were relatives of a Mr Owens, who worked with the children's father in the mines.

'Will you be with us until' – Fergus gulped – 'until we have to go with them?'

'Oh, Fergus.' Ruth put an arm around him and pulled him into her side. 'Of course I will.'

'And I'm to stay with Rosie? We won't be split up?'

'I have been assured you will remain together; you mustn't worry.'

Rosie waved at another small motorboat nearby. Two children sitting in the back of the boat waved back. 'Wait till I tell Ma about everyone coming to see us arrive, Fergus. It's like we're royalty,' Rosie said.

'They think you're extremely brave children coming all the way out here on your own,' said Ruth.

'We are brave, miss,' said Will, wedged against the railing. 'We're the lucky ones getting to come here.'

'That you are, Will,' Ruth said, a lump in her throat threatening to cut off her breath. 'The brave and lucky few.'

She thought back to the long and wearisome previous few weeks at sea. After the sinking of the *City of Benares*, a veil of melancholy had shrouded the ship for several days. The soldiers, crew and passengers all helped the escorts to comfort the children, but even though they had been showered once more with generosity and kindness during their stopovers in Bombay, Colombo and Singapore, the children lacked their usual boisterous enthusiasm. Leaving Singapore had brought another wave of sadness as the children said goodbye to the several hundred soldiers who left the ship. Many of the children had developed close bonds with the men, and the men, for their part, had treated the children as if they were their own.

The oppressive tropical heat had also taken its toll. The children suffered from heat rash, impetigo, influenza and fatigue (many had found it impossible to sleep in the stifling conditions).

All in all, it was a relief to have finally reached their destination. A relief, yes, but also bittersweet, Ruth thought. Soon she would return to England having discharged her duties. She'd barely had time to think of returning home, and now the time had come she didn't feel ready.

As they pulled into the dock and waved down at the smiling crowds, the children began to sing the special song Meta Maclean had written about their journey aboard the *Batory*. Ruth had helped to teach the children the lyrics, and they had been so proud to have a song written just for them that they sang it at every opportunity and at every port of call. The *Batory* had been nicknamed the 'singing ship' as a result.

We heard your voices across the sea,
And we're proud to answer the call.
With heads held high,
'Neath friendly sky,
For we know you will welcome us all.

As their sweet, clear voices rang out, Ruth wanted to join in, but she was too choked up to try.

~

Eventually the children were given permission to walk down the gangway with their escorts, the sounds of cheers from the crowd on the wharf reverberating in their ears. Most of the children smiled and chatted and waved with excitement, while a few, Fergus among them, stared stonily ahead.

They were herded into a large warehouse, where for the next couple of hours organised chaos reigned. Ruth kept her group of boys, and Rosie, close by as names were called and children handed to smiling adults.

When it was Will's turn, the man stepping forward to collect him could have been his older brother, they were so similar in appearance. 'Well, hello there, Will – I'm your uncle Tim, and I promised your dad that we'd have a ball. How would you like to learn to surf, eh?'

Will was smiling so hard as he left, Ruth felt sure his cheeks must be hurting.

Eventually, only Fergus and Rosie remained, and Ruth scanned the thinning group of adults, wondering who would be the ones to collect them.

'Fergus McKenzie,' shouted the official who had introduced himself as a representative of the Child Welfare Department. 'Can we have a Fergus and Rosemary McKenzie, please.'

Ruth took each of the children by the hand and stepped forward. 'Here,' she croaked. Clearing her throat, she tried again. 'Here,' she shouted.

As they walked towards the official, Ruth quickly assessed the couple standing beside him.

They looked nice enough, she thought, taking in the woman's neat frock and the man's casual shorts and shirt. While neither of them were smiling, they both had friendly faces. They're nervous, Ruth realised. She felt Fergus's grip tighten and wondered if it was her hand that was slick with perspiration or his.

'Right then, Fergus and Rosemary, Mr and Mrs Shirley have kindly volunteered to take you in. How about you say hello?'

For a moment no-one moved, then Mrs Shirley rushed forward and gave first Rosie and then Fergus a hug. 'Oh, you poor lambs,' she said. 'This must be overwhelming for you. I'm going to do my very best to make sure you are happy here. We have a little girl slightly younger than you, Rosemary, and a small house, but a big garden, and a dog who will just love having some more children to play with. Our neighbour has a boy about your age, Fergus, and there's a lovely school just down the road.'

Fergus and Rosie stared at her without speaking. Fergus was still squeezing Ruth's hand so tight she could feel her bones pressing together.

'It's very kind of you to take Fergus and Rosie into your home, Mr and Mrs Shirley,' Ruth said. 'They have been extremely brave on their voyage out here, especially as Rosie suffered from the most terrible seasickness.'

'Oh, what a shame.' Mrs Shirley held out her hand to Ruth. 'I'm Peggy,' she said.

'Ruth.'

They shook hands.

Peggy turned to look behind her. 'And this is my husband, Steve.'

It seemed like Steve couldn't quite decide what to do. Abruptly, he shook Ruth's hand, then held out his hand to Fergus. 'Hello, young man,' he said gruffly. Fergus hesitantly let go of Ruth, wiped his palm on his shorts, and shook Steve's hand. 'Hello, Mr Shirley,' he stammered.

Ruth noticed Rosie's lower lip had started to wobble. Steve must have seen it too, because he scooped her up and rested her on his hip. 'I imagine you're exhausted,' he said softly. 'How about we take you to see your new home?'

Rosie glanced down at her brother, then at Peggy, who had rested a hand on Rosie's back. She ducked her head into Steve's chest. 'Yes, please, mister,' she said.

Smiling as widely as her breaking heart would allow, Ruth said goodbye to Rosie, kissing her on the cheek, then she bent to give Fergus a final hug. 'Be good,' she whispered. 'Be sure to write to me with all your news.'

Fergus hugged her back. 'Aye, miss.'

They let each other go, and Fergus blinked at the ground. 'Don't forget about me,' he said softly.

Ruth wanted to grab Fergus and make a run for it. They could get on a boat to New Zealand and hide out with her father until the end of this dreadful war. 'Of course I won't,' she said, trying to ignore the lump in her throat. Reluctantly, she took a step back. Steve picked up the satchels containing the children's belongings and Peggy reached for Fergus's hand.

Watching them leave, the pain in Ruth's chest was so agonising she could hardly breathe.

Sensing movement beside her, she turned to see a breathless Bobby. 'I was hoping to catch Fergus and say goodbye,' he panted. 'Am I too late?'

Ruth nodded. 'He's gone.'

'Bother.' Bobby took a deep breath in and blew it out. 'This is awful, isn't it? I know we are supposed to be all smiles but gosh . . .' He stopped and studied Ruth's face. 'Oh, Ruth.' Then he was throwing his arms around her and pulling her into a tight hug. 'They'll be all right – I'm sure they will.'

Ruth slid her arms around his waist and leant her head on his chest. 'I hope so,' she whispered. They hugged silently for several seconds, then drew apart.

'I have to go,' Bobby murmured. 'I've still got one lad to look after until his aunt arrives.'

'Yes, of course.'

She watched Bobby cross the room and wished he would turn around and come back. Her body felt heavy with sadness.

'Keep it together, Ruthie.' Betty slipped her arm through Ruth's. 'We've come to whisk you away.'

Devan appeared on her other side. 'We have been with these children constantly for nearly three months and we deserve a rest,' he declared, as if trying to convince himself. His dazed expression and white face indicated that parting from his group of children had been difficult too.

'I've been so looking forward to a break,' Ruth said. 'Yet now we're . . . the thing is . . . I don't know what I'll do without them.'

'That's where we come in,' announced Betty, the tears in her eyes giving away her own distress at seeing the children go. 'Come on – the lovely people of this country have arranged for us to stay at the Australia Hotel, which is the best in town, apparently. I plan to have the longest bath possible, and then you and I are going to hit the town.'

20

HAZEL

When Hazel eventually returned to her seat – she couldn't hover around the toilets forever – Joe was watching a movie. The second she sat down he tapped the screen to pause it and removed his headphones. 'Look, Hazel, I think we should talk.'

There were a million things Hazel would rather do than talk about what a complete fool she'd been, acting like some pathetic, infatuated schoolgirl. What had she been hoping to achieve by telling Joe she was sorry he was married, apart from extreme mortification? She wasn't even sure why she'd said it. It had come out of nowhere. 'Okay.'

'I've only just met you, right? And we basically don't know each other at all.'

'True.'

'But I'm going to come out and say this, even though I know I shouldn't. I've really liked meeting you. A lot. And I'd love to be able to ask if we could catch up in London, like for a date or something, only I'm married and you might have a boyfriend.'

Hazel nodded. 'I *do* have a boyfriend.' She wasn't entirely sure this was correct, since she'd left her relationship with Matt in limbo. But they hadn't broken up, so technically . . .

'Okay, so there you go: I can't ask you. Which is fine – well, it's not fine, but my point to this garbled mess of a conversation is this: if I want to be asking you out, should I be going back to my wife? Is this a sign?'

Hazel blinked. 'Maybe you've been looking for a sign and it's nothing to do with me so much as you wanting a convenient way out.'

Joe widened his eyes. 'You're not one to mince your words, are you?'

Hazel grimaced. 'It's probably sleep deprivation making me slightly mad.'

Joe smiled and shook his head. 'See, when you make that face and give that little tilt of your head, it tells me I wasn't looking for a sign, Hazel, I was . . .' He hesitated. 'I know this sounds cringe, but, well . . . I think I might have been looking for you.'

'You're right,' Hazel said. 'That does sound cringe.'

'Thanks.'

'Joe, this is the most bizarre conversation I've ever had. I can't even . . . Do you have any idea how dodgy this makes you?'

'Dodgy?' Joe retorted. 'You think I'm dodgy because I've confessed an attraction to you? You just told me you were sorry I was married!'

'Would you lower your voice?' Hazel hissed.

'So you're simply sitting there wishing you'd never ended up beside some weird British guy and there's nothing going on here?' He waved his hand between them. 'Nothing at all?'

Hazel closed her eyes briefly. 'Joe,' she whispered. 'You're married.'

'You didn't answer the question.'

A sharp pain pierced Hazel's chest. 'I don't need to. You should never have asked it in the first place.'

21

Sydney, 1940

Ruth pushed the letter to her mother aside and stood up. She stretched her arms over her head, peered out of her hotel window, sighed, and sat back down. It had been over a week since she'd said goodbye to her group of evacuees, and she wished she could visit them to see how they were faring. She had enjoyed her time in Sydney, but she was restless. Especially now she knew she was headed to New Zealand with most of her fellow escorts. They'd be boarding a ship in the morning bound for Wellington, with some, like Bobby, in charge of ensuring a small remaining group of children who had come out on the *Batory* were delivered safely to their new host families in New Zealand. The escorts would then continue on to Auckland by train before beginning their long voyage home to England.

Ruth had written to her father in the hope he would be able to meet her in Auckland. She was excited at the prospect of seeing him again, but couldn't shake the sense that it was a betrayal of her mother.

A loud knock on the door startled Ruth.

'Let's go, lazybones,' came Betty's voice.

Ruth opened the door and smiled at her friend, who was dressed in a new, bright yellow sundress and straw hat. Betty had lost her gaunt, overtired look from weeks of nursing sick children and practically glowed with her golden tan and shining eyes. 'The Australian lifestyle agrees with you, Betty,' said Ruth.

'No offence, Ruth, but I honestly can't see how New Zealand can top this place. Now, let's get a wriggle on.'

'Betty, I'm sorry, but I haven't an ounce of desire for any more shopping. And I know it sounds terrible, but I don't think my skin can handle another afternoon at the beach. You're on your own.'

'We're not going shopping or swimming. We're off to the zoo to see these koalas everyone keeps talking about. Come on, Devan and Bobby are waiting for us in the lobby.'

'Bobby's coming?' Ruth hoped her tone sounded casual. She had barely seen Bobby since their arrival in Sydney and, if she was honest, ever since their hug she'd been doing her best to avoid him, though she wasn't entirely sure why.

'Yes,' said Betty, arching her eyebrows. 'Is that a problem?'

Flushing, Ruth reached for her handbag and hat. 'Not at all.'

As they walked down the hall, Ruth thought of Fergus. She hoped he was as much in love with his adopted country as Betty was, with a tan and smile to match.

Thankfully, Bobby was his usual relaxed self, and after a brief friendly hello to Ruth, spent the rest of the tram ride to the zoo chatting and joking with Devan. Like Betty, he'd developed a tan, which was nicely accentuated by his crisp white shirt, and several times Ruth found herself catching his eye before quickly looking away.

By the time they arrived at the zoo, Ruth was as excited as the others, and they had a wonderful time visiting the various exhibits, the undisputed highlight being the chance to hold a koala.

As the day grew warmer, they bought ice creams and found a bench in the shade. At some point the conversation turned to films and Ruth discovered Bobby shared her enthusiasm for the cinema. A lively discussion ensued about the various movies they'd been to, and Ruth was so enjoying talking to Bobby she barely noticed when Devan and Betty wandered off.

'I went to see *The Wizard of Oz* three times before they closed the theatres in Edinburgh,' Bobby said.

'Me too!' exclaimed Ruth. 'It might be my favourite film of all time – but I didn't imagine it would be your cup of tea, Bobby.'

'Why ever not?'

'Because of all the singing. I barely saw you sing at all on the *Batory*.'

Bobby tipped back his head and laughed. 'Oh, I enjoy singing, Ruth, but I kept it a secret because I was terrified Meta Maclean would find out and coerce me into participating in one of her concerts.'

Ruth grinned. 'If I'd known I might have coerced you myself.'

'Is that right?' His smile softened and his voice dropped low. 'It's wonderful seeing you like this, Ruth.'

'Like what?'

'Happy. Relaxed.'

Ruth realised it was true. She was calm and content, yet strangely energised. There was nowhere else she would rather be.

'You seem happy too,' said Ruth.

'I am.' Bobby held her gaze. 'Right now.'

Blinking, Ruth concentrated on eating her rapidly melting ice cream. 'You must be looking forward to getting home to New Zealand,' she said lightly.

'It will be grand to see my family and friends, though' – Bobby grimaced – 'I expect I will face certain pressures from my father.'

'Pressures?'

'My father always expected that I would grow up to run the family farm. I loved being on the land, but I couldn't bear the thought of being in one place doing the same thing for the rest of my life – especially with Dad looking over my shoulder and telling me everything I was doing wrong. So I told him I wanted to become a teacher instead and he didn't take it well.' Bobby gave a short, bitter laugh. 'Thankfully my sister stepped in and said that she and her husband would take over the farm. By that stage my father was far more focused on the fertiliser company he'd founded, and he set his sights on me joining the company, but I honestly couldn't think of anything worse.'

'So you ran away to Scotland?' Ruth hoped her lighthearted tone might help to relieve some of the tension in his stiff shoulders.

'Something along those lines.' His eyes bore into hers and she felt an ache in her lower belly as his gaze travelled to her lips.

'Your girlfriend must have found it hard,' she blurted, shifting back a fraction. 'When you left New Zealand?'

Bobby's face froze then he dropped his head and spoke to the ground. 'I nearly convinced Nell to join me in Scotland, but she didn't want to travel so far from her family. And I was enjoying teaching, exploring, having some distance from my father. I should have returned home after a year, but then the war started and the children were going through such upheavals I felt it was my duty to remain. Shortly after the schools closed I heard about the CORB scheme and I thought' – Bobby shrugged – 'time to go home.'

Neither of them spoke for several seconds.

'I imagine your pupils thought you were wonderful,' croaked Ruth. 'You were certainly worshipped by most of the evacuees on the *Batory*.'

Bobby's brown eyes were intent and serious as they met hers. 'I miss them,' he murmured.

'Me too.'

Frowning, Bobby shook his head and leapt to his feet. 'Come on, Ruth, we'd best find the others.' He held out a hand to pull her upright then quickly released his grip.

As they headed down the path, Ruth made sure she didn't walk too close to Bobby. 'Will you continue to teach?' she asked politely. 'In New Zealand?'

'I'm not sure what I'll do,' Bobby said gruffly. 'I could always make my father proud by enlisting.'

Ruth stopped walking and grabbed his arm. 'Would you?'

Bobby stared at her hand resting on the sleeve of his shirt. 'I've been considering it.'

'But . . . But . . .' Ruth wanted to tell him not to do it, that the thought of him joining the war terrified her. It wasn't her place, though. Lifting her hand, she pointed at Betty's distinctive straw hat in the distance. 'There they are,' she said brightly. Stepping ahead of Bobby, she quickened her pace, the happiness she had felt moments earlier evaporating around her.

22

Auckland, 1940

'Dad!' Ruth called, spying her father's face on the crowded platform.

He turned her way and grinned. 'Ruthie!' he shouted.

Stepping off the train, Ruth jostled through the throngs of people towards her father. He threw his arms around her and lifted her off the ground. 'Look at my girl, all grown up and glamorous.'

'I'm so glad you could come and meet me,' Ruth said, kissing him on the cheek. She'd barely managed a wink of sleep on the overnight train from Wellington, yet she didn't feel at all nervous or tired. If anything, she was fizzing with energy. 'I can't believe I'm finally here.'

'How was Wellington?' her father asked.

Ruth took a second to absorb the fact she was face-to-face with him. He hadn't aged at all; if anything, he seemed younger, tanned and more handsome. 'Cold. And wet. But I'm sure it would be a lovely city in better conditions.'

'That's my Ruth, always finding the positive.' He hooked his arm through hers and grabbed her suitcase. 'Come on, let's get out of this zoo.'

Hearing the word 'zoo', Ruth was instantly reminded of her outing to the zoo in Sydney, and *that* made her think of Bobby. She'd spent much of the short voyage from Sydney to Wellington with Betty, Una, Devan and Bobby. They'd shared many enjoyable moments, but Ruth had been wary of getting too close to Bobby, of spending time alone with him. They'd said a brief, polite goodbye to one another as they'd parted ways in Wellington, yet she couldn't get him out of her thoughts. Sighing, Ruth shook her head in frustration and instead focused on the back of her father's head as they fought their way to the exit.

'Any word on Frank?' her father asked, leading Ruth past a public garden bursting with colourful dahlias.

'Oh, wait.' Ruth pulled him back. 'Would you look at this garden? I've never seen such a beautiful display.'

'There's been a resurgence in all things beautiful since the war began. Every week they're planting more trees in the parks. I guess it's a form of rebellion against all the evil happening else-where in the world.'

Ruth wished suddenly the flowers weren't quite so colourful and gay. 'There's been no word from Frank at all,' she said quietly. 'It's frightfully hard, Dad, not knowing.'

Her father nodded, his eyes fixed on the garden before them. 'He's a brave lad, Ruthie; always has been.'

Frowning, Ruth nodded. She was sure Frank hadn't been in contact with their father for years, possibly since the day their father had abandoned them. Her brother was almost as tight-lipped as their mother when it came to talk of Ruth's previous visit to New Zealand.

'Can you stay long?' Ruth asked as they continued to walk.

'Long enough for tea and a catch-up, I daresay.'

'Right.' Ruth tried to hide her disappointment.

'With all the troops in port and the various comings and goings, it's very difficult to find a room. Also, I have to get back to the dogs.'

'How are Bob and Sal?' Ruth's father often mentioned his sheepdogs in his letters. Not that they were required to herd sheep. Instead they chased rabbits and kept her father company on his orchard.

'I hear you're leaving on the *Rangitane*,' he said, ignoring her question. 'A grand dame that one. She's down in the port now being loaded with supplies.'

Ruth's chest tightened. She'd only just arrived in New Zealand and tomorrow she'd be leaving, heading back across endless miles of ocean. 'Yes, I've heard she's lovely.'

They arrived outside a smart-looking hotel and her father led her to the tearooms. 'Where are the other escorts?' he asked, pulling out a chair and waiting for her to sit.

'I wanted to come a day earlier to spend some time with you,' Ruth said. 'They'll be arriving in the morning.'

'Jolly good.' Her father picked up the menu and Ruth studied his freckled hands.

'I wish I didn't have to go back to London straight away,' she said softly.

Her father lowered his menu. 'You could always delay your return? There's a shortage of teachers, especially in the rural areas. I've a spare room you can stay in as long as you need.'

Ruth stared open-mouthed at her father. For months – years, even – she'd been hoping he would say those words.

'You'd be safe in New Zealand,' he continued. 'Why go back? Your fiancé and brother are away in France, you told me your mother is staying with the dreaded Aunt Audrey. This is an opportunity for the two of us to spend time together. We could take some trips, maybe visit the Southern Alps. If you go back to London you'll just be another mouth to feed, another burden.'

'I'm not a burden, Dad.'

'Look around you, Ruthie,' he continued. 'Why would you want to leave all this to go back *there*?'

Ruth had to bite her tongue hard to stop herself yelling. It wasn't just that his enthusiasm for his adopted homeland overwhelmed his loyalty to his birthplace; she was angry because he had touched a sore spot: a part of her wanted to stay in New Zealand, even as she tried to deny it. 'London is my home, Dad.'

He frowned as he sipped his tea. 'It doesn't have to be.'

Ruth stood up, her heart pounding, her mouth dry. 'You may have abandoned everything to come here, but I'm not going to do the same.'

Her father studied her for a second or two. 'All right, Ruthie, I won't bring it up again. I only want you to be safe . . . and happy,' he added.

'Thank you,' she muttered.

As she sat down, her father began to talk about his recent planting of orange trees and the differences in soil quality, but she wasn't able to shake their conversation, or how much it had affected her.

Ruth quietly sipped at her tea as her father talked on. He seemed unconcerned by her silence and failed to ask her another question. For years she'd been jealous of her father's audacity. She'd put him on a pedestal, and now, for the first time in her life, he had tumbled off. She loved him, of course. And a part of her still admired the way he'd refused to accept the confines of his life in England. But he was selfish, Ruth realised. His own desires and dreams came before anything else, including his wife and children.

Eventually, her father pushed back his chair. 'I'll need to dash, I'm afraid, Ruthie. The dogs have to be exercised and fed.'

Ruth stood too.

'Can I walk you down to the docks?' he asked.

'No, it's fine. I'm sure I'll find my way.'

They hugged, more awkwardly this time.

'Stay safe,' her father said, giving her a squeeze before letting go.

'Bye, Dad.' Ruth wished she could reverse time and they could start again, only this time it would unfold as she'd imagined, with her eagerly telling him about her adventures on the voyage to Australia, and her father saying how much he missed her, how his life wasn't fully complete without his children in it.

Ruth strode down the main street, her suitcase banging against her leg as the trams clanged and screeched beside her. The past few months had been the most rewarding and challenging of her life. She would never regret her decision to be a CORB escort, and she was glad she'd been able to see her father, however briefly. If only she felt more ready to return to England.

Her pace slowed as she crossed a square and approached a flowerbed overflowing with roses. Standing next to the flowers were two women around Ruth's age in matching blue frocks with name badges. They were laughing loudly with no hint of tension or worry on their happy, tanned faces.

Ruth thought of Fergus and hoped he was settling into his new life. Then she thought of Bobby. No doubt he would be reunited with his sweetheart by now. He might even have proposed, and surely Nell would have said yes.

Fixing her eyes on the docks in the distance, Ruth straightened her shoulders and resumed walking. It was time for her to return home to her family, her friends and her fiancé.

23

JOE

'We will shortly be starting our descent into Heathrow,' came a voice over the cabin PA system. 'Please ensure that your seat-back is upright, your tray table is stowed away and your window blind is raised.'

Slowly, Joe made his way back to his seat. He'd asked Hazel if she could let him out to stretch his legs about twenty minutes ago. It had been the first time they'd spoken in four hours.

'Excuse me,' Joe said politely on reaching their row.

Hazel scrambled into the aisle and her book fell to the floor.

They both bent over to pick it up at the same time and banged heads. Hazel clung to Joe's arm to stop from falling backwards, and he gripped her by the waist.

'Sorry,' he said. 'Are you okay?'

They straightened and quickly let go of one another.

'Ouch,' Hazel said, rubbing her forehead. 'That was a decent knock.'

Joe touched a finger to his eyebrow. 'You're not wrong.' He watched her bend to retrieve the book and wished he could think of the right thing to say. He sighed and shuffled sideways to his seat.

Hazel sat down. 'Almost there,' she said to her blank screen.

Joe looked at her profile. The curve of her neck, her long dark eyelashes, the constellation of freckles on her cheek. 'Yep,' he said, nodding at his own screen. 'Better finish this movie before I run out of time.'

He could feel her eyes on him, but he was too afraid to look back.

'I'm sorry if I upset you,' said Hazel softly.

Joe steadied himself and turned to her. 'You didn't.'

'We'll be in London soon; we can go our separate ways and never see each other again.'

Joe held her gaze. 'I don't want that.'

Hazel bit her lip. 'Neither do I,' she said at last.

If things were different, Joe would be moving closer to Hazel. Instead, he stayed very still. 'So what do we do?'

'I guess we could try to be friends? Forget about what we've said and . . . and any attraction we may feel to each other.'

It was the most sensible and idiotic suggestion he'd ever heard. 'We could.'

Hazel looked past Joe to the window. 'Can you see anything through all that grey?' she asked brightly.

Joe looked outside. 'Not much. Appears to be a typical drizzly London afternoon.'

'Is anyone collecting you from the airport?'

'I'm not sure. Klara, maybe.'

He saw her flinch and cursed himself. She was making an effort; why couldn't he?

'Right,' said Hazel quickly. 'I thought it might be your mum or dad.'

Joe shook his head. 'I told them not to bother. If Klara isn't there, I'll get the express.'

'The Heathrow Express? That's what I'm supposed to catch – if I can figure out how.'

'It's not hard.' There he went again, sounding all bitter and twisted. What was wrong with him?

They lapsed into silence and Joe reached up to press play on his movie.

'I've always wanted to go to Paddington,' Hazel chirped.

Joe's hand dropped. 'Why is that?' He was getting annoyed now. Judging by her tone, she obviously didn't feel as angst-ridden and conflicted as he did.

Hazel hesitated. 'It's silly.'

Joe shifted to face her and tried to act relaxed. 'Let me guess. Does it have anything to do with a small stuffed bear?'

Hazel's eyes crinkled. 'Maybe.'

'What a surprise.' Joe couldn't help but smile back.

'Gramps read me the Paddington Bear books all the time when I was young. He used to say . . .' she paused. 'He used to say he had a soft spot for Paddington because –' Hazel stopped abruptly.

'Because?'

Hazel took a deep breath in and let it out with a sigh. 'Because he understood how the bear felt, being abandoned with a tag around his neck. I never asked him what he meant by that. Oh

God, Joe, it must have been so hard for Gramps. I'm sure his parents didn't want to send him away, just as Ruth didn't want to leave him with a couple of strangers in Australia.'

'Ruth was doing her job, Hazel.'

'That sounds heartless.'

'I just meant Ruth knew from the start that her role was to get the children to Australia safely. Becoming attached to Fergus was an occupational hazard, and I'm sure she felt sad at leaving him, but she had no cause for guilt.'

'You're so black and white,' says Hazel. 'Except when it comes to sorting out your own life.'

Joe felt a painful spasm in his stomach. 'What's that supposed to mean?'

Hazel started to speak, then stopped. 'Nothing. I don't know you at all.'

'No you don't, and I haven't a clue about you, except you're like a bloody yo-yo.'

'Excuse me?'

'It's impossible to get a handle on you. One minute you act like I'm some crazy guy you can't wait to get away from; the next you're chatting away as if we're best friends. One second you're cracking jokes and throwing pillows at me, and then you're telling me you're sorry I'm married.'

Hazel stared at Joe, her face expressionless. 'That's the longest speech I've heard you make.'

'Don't, Hazel. Please don't turn this into something light and breezy.'

'You're the one who announced you liked me then proceeded to zone me out like I didn't exist.'

'Are you always this –' Joe stopped.

'What?'

'Emotional.'

Hazel's eyes widened. 'No, I'm not this emotional. Ever.'

Joe gripped his hair and groaned. 'Hazel, this is ridiculous.'

'I agree,' Hazel snapped.

'Can we just go back to being two normal people having a normal conversation?'

'Fine.'

In the ensuing strained silence, Joe could hear their shallow breaths.

'I'm going to finish my movie,' he said firmly. He was a thirty-three-year-old married man, for God's sake – it was time to get a grip on himself.

Soon he was going to be reunited with Klara.

24

Rangitane, 1940

The docks hummed with vitality as Ruth dodged out of the way of a fast-moving cart being shoved along metal tracks. She wondered briefly what lay beneath the army green tarpaulin and whether it was urgent supplies destined for Britain. Men with rolled-up shirtsleeves were bustling around carrying parcels, pulling on ropes and pushing carts much like the one that had almost bowled her over. Chains clanked loudly as supplies were lifted onto ships, and whistles and shouts came from every direction.

Boats of all shapes and sizes were tied up at the docks, from bulky grey naval ships to vulnerable-looking dinghies. A heavy smell of diesel mingled with the briny smell of the sea wafting up from between the wooden boards beneath her feet. Everyone seemed to be in a good mood as they went about their business, the day bright and warm. It was a stark contrast to the grey and sombre Liverpool docks, surrounded by bomb-damaged buildings and echoing with the eerie *clump, clump* of marching soldiers.

Ruth squinted into the afternoon sun, trying to spot the vessel that would return her home.

'Can I help you, love?' asked an older gentleman in overalls.

'I'm after the *Rangitane*,' she replied.

''Course you are; I heard she was leaving tomorrow. Just over there.' He pointed to a moderate-sized white ship with a black hull and two large black funnels. 'You'll be travelling in style on that beauty,' he said, winking.

'Thank you,' Ruth said, hurrying on.

Drawing close, she had to agree the *Rangitane* did look quite charming — smaller than the *Batory*, with rows of glinting portholes, shining wooden railings and a more genteel air. Ruth could almost believe she was about to embark on a luxury cruise.

Making her way up the gangway with her suitcase, she was immediately greeted by a young Māori man in a smart crew uniform.

'Hello, ma'am,' he said. 'I'm Rewiri, the head steward, and it's my great pleasure to welcome you on board. Please let me assist.' He grasped her suitcase and Ruth sighed with relief, swinging her arm around to relieve the ache.

'Thank you,' she said. 'It was getting heavier the longer I carried it.'

'I can imagine.' Rewiri glanced at a crew member nearby who immediately stepped forward.

'If you could please show me your ticket,' said Rewiri, 'then Mark will show you to your cabin.'

Ruth rummaged in her coat pocket and proffered the ticket CORB had issued to her the day she arrived in Wellington.

After a brief inspection, Rewiri handed it back. 'Well, Miss Best, I hope you will enjoy your trip home. If you should need anything, please don't hesitate to ask.'

Following the silent steward and her suitcase, Ruth walked across a wide deck and through polished wooden doors. Descending a set of stairs, she paused to admire the long passageway stretching before her. It was silent and serene, with thick red-patterned carpet and gold-etched wallpaper lined with shiny brass sconces. 'Goodness,' she murmured.

'You'll be travelling first class, miss, and you're one of the lucky few to have a cabin all to yourself,' said Mark over his shoulder. 'Here you are.'

As he pushed open the door, Ruth gasped. Her cabin had a proper wooden dresser, curtains over the large porthole, a beautiful white damask cover on the bed and a lamp on the bedside table emitting a warm golden glow. 'This is lovely,' she exclaimed.

Mark placed her suitcase on a wooden rack behind the door. 'I'll leave you to settle in,' he said. 'There's a ship's guide over on the desk, and dinner will be served in the dining room at six.'

'Thank you.'

Ruth stood in the middle of her cabin without moving. Silence filled her ears as she sank onto her bed. She wondered how many passengers were on board and wished she didn't have to wait another day for the other escorts to arrive. It felt strange being here on her own. Ruth wondered what Fergus and Rosie were up to right at this moment. She hoped that they were happy and didn't miss her as much as she missed them.

Feeling her spirits start to sink, Ruth leapt to her feet. She should explore her new surrounds rather than sit and mope.

⁓

'Gosh, I'm sorry,' Ruth gasped, knocking into someone as she charged out of the ship's lounge and rounded the corner. Her heart thumped as she realised who it was. 'Bobby?'

'Hello, Ruth.' He gave her an uneasy grin. 'Bet you didn't expect to see me again.'

He'd had a haircut since she'd last seen him, and he was in a new, pale blue-checked shirt.

'I am surprised.' Ruth wished her voice was more even. 'What on earth are you doing here?'

Bobby's smile wavered. 'This was, I'll admit, a fairly rash last-minute decision, but I'm returning to England to join the Fleet Air Arm.'

'The what?'

'I'm going to train to fly for the Royal Navy; I understand they're desperate for men.'

'But why on earth did you enlist?' Ruth tried to keep the panic from her voice. 'You've only just arrived back in New Zealand; why are you rushing off again? And what about . . .' Ruth's voice trailed off. For some reason she couldn't bring herself to say Nell's name.

As if reading her thoughts, Bobby took a step back and looked over the railings. 'Turns out my sweetheart wasn't prepared to wait for my return,' he said quietly. 'She could have written to tell

me, of course, before I made the long journey out here, but . . .'
Bobby shrugged, his eyes fixed on the busy docks below.

'I . . . I'm sorry,' said Ruth.

Bobby glanced at Ruth briefly, his face impassive, then looked
away again. 'I was going to stay in New Zealand for the summer,
but then I had an argument with my father.' Bobby rolled his
eyes. 'No surprises there. Anyway, my mate Gary was keen for
me to join up with him and I thought, hey, why not try to make
the old man happy? Make him proud and all that.'

'Oh, Bobby.' Ruth touched him gently on the arm. 'Are
you sure?'

Bobby stepped further back to lean against the wall and her
hand fell away. Crossing one ankle over the other, he gave his
familiar lazy grin. 'I'm afraid it means you'll have to put up with
me a little longer, Ruth.'

She had an alarming urge to step forward and throw her arms
around his neck, but instead she tried to match his laidback air.

'I'm sure I'll cope,' she said.

'It should be a very pleasant trip back to England. I hear
there's more crew than passengers, so we'll be well taken care of.'

'It will make a quite a change from the journey out here.'

Bobby laughed. 'Indeed, Ruth. Indeed.'

'Well . . .' Ruth risked a quick glance at his face and her
stomach flipped. He was looking at her far too intently with
his big brown eyes.

Bobby pushed himself off the wall and ran a hand through
his hair. 'Better let you go.' He looked past Ruth as if searching
for someone behind her. 'Cheerio.'

As she watched him stride away, she shook her head. What on earth had got into her?

Ruth walked to the main deck to watch the sunset and wait for dinner. She leant her forearms on the railings and closed her eyes, letting the last rays of sun rest on her face and eyelids. If only she was back running about on the deck of the *Batory* under the spray of the hose, her group of boys jumping about beside her. She'd felt valuable then, appreciated. Now she didn't know what her purpose was. What would she do when she returned to London? Perhaps she could become an ambulance driver, like Florrie, or maybe she could help in the CORB office. There might even be another group of children she could accompany to Australia or New Zealand, if her mother would allow it. She could visit Fergus and the rest of her boys, check how they were getting on and bring them first-hand reports from home.

Opening her eyes, Ruth admired the yachts gliding down the harbour, their spinnakers glowing white in the softening light. Her stomach growled. With a last look at the glistening water, she headed to the dining room, hoping it would be as empty as the rest of the ship; hoping Bobby wouldn't be there almost as much as she wished he would.

⁓

Waking early the next morning, Ruth listened to muffled sounds coming from the wharf. Her room felt confined and stuffy, the smell of the sea combined with diesel cloying and sickly.

After dressing, she headed to the deck to get some fresh air and watch the goings-on. Peering over the railings, she saw crate after crate of frozen meats, butter and various other supplies being loaded on board.

A ship's purser walked past her and smiled. 'That should help relieve some of the food shortages of our friends in England,' he said.

'It certainly will,' said Ruth. 'Will it survive the trip?'

'Let's hope so. Though —' he gave a wink, 'I wouldn't be too unhappy if we were served a roast lamb every now and again.'

When the sun beating on her neck became too intense, Ruth headed to the dining room for breakfast. Occasionally she glanced around, looking for Bobby. He hadn't appeared at dinner the previous evening and Ruth was annoyed with herself for being disappointed.

After breakfast, Ruth returned to her cabin and wrote a short letter to Florrie, followed by an even shorter one to Peter. Then, deciding the day was far too bright and sunny to stay indoors, she took the book she had obtained from the ship's library to the deck to read. Ruth positioned herself with a view of the wharf so she would be able to see the other escorts arriving, and less than forty minutes later she was rewarded with the sight of Betty stepping onto the gangway.

'Betty!' Ruth stood and waved.

'All set for another cruise?' Betty called out, grinning.

Moments later, they were hugging each other on deck.

'I hope this trip is going to be less exhausting than the journey out,' said Ruth.

'If anyone contracts measles, I do *not* want to know,' said Betty. 'I am officially off all nursing duties.' She plonked her suitcase down and whipped off her hat. 'Phew, but it is warm today.'

'Hello, Ruth,' said Una, appearing behind them.

'Hi,' said Ruth, giving her a far more sedate hug.

'Where's Devan?' Ruth asked, waving at Reverend Kelly, Mrs Ellis and the other escorts making their way up the gangway.

'Oh, he'll be along later. Apparently he wanted to do some last-minute shopping.' Betty raised an eyebrow. 'I might have let slip it's my birthday in a few days.'

'It is? Well, we'll be sure to celebrate. The dining room is simply lovely; I'm sure we can organise something special.'

Ruth picked up Betty's suitcase, leaving Una to carry her own. 'Come on, I'll show you to your room. The purser told me the two of you are sharing a cabin just a couple of doors down from me.'

'Who's your roommate?' Betty asked.

'I don't have one.'

'No fair,' moaned Una. 'Want to swap? I wouldn't mind a room of my own. No offence to Betty.'

Ignoring her, Ruth sped up. She was finding it hard to resist snapping at Una and wondered if she was unusually grumpy from lack of sleep. Much of the previous night she had lain awake tossing and turning, images of Bobby returning again and again. She needed to get back to her life in London. The longer she stayed away, the more distanced and confused she became.

～

'It's a beautiful harbour,' Devan said, gazing at the green peninsula dotted with villas as they glided past. 'Shame we have to head back to winter.'

'And the war,' muttered Betty.

The three of them were standing at the railing on the top deck. It was a calm, clear afternoon as the *Rangitane* left the port of Auckland.

'Funny to think all those hills are volcanoes.' Devan pointed at the various mounds sprouting out of the mostly flat landscape.

'Goodness, are they really?' Ruth studied the grass-covered hills more closely. 'How do you know?'

'The Reverend told me over lunch.' He pointed. 'That one over there is called North Head. The buildings on top are a military camp and apparently there are hidden guns up there, and tunnels. Preparing their defences, just in case.'

'Do you think there's a risk of attack?' asked Betty.

Devan shrugged. 'There've been reports of German ships scouting the waters and some mines were laid further north. They sunk a ship carrying gold a few months ago. I'm sure it's safe, though, otherwise we wouldn't be going.'

They fell silent as their ship slowly rounded North Head. A distant sound of children shrieking and laughing caused Ruth to spin around. On a long sandy beach small bodies were leaping about in the water while adults stood in the shallows watching and chatting. Ruth remembered running about with her boys beneath the spray from the hose on the deck of the *Batory* and her heart contracted.

'I'd like to come back when this war is over,' said Ruth. 'With Peter,' she added quickly.

'I might come with you,' said Betty, putting an arm around Ruth and giving her a squeeze.

'What about me?' Devan asked, giving Betty an odd look. 'Am I invited?'

Betty shrugged. 'If you're lucky.' Without taking her eyes from the view, Betty slid her gloved hand along the rail and placed it on top of Devan's.

'I am lucky,' he said with a smile.

The previous evening Betty had popped into Ruth's cabin to say goodnight, then thrown herself onto Ruth's bed and confessed she was secretly engaged to Devan. He had taken Betty out for a candlelit dinner in Wellington and declared his love for her. She'd told him she felt the same way and they had agreed to a secret engagement until they returned to Britain, where they would make it official. Not that either of them seemed particularly concerned about keeping their obvious affection for one another a secret.

Ruth turned away from the happy couple and surveyed the other passengers on deck. Around her was a group of about twenty other escorts returning to Britain, many of whom had been on the *Batory*. While Ruth could recall most of their names, she realised how little she really knew them. They'd been so busy taking care of their evacuees there'd been little time for a proper conversation. It would be nice to spend the next few weeks getting to know them better.

Catching the eye of Reverend Kelly, she smiled and edged towards him. 'Hello, Reverend, it's lovely to see you again.'

'And you, Ruth.' He leant forward to kiss Ruth on the cheek. 'You're looking well rested.'

'I am, thank you.' Her smile faltered.

'It feels strange, doesn't it?' the Reverend said softly. 'Without the children for company.'

Ruth nodded, her throat thick.

'I'm sure they're being well cared for, Ruth. They are safe from harm now.'

Busying herself adjusting her hat, Ruth decided to steer the conversation in another direction. 'She's an impressive vessel. It should be a pleasant voyage.'

The Reverend frowned. 'Let's hope so.'

'Is something wrong?'

'I'm sure we'll be fine,' he said, giving her a half-hearted smile.

Ruth frowned. 'You don't sound entirely confident.'

Reverend Kelly patted Ruth's arm. 'No point in worrying, my dear. Let's just relax and enjoy the voyage.'

'Let's,' said Ruth. She would make the most of the next few weeks on board, she decided. After all, who knew what lay ahead for her once she reached England? Realising that she was scanning the deck for Bobby again, she forced herself to conjure up an image of Peter instead – without much success.

⌒

'Good evening, all.'

Caught with a mouth full of food, Ruth swallowed quickly then glanced up at Bobby.

'This is my mate, Gary,' Bobby said, introducing the red-headed man beside him. 'Gary, this is Una, Betty, Devan, Reverend Kelly and Ruth.'

'We heard a rumour you might be gracing us with your presence again,' said Devan, standing to slap Bobby on the back before shaking Gary's hand.

Bobby and Gary took seats at the opposite end of the table to Ruth.

'So are you joining the Fleet Air Arm too?' asked Una, gazing at Gary with wide eyes.

'Yes, ma'am,' he said, grinning back. 'I was the one to convince Bobby to join. Not that he needed much encouragement.'

Una gave a high-pitched giggle and Ruth winced.

'What's on the menu tonight?' Gary asked, rubbing his hands together, his gaze still on Una. 'I'm starved.'

'You're always starved,' said Bobby. 'Even when you've just eaten.'

Gary patted his stomach. 'I have exceptional digestion.'

Everyone at the table laughed, Una loudest of all.

Gary leant towards her. 'Best enjoy it while we can,' he said, in a strange echo of Reverend Kelly's words on deck earlier.

'What do you mean?' asked Una.

'The enemy are swarming all over the Pacific, I reckon.'

Una put a hand to her throat. 'Oh no!'

Gary straightened his back and puffed out his chest. 'Don't you worry, Una; the *Rangitane* will outrun anything.'

'I hope you're right,' she purred.

Ruth caught Bobby's eye, and he lifted his eyebrows. She smiled and was pleased when he gave a small conspiratorial smile in return.

'I missed you last night,' said Bobby, sitting down opposite Ruth at breakfast.

They'd all agreed to meet on the top deck shortly after dinner to look at the stars through the telescope, but Ruth had decided not to join them for reasons she'd hoped to avoid talking about.

She stared at her plate. 'Sorry, I lay down for a rest and must have fallen asleep.'

'Right.' Bobby sounded unconvinced.

With a shaking hand, Ruth picked up her cup of tea. She hadn't been able to settle after dinner, instead pacing about her room wishing she could find a way to get off the ship. How could she begin to explain to Bobby the dread that was suddenly consuming her?

'Ruth,' Bobby said, 'are you all right?'

Nodding, Ruth took a sip of tea. 'I'm fine,' she murmured.

'You appear to be less than fine.'

When Ruth saw the concern on his face, tears sprung to her eyes.

He leant forward and touched her arm. 'What is it?'

Ruth shook her head and blinked. 'Nothing. I'm not myself for some reason. It will pass.'

Bobby squeezed her arm gently. 'Is something worrying you?'

Ruth wished he would leave her alone almost as much as she wished he'd wrap his arms around her. 'Really, Bobby. I'm fine.'

He sat back, crossing his arms over his chest. 'Would you prefer to be left in peace?'

Ruth took a deep breath in and shook her head. 'I have a feeling I've taken a wrong turn,' she whispered to her lap.

'In what way?'

She lifted her eyes to meet his. 'I don't know why, but I have this strong sense we need to turn around. Go back.'

Bobby studied her, a frown creasing his forehead. 'Have you left someone important behind?'

'It's not that.' Ruth didn't know how to explain it. 'I have this feeling of . . . of darkness. I've never felt anything like it before. Well, perhaps once before, when Brenda —' Ruth stopped herself just in time. 'I just want to beg the captain to turn back before it's too late.'

'Too late?'

Ruth shook her head. 'I'm being ridiculous.'

'Not at all.'

'I keep imagining Fergus is calling out to me,' Ruth blurted. 'And he's upset, panicked; I can hear it in his voice.'

Bobby nodded but remained silent.

'It's as if he's trying to warn me,' she muttered, rubbing her hand across her eyes.

'About what?'

'I wish I knew.'

For a moment neither of them spoke. Then Bobby unfolded his arms and leant towards her. 'Ruth, if I thought it would work, I'd go and find the captain now and ask him to turn us around.'

She gave him a wobbly smile. 'Thank you.'

Bobby reached for her hand and squeezed it gently. 'Ruth, Betty told me about Brenda. After I found Rosie and you were . . . upset with me, Betty felt she should explain.'

Ruth stared at her hand enclosed in Bobby's. It felt comforting, yet far too dangerous. 'I'm sorry,' she said. 'I shouldn't have been so rude.'

Bobby squeezed her hand again. 'Please don't apologise. War is rife with senseless tragedies. I am sorry about Brenda, truly I am. Besides . . .' He released her hand and sat back in his chair, a mischievous twitch at the corners of his lips. 'It helps explain your fairly robust attitude to your role as escort.'

Ruth smiled. 'Is that a polite way of saying I was a tad uptight, Bobby?'

She was rewarded with his booming laugh. 'Not at all.' He slapped a hand on the table. 'Come on, Ruth, it's a beautiful morning. How about after breakfast we go and play some ping-pong on deck? Take your mind off things.'

'That would be nice,' she said, her sense of darkness dissipating.

⁓

Thankfully, as the day went on, Ruth's mood lifted further. Bobby did his best to cheer her up, and they ended up spending most of the day on deck with the others, the overt flirtation between Gary and Una causing much amusement. There was a festive atmosphere on board, with passengers chatting and playing games. A young mother was being run ragged chasing after her two small boys, and Ruth offered to play with them for a while to give her some respite. The mother explained they were disembarking at Papua New Guinea, where she and her boys would be joining her husband, who ran a coconut plantation. They'd been visiting her parents in New Zealand, which had been lovely, she said, but she was looking forward to returning home.

The sapphire water was flat and sparkling, and there were cries of joy as two albatrosses appeared, shrieking and swooping back and forth in front of the ship, their giant wings magnificent against the bright blue sky.

By evening, Ruth was almost back to her old self. She felt dopey after a combination of too much sunshine and lack of sleep the previous night. Turning down Betty's suggestion of a game of draughts after dinner, she retired early to her cabin, where she quickly fell asleep.

In her dream, Fergus soared towards her over the sea, as effortless and graceful as an albatross, his arms held wide, his expression determined.

Ruth woke to the sound of gunfire. She lay still and listened, her heart racing. The lights in the hallway shone brightly through the gap in her door, and the *Rangitane* continued to motor full steam ahead. Ruth wondered if she'd imagined the noise until she heard others in nearby cabins begin to shift about. One or two called out, asking what was going on, and Ruth decided she'd best get up and dressed. As she got to her feet, a series of ear-splitting bangs shook the ship, accompanied by the sound of shattering glass. In horror, Ruth saw the wall of her cabin fall in, and she was thrown down, her cheek slamming into the floor.

When she opened her eyes again, all the lights had gone out and she lay in terrifying darkness, smoke filling her lungs. The ship's engines had stopped and there was an eerie silence. Ruth's head pounded and pain radiated through her body.

'Help me!' a man yelled.

Dragging herself to a sitting position, Ruth began to cough. The smoke was suffocating.

A high-pitched scream echoed in the darkness. Ruth extended a hand, planning to crawl in the direction of the passageway, but as she put her weight on it, a searing pain in her wrist caused her arm to collapse beneath her. She gripped her arm and rolled onto her back, tears filling her eyes.

Get up! Fergus spoke so clearly it was as if he was next to her. *You have to get out,* he urged.

Still coughing, Ruth managed to get to her knees, her breathing ragged. The coat she had reached for as she'd climbed from her bed snagged on her foot and she used her good arm to drape it over her head. Her lungs burnt as she staggered to her feet and stumbled out of what remained of her cabin.

Turning in the direction of Betty's cabin, Ruth gasped as flames lit up the passageway. 'Betty!' she called, her voice hoarse. A body lay face down on the ground outside her friend's cabin. Recognising Betty's hair, Ruth screamed her name again.

There was no response.

'Help!' called a woman. 'Please!'

Ruth turned in the direction of the voice. 'Una?'

'Ruth, I'm stuck.'

'I'm coming,' Ruth rasped. 'I just need to help Betty first.'

Ruth stumbled forward, faintly aware of a sting as her feet were cut by broken glass. She knelt beside Betty and lifted the hair off her face. One side of Betty's skull was missing, thick blood seeping from the wound. Betty's eyes were wide open and glazed, her face devoid of life.

Ruth groaned and leant to one side to be sick.

'Ruth,' called Una. 'Help me.'

Still retching, Ruth got to her feet once more and numbly made her way to the doorway of Betty and Una's cabin. Though it was dark, Ruth could see the walls were still largely intact. The floor, on the other hand, had disappeared. Peering into the void, Ruth could just make out Una lying on the floor of the dining room below. A large wooden beam lay across her legs.

'Una,' Ruth called. 'I'm here.'

'I can't move,' Una gasped.

'It's all right, Una — try to stay calm. I'm going to get help.'

'Don't leave me,' Una screamed. 'What if they shell us again?'

'I have to get help, Una. You need to be brave.'

'Okay,' Una whispered. 'Hurry, Ruth, please.'

Ruth glanced back towards Betty's lifeless body then stumbled towards the stairs that led to the upper deck. Devan appeared at the top. 'Ruth,' he yelled, hurrying down with a torch in his hand. 'Is everyone okay? Where's Betty?'

A strangled gurgle was all Ruth could manage. Devan peered down the passageway. 'Oh God, please tell me she's not down there?' Smoke surrounded them like fog and he began to cough.

Ruth could only grip his arm. 'She's dead, Devan,' she said, hoarsely.

With a strangled cry, he tore his arm from hers and charged in the direction of Betty's cabin.

'Devan, don't,' called Ruth. She heard a crash and a scream.

'Ruth!' Una yelled.

Staggering to the top of the stairs, Ruth burst onto the deck.

Immediately Bobby was at her side. 'Oh, thank God. Ruth —'

'Una needs help,' Ruth gasped. 'She fell through the floor into the dining room. She's trapped.'

Placing an arm around Ruth's shoulder, Bobby led her to a group of passengers who were huddled together by the lifeboats. Many were nursing injuries, from swollen lips to cuts to burns. One woman lay on the deck, her face twisted in pain. Someone was wrapping a piece of cloth around her leg.

'Stay here,' Bobby whispered, rubbing Ruth gently on the back then leaning in to kiss her softly on the cheek. 'I'll help Una.'

Ruth watched him go, wanting to shout for him to stay.

One of the passengers glanced at Ruth and then pointed out to sea. 'Look.'

Ruth squinted at the bright spotlight shining on them from a ship lying several metres off their bow. It was dark and ominous-looking, and Ruth's heart skipped a beat as she realised the ship had its guns pointed towards them. Two other ships flanked it on either side. Smaller than the *Rangitane*, they had a stark, hostile look about them. Ruth's ears rang as she recognised the Nazi flag flying from the smallest of the three ships.

A motorboat approached across the choppy sea at speed. In the blazing light from the ship, Ruth could make out the swastika on the arms of several men in smart white uniform standing on board. She gasped.

This can't be happening, she thought.

'Lucky you have your coat,' said the passenger who had pointed out to sea. 'Best you put it on before you get too cold.'

Ruth nodded but made no attempt to move. Most of the people standing around her were still in their nightwear. Some had managed to grab a pair of trousers or a coat. One or two pressed small bags to their chests. No-one wore shoes.

'Do you think everyone made it out okay?' asked a middle-aged man in torn pyjamas, a bead of blood dripping down his forehead.

A picture of Betty's damaged lifeless face rushed into Ruth's head and she groaned softly. Her body began to shake. 'No,' she whispered. 'Betty's dead.'

25

HAZEL

Hazel wiped her eyes and sniffed, a teardrop landing on the page.

'You all right?' Joe asked.

She nodded. The tension between her and Joe had dissipated, replaced by a strange calm. 'I never knew the Germans were attacking ships so close to New Zealand.'

'Did someone die?'

'An escort. She had half her face blown off.'

Joe grimaced, then fumbled in his backpack and pulled out a small packet of tissues. 'Help yourself,' he said, handing them over.

'Thanks.' Hazel wiped her face and blew her nose. She tried to imagine herself on the *Rangitane* and how terrified she would have been.

Hazel flung the book onto the seat beside her. 'This is torture having to sit here and wait. It's bad enough we've been flying for over twenty-four hours, now we're stuck on the bloody tarmac.'

'Yeah, it's frustrating all right.'

Joe didn't look frustrated at all. He looked his usual chilled, unfazed self. It was insanely irritating.

'I mean, this airport is huge,' she said. 'How can there be no available air bridges, for heaven's sake?'

'I guess this is what they call a lesson in patience.'

'Oh, shut up, you sound like a teacher.'

Joe's smile was serene. 'What's the point in getting all worked up? I can't do anything.'

'But aren't you desperate to get off?'

Joe shrugged. 'Sure, but I'm not in a rush to *be* anywhere.'

Hazel frowned. Was he saying he wasn't in a rush because he wanted to stay on the plane with her? *Stop it*, she told herself. *You aren't going there, remember?*

'I'm always rushing, apparently,' Hazel said, trying to push her errant thoughts aside.

Joe laughed. 'And I'm always being told to hurry up.'

Hazel leant back in her seat. 'I wouldn't even know how to slow down, if I'm honest.'

'Why are you always rushing? Is there some place you're trying to get to?'

'Literally or metaphorically?'

'Both.'

'I've always been desperate to get as far away from my home town as possible, and London is on the other side of the world, so I've been impatient to get here. And in terms of myself and who I am, I'm in a rush too. I figure wherever I'm going has to be better, so why not get there quickly.'

'Better than what?'

'Than my mediocre life.'

'Right.' Joe frowned in thought. 'I wonder which of us will get there first.'

'Where?'

'To a better place. I mean, I'd definitely say my life is in the mediocre category and I'd like it to be better, but I'm not sure that rushing will get me there faster, if that makes sense.'

Hazel pursed her lips and blew air out of them. 'Shit, that's a depressing thought.'

'Is it?'

'Yeah. I mean, what's the answer?'

Joe shrugged.

It was nice talking to Joe again. Hazel had never had conversations like this with Matt . . . or anyone, now she thought about it. Even with Gramps she wouldn't have talked about how she was in a rush to figure herself out. It was as if Joe had a special knack for making her open up more. It was scary, but also extraordinary. Maybe they *could* find a way to be friends, because Hazel liked the idea of having someone to talk to in London. She barely knew a soul in the city. Joe would not only be a friendly face, but he could share his local knowledge. Maybe they could even help one another in their search for that elusive something they were seeking.

26

Prisoners, 1940

A middle-aged German in uniform strode towards them, flanked by younger soldiers holding rifles. 'Get on boats,' he barked, pointing at the lifeboats. 'Abandon ship.'

'What about our belongings?' a passenger asked boldly.

The German officer frowned and shook his head. 'Abandon ship,' he repeated. 'No things.'

Ruth pointed to the door leading to the cabins. Smoke was billowing from the dark void. 'There are people still in there,' she choked.

For a moment his frown softened. 'No people. All out.'

'Where are they?' Ruth cried.

His face hardened. 'Get on boats,' he ordered. 'Now.'

'But Una is in there, and Bobby, and Devan!'

The officer glowered and turned away.

Someone placed a hand on Ruth's back and guided her towards a lifeboat. 'Come on, love. We'd best do as we're told.'

Numbly, Ruth queued with the other passengers until it was her turn to step into the boat. Silently she watched as ropes lowered them to the water. There was a jolt as the boat landed in the sea, and Ruth gasped as pain shot through her arm. The sleeve of her pyjamas had been torn, revealing an angry swollen lump.

An elderly man perched opposite caught Ruth's eye. 'We'll get through this,' he said firmly, his expression determined. 'Chin up.'

An officer from the *Rangitane* stood in the stern of the lifeboat and instructed two men to take up the oars. Slowly they moved away from the burning ship.

'She's on a lean,' someone said.

'We have nothing,' another voice whispered.

Ruth felt a flicker of anger. 'We're alive,' she said, her throat raw.

A motorboat pulled up alongside them and one of the German officers pointed to the largest of their three ships. 'You go there. Hurry,' he said, urgency in his voice.

The men picked up the oars, having no choice but to obey instructions.

As they arrived alongside the enemy's ship, Ruth was dismayed to discover they would need to climb a rope ladder. Her ascent was slow and painful; each time she gripped a rung with the hand of her injured arm, she had to bite down on her lip to stop from crying out.

Once everyone had scrambled on board, stern-looking soldiers with rifles quickly herded them below deck. Ruth noted with dismay that they were led well below water level before they were divided, men into one room, women another. Ruth trembled at the sight of the dim, windowless hold with painted metal floors and a couple of long trestle tables with fixed benches alongside.

The door to the hold slammed closed the moment all the women were inside, and they stood in silence listening to the rattle of a key turning in the lock. No-one spoke or moved as footsteps pounded overhead, doors banged, the engine grumbled and the ship began to move.

'We're prisoners,' someone whispered at last.

Ruth felt her legs give way and she collapsed onto the hard, unforgiving floor.

Mrs Ellis hurried over and crouched beside her. She began to rub Ruth's back in small, firm circles. 'You're all right, Ruth, my dear.'

A woman plonked onto the bench nearby, wet hair and wet clothes plastered to her body. 'My lifeboat sank,' she murmured, her teeth beginning to chatter.

Mrs Ellis stood. 'You poor dear. Let's see if we can find something for you to change into.'

The woman appeared not to hear her; she gazed blankly at the water pooling around her bare feet.

Ruth used her good arm to offer the woman her coat. 'Here,' she said hoarsely.

Mrs Ellis helped the woman to remove her soaked pyjama top and put on Ruth's coat. Others in the room began to shuffle about attending to those with injuries.

Crouching beside Ruth once more, Mrs Ellis examined her wrist. 'I hope it's not broken.'

Ruth met Mrs Ellis's eye. 'Betty's dead,' she said, her body beginning to shake.

Mrs Ellis froze momentarily, then she nodded. 'We can't show any weakness, no matter our despair,' she said tightly. 'We must do all we can to show these Germans how strong we can be, Ruth. Do you understand?'

'Yes,' whispered Ruth. 'We must.'

27

JOE

'Good luck, then,' Joe said, as Hazel tucked her book into her bag and moved into the aisle.

'You too,' she said, barely glancing up.

Joe wanted to say more. To suggest they exchange email addresses so they could contact one another. Catch up for a drink somewhere. Or maybe he could show Hazel some of the sights. Not the usual spots tourists flocked to, but lesser-known places, like the canal boats at Little Venice, or his favourite Italian place in a tiny lane in Soho.

'I'm sorry I won't get to hear how the book ends,' he said, shuffling across the seats, hoping to squeeze into the aisle beside her. 'I'm intrigued to find out what happened to Ruth and how your grandfather ended up in New Zealand.'

A man from the row behind pressed forward impatiently, knocking Hazel's shoulder in his attempt to get her moving. Joe had to restrain himself from giving the prick a shove.

Hazel scowled as she swung her bag onto her shoulder. 'Bye, Joe,' she said, looking back and giving a brief wave. Her smile was strained and Joe couldn't read her expression. He'd missed his chance. Soon she'd be stepping off the plane and they'd probably never see each other again. Joe tried to manoeuvre himself into the aisle, but two more aggressive types jostled into the queue ahead of him. Hazel was getting further and further away.

'Bye, Hazel,' he called, his chest tight.

Her head swivelled in his direction just as he managed to step into the aisle, and he lost sight of her among the sea of heads and bags ahead.

It wasn't until he was standing in line at passport control, waiting for his turn to speak to the sour-faced official at the counter, that he spied Hazel again. She was in another line, a few metres ahead. Joe could tell she was anxious from the way she shifted from one leg to the other and kept biting her lip. Occasionally she scanned the crowded room, and Joe wondered if she was looking for him.

When Joe finally reached the baggage carousel, he spotted Hazel again. She was on the other side of the conveyor belt, partly obscured by a woman in a bright orange jacket. Joe watched Hazel wrestle a heavy suitcase onto the floor then stride towards the exit, her face determined.

It had to be pretty overwhelming to arrive in a new country on the other side of the world entirely on your own. Out in the arrivals hall there would be hundreds of people milling about and holding up signs, but none of them would be waiting for Hazel.

Retrieving his pack, Joe slung it over his shoulder and edged past a large group of young people in matching tracksuits chatting excitedly in a foreign language. He hastened to the arrivals area and scanned the crowd. He didn't know why he'd told Hazel his wife might be there to meet him. He hadn't told Klara what flight he was on.

'Hazel!' he called. She was heading in the wrong direction and he ran towards her, his giant backpack banging up and down on his back.

'Thought I'd show you where to get the Heathrow Express,' he said as he caught up. 'Looks like I'll need to catch it too.'

She hesitated. 'Aren't you being picked up?'

'Apparently not.'

'Well that's lucky for me, because I seriously don't know where the hell I'm going.'

'I thought as much. Come on, we need to get to the other terminal.' Joe turned back the way they'd come and they fell into step beside each other.

'This place is bigger than I ever imagined,' said Hazel, her suitcase bumping loudly behind them. 'And there're so many people.'

'It seems fairly quiet to me.'

They laughed and Joe felt a fizzing in his arms and legs, as if he'd achieved something important.

'I'm glad to be off that plane,' said Hazel. 'I felt like a prisoner.'

'It does feel a bit like we've been set free,' Joe agreed. He caught her eye and they smiled at one another. *Just friends*, Joe told himself. That would have to be enough.

28

Pacific Ocean, 1940

A Nazi soldier unlocked the door and entered their room. He placed a large enamel jug and one cup on the table. 'Coffee,' he stated, before leaving the room and locking it once more.

Everyone stared at the jug till eventually Mrs Ellis moved to pour some coffee into the cup and pass it around.

'Ew, it's all coffee grounds,' said the first woman to take a sip, swallowing with a grimace.

The next person to receive the cup eyed it suspiciously. 'If only I wasn't so thirsty,' she muttered, before taking a quick swig.

Ruth did her best to swallow a couple of mouthfuls but it was like drinking bitter black water and sand.

A short while later, the same soldier returned with a tin tray of black bread sandwiches. There was nothing inside the two thick slices except for a smear of some kind of lard. The dry, sour bread lodged in Ruth's parched throat. She only managed to nibble one corner before returning her sandwich to the tray.

Several hours passed. Ruth sat in silence as those around her talked about what had happened and speculated on where they might be going. There were a few escorts she recognised, though none she knew well, apart from Mrs Ellis. She hoped Bobby had found Una and they'd made it off the *Rangitane*. Devan and Reverend Kelly, too.

'What if they take us to one of those camps?' asked a pretty young woman, her eyes wide with terror. 'They sound dreadful.'

'Surely they won't take us all the way back to Europe? Not in these conditions,' said another voice.

One of the women who'd managed to leave the burning *Rangitane* fully dressed in slacks, blouse and a coat said the Germans had sent a torpedo through the *Rangitane* once all the passengers and crew had been removed. She reported it was already sinking fast by the time she was brought down to the hold.

Ruth wondered if Betty had gone down with the ship into the depths of the Pacific Ocean. The thought made her curl into a ball trying to contain her pain.

⁓

'What were you doing in New Zealand?' asked the German officer. He was sitting straight-backed at the table, the women being summoned one by one to answer his questions.

Ruth was the last in the room to be interrogated, and she struggled to concentrate on the officer's words. A few hours ago she'd been asleep on board the *Rangitane*. A few hours ago Betty was still alive.

'I was an escort for child evacuees,' Ruth explained. 'I was passing through New Zealand on my way home to Britain.'

'What port were you heading for?' asked the officer.

'I don't know.' Ruth gave the same reply as everyone else. It was the truth. The *Rangitane* would have stopped somewhere to refuel and load supplies, but the captain had deliberately kept their route to himself. Now Ruth understood why.

'Which English ports are still in use?'

'I don't know.'

'Did you hear of any German activity near New Zealand?'

'No.' This wasn't entirely true, but since no-one around her had mentioned anything about the mines, she kept the information to herself.

The officer left the hold at last, clearly exasperated by his fruitless efforts.

For a few moments there were winks and hugs. 'We got one up on them then, didn't we, girls?' someone whispered.

There was even a brief burst of laughter, before everyone grew silent and tense once more.

By now Ruth's wrist ached constantly. When the ship's doctor arrived, he took one look at it and shook his head.

'You come.' He gestured to the door. Two other prisoners had been sent to stand by the door during his examination of the injured. One held a wad of blood-soaked cloth to her head, the other had blistering burns to her legs and was white-faced with pain.

Ruth went to join them without a word.

Eventually, the doctor and his assistant finished patching up the various cuts and burns and led Ruth and the two others to the hospital.

When they arrived, Ruth was dismayed to see six crude cots set up in a small room with scant evidence of medical supplies. All the cots were occupied with badly injured men. One man groaned continuously, his left leg now a heavily bandaged stump. Ruth was relieved to see it was no-one she recognised.

One bunk, separated from the rest, sat at the very end of the room, concealed behind a makeshift curtain. Ruth wondered about the state of the patient lying behind it. She sagged against the wall as a thin slip of a woman in a nurse's uniform stepped out from behind the curtain. 'All right there, love,' the woman said. 'It's a shock, but we'll sort you out.'

Ruth stared at her. 'You're British,' she whispered.

The woman nodded. 'I was travelling on the *Holmwood* when it was attacked two days ago.' She led Ruth to a chair and helped her to sit.

'Oh my God,' Ruth said. 'Was everyone . . . did they . . . ?' Ruth couldn't bring herself to voice the question.

The woman squeezed Ruth's shoulder. 'We were lucky; we all made it off the ship without injuries. Not like you lot. It was dreadful listening to the blasts. We couldn't see a thing, as they'd shut us away, but the noise was bad enough.'

Nodding, Ruth blinked back tears. 'My friend was killed,' she murmured, the woman's kindly face now a blur.

'Oh darling, that's terrible.' She shook her head in dismay. 'There's one of your ladies here.' She nodded towards the curtain. 'We're doing what we can, and I daresay I can't accuse the doctor of not doing all he is able, but . . . I'm afraid it's not looking good.'

Ruth stared at the curtain. 'Who . . . who is it?'

'Miss Herbert-Jones.'

'Elinor,' Ruth gasped.

Elinor had been the youngest of the escorts on board the *Batory* and all the children had adored her. While Ruth hadn't spent much time with Elinor, she recalled her infectious smile.

'Oh no,' whispered Ruth.

The doctor arrived by their side and snapped at the nurse. 'You help, not talk.'

'Keep yer knickers on,' the nurse said calmly.

He frowned, obviously not understanding what she had said, then pointed to the woman with the bandage around her head. 'Clean and dress wound,' he growled.

The woman curtsied briefly. 'Yes, doctor,' she said. As she turned away, she winked at Ruth. 'Chin up.'

Ruth felt a glimmer of determination. She sat up straight, fixed the doctor with a glare and held out her arm for inspection.

Mrs Ellis faced Ruth, her snores loud and guttural. Ruth had no idea what time it was, but it felt as if the night would never end. For hours she'd laid in the dark listening to guards stomping overhead and the slapping of water against the hull as the ship motored on. The Germans had given them brand-new hammocks to sleep in – as well as bedding, cutlery and plates, all bearing a Japanese trademark – though instead of hanging them, most of the women had decided simply to lay them out in rows on the metal floor, with their lifebelts as pillows. Every hour or so, a torch shone through a small grating in the wall and a guard's face would appear, only to disappear and return the room to darkness.

Ruth prayed morning would arrive soon. Her wrist throbbed and she couldn't get comfortable. At least it wasn't broken, just badly sprained, the doctor had said as he'd bandaged it.

Ruth was hungry and thirstier than she'd ever been in her life. It was as if someone had poured talcum powder into her mouth. For supper, the prisoners had been given a bowl of dark brown stew containing a handful of peas and the odd strand of beef. Barely anyone had managed more than a mouthful. It tasted of nothing Ruth had ever eaten before or wished to ever eat again. A short while later a guard had removed the uneaten stew with a shake of his head, turned out the light and locked the door. They could do nothing except lie down and wait for morning.

Ruth wondered if anyone knew the *Rangitane* had been attacked. Were people looking for them, or had the captain been unable to radio for help? What if no-one knew? When would the alarm be raised? How could the New Zealand or Australian navies hope to find them? What if allies shelled the German boat without realising there were prisoners on board? Being so far down in the hull, the prisoners would be the last to reach the deck, if they managed to make it there at all.

Ruth tried not to think about where the Germans were taking them and what their fate would be. Would she ever make it home? Would she be taken to a prison camp somewhere? Images of her mother and brother, Florrie and Peter flashed through her mind. And Fergus: she'd promised to stay in touch – he'd think she had forgotten him. That she no longer cared.

Finally, Ruth thought of Betty. Her birthday was tomorrow. Devan had been planning a surprise party. Oh, how happy and in love they had been. The last Ruth had seen of Devan, he'd been racing down a smoke-filled corridor towards his dead fiancée. Had he made it out alive? If so, how grief-stricken he must be.

Breathe, Ruth told herself as her chest tightened and her body began to shake. She had to keep it together. Everyone else in the suffocating room was in the same situation. They were coping, with only a few brief episodes of tears or hysteria. Ruth would have to be strong as well. She concentrated on the sounds of others shuffling about unable to sleep and wished she could say something out loud in order to hear a reassuring voice in return. Ruth imagined she was back in Auckland having tea with her father. This time, when he suggested she stay in New Zealand, instead of getting angry and indignant, she hugged him and said yes.

After an eternity, a guard opened their door and turned on the light, signalling the morning had arrived. Two basins of fresh water were brought in and each of them was issued with a small towel and a tiny bar of soap. 'This is to last you one month, ladies,' the soldier said.

One month! Ruth reeled, taking in the other shocked faces around the room.

They took it in turns to wash, before the basins were removed and replaced with breakfast. Ruth swallowed bile as she saw the reheated stew from the night before, with the same sour black bread and jug of coffee. Was this to be their only food for an entire month? A woman beside her turned away and retched.

After breakfast, the guards brought in a bucket of sea water and told them to wash their dishes and clean the room.

They obeyed orders without question, though Ruth was little help, with only one good arm.

'I'd give anything for a proper lungful of fresh air,' muttered a stewardess from the *Rangitane*. She stood next to the only ventilating shaft in the room, inhaling deeply.

'Come on,' another stewardess said, leaping to her feet. 'Let's exercise.'

Everyone looked at her as if she'd grown another head.

'We'll go mad if we sit here all day long.' The stewardess stretched her arms above her head. 'How about we do some stretches to start.'

Mrs Ellis stood up. 'Anything to pass the time,' she said.

Everyone did their best to move their bodies about, but it didn't last long. Ruth suspected the adrenaline that had kept them all going was fast draining away, leaving them bone-weary.

When the door to their prison was eventually opened, Ruth hoped desperately for some good news to boost their spirits.

The doctor entered, his expression grim. Beside him stood the nurse Ruth had met the day before. 'Hello, ladies,' she said softly. 'My name is Kathy. I'm a nurse and fellow prisoner. I'm afraid I have some sad news. Miss Herbert-Jones died a short while ago.'

The escort standing in front of Ruth wailed and dropped to her knees. Mrs Ellis rushed to comfort her. Ruth made no attempt to wipe away the tears running down her own cheeks as she pictured Elinor's young smiling face.

Kathy continued. 'The doctor did everything he could for her, but her injuries were too great. She was incredibly brave till the end and we can assure you she was as comfortable as it was possible to be.'

'I am sorry, ladies,' said the doctor, a crack in his voice belying his staunch demeanour. Then, with a salute, he turned and walked away.

Kathy caught Ruth's eye, gave a weak smile of recognition and followed the doctor. The door was locked once more and for a long time no-one spoke. Sadness seeped into the air like an invisible fog and the women involuntarily reached for one another, giving hugs and squeezing hands as if they might become lost in the haze.

The day wore on, slow and relentless. With each minute the atmosphere turned more stale and bleak.

Finally, the officer who had questioned them the day before entered. In broken English he explained they were stopping the ship for a burial service and asked for all prisoners to follow him onto the top deck. With stiff legs, they left the room and began to climb. As Ruth stepped out into the open, squinting in the brightness of the evening light, the boat stopped. She immediately looked about and was gripped with a sensation of vertigo as she took in the vast ocean all about them.

In rows along one side of the deck stood over a hundred German sailors in white uniforms and caps. Ramrod-straight, their eyes were fixed on some invisible mark, faces mask-like. Before them, in dark uniforms and grey gloves, stood around fifty German officers with similar impassive expressions. At the far end of the deck were short rows of far less well-presented male prisoners. Scanning their faces, Ruth found herself seeking out a familiar face – Bobby, Devan or Reverend Kelly – but saw no-one in the brief glimpse afforded her before she was led to a row of chairs. Sitting down, Ruth looked up to see a swastika flag fluttering at half-mast and she felt herself sway to the side as if she might fall or, worse, faint.

A voice barked an incomprehensible order, and the German officers and sailors stood to attention as the captain strode past his men, faced the prisoners and gave the Nazi salute.

Ruth shuddered as she took in his stern face and hard grey eyes. Facing the bier on which lay Elinor's covered lifeless body, the captain gave a loud, passionate speech in German, similar in tone to some of the lectures Ruth had heard the headmaster give to unruly children at school. Then a British chaplain Ruth recognised as another escort from the *Batory* stepped out from among the rows of prisoners and said a prayer.

As a German military march blared from speakers fixed to the mast, Elinor's body was lowered into the Pacific. Behind Ruth, a woman sobbed loudly. Ruth felt nothing but a great emptiness she feared would swallow her whole.

After a few seconds of silence, the captain faced his men, saluted, and with a firm, 'Heil Hitler,' strode away.

Goosebumps rose on Ruth's skin. As she watched the captain's retreating back she imagined herself running across the deck and throttling him. Anger made her vision darken, but she knew there was nothing to be done except join passively with the other women as they were led back below deck.

Ruth sleepwalked through the rest of the evening and the night. She observed herself from afar, in the same way she'd felt disconnected from her body when she'd arrived in Liverpool. This time, however, rather than being disconcerting, she welcomed the sense of remoteness from the current situation. Even the few mouthfuls of stew she swallowed tasted of nothing.

⌒

In the morning, after a repeat of the grainy coffee and black bread for breakfast – thankfully still tasteless to Ruth – the women were taken to the deck for ten minutes of fresh air and exercise. They walked back and forth, scanning the boat in the hope of seeing other prisoners before being led below deck once more.

Lunch was plain white rice boiled in sea water. Impossibly bland and gluggy, it stuck in the throat like a fistful of wet cottonwool.

Ruth's wrist now hurt less, but the bandage was hot and uncomfortable.

The next few hours revolved around whose turn it was to stand beside the ventilation shaft. There was no suggestion of doing exercises or stretches. Instead, the women sat drooped over the table, or lying on their hammocks staring at nothing.

At some point in the afternoon – all sense of time having disappeared – the officer who had taken them out for their fleeting taste of fresh air on deck entered the room smiling. 'Ladies, you are being moved to another ship. Get ready.'

The room burst into life. 'Oh, thank goodness,' a stewardess muttered. 'Another day in here and I would have started banging my head against the wall.'

'There's no guarantee our next lodgings will be any better,' said her companion.

'Frankly, I don't care, as long as we are doing something.'

Everyone set about gathering the few belongings they had, then they were told to say goodbye to the male prisoners, who were remaining on board. Ruth waited for her turn to stand at the doorway to the men's quarters, hoping to spot someone she knew. Suddenly she spied Reverend Kelly and called out his name. He was towards the back of the room, and when he caught her eye he smiled. 'Good luck, Ruth,' he called, blowing her a kiss. 'Stay strong.'

She blew him a kiss in return, scanning the room once more for Devan or Bobby. There was no sign of either.

From here she was led to a gangway and onto a motor launch, her eyes stinging in the brightness. The blue sky and sun warmed her back, the water slapped at the side of the boat, the air was salty and clear. It was all so remarkable. *I'll never take this for granted again*, Ruth vowed, breathing in deeply.

The women looked at one another with tremulous smiles as they motored across the sea, then they collectively straightened and took a deep breath as their launch approached another boat – smaller and less foreboding than the one they had just left.

'Look!' a woman cried, pointing to the deck. 'It's Emily.'

Ruth recognised some escorts standing on the top deck and instinctively began searching for Betty. Then realisation hit, and she bit down on the inside of her cheek, welcoming the pain and accompanying taste of blood.

The sea was rough and it took a while for the women to time their leap onto the gangway. Eventually Ruth arrived on deck and spotted Una standing quietly to one side. She had a thick bandage around one leg and a large angry graze across her cheek.

They stared at one another wordlessly for several seconds, then Ruth slowly walked over to the other woman and they put their arms around each other.

'Betty's dead,' Una croaked.

'Yes,' murmured Ruth.

'It's not . . . it's just not possible,' said Una, before breaking into loud, gut-wrenching sobs.

They held one another tightly until at last Una's sobs eased.

She took a deep shuddering breath and stared at Ruth's arm. 'Is it broken?' she asked.

Ruth shook her head. 'A sprain. What happened to your leg?'

Una shrugged. 'Burns and bruises. It'll be fine.'

Ruth saw no remnant of the flirty girl she was used to in Una's pale, sombre face.

They were interrupted by soldiers who quickly corralled all the women into a roped-off area, where they were left to watch as male prisoners were transferred. A handful of RAF men who had been on the *Rangitane* were ordered into the transfer boats first, followed shortly after by officers of the *Rangitane*. Ruth scanned every face, still hoping for a glimpse of Bobby, even though she knew he wouldn't be one of those transferred, as he wasn't in uniform.

As the men pulled away, they looked up at Ruth and the other women, raised their thumbs and shouted messages of good luck. Mrs Ellis, standing beside Ruth, dabbed at her eyes. 'I fear they are on a different path to us, now,' she murmured.

'Whatever do you mean?' asked Ruth, ignoring the part of herself that already knew the answer.

Mrs Ellis sighed. 'There must be a reason all the uniformed men are being separated out, Ruth.'

Ruth stared at the retreating boats, the men getting smaller and smaller.

A German officer strode over, removed the rope and led the women to a lower deck. Ruth's heart sank as she saw their dark, dank new lodgings. Tiny bunks with straw mattresses were placed one above the other. There were small, closed portholes, no signs of ventilation, and the only entrance to the room was through a heavy iron door.

We truly are prisoners, Ruth thought bitterly.

She had lost sight of Una while they were on deck but now noticed her lying on a narrow bunk staring blankly ahead, her body eerily still.

Ruth stepped closer. 'Una?' she said. 'Are you all right?'

Una blinked but kept her gaze on the bunk above her. 'I'm fine, Ruth,' she said flatly. 'Just wanting a rest.'

Ruth backed away and moved towards a porthole. If only she could open it, just for a few minutes.

Thankfully they didn't have to stay in the depressing room for long and were allowed back on deck as the ship began to move across the vast expanse of the Pacific Ocean. Ruth had gently urged Una from her bed and they now stood side by side, staring at the water as the sky turned grey.

The sound of a gong caused Ruth's stomach to grumble. 'I hope the food on board this ship is nicer,' she said. 'If I have to force myself to eat plain white rice again, I will surely vomit.'

Una smiled faintly but didn't speak.

Entering the dining room, they were confronted by a giant portrait of Hitler on the wall. Catching Ruth's eye, Mrs Ellis raised her eyebrows and gave a surreptitious wink. Ruth winked back before quickly finding a seat for herself and Una at one of the round tables.

'Cor blimey,' someone beside Ruth murmured. 'Real china.'

Ruth desperately hoped the blue-and-white china was an indication of the quality of the food to come, but was disappointed when a plate containing two small black bread sandwiches was placed in front of her. On closer inspection, she discovered one sandwich contained a slice of cheese and the second some type of German sausage.

The woman beside Ruth began to choke and Ruth thumped her on the back.

'Thank you,' the woman gasped, discreetly spitting out the offending chunk of sausage. 'I should be used to it by now.'

'Is this a regular meal?' Ruth asked.

The woman nodded. 'Best one of the day.'

'You're kidding,' piped another voice at the table. 'Here I was thinking this had to be the worst.'

'Oh, we shouldn't complain – the men have it far worse.'

'Are there more male prisoners on board?' Ruth asked.

She nodded. 'There's at least a hundred in the hold, though Lord knows how they fit. They're only allowed out twice a day for exercise. It must be dreadful.'

Ruth hoped Bobby, Devan and Gary were among them. As terrible as the conditions were, at least it meant they were alive.

'Do you ever get to see or talk to the male prisoners?' Ruth asked.

The woman shrugged. 'Occasionally we might give them a wave, but we're never close enough for conversation.'

Ruth wanted to ask more, but at that moment the captain entered, cigar in hand and a welcoming smile plastered on his face, as if they were his guests on a luxury ocean liner. 'Welcome,' he said. 'This is not the right way to treat ladies, but I will do my best to make sure you are well looked after.'

Mrs Ellis stood up and thanked him for his kindness, and the others murmured their agreement.

'We do not make war on women,' said the captain, smiling broadly.

'Sure,' muttered Una.

'He's nice enough,' said the woman beside Ruth once the captain had left. 'Yesterday he said the war was senseless. I don't believe he likes this situation any more than us.'

'I bet he's not eating these sandwiches, though, and he's probably sleeping in a very comfortable cabin all to himself,' said someone sitting across the table.

After the meal they were escorted back to their quarters. Ruth tried her best to sleep, but her racing thoughts kept her awake in the dark, airless room. She thought of Peter and her brother; of her mother battling Aunt Audrey; she thought of Florrie in London and of her father on the orchard with his dogs. She thought of Bobby, and hoped he had made it off the *Rangitane* alive. Finally, Ruth wondered how Fergus and Rosie were getting on in Australia. She hoped they were happy. She hoped that one day she would see her loved ones again.

The following morning, the women rose early, desperate to escape the heat. The days were growing ever hotter and everyone assumed they were nearing the equator. Ruth's pyjamas stuck to her sweaty body and she wished there was something to change into. She knew she must smell as bad as the others in her cabin. Sighing, Ruth decided it was time to brave a trip to the bathroom. The facility may have been pleasant enough once, but it was now a filthy room with at least two inches of murky water on the floor. The women were given only a single bucket of fresh water to use between them, which worked out to be no more than a glassful each – barely enough to clean their face and hands, let alone any other body parts.

Finally, they were allowed out on deck. Those first big lungfuls of fresh salty air each morning turned out to be the highlight of Ruth's day as time dragged on.

Every day was the same. Rice boiled in sea water with the occasional maggot for breakfast, accompanied by a mouldy slice of bread and a smear of jam.

At midday, they were served the same boiled rice with tinned peas or a tiny piece of carrot. For supper it was the usual black bread sandwiches with cheese and chewy sausage – which, as the woman had told Ruth on her first day aboard, was the most palatable of the meals, and often the only one Ruth and the other prisoners could stomach.

One morning, after more than a week of the same dreadful conditions, a stewardess from the *Rangitane*, who had spent the night tossing about on the bunk beneath Ruth, collapsed in a heap on the floor and began to wail. 'What if they plan to take us back to Europe and lock us up in those camps we keep hearing about? It will take weeks to get there, and I can't take it, I really can't. There is simply no *air*.'

'That's enough.' Mrs Ellis put her hands on her hips and glared at the woman. 'Get up at once. We must show our British spirit at times like these. Our men are out there fighting for their lives; the least we can do is stay strong.'

Ruth crouched down beside the stewardess and helped her to her feet. 'Chin up,' Ruth whispered. 'I know it's hard not to despair.'

The stewardess leant against Ruth, tears in her eyes. 'I want to be clean and I am hungry every minute of the day and night. You are too of course, we all are, but it's harder for me. Don't ask me why, I just know it is.'

Ruth suppressed a smile. 'I'm sure you're right.' She was reminded of Rosie, who could be similarly indignant. Then she thought of Fergus, and how he would have done anything to help his sister.

Something stirred inside her. Ruth strode towards the door and banged on it with her fist.

The guard wrenched it open, a scowl on his face. 'What?' he barked.

'We need air. And water. And better food.' Ruth put her hands on her hips and returned his scowl. 'I want to speak to the captain.'

They continued to eyeball one another, Ruth refusing to look away. Suddenly the soldier reached out and gripped her arm.

'Now see here!' Mrs Ellis moved beside Ruth. 'Let her go immediately.'

The other women pressed in behind Ruth, muttering, and the guard placed his hand on the gun holstered to his hip. 'Step back,' he barked.

It was as if for one long drawn-out second everyone froze. Then the guard let go of Ruth and nudged her back into the room. 'I get captain,' he barked, before closing and locking their door.

Mrs Ellis raised her eyebrows. 'That was bold, eh, Ruth?'

There were several cheers from others in the room.

'We shall see if anything comes of it,' said Ruth, staring at the locked door.

Ten minutes later, the door was unlocked and the captain stepped into the room. 'Ladies,' he said politely. 'There is a problem?'

Ruth no longer felt quite as confident, especially now the captain stood before them. 'Yes,' she croaked. 'We need more air.' She pointed to the covered portholes.

The captain pursed his lips, his eyes sweeping about the room. Surely the unpleasant smell of unwashed bodies that hung in the hot still air must have been enough to persuade him. He nodded once, decisively. 'You may open the portholes when it is light. At night they stay closed.'

A murmuring went through the crowd of women.

'Thank you,' said Mrs Ellis, who was standing nearby.

'Is that all?' asked the captain, already turning on his heel.

'Water,' Ruth blurted. 'We aren't getting enough.'

Slowly, the captain spun back. His jaw was clenched and Ruth knew she had annoyed him. He stepped towards her, his eyes narrow slits. 'We ration water. There is no more.'

Ruth knew from his expression she should not test his patience any further. She looked down at her feet. 'I understand,' she said.

'Good.' The captain marched to a porthole and opened it wide. 'Happy, ladies?'

'Yes, sir,' they chorused.

Ruth kept her head lowered as he left, hoping no-one could see the tremor in her legs.

'Well done, Ruth,' said Mrs Ellis as the door closed behind the captain.

'That was very courageous,' said another woman.

Ruth sat heavily on the nearest bunk, her burst of bravery well and truly spent.

29

HAZEL

'It's like I'm in a Harry Potter book,' Hazel squealed as she stepped off the Heathrow Express and onto the platform at Paddington. 'Look at that.' She pointed to the elegant arched roof of the station. 'I can't believe I'm really here. I'm actually in London.'

Hazel spun around, arms outstretched. Her bag whacked an elderly gentleman in the ribs as he strode past.

'Oh, I'm sorry,' she gasped.

The man glared and cursed under his breath before continuing on his way.

'Ease up there, Hazel: you don't want to get arrested on your first day in England.' Joe was standing a few steps away, smiling.

Hazel's eyes widened. 'Arrested? For what?'

'Disturbing the peace. Assaulting a grumpy old man. Acting in a distinctly un-British manner.'

'How so?'

'We don't squeal with excitement and we certainly don't twirl with joy. You'll have to learn fast if you're going to fit in around here.'

Hazel grinned. 'Hassle me all you want, Joe. When you've been wanting to travel the world for as long as I have, you don't care how ridiculous you might look.'

Joe hoisted his pack onto his back. 'Come on – since you're so bloody happy to be here, how about I show you what real British life is like. There's a great pub around the corner.'

'What about Klara? Won't she be waiting for you?'

'Probably,' Joe called over his shoulder. 'And if I'm honest, I need a drink before I see her.'

Hazel grabbed her suitcase handle. 'I wouldn't say no to a pint,' she said in a poor attempt at a Cockney accent.

Joe groaned. 'Hazel, how can you be so goddamn sprightly? We've been travelling for more than twenty-four hours, we've barely slept, and I would murder a hot shower because I feel and probably look like shit.'

Hazel giggled. 'I'm high on life, Joe.'

'Yeah, well, a few days in this city should knock that out of you.' Joe's wink let Hazel know he was joking.

'After our pint, I'm going to hail a black cab.'

Joe rolled his eyes. 'Of course you are.'

'Do you know how many British TV shows I've watched where someone leaps into a black cab? A gazillion at least.'

'The jet lag is going to hit you soon, and when it does you're going to wish you'd never left little old New Zealand, trust me.'

'Are you always this positive?'

'Oh, shut up.' Joe smiled at Hazel and she smiled back.

Moments later, she was sliding into a booth at a pub that looked exactly like an English pub should. 'God, I wish there were places like this back home,' she said, taking a sip of the beer Joe placed before her.

Hazel swallowed then grimaced. 'It's warm,' she spluttered.

Joe laughed as he sat opposite. 'You'll find we drink our beer warmer over here, Hazel.'

'Why?' she asked, horrified.

'No idea. I have to admit I got used to drinking icy cold beer in New Zealand. It's going to take me a while to readjust.'

Hazel eyed her pint glass with suspicion. 'I suppose I'll have to get used to it,' she said, cautiously taking another sip.

'So, tell me more about this friend you're going to stay with.'

'Nothing much to tell. We were both doing a pharmacy degree in Dunedin and flatted together for a year. I lost touch with her after university, but then I heard she was living in London, so I sent her an email and she said I could doss on her couch until I found somewhere to live.'

Hazel took another sip of beer and wiped her mouth. 'Anyway, I feel like you know all about me and I know next to nothing about you. What are your parents like? Do you get on?'

'We do, actually. I don't think I've ever had an argument with them, unless you count the time I let a couple of my schoolmates into the pub and served them drinks when they were underage.'

'I bet your friends were jealous your parents ran a pub.'

'Oh yeah. Though there were a few snobs who thought it was too lowly.'

'Assholes.'

A waiter arrived and placed a basket of chips between them.

'Thought you might be peckish,' said Joe.

'Thanks.' Hazel reached for a hot chip, her stomach grumbling. 'Have you got any brothers or sisters?'

'A younger sister, Maggie. The golden child. She married a wealthy lawyer and they live in a beautiful house near Hampstead Heath with their two gorgeous girls, Bea and Lily, and a nanny, because Maggie has some important job in finance. It's a miracle I don't hate her really.'

'She sounds nauseatingly perfect.'

Joe's smile lit up his face. 'She's really nice too. You'd love her.'

'Let me guess: she belongs to a gym and has a personal trainer, right?'

'Of course. And she eats salad for lunch and hardly touches alcohol.'

'No offence, but she sounds terrifying.'

'Oh, she's not. Everyone gets on with her – except Klara, for some reason.'

Hazel was pleased to observe the mention of Klara had no effect on her. 'Why is that?'

Joe shrugged. 'Not sure. I do remember at our engagement party Maggie asking me in a polite roundabout sort of way if I was sure about getting married. Maybe she could see something I couldn't.'

They both reached for the fries and their hands knocked together. Joe withdrew his quickly. 'You first,' he said, avoiding her eye.

Hazel took some fries and wolfed them down. 'Is there anything you dream about doing? You said you were happy working in your parents' pub, but do you ever think about doing something else?'

Joe eyed Hazel over the rim of his glass as he took another sip. 'Not really. Maybe I should have some big ambition to make lots of money, or have some super-rewarding job helping the poor, or becoming a builder or architect or something, but I don't.'

'You make it sound like that's a bad thing.'

'Isn't it?'

'Not at all. You're content with what you have. That's pretty rare, you know.'

'Definitely not how Klar—how other people see it. And before you ask, I don't play a sport or have any interesting hobbies or secret talents. When I'm not working, I'm out aimlessly walking or at the pub with a mate or eating a late-night kebab on Edgeware Road. I don't offer much to the world at all.'

'Christ, you sound like one of those penniless artists in some period drama like *Downton Abbey* who says' – Hazel struck a dramatic pose and put on a posh voice – 'I have nothing to offer you, my dear.'

Joe laughed. 'Don't quit your day job, Hazel.'

'I won't.' Hazel took another quick sip of her beer. 'Okay, what about travel? You went to New Zealand, which is bloody miles away, but I bet you've been to all sorts of places in Europe.'

'I got the Eurostar to Paris once.'

'That's it?'

'Yep.'

'I have a list of all the places I want to go and it's at least five pages long.'

'I bet you do.' Joe rubbed his cheek. 'You know, I never thought about it much. In the back of my mind, I figured I'd end up travelling around Europe eventually. Except now that I see how excited you are, I feel guilty. I enjoyed my time in New Zealand. It was refreshing to be in another culture.'

'Do you think it's very different from here?'

Joe nodded. 'Sure. It's more laidback. Everyone is way too friendly, of course.'

Hazel laughed. 'And that's a bad thing?'

'It was tiring. I'm used to being able to stay in the background and watch what's going on without people trying to include me, but the second anyone realised I was on my own they were right up in my face. I guess I prefer to be an observer rather than a participant. I think that's why I like working in the pub. And why I spend so much time out walking.' Joe winced. 'Man, that makes me sound weird.'

Hazel reached over and put a hand on top of Joe's. 'No, it doesn't.' Then, realising what she'd done, she quickly took her hand away and wrapped it around her glass. 'If you ask me, there aren't enough observers in the world,' she said. 'Everyone's trying to get out in front, to be the one other people watch, instead of slowing down and taking the time to appreciate what's around them.'

'Thanks. That's the first time anyone has come close to understanding me.'

Hazel risked looking up to find Joe was watching her intently. Her heart skipped a beat. *Just friends*, she reminded herself.

When Hazel had finished her beer, Joe stood beside her on the footpath as she hailed a black cab heading down the street towards them.

'Look,' she cried. 'It's stopping.'

Joe shook his head. 'Contain yourself, Hazel.' He was clearly trying to look stern but failing dismally. It was about the worst attempt at a frown Hazel had seen.

The cab stopped beside Hazel, and Joe opened the side door. 'Madame,' he said, holding out his arm and giving a small bow.

'Why, thank you.' Hazel curtsied and clambered in, Joe sliding her suitcase in beside her.

'Where to?' called the driver through the glass divider.

Hazel cleared her throat and recited the address in Camden.

Joe leant heavily against the open door. 'Did you just attempt a British accent?'

'Don't be ridiculous,' she said, doing her best to sound British.

Laughing, Joe stepped back. 'Bye, Hazel. Don't be a stranger. You still have my number, right?'

Hazel nodded and patted her pocket. 'As soon as I buy a mobile, I'll call you.'

Joe nodded decisively. 'Right, well, bye then.' He hesitated, as if about to say more, then carefully closed the door.

'All right, love?' asked the driver, looking at Hazel in the rear-view mirror.

Hazel cast one last look at Joe, who was heaving his pack onto his back. 'Yes,' she said firmly. 'I'll be fine.'

30

Emirau Island, 1940

During the next three weeks, the German raiders attacked several more unsuspecting vessels. After each attack, more prisoners were taken aboard their ship. Ruth gasped to see some children among the prisoners as they were herded into the now-overflowing cabins. All the younger women, Ruth included, offered up their beds to the children and their mothers, instead sleeping in cramped rows on the floor. The prisoners tried to maintain high spirits, but as the days wore on they became listless.

In a fit of frustration at the heat, Ruth ripped off the bottom of her pyjama legs, turning them into shorts. She used the strips of material to tie up her hair. Many of the other women immediately followed suit, relishing the cooler air on their legs and necks.

The hours were endless, and they spent most of their time either playing cards or talking about food, each of the prisoners describing in detail all the wonderful meals they would eat if they could.

Fresh drinking water continued to be scarce. Ruth, whose mouth was permanently parched, would have given up food for an entire day just for an extra glass of water.

The one day it rained there was a stampede as everyone was allowed to race on deck with any receptacle they could find to catch drops of water. Ruth simply stood there, feeling the rain on her hair and face and licking the drops as they fell from her nose. All too soon, the sky cleared to blue once more.

There were occasional rare glimpses of the male prisoners, and Ruth thought at one point she might have caught sight of the back of Bobby's head. She'd called his name, but her voice didn't carry far enough for him to hear – or perhaps it wasn't him at all.

Then one day Una entered the dining room and, her cheeks flushed, rushed to Ruth's side. 'I've seen Gary,' she whispered. 'And Bobby too.'

Una had gradually improved, though she still avoided any talk of Betty. She'd been called on to help in the hospital, so Ruth only saw her in the dining room and at bedtime. Ruth was jealous of Una, bandaging wounds and providing comfort to those in pain. At least she was able to do something useful.

'Really? They're here on the ship?' Ruth asked. 'Are they all right?'

Una nodded. 'They've been here since the start. Gary was thrilled to see me, and Bobby asked after you.'

'However did you manage to talk to them?'

Una grimaced. 'They'd carried one of their friends to the hospital. He was very sick, Ruth. I've never seen such yellow skin before and there was nothing to him. He was like a stick insect. The doctor thinks he might not make it through the night.'

'Oh no.'

'Gary and Bobby were skin and bone too. It took me a moment to recognise them, especially with their beards and shaggy hair. They really were a sight, Ruth. But, then, I wasn't exactly looking my finest either.'

'Thank goodness they're alive.'

'Gary said he overheard someone saying we're heading towards an island.'

'Which one?'

Una shrugged. 'No idea. I hope we get to go ashore, though. I'd give anything for some time on land.'

'So would I.' Ruth didn't think she could bear it if she saw land and wasn't able to get to it. At least when all she could see was ocean she knew there was nowhere to go, but to see land and not be allowed to touch it, well, that would be the worst torture of all.

~

Harry, the chubby-cheeked British four-year-old to whom Ruth had given up her bed, was given permission by his mother to open the porthole – a task he took great pride in performing. The moment he opened it, he gave a yelp. 'Trees!'

Everyone crowded around him, trying to get a glimpse.

'I've never seen anything more glorious in my life,' Mrs Ellis declared.

At some point during the night, their ship had dropped anchor. Less than a hundred yards away was a long, low-lying island covered in trees. The sparkling turquoise water surrounding the island was so clear Ruth could see the sandy bottom.

'It's paradise,' Una breathed. 'Oh, I want to jump into that water right this minute.'

'Me too,' said Harry, jiggling about with excitement. His mother placed a firm hand on his head and he froze, his lips forming a disappointed pout.

Footsteps pounded back and forth on the deck overhead, and they waited impatiently for the guard to unlock their door. Only, he didn't come. The wait was unbearable, especially as the day grew hotter and their cramped room became a furnace.

'I'll pass out if they don't let us out soon,' Una whispered, wiping her brow dramatically. 'This treatment is barbaric.'

Suddenly the iron door swung open. 'Gather your possessions,' yelled the guard.

Everyone stared at one another. Did this mean they were leaving the ship?

'Now!' he shouted.

Hurriedly, they did as they were told. Ruth took her coat, not imagining for a moment it would ever be cool enough to put it on but unwilling to leave the one thing she still owned behind.

They filed out of the room, whispering together in excited, hushed voices, and were greeted on deck by their smiling captain. 'Ladies, you are being released onto this island. We have kindly left supplies for a few days.' He stared at them expectantly, as if they should be cheering or clapping, but they remained silent.

'Very well,' he said, his smile slipping away. Then he gave the Nazi salute and strode off.

They gathered at the rail and inspected the island. Ruth guessed it was around ten miles long, with a small jetty and boathouse at one end. Dark-skinned islanders darted among the trees, no doubt terrified by the spectacle before them.

Turning her head, Ruth saw the ship that had first taken the passengers of the *Rangitane* prisoner was anchored beside them. Several small boats flying the swastika were loaded with prisoners and making their way from the ship towards the island.

Soon it was their turn. Ruth was in the fourth group of women and children to hurry down the gangway onto a waiting lifeboat. With the sun beating down on them, they slowly made their way to the jetty. As they drew close, Ruth saw a middle-aged, red-faced man in khaki clothes and a straw hat greeting prisoners as they disembarked. Beside him stood a short, plump woman with a good-natured, friendly face.

'Welcome to Emirau,' the man boomed. He had an unmistakable Australian accent. 'We are Mr and Mrs Cook.'

Behind the Cooks stood two other Europeans, who smiled and nodded nervously.

Ruth's legs shook as she stepped onto the jetty and wobbled towards hundreds of prisoners gathered on the beach. The ground seemed to shift about under her feet, causing her to stumble.

'Ruth!'

Turning, Ruth saw a gaunt, hairy man grinning and waving as he rushed towards her.

'Bobby?' she whispered.

'You're okay!' He lifted her off her feet and spun her around.

She gripped him tightly as laughter bubbled up inside her and tears welled in her eyes.

～

'I'm sorry about Betty,' said Bobby.

They were sitting side by side in the sand, waiting for the remaining prisoners to be offloaded. Ruth kept staring at Bobby, not just because of his shockingly changed appearance, but because she had to keep convincing herself that he was actually there.

'I still have trouble believing she's dead,' murmured Ruth. 'It's all been so dreadful, Bobby.'

'It's been an ordeal, I'll grant you. But we're free, Ruth.' He cleared his throat. 'Most importantly, you're safe,' he added.

Ruth leant against Bobby, their shoulders pressing together. 'We both are.'

Bobby opened his mouth to speak, then closed it again.

'Have you seen Devan?' Ruth asked.

'We were in the same hold together.'

'How is he?'

Bobby shrugged. 'He's had his struggles, but he's improving.' He pointed further along the beach. 'That's him down there.'

Devan was standing at the water's edge staring out to sea. 'Oh goodness,' said Ruth, taking in his thin, hunched frame. She knew she should go over and offer words of support, but she couldn't do it. Not yet.

'Do you have any idea what happens now?' she asked.

Bobby dipped his head at the man in the straw hat on the jetty. 'Mr Cook there runs a copra plantation on the island. That's his

wife beside him, and the younger man behind him is the plantation manager with his wife. They're the only ones who live here
on the island, believe it or not, with a group of islanders who
work on the plantation. He told us when we arrived that we're to
make our way to his house on the other side of the island, where
we'll be fed and looked after until we can be rescued.'

'I can't believe we're free. In fact, I won't believe it until those
wretched Germans leave.'

Bobby chuckled and Ruth felt a surge of elation. She noticed
his hand was buried beneath the sand. Impulsively she dug her
hand into the sand next to his and moved a finger until they
were touching.

He glanced at her then back at the German raiders anchored
out at sea. 'Ruth, I promised if I ever saw you again, I would tell
you something.' He sounded hesitant, and Ruth was immediately on alert.

'What is it?'

He took a deep breath. 'I wasn't entirely honest with you about
Nell. It was a mutual decision to go our separate ways. You see,
after Nell confessed she had developed feelings for another man,
I . . . well, I admitted I had developed feelings too.' He turned
to face Ruth with a look that made her lower stomach quiver.
'For you,' he said softly.

Ruth held herself still. If she moved even a fraction, she knew
it would release a flurry of emotions churning inside her.

'Ruth, please say something,' said Bobby.

Closing her eyes, Ruth concentrated on breathing in and out.
What could she say? What was she to do? It was too much. She'd
been a prisoner for the last four weeks. She was on an island

in the middle of nowhere with nothing but the tattered clothes sticking to her body. She was dirty, hungry, thirsty and tired. For so long she'd been focused on surviving, on coping with the loss of her friend, and now . . .

'Look, I'm sorry,' Bobby said. 'I should have waited. It's just . . . I just . . .'

When he didn't finish his sentence, Ruth opened her eyes. 'Bobby, this is not the right time,' she whispered.

Bobby nodded briskly and lifted his hand out of the sand. 'Absolutely,' he said, clambering to his feet.

Awkwardly, Ruth scrambled upright, brushing the sand off her clothes and wishing she had not been so abrupt.

⁓

Mr Cook had one lorry on the island and offered to take as many of the children, mothers and injured as he could to his plantation house. 'The rest of you will need to walk the ten miles, I'm afraid.' Ruth, already exhausted from the heat, would have dearly loved a ride in the lorry, but she knew the others should get priority.

The expedition across the island was slow, painful and unbearably hot. Days in cramped conditions with very little exercise, along with a lack of proper nourishment, had left them weak. Bobby and Gary joined Ruth and Una for the walk and it was clear from the way the men struggled they had suffered far worse than the women during their imprisonment. After less than half a mile they both had to sit down and put their heads between their knees, their faces pale.

'Sorry, ladies,' said Gary. 'Not quite as sturdy as we'd like.'

Una sat beside him. 'I can't believe they only gave you one tiny meal a day.'

'If it had been edible we would have been all right, but often . . .' Gary shrugged.

Ruth looked at Bobby's lowered head. Since his declaration on the beach they'd been acting as if everything between them was fine. As if he'd never said a word about his feelings for her. She knew it was cowardly, but she was relieved. Some things were easier to ignore than face.

A small boy with thick, curly hair approached. He smiled and held something out to Ruth. She gasped and immediately grabbed at the fruit. 'It's a pawpaw,' she exclaimed. Thanking the boy profusely, she ripped the yellow skin apart, handed a chunk to each of her companions and bit into the brightly coloured flesh. The juice ran down her chin and she licked at it with a grin.

'Best moment of my life,' Gary said, taking a large bite.

They ate silently but for their regular groans of delight.

'Look,' Ruth said, pointing into the trees. 'There's more.'

Bobby took one look at the fruit hanging from the limbs of the tree to the side of the path and leapt to his feet. Seconds later, he was back with four more pawpaws in his arms.

They all sat down on the sandy path and devoured the fruit. It was so sweet Ruth felt an immediate rush to her head.

'We should slow down,' muttered Una, her mouth full. 'Our stomachs won't be used to it.'

The small boy returned, this time holding a coconut. He pointed to the hole he had made at the top. 'Thank you,' Ruth said, beaming. The boy's crooked teeth shone as he smiled back.

Ruth held out the coconut to Bobby. 'You go first,' she said lightly. 'You need this more than me.'

Bobby gently pushed the coconut towards Ruth. 'Ladies first.'

Ruth knew she should argue, but she was thirsty and couldn't muster the will. She tipped the coconut and gulped at the water spilling from its centre. It tasted so fresh and glorious that tears sprang to her eyes.

The coconut was handed around and drained quickly.

'Well,' said Gary, standing, 'I feel a million times better now – don't you, Bobby?'

'Absolutely.' Bobby stood and held out a hand to help Ruth up.

Ruth let herself be hauled to her feet. 'I fear most of the others have gone on ahead.'

'There are plenty of them still to come.' Bobby turned and pointed to the men and women walking slowly or resting by the side of the path. Most were holding pawpaws or drinking from coconuts as children ran among them.

'At this rate it will take us all day,' said Una. 'And I've already cut my foot.' She lifted her leg and Ruth saw a thin red line of blood on her big toe. Less than a handful of passengers had escaped the *Rangitane* with shoes, and the thought of wearing something on her feet again seemed foreign. 'I think you'll live,' she said.

Bobby laughed and gave Ruth a wink, causing her heart to thump erratically.

Their progress was gradual but steady over the next few hours, though at one point they had to stop while Gary escaped into the bushes, his stomach in cramps.

'I thought this might happen,' said Una. 'He's barely stopped eating those pawpaws all day.'

'I'll admit my stomach feels rather sensitive too,' Ruth said, underplaying the powerful ache in her abdomen.

After almost six hours of walking they came to an open gate and entered a fenced-off area of garden. Before them was a large wooden house raised on wooden poles. Deep verandahs wrapped around two sides, their posts covered in purple flowering creepers, and bright red hibiscus bushes framed the house. Women and children from the ships were scattered along the verandahs.

'Well, this is a sight,' said Una, picking up her pace.

'Ruth,' Mrs Ellis called from the front door. 'There's tea — with milk and sugar, no less.'

'Goodness,' Ruth breathed.

Bobby and Gary said a quick goodbye then headed to a building a little way off from the house, where the men had gathered.

'Come on,' Una said, grabbing Ruth's hand. 'You'll see him again soon enough.'

Embarrassed, Ruth realised Una had caught her watching Bobby go.

They hurried inside, where they were greeted by their hosts, Mr and Mrs Cook, who poured the tea Mrs Ellis had promised. Una let out a small squeal of joy when a young girl then handed them a plate of white bread smeared with butter.

Ruth did her best to chew slowly and politely, but it was difficult not to gobble it up in one go.

'Where exactly are we?' asked Mrs Ellis.

Mrs Cook smiled. 'We're on Emirau Island, a mere two degrees from the equator. It's part of New Guinea. We're around seventy miles from Kavieng, which is where we go for supplies – though I find myself a little short, as I hadn't anticipated quite so many guests today. It is going to be a challenge to ensure you're all adequately cared for.'

Ruth put down her empty cup. 'What can we do to help?' she asked.

'They're setting up a makeshift hospital for the sick and wounded over there.' Mrs Cook pointed through a window at a small hut a little distance away.

'That's me then,' said Una.

'And a number of women are helping in the cookhouse out back. I believe they're trying to make scones for everybody.' Mrs Cook shrugged and laughed.

'Righto,' said Ruth. 'I'll go and lend a hand.'

'I'll join you, Ruth,' said Mrs Ellis.

The three women stood and, after thanking the Cooks for their hospitality, hurried off.

The cookhouse was a hive of activity and Ruth was soon put to work measuring out flour for the scones. It was wonderful to move about freely with no guard watching over them, and there was much laughter and more than a few tears of joy.

The question of utensils was raised, and soon men were whittling spoons from pieces of driftwood, and the women were gathering up any receptacle they could find to hold tea. After an hour in the hot confines of the cookhouse, Ruth volunteered to help gather coconuts and turn them into bowls. Once the islanders split the coconuts in two, the milk and flesh were eagerly consumed by whoever hovered nearby, then the shell was scrubbed with sand and sea water, and left in the sun to dry.

Ruth enjoyed being outside, the sea breeze on her face and the sound of gentle waves lapping against the shore. She kept an eye out for Bobby among the large group of men constructing sleeping quarters out of palm fronds down near the beach, but she was unable to spot him anywhere.

'Ruth!' Reverend Kelly rushed towards her. 'I was hoping to find you somewhere on this island.'

He was as emaciated and scrawny as the rest of the men. 'It's so good to see you, Reverend,' said Ruth, giving him a hug.

'I trust you are as thrilled as I am to be on solid ground,' he said.

'I am indeed.'

They chatted a little longer before the Reverend excused himself to see if he could assist the men.

By dusk, the final stragglers had arrived and Mr Cook gathered everyone together to inform them that the German boats had departed. Ruth suspected they were all experiencing the same combination of relief at their freedom and sadness at the realisation that so many RAF men and officers had remained as captives, most likely on their way to prison camps.

As they all broke apart to find somewhere to sleep for the night, Bobby approached Ruth. She did a double take at his transformation. He was scrubbed clean, his beard gone and his hair trimmed rather unevenly to his ears. 'Look at you,' Ruth exclaimed, before blushing furiously. She felt a mess in comparison – her hair was so unruly she could no longer get a comb through her knotted curls.

'I spent an hour floating and swimming in the sea. It's so warm, Ruth, and there are tropical fish everywhere. One of the lads, Charlie, offered to trim my hair, and Mr Cook procured a barber of all things. I feel a million times better than I have done in weeks.'

'I wish I could swim too,' Ruth said wistfully, staring down at the beach lit by the last rays of fading pink sunlight.

'Why don't you? Not that you have to . . .' Bobby added hastily. 'You're fine as you are.'

Ruth laughed. 'Bobby, there's no need to be polite; I know I must be a dreadful sight.'

Bobby shook his head, his cheeks red. 'Not at all.'

'Do you think we will be here long?' Ruth asked, changing the subject.

'On the island? I couldn't say, though I understand Mr Cook is setting off in his boat in the morning with a couple of *Rangitane* crew. They're going to Kavieng to send word of our whereabouts.'

'Just imagine, all those people who had no idea what happened to us. Do you think they believed we went down with the *Rangitane*?' Ruth thought of her mother and Florrie, to whom she'd written the day before she left Auckland harbour. She'd said how much she was looking forward to being home for Christmas. 'What's the date, Bobby? Do you know?'

'It'll be Christmas Eve the day after tomorrow.'

'Not exactly where I planned to be.'

Bobby touched Ruth on the arm. 'I can't think of a better Christmas present in the world than our freedom, can you?'

Ruth blinked back tears. 'You're quite right.' What did it matter if she hadn't had a bath in more than a month and she was marooned on an island in the middle of the Pacific? At least she was free. 'I'm just tired and in need of a good rest. Have you organised a place to sleep?'

Bobby nodded. 'Gary and I have rigged up a shelter, though some of the lads are going to sleep on the beach under the stars. I might join them, if Gary sets to snoring.'

Ruth laughed. 'There's certainly no fear of being cold; it's still warm, even though it's nearly dark.'

'Will you be sleeping inside?' Bobby asked, dipping his head in the direction of the main house.

'That's the plan. It'll be a squeeze, but with luck I'll find a little floor space. I'm so tired I'm sure I'd sleep almost anywhere.'

They smiled at one another shyly. Ruth felt connected to Bobby in ways she'd never felt with Peter. If she'd met him under normal circumstances, would there have been the same current of energy passing between them?

'Goodnight, Ruth.' Bobby leant in and gave her a quick peck on the cheek. 'Sleep well,' he murmured, his lips still close to her ear.

Ruth took a quick step back. 'Goodnight,' she said, her voice clipped. Ignoring the hurt expression on Bobby's face, Ruth quickly turned away and headed towards the house.

As she climbed the steps to the front door, she spied Mrs Ellis lying on the verandah with a row of other women. They were using their lifebelts as their pillows. 'It's very full inside now, Ruth dear. Perhaps you'd like to bunch up here with us?'

Ruth nodded. Hopefully she would drop off to sleep quickly and wouldn't replay the last few minutes in her head.

Unfortunately, it was clear within moments of lying down that Ruth and the others would struggle to get any sleep at all. The mosquitoes, sandflies and hordes of tiny red ants drove everyone mad. While Ruth initially tried not to scratch, she soon gave up as the itching became too intense to ignore. Add to that the crickets and other insects – so loud and insistent it reminded Ruth of being in a school assembly before the children had been hushed – and sleep proved all but impossible.

Everyone was up early, eager to put the uncomfortable night behind them. Apart from the odd disgruntled remark as they compared the red welts blooming across their bodies, no-one complained. After being prisoners at sea for a month, a few insect bites on dry land were a small price to pay. Ruth's spirits were significantly improved when Mrs Cook appeared and handed out enamel bowls filled with warm water, along with soap and towels. After a quick wash under the trees, Ruth felt refreshed and headed off to help in the cookhouse. Some of the locals must have been up most of the night, as there were several huge urns filled with bullock stew and everyone queued politely with their half coconut shells and recently carved wooden spoons. Ruth spied Una with her back against a tree. Sitting next to Una was Devan. Ruth took a deep breath and went to join them.

'Look who I bumped into,' said Una.

Ruth met Devan's eye and forced a smile. 'Hello, Devan.'

He offered a faint smile in return. 'Ruth.'

'I'm so sorry, about . . . Betty was . . .'

Devan nodded. 'I know, Ruth.'

Una touched his arm. 'We were blessed to have her in our lives.'

'That we were,' he croaked.

After a few seconds of awkward silence, Ruth sat down next to Una and inspected the contents of her coconut shell. 'How is it?' she asked, keen to talk of something less painful.

'It's the most delicious thing I've ever eaten,' said Una, slurping from her spoon. 'And I can tell you now I never in a bunch of Sundays would have expected those words to leave my mouth.'

They laughed, which helped to ease the strained atmosphere, and Ruth dug into her stew. 'It's a tad different to the breakfasts my friend Florrie and I used to enjoy at the Savoy.'

As they ate, they discussed where and when they had eaten their best breakfasts, and it was almost as if they were back on the *Batory* and Betty would be rushing over to join them at any moment.

By the time they'd finished their stew and had a couple of slices of pawpaw with a squeeze of fresh lime juice, Ruth decided that even a meal at the Savoy could not have been tastier.

The sun was high as they rinsed their bowls and said goodbye to Devan, who headed off to help the lads build more shelters down by the beach. Ruth dripped with sweat, her earlier wash nothing more than a distant dream as her clothes stuck to her body. 'Phew, it's going to be a scorcher,' she said, fanning her face.

'That's it.' Una grabbed Ruth by the hand and began pulling her towards the beach. 'We're going for a swim.'

'We have nothing to wear,' Ruth objected as they stepped onto the sand. She glanced at the men dotted along the shore.

Most were wading in the shallows, chatting and laughing with one another, their shirts tied around their waists.

'Don't be daft, Ruth,' Una said, pulling off the yellowed, stained blue blouse she had worn every day for the past month and exposing her tattered grey brassiere. 'After what we've been through, let's not concern ourselves with propriety, especially out here on an island in the middle of nowhere.' She grinned at Ruth before slipping her skirt down, stepping out of it to reveal a short, torn petticoat, and running into the water. With a shriek, she disappeared beneath the surface, before her head popped up with a bright smile spread across her face. 'It's wonderful, Ruth,' she called. 'Come on.'

Glancing along the beach, Ruth saw no-one appeared to be looking in their direction. Taking a deep breath, she whipped off her pyjama top and bottoms, covered her brassiere with her arms and quickly dashed into the clear blue water. As she sank into the sea, her heart almost burst apart with joy. Having the water wash over her head was the most wonderful sensation she'd ever experienced in her life. Never had she felt so vibrant and alive.

For several seconds Ruth stayed beneath the surface, listening to the faint pop and hiss of the ocean and letting the light current rock her backwards and forwards. Then she slowly emerged. 'It's the first time I've felt cool, comfortable and clean in weeks,' she said, wiping the water from her face and grinning at Una. 'Isn't it glorious?'

Una said, 'It makes one so very grateful to be alive.'

Ruth's smile disappeared. 'If only Betty were here,' she whispered.

'I wish she were here too, Ruth,' Una responded, her expression grave now. 'Every single day.'

'She will be missed.' Blinking hard, Ruth gave Una's arm a squeeze. 'And we will never forget her.'

Ruth flopped back into the water and floated on her back, her arms and legs spread wide like a starfish. She could do nothing to bring her friend back; all she could do was embrace the precious gift of being safe and alive, with food in her belly and cool water on her skin.

Eventually, Ruth and Una returned to the beach, pulled on their clothes and lay on the sand to dry off.

'It still seems so unreal, to think we're lying here on a beach in the middle of nowhere and the entire world has no idea where we are or what happened to us,' murmured Una.

'I wonder what *is* happening,' said Ruth, shielding her eyes from the sun with her forearm. 'With the war, I mean.'

'Maybe it's nearly over,' said Una, little conviction in her voice. 'Maybe.'

Before they grew too hot again, the women retreated to the shade of a coconut tree. 'I should get back to the patients,' said Una, grimacing. 'A couple of the men are in a very bad way.'

'What's wrong with them?' asked Ruth.

'They were both injured during the attack on the *Rangitane* and their wounds have become infected. We're giving them penicillin, but it doesn't appear to be helping. The heat makes it all worse. And the lack of proper food.'

'Hello, ladies.' Gary threw himself onto the sand at Una's feet. 'Looks like you've been swimming.'

Una gasped. 'I hope you didn't spot us in our undergarments.'

Ruth smiled to see Una flirting again.

'Sadly, no.' Gary winked at Una. 'Though word did get around that two lovely ladies were scantily clad.'

Una squealed. 'Oh dear, don't tell Ruth. She'll never swim again.'

Ruth laughed. 'Honestly, I hardly care,' she said, almost believing the daring words herself. 'Where's Bobby?' she asked, inwardly cursing herself for sounding so eager.

'I left him a mere moment ago at the cookhouse looking for you.' Gary raised his eyebrows at Una. 'Anyone would think they fancied each other.'

Una feigned shock. 'Whatever do you mean, Gary? Ruth is engaged to be married; she couldn't possibly be entertaining thoughts of another man.'

As Gary and Una burst out laughing, Ruth scrambled to her feet. 'I'm going to see if I can be of help somewhere else,' she said, stumbling across the soft sand.

'Oh Ruth, we're only teasing,' called Una. 'I'm sorry.'

Ignoring her, Ruth kept her head down, trying to hide her flaming cheeks. How could Una behave that way, just when Ruth had thought they were becoming friends?

Scowling at the ground, Ruth was so absorbed in her thoughts that she caught her toe on a fallen branch and crashed to the ground. Before she could clamber back to her feet, hoping no-one had witnessed her ungainly fall, a hand clasped her elbow. As she looked up into Bobby's smiling face, Ruth's heart skipped a beat.

'That was an unfortunate tumble,' said Bobby, helping her up. 'Are you all right?'

Ruth forced herself to smile. 'Silly me. I'm fine, thank you, Bobby.' She took a step back, and his hand dropped from her arm.

Bobby assessed her for a moment. 'I've upset you,' he said softly.

'I'm engaged,' exclaimed Ruth.

Bobby stared at her, frowning. 'I know,' he said.

Ruth straightened. 'So, I don't feel this' — she waved a hand back and forth between them — 'is appropriate.'

'We haven't done anything wrong, Ruth.'

'No, but I . . .' Ruth didn't know what to say.

Sighing, Bobby shook his head. 'I'll leave you be,' he said flatly. 'Sorry to bother you.'

Watching Bobby's back as he walked away, Ruth had the strong sensation she'd made a terrible mistake.

31

JOE

'Sorry I'm late. Bloody rain.' Joe shook himself and droplets flew off his raincoat, landing on the table.

'No worries,' Hazel said through her mouthful of croissant. 'I ordered you a coffee.' She indicated the mug next to her half-drunk one. 'Hope a flat white is okay.'

Shrugging off his coat, Joe hung it over the back of his chair. 'I didn't even know what flat whites were until I went to New Zealand, but thanks, that's great.'

'Ha! I wondered why the girl at the counter looked at me funny. She had to go and ask the guy on the coffee machine if he knew what I was talking about.'

Joe sat opposite Hazel and immediately raised the mug to his lips. 'Thanks,' he said again, after a large gulp. 'I needed that. The bus was going nowhere so I got off and ran. Have you been here long?'

'Twenty minutes maybe, but I've been enjoying just sitting back and watching everyone. I'm doing it a lot more, thanks to you.'

'Doing what?'

'I'm trying to be more aware of my surroundings – you know, be an observer.'

'Is that a compliment?'

'Yes, it is, Joe. Don't look so shocked.'

Joe had another sip of coffee. 'So how are you finding our delightful English weather? Believe it or not, it's actually still summer.'

Hazel laughed. 'I might have to buy a winter coat and gumboots if it continues.'

'We call them wellingtons here – or wellies, if you want to be down with the locals.'

'Oh, right. Why wellingtons?'

'I think it's after the Duke of Wellington. Why gumboots?'

'I have no idea. They're boots made of gum-like material, maybe?'

There was a heavy silence and Joe tried to think of something to say. It was so good to see Hazel again, but at the same time, it brought back feelings he'd hoped would have dissipated. 'Have you finished the book? I've been wondering what happened to Ruth after she was taken prisoner.'

Hazel shook her head. 'Not yet. I've been so busy and it's been hard to find anywhere quiet to read. But Ruth is no longer a prisoner. She's now on an island in the middle of nowhere.'

'What?!'

As Hazel filled him in, Joe began to relax. He remembered how much he'd enjoyed talking to her on the plane and at the pub in Paddington. The truth was, he'd missed Hazel. He wanted to ask her what she thought about Bobby's declaration and whether she thought Bobby and Ruth would get together. But the question seemed too personal. Too intimate.

'How's it going with Klara?' Hazel blurted.

Joe tensed. 'You're not afraid to jump right in there, are you?'

'Sorry. Do you want to talk about it?'

'Not particularly.'

He felt annoyed with Hazel for bringing up his wife, and annoyed with himself for being annoyed.

'Are you fully recovered from the jet lag?' Hazel asked, seeming to realise she'd be wise to switch to a more neutral topic.

'Yeah, pretty much. You?'

'Finally, though I can't believe it's taken almost a week. I blame you, by the way. You should never have taken me to the pub and forced me to drink warm beer after a long flight.'

Joe wanted to say something light and funny, but he didn't have it in him. 'How's it going in Camden?' he asked.

Hazel sighed. 'They say I'm not in the way, but I totally am. I'm sleeping on the couch in their living room and it's not exactly comfortable. Plus, I can't go to sleep until everyone else goes to bed. Not that I'm getting a lot of sleep anyway.'

Hazel didn't look like she'd spent the last week crashing on a couch getting next to no sleep. Her face glowed with its usual animation.

Joe sat forward. 'I'm glad you called yesterday. I was beginning to think you'd cut me loose.'

'It's taken me a few days to get the whole phone thing sorted. And don't get me started on the trials of setting up a bank account or working out the buses and tubes. Not that it matters; I've been able to walk everywhere so far. No-one tells you that Central London is so compact. I walked from Camden to Buckingham Palace yesterday.'

'That must have taken forever. So you've been visiting a few of our tourist sites then?'

Hazel nodded over the rim of her mug. 'I went to Madame Tussauds a couple of days ago.'

'You didn't!'

'I know, it was totally kitsch — but also bloody awesome. I must have taken a hundred photos with Han Solo.'

Joe groaned. ''Course you did.'

They both grinned and Joe was relieved to find the tension in his body was easing.

'Enough about me,' said Hazel. 'How's it going back at the pub? Are you regaling all the regulars with stories about your trip to the incredibly beautiful New Zealand and some weird Kiwi girl you got stuck next to on the plane?'

'It's like I never left, to be honest. Apart from . . .' He paused. 'Apart from the fact that suddenly my wife is always around.'

'Joe! That's an awful thing to say.'

'I know. But Klara is there literally all the time. When she went back to Sweden I gave up our apartment, so we're living in one of the rooms above the pub. Plus we're both working in the pub, because she also gave up her job when she left. I should be happy she wants to spend every minute with me, but I feel like she's forcing herself to do it. Like if we're around each other for long enough we'll start to be a happily married couple again.'

'Have you tried talking to her about it?'

'Hell, no! I'm pretending everything's fantastic in the hope that it soon will be.'

Hazel opened her mouth to say something and hesitated.

'What?' asked Joe.

'Does she know you're meeting me for coffee? You could have invited her along; I wouldn't have minded . . . much.'

Joe tipped his head to one side. 'Care to elaborate?'

Hazel's cheeks turned red. 'After . . . well, after some of the things we said on the flight, I'd probably feel uncomfortable seeing her, but maybe it would be a good thing for me to meet your wife.'

Leaning back in his chair, Joe folded his arms and frowned. 'Hazel, it was wrong of me to say I was attracted to you and all that other soppy stuff. I'm sorry.'

Hazel leant back in her chair and crossed her arms too. 'Does Klara know about me at all?'

Joe tapped his toe against the table leg. Why did Hazel have to ask so many probing questions? 'I didn't mention you.'

'Right.'

'It was easier, that's all.'

Hazel stared at him silently and Joe looked everywhere but at her face.

'So, you start your job Monday?' he asked politely, tapping his foot harder. 'Feeling nervous?'

'A little.'

A young woman pushed past their table with a pram and knocked Hazel's elbow.

'Sorry,' said Hazel quickly.

The woman glared and muttered as if Hazel had somehow been in the wrong.

Rubbing her elbow, Hazel blinked back tears as the woman moved on. 'Is there some rule I just missed there?'

Joe unfolded his arms and leant forward. He wanted to move around the table and put his arms around her, but he resisted. 'You okay?'

'Yeah, it's just . . . well, I don't miss home, and I'm really glad I'm here, but it's all quite daunting. I wouldn't mind going to see Gramps for an hour of familiarity, if that makes sense.'

'Of course it does. Have you spoken to him since you arrived in London?'

'I phoned him last night. I had so many questions about the book, only he refused to answer most of them.'

'Why?'

Hazel threw her hands in the air 'I don't know! Because he's a grumpy bugger. One thing he did tell me was that Una sent it to him.'

'Which one was Una again?'

'She was a nurse, a friend of Betty's. She was also June Sullivan, one of the authors of the book.'

'Seriously?'

'Apparently Una was her middle name.'

'Huh, so she sent it to him. When? Why?'

'Gramps said it arrived in the mail shortly after the war ended. There was a note from Una explaining that she and Florrie had written the story based on notes they'd found in Ruth's journal.'

'What happened to Ruth?'

'He didn't say. He started to have one of his nasty coughing fits and had to hang up.'

Joe wished he could stay and talk with Hazel for the rest of the day. He was a different person when he was with her. When they talked, he didn't feel as if he was some guy hovering in the background the way he did when he spoke to other people. She noticed him in a way no-one had before. But the reality was he needed to get back to work soon. And to his wife. He had to make sure things didn't get any more complicated with Hazel. He drained his coffee and got to his feet.

32

Christmas, 1940

Ruth avoided Una and Bobby for the rest of the morning. She tried to keep herself busy helping Reverend Kelly sort through the supplies the Germans had left with them, but it was difficult to stop her thoughts from wandering. She missed home dreadfully, Florrie especially, and she felt a desperate need for news. After a basic lunch of rice boiled in coconut milk (a welcome change from rice boiled in sea water), all the men, women and children who less than twenty-four hours earlier had been hungry, weary prisoners, gathered at the jetty to see off the men tasked with initiating their rescue mission. On board the small motorboat were Mr Cook, two crew from the *Rangitane* and three islanders. 'Now we just have to wait,' said Mrs Ellis, who was standing beside Ruth.

'How long for, do you suppose?' Ruth asked, glancing towards Bobby, who was chatting with a group of men further down the jetty. He wore his usual friendly smile and Ruth felt a pang of jealousy. If only she could be standing there enjoying his company too.

When he turned his head in her direction, she quickly looked back at Mrs Ellis.

'I'm sure it won't be long, dear.' Mrs Ellis patted Ruth on the arm. 'Now, Ruth, I can't help but notice things are strained between Una and yourself.'

Ruth grimaced. 'I realise we're all in this together, but she is frightfully hard to get on with sometimes.'

Mrs Ellis frowned. 'I've always found Una to have a very giving nature. Her dedication to nursing is commendable.'

Guilt made Ruth's skin crawl. She had been shamefully self-absorbed, she realised. So Una had teased Ruth in front of Gary; that hardly made her a dreadful person.

Making her way back towards the main house, Ruth hoped she would run into Una so she could apologise for charging off in such a huff earlier, but Una found her instead.

'Ruth,' Una called, jogging towards her. 'Have you forgiven me yet?' She hooked her arm through Ruth's and fell into step beside her. 'I know I can be a fool sometimes. Betty was always telling me off.'

Ruth smiled. 'I was the fool, Una. I'm too sensitive for my own good.'

'Not at all. I should have kept my trap shut. But, Ruth, you'll need to face up to it at some point.'

'Face up to what?' Ruth asked uneasily, already knowing what Una was going to say.

'To your feelings for Bobby. I can see it every time you look at him. And the way he looks at you is no different. I know you're engaged, but are you really going to keep denying what is happening?'

'I don't know what to do,' murmured Ruth.

Una gave Ruth's arm a squeeze. 'Well, if you want to talk about it, I'm here. And I promise not to tease you again.'

'Thanks, Una.'

They continued to chat amicably as Ruth accompanied Una back to the makeshift hospital. 'See you at supper?' said Ruth.

Una smiled. 'Save me a seat,' she said.

~◠

The following morning was Christmas Eve, and Ruth woke to the unexpected sound of carols.

Reverend Kelly had gathered together a handful of escorts, along with a few of the stewardesses and passengers from the sunken ships, and they were practising for a midnight mass they planned to hold that night. A gaggle of children dashed about among the group, enjoying the singing and occasionally dancing along.

Smiling, Ruth sat on the step of the verandah to watch.

'What a lovely sound,' said Mrs Ellis, sitting down beside her. 'But it does make me dreadfully homesick.'

'It feels so very unlike Christmas,' Ruth agreed, as a bead of sweat trickled down her back.

'There's little chance of snow.'

'Or a roast with all the trimmings.'

They both laughed, then Mrs Ellis patted Ruth on the back and stood. 'Time to help serve the tea,' she said brightly. 'Come on there, Ruth. Chin up.'

Ruth leapt to her feet. 'Lead the way.'

After tea and another round of bullock stew, the day passed quickly. Ruth and Una risked another long swim in the sea and spent a lovely few hours lying beneath a tree with a group of female escorts, chatting about their hopes for when they returned to England and about their families' Christmas traditions. While there were occasional tears, it was mostly a happy time.

The sun dropped quickly, and with little warning the day turned to night.

'Look,' someone yelled, pointing out to sea.

Everyone raced down to the beach as lights flashed from a boat offshore.

'Who is it?' Una cried, clutching Ruth's hand.

Exciting news soon reached them. The boat was signalling to say they had doctors, medical supplies, food and cigarettes, and they would land in the morning when the tide allowed.

Those on the beach erupted into cheers.

'Oh, Ruth,' said Una, tears in her eyes. 'We're saved.'

One man with a beautiful baritone voice began to sing 'O Holy Night' and everyone joined in. People began to mill about, hugging each other and shaking hands as they continued to sing. 'Hark! The Herald Angels Sing' was followed by 'O Come, All Ye Faithful', and Ruth sang with all her might.

When Devan, Gary and Bobby appeared, Ruth didn't hesitate. She hugged them each in turn, leaving Bobby till last.

'Merry Christmas, Ruth,' said Bobby, planting a light kiss on her cheek.

'Merry Christmas, Bobby,' Ruth replied. Then she gripped his arms, tipped her head back and shouted up at the stars. 'I will never take a minute of ordinary life for granted again.'

'Hear, hear,' cried Gary and Una.

'Well said,' Bobby murmured, his large brown eyes fixed on hers.

Then everyone hushed and Reverend Kelly began the midnight mass. Ruth and Bobby stood leaning slightly against each other. Five hundred or so people with bare feet, unkempt hair, ripped clothing and broad smiles on their faces gathered around the makeshift altar to listen to his sermon. The moon shone brightly in the cloudless sky, waves lapped gently, palm leaves swayed and rustled in the breeze, and as the stars shone down, loved ones who had been lost were remembered. The Reverend announced one by one the names of those who had died, and when he spoke Betty's name, Ruth and Una stepped towards Devan and each put an arm around him in support.

When the Reverend finished speaking, there was a moment of stillness before the group raised their voices in the national anthem. Never had 'God Save the King' sounded so magnificent and many eyes were wiped with dirty sleeves, Ruth's included.

'Well,' sniffed Una. 'This might be the most beautiful Christmas Eve I've ever known.'

'Indeed,' said Gary.

Bobby placed a hand lightly on Ruth's back. 'I'll never forget this night,' he said.

'Nor will I,' Ruth whispered back.

Less than an hour later, as they were readying for bed, a storm arrived. It blew in without warning, bringing heavy rain and ferocious winds.

'Mrs Cook says another name for Emirau is Squally Island, and I can see why,' shouted Mrs Ellis as she huddled with Ruth under the shelter of the verandah.

'Think of those poor men down by the beach,' Ruth said, raising her voice over the keening of the wind. 'I imagine there can't be much left of their sleeping quarters now.'

Though dark, Ruth could see leaves and branches strewn about. Every now and then she'd hear a man's deep call. They sat silently, watching the storm, then as the wind finally dropped and the rain turned into a steady drizzle, they lay down, exhausted, and slept.

—◡

Christmas Day dawned overcast but did little to dampen the air of excitement as supplies from the rescue ship were offloaded and delivered by lorry. In the daylight, it was clear the small government boat sent from Kavieng would not be capable of carrying them all off the island, but they were reassured to hear a larger ship was on its way.

Ruth offered to help at the cookhouse but was sent away by the cooks from the *Rangitane*, who were preparing a celebratory breakfast.

A short while later, coconut shells were being filled with porridge and stewed pears, tinned milk was poured into tea and real butter was spread onto fresh white bread.

'Have you ever had a Christmas breakfast as fine as this?' Una asked. A group of the female escorts were sitting together, their backs against the trunks of trees.

'Never,' Ruth declared.

Giggling, they clinked their tins of tea.

Mr Cook strode out of the house and called for everyone's attention. 'The ship that delivered these supplies has informed us they will be taking all the women and children. Your departure is imminent.'

Squeals of delight erupted from the women and children, while the men cheered heartily. Ruth searched the sea of faces until she found Bobby's. He was with Gary and some other men on the opposite side of the grounds. She stared at him a moment longer, hoping to catch his eye. Just as she was about to give up, he looked over at her and gave a thumbs-up. Her heart skipped a beat.

Devan called her name and she walked over to him, flustered. 'Oh, Devan, we should all be leaving together.'

'The rescue ship won't be far behind.'

'Yes, but if we're separated, anything could . . .' She trailed off, unwilling to voice her fear.

He put a reassuring hand on her shoulder. 'We'll be fine, Ruth.'

Ruth nodded. She couldn't wait to leave the island, but she was anxious about the future. A part of her wished she could stay there, away from the realities of war, with people she had grown to care for greatly. Truth be told, she was also terrified at the prospect of being out on the Pacific Ocean once more.

A short while later, the men gathered on the jetty to bid them farewell. The wounded were taken out to the waiting boat first, followed by the women and children. They had to be ferried out in small loads and Ruth hovered towards the back of the group.

'Off you go there, Ruth,' said Reverend Kelly. He held the small transfer boat steady with one hand and reached out to her with the other. She gripped his hand firmly, took a deep breath, and stepped gingerly into the rocking boat.

Stumbling onto a wooden bench seat, she glanced back along the jetty filled with men. She spotted Devan, then Gary beside him. They waved and shouted, 'Bon voyage, Ruth.'

Ruth smiled weakly. Bobby wasn't with them, and she was unable to spot him anywhere. As a sailor took up the oars, Ruth glanced at the three other women in the boat with her. They were waving, smiling, calling goodbye to the men. Ruth was unable to join in. She sat in silence as the faces on the jetty grew distant, an aching emptiness swelling inside her chest.

Reaching the government boat, Ruth was surprised to see it was already overflowing. There was only enough seating for around twenty people and everyone else was sitting on the deck, packed in like sardines. Una called out to Ruth and, with great difficulty, Ruth made her way over to her friend.

The moment she was seated on the deck, the motor roared and the boat began to speed away from the island. Within seconds, there were moans and groans as the boat started to pitch and roll in the rough seas. Water splashed over the side, soaking them all. Ruth's stomach began to heave and she was forced to look away from the retreating island to fix her gaze on the horizon.

For ten long hours the boat motored towards Kavieng. With so many on board, they were unable to make great headway. Initially Ruth had felt mildly chilly in her damp clothes, but as the sun beat down she grew hotter and more uncomfortable. It was remarkable how little the children complained, though many sat staring at the waves, their faces green as they battled seasickness.

Finally, through the dark night, they were able to see lights and the faint shadowed outline of land.

'Thank goodness,' said Una, who had been sick overboard numerous times. 'I couldn't have taken much more.'

They were approaching a jetty when suddenly the boat changed direction and continued along the coastline. Some of the children began to cry from tiredness and hunger, but their tears soon dried as the boat rounded a corner to reveal a passenger liner glowing with lights. On the decks were rows of officers and crew in smart white uniforms, the Union Jack flapping in the breeze above them.

'Put down your gangway,' hollered the skipper of the smaller boat. 'Women and children are coming aboard.'

One by one, the members of the worn-out, bedraggled group stumbled up the gangway. Self-conscious in her filthy attire, Ruth kept her gaze averted from the officers and crew. Una, weak and limp after her ordeal, leant on Ruth heavily. 'All I want is water and bed,' she murmured.

They were greeted by a smiling stewardess who led them to the dining room, where they were given white bread and butter, cheese and coffee. Una nibbled tentatively on a crust. 'That's actually quite lovely,' she said, taking another bite. Ruth was relieved to see colour return to Una's face.

Looking about, Ruth noticed most of the children had fallen asleep in their mothers' arms and were unable to be roused to eat.

A short while later, people were shown to their cabins. Ruth gave a cry of delight when she and Una entered their immaculate cabin to see proper beds made up with crisp white sheets. Collapsing onto the nearest one, Ruth fell instantly asleep.

In the morning, Mrs Ellis sat with Ruth and Una at breakfast. 'I've just been having a lovely chat with the chief steward, Mr Jones.'

Una sat forward. 'Tell us everything.'

'We're aboard the *Nellore*, which was bound for Sydney until the Australian government requisitioned them to come to our rescue. We're going back to Emirau today to collect the men.'

'Wonderful news,' Ruth exclaimed.

'Yes, indeed,' said Una. 'Though if I'd known we'd be going straight back, I might have stayed the extra night on the island and saved myself yesterday's miseries.'

Mrs Ellis smiled sympathetically before continuing. 'Can you believe that before we turned up, there were only two passengers on board? Mr Jones is in quite a fluster, as he now has to prepare food for close to five hundred. He's grateful to have a generous store of supplies on board, but he'll still need to ration meals until we reach Australia.'

Ruth's thoughts immediately turned to Fergus. 'They're taking us to Australia? Where?'

'I understand we'll dock in Townsville first, in the north, before travelling south to Sydney.'

Una laughed. 'Back to Sydney again, eh, Ruthie? Full circle, it seems.'

'Ladies, a Christmas gift.' The stewardess who had greeted them when they arrived handed them each a comb. 'I understand you've been short of a few things lately,' she said with a wink.

Una squealed and clutched the comb to her chest. 'Who would have thought I'd be so pleased to have something as basic as a comb?'

Ruth twisted her comb around in her hand in wonder. 'If I ever manage to get this through my mess of curls it will be a miracle.'

⌒

Soon they were heading back to Emirau at a much faster pace than they'd managed the previous day. A British seaplane accompanied the *Nellore* on its journey, keeping an eye out for signs of the enemy.

As they approached Emirau, the plane swooped lower and circled the island, the colours of the Union Jack visible on its wings for all to see. Tears filled Ruth's eyes as she heard the shouts and cheers from the men waiting on the beach.

Five boats were tied together, each one proudly displaying the British flag. Then they were loaded with men, and Mr Cook's launch pulled the lot towards the waiting ship anchored further out.

The women and crew shouted words of welcome as the unshaven, sunburnt, scruffy men filed up the gangway, a look of stunned relief on their tired faces.

'I can't see Gary,' said Una, leaning over the railing.

Ruth had been unable to spot Bobby either. 'There's still a few more to come,' she said, glancing back at the dwindling numbers standing on the jetty. They were too far away for her to make out individual faces.

Finally, as the second-to-last boatload of men pulled up alongside the *Nellore*, Una cried out, 'There,' and pointed. 'Gary!' she yelled, waving frantically.

He looked up and grinned. 'Hello, lovely ladies. Thought you'd got rid of us, eh?'

Behind Gary stood Devan, and next to Devan was Bobby, waving up at Ruth.

'Hello,' he called.

Ruth let out the breath she hadn't realised she'd been holding, and waved back.

33

HAZEL

Hazel watched Joe from her booth in the corner as he worked behind the bar. He moved in his usual unhurried way, pouring pints and clearing glasses. His relaxed attitude put everyone at ease and most people in the pub seemed to know him by name. Joe had been past Hazel's booth a couple of times to apologise. His parents had decided at the last minute to take the afternoon off and he hadn't had time to message Hazel to let her know he'd be getting off late. But she didn't mind waiting. She liked watching him work.

'It's getting quieter now,' said Joe, stopping beside Hazel once again. 'I promise I won't be much longer.'

'It's fine.'

'How was the chowder?' He'd delivered a bowl of soup and toast to Hazel's table earlier.

'Delicious,' said Hazel. 'Thank you.'

Joe glanced at the bar, gave Hazel an apologetic look and dashed away again.

Twenty minutes later he returned with two pints in hand and sat down opposite. 'I'm all done,' he said. 'Robbie can handle it from here.'

'You sure?' Robbie from Brisbane had spent most of the past two hours chatting up some girl at the bar and doing very little else.

Joe smirked. 'Yeah – now that girl has left he should be able to focus on actually doing his job. Speaking of jobs, how's yours going?'

'Great! Everyone keeps telling me I'm working hard but honestly I'm not. I start at nine, check through the drug orders and chat to the other pharmacists, then I might spend a couple of hours cruising around the wards, chatting to nurses and looking at drug charts before grabbing a cheap lunch in the staff cafeteria. In the afternoon I chill in the pharmacy dispensing a few drugs, head out the door bang on five with the others, and we generally go to the nearest pub for a meal. I love it.'

'So you're making friends at work? That's good.'

Nodding, Hazel took a sip of her beer. 'There's this guy Scott, from Yorkshire, he's hilarious. He's the pharmacist in charge of the plastic surgery ward, and you should hear some of his stories about famous people he's met there.'

'Glad you're settling in,' said Joe abruptly. 'And the new flat?'

Hazel wanted to ask if something was wrong, but she had made a vow to herself not to probe. 'So far, so good. It's a little weird sharing with a couple, especially when they're cuddling up on the couch. I usually end up going to my room because I'd rather not watch them feel each other up.'

'Awkward.'

'Yeah, I think it's an Italian thing. But it is so great to have my own room and be able to walk to work.' Hazel shifted in her seat. 'Your parents were nice,' she said. 'At least, in the five seconds I spoke to them.'

They'd been hurrying to get a train but Joe had brought them over to meet Hazel, introducing her as a Kiwi girl he'd met on the plane, explaining that he'd suggested she pop in to the pub if she was ever nearby. Hazel wondered if Joe had told Klara about her now too.

'Mum and Dad are great – except when they decide to take Sunday afternoon off without telling me,' said Joe, rolling his eyes.

'Well, I didn't mind. I've enjoyed sitting listening to everyone being delightfully British. It's a lovely pub. I bet there's quite a bit of history behind it.'

Joe smiled. 'Ah, Hazel, I thought the reality of London might have dented your enthusiasm but I'm glad to see it hasn't yet. I promise to bore you with the history of this place some other time.'

Hazel rubbed at a mark on her hand to avoid Joe's gaze as she said, 'I thought Klara might be here.' So much for not probing. She was hopeless.

He was silent for several seconds before he spoke. 'She's gone back to Sweden for the weekend. I was going to go with her, but . . . we had a fight and she went without me.'

A group of rowdy blokes at the bar cheered loudly. They were watching football on the big screen in one corner. Joe swivelled around and squinted at the TV. 'Chelsea scored,' he muttered. 'Bastards.'

'What was the fight about?' asked Hazel, before clamping her lips together. Why couldn't she leave well enough alone? 'If you don't mind me asking,' she added sheepishly.

Joe took a couple of quick sips from his beer and wiped his mouth. 'You.'

'Me?' squeaked Hazel. 'What about me?'

'When you rang a few days ago and I suggested you come here for a catch-up, Klara overheard. She asked me who you were, so I ended up explaining we'd met on the plane and she got mad.'

'It's not like we're having some sordid affair,' Hazel protested.

Joe gave Hazel a funny look. 'I told her nothing had happened between us, but I wanted to be completely honest so I –' Joe's eyes travelled to the bar, as if he needed something stronger to drink – 'I said I'd been conflicted.'

'What the hell does that mean?'

'Ha – that's exactly what she said.'

'No wonder she's pissed at you.'

'Look, Hazel, I feel bad enough, okay? In retrospect it was a shitty thing to do, but I thought Klara deserved the truth. Can we leave it and talk about something else?'

Hazel picked up her glass, stared at its contents and put it down again. 'Okay,' she replied carefully. It would be easy enough to change topic, but not so easy to alter her feelings for Joe.

34

Nellore, 1940

'Most of the men are sleeping on the decks.' Una slipped into the seat beside Ruth in the dining saloon. 'We're lucky to have a berth.'

'Indeed we are.' Ruth sipped her tea, still revelling in the simple joy of drinking from a proper china cup and sitting at a table set with clean, starched linen.

Una leant forward, her face alight with excitement. 'Did you notice all those packing cases coming on board earlier?'

They were anchored not far from land, having arrived at Rabaul overnight for supplies, and though no-one had been allowed ashore, most of the passengers had crowded onto the deck to observe the action, Ruth among them. She'd wondered how long it would take Una to bring up the mysteriously labelled crates. 'I did.'

'Guess what was written on them? *Red Cross Comforts.* What do you suppose that might mean? Do you think it could be some provisions for us?'

Ruth smiled. 'I believe it might. I understand the lounge is closed while everything is unpacked.'

Una grabbed Ruth's hand. 'Why, you know more than I do, Ruth! When will we be able to go and look? Tell me everything.'

Ruth laughed so hard her cup wobbled in its saucer as she tried to place it down. 'All I know is that Mrs Ellis was put in charge of unpacking the items and she said we'd be very pleased.'

'What does that mean? Oh, I'd give anything to change into some fresh clothes. I feel as if this skirt and blouse are glued to my body, I've worn them for so long.'

Ruth shook her head. 'Drink your tea and have something to eat, and then we'll go and take a look.'

Una gulped down her tea and sandwiches in a flash. 'Right,' she said, standing. 'Let's go.'

As they made their way to the lounge, Ruth once again kept an eye out for Bobby. Since the men had arrived on the *Nellore* they had been busy sorting out their sleeping arrangements, having something to eat and washing. The generous crew had offered many of the men a change of clothes, and the ship's barber had been hard at work. It was strange seeing her fellow prisoners looking so clean and tidy; it made her feel shabbier than ever.

As they approached the lounge they heard the din of women chatting and laughing. At least fifty women were lingering outside the closed doors, waiting to be let in.

'Come on.' Una grabbed Ruth's hand and began to push her way towards the front.

'Oi!' cried a woman. 'We were here first.'

'Excuse me,' Ruth said. 'I do apologise.' She yanked her friend back. 'Stop, Una! What's got into you?'

Glancing about, Una saw the angry faces and hung her head. 'Sorry,' she said softly. 'I just want to feel human again.'

Before Ruth could respond, the lounge doors were flung open and there was a great cheer as the women surged forward.

Soon, squeals of delight filled the air. Trestle tables had been set up in the middle of the room and they were laden with an assortment of everyday comforts the prisoners had so sorely missed. Toothbrushes, toothpaste, combs, soap, talcum powder, hairpins and all other manner of grooming products covered one table, while another two were filled with clothes and shoes in all shapes and sizes.

'Ladies,' called Mrs Ellis. 'The women of Rabaul have donated all they could. As you can see, they have been very generous.'

The rest of the afternoon was spent happily trying on clothes and shoes, with only the occasional raised voice or disagreement over who had put their hand on something first.

Ruth was content to stand back and wait until Una thrust an armload of blouses, skirts and dresses at her and insisted she try them on.

Standing before a mirror and looking at her reflection for the first time in over a month was a disconcerting experience. She had lost weight, and her skin was striped with tan lines. Her face was browned by the sun and the skin on her nose and neck was peeling, while mosquito bites and the odd scratch marked her body. Her hair was a frightful mess.

Conscious of the queue of women waiting to use the rigged-up changing room, Ruth quickly finished trying on the clothes, the most exciting of which was some clean underwear, settling on a couple of blouses, a skirt and a dress which had fit well enough.

While Ruth was busy selecting a toothbrush, toothpaste, a couple of hairpins and a nailbrush, Una, now clad in a pretty blue floral blouse and matching skirt, had been scouring the shoe table. 'These lovely black ones look like your size, Ruth. Here – try them with some socks.'

Ruth sat on a nearby chair and pulled on the socks and low-heeled shoes. When she stood, her feet felt compressed and uncomfortable. Taking a step, she nearly toppled over.

'I've grown so used to bare feet,' she said, placing a hand on Una's shoulder for support. 'Isn't this all so strange?'

Una grinned. 'It's wonderful, that's what it is. Wait till Gary sees me in this.' Giggling, Una spun around in a circle, her skirt fanning out. 'He's sure to propose.'

Ruth stared at her wide-eyed. 'Una, you've only just met. I understand we've all been through an ordeal together and that can make us –'

Una threw her arms in the air. 'Oh, Ruth, don't spoil it, please. I know all I need to know about Gary. He's kind, funny, good-looking, and he fancies me. What more could I ask for?'

'How do you know he fancies you?'

'Because I can see it in the way he looks at me, and the way he kisses me.'

Ruth shook her head. 'I had no idea things had gone so far.'

'Oh, Ruth, why can't you be happy for me?'

Sitting back down, Ruth yanked the shoes from her feet. 'Have you talked about the future, Una? What happens when we get to Sydney?'

Una shook her head. 'I have no idea. And if there's anything I've learnt over the past few weeks, it's that we can't predict the future. We can only live in the moment, make the best of the situation we're in and follow wherever our heart takes us.'

'I'll see you at dinner,' muttered Ruth, gathering up her things.

Ignoring the hurt expression on Una's face, she strode quickly out of the lounge and headed towards their cabin.

Dropping her new possessions on the floor, Ruth collapsed face down on her bed and let out a cry of frustration. What was wrong with her? Why hadn't she been happy and supportive of Una's relationship with Gary? Why did she have to be so righteous and negative? Ruth rolled over and sat up. *Oh no!* she thought, a hand flying to her chest. She had reacted to Una's news the way her mother would have done. Ruth loved her mother but there was no way in the world she wanted to be *like* her.

Groaning, Ruth flopped back and stared up at the ceiling. She wished she were back in London with Florrie. Her friend would be able to talk some sense into her and help her to understand all the emotions swirling about inside.

Closing her eyes, Ruth made herself think of her fiancé, Peter. Where was he at this moment? Did he know the passengers of the *Rangitane* had been found, or did he think Ruth was still missing, perhaps lost at sea forever?

Ruth remembered Peter's last kiss goodbye before he'd left for military training. She had been filled with love and affection, and yet a part of her had felt relief watching him go.

With a jolt, Ruth's eyes flew open and she sat up. She knew with absolute certainty she couldn't marry Peter. Even if she'd never met Bobby, she couldn't marry Peter. Not now.

Suddenly, the door of the cabin was flung open. 'Do you want to tell me what that was all about?' Una stood in the doorway, hands on her hips.

Ruth leapt to her feet. 'Oh, Una, I'm so sorry. My reaction was entirely unfair. I'm happy for you, really I am. And I'm sure you'll figure things out together.'

Una sat on Ruth's bed and patted the mattress. 'Sit,' she ordered, her expression serious.

Ruth did as she was told and was surprised to notice herself shaking.

'If Betty were here, she'd say you're acting like a right ninny,' Una said.

Ruth mustered a wobbly smile. 'True.'

'What's troubling you, Ruth?'

Ruth sighed. 'I feel all over the place,' she confessed. 'Ever since we boarded the *Rangitane* – no, that's not it – ever since we left Liverpool all those months ago, the days have been so challenging there's been no time for reflection. We simply had to deal with each day and do the best we could.'

'It has certainly felt that way.'

'This will sound crazy, but the moment we were set free on Emirau Island that feeling lifted. I didn't feel lost or confused or overwhelmed. I felt . . . whole. And now . . . I don't know how to fully describe it, but for the first time in this entire journey I feel genuinely terrified. It doesn't make any sense. It's like I've woken up and the whole nightmare of the *Rangitane* being bombed, and Betty dying, and being held captive by the Germans, it's all caught up with me. I can't relax, Una.'

'I've talked to a few doctors about this,' Una said. 'Often patients can be stressed and anxious after a traumatic incident. Be kind to yourself and give it time.'

For a long time neither of them spoke. Ruth considered opening up about her revelation that she couldn't marry Peter anymore, but she felt it was unfair to tell anyone until she'd broken the news to Peter himself. 'Thank you, Una,' Ruth whispered. 'You're a grand friend.'

Una stood up. 'How about you have a lie-down and I'll come and get you for dinner?'

Ruth glanced at the nailbrush sitting atop her pile of things on the floor. 'Actually, I'm going to have a good long wash, sort out my hair and nails, and put on some new clothes.'

'A superb idea. I might just do the same.' Una clapped her hands in excitement. 'I managed to get hold of some varnish too. We can paint each other's nails.'

'I'd like that.' Ruth got to her feet. 'Hopefully it's just what I need to perk me up a bit.'

By dinnertime, Ruth's mood had improved. It was impossible not to feel better when she was wonderfully clean, dressed in a new outfit, and her hair was mostly knot-free and pinned back tidily. With her newly polished nails and lipstick, she was no longer embarrassed by her appearance. All of the men and women in the dining room were looking more presentable than they had done in a long time.

Ruth was keeping the seat beside her free for Una; on their way to the dining room they'd bumped into Gary on the deck, and Una had stayed behind for a quick chat. Ruth's stomach grumbled and she wished her friend would hurry.

Devan approached the table. 'Mind if I join you?' he asked, looking very dapper in a new shirt, his face clean-shaven.

'Of course not.' Ruth gave him welcoming smile, but Devan didn't return it. Instead, he sat down opposite Ruth and leant forward. 'Ruth, there's something you should know.' His voice was hesitant. Ruth knew bad news was about to be delivered, and her heart beat faster.

'What is it?'

'Bobby's not well.'

'What do you mean?'

'He's had a nasty cut on his leg for a few days and it's become infected. The doctor says he has sepsis. They're giving him antibiotics, but he's not responding as well as they had hoped.'

'Where is he?' Panic and fear made her voice shake.

'He was admitted to the ship's hospital shortly after he came aboard.'

She was about to ask more questions when Una rushed over and threw herself into her seat. 'Phew, is it hot. I have to say, I'm looking forward to us moving further south.' Then, clearly sensing something was wrong, she glanced back and forth between Devan and Ruth. 'What's wrong?'

'Bobby's not well,' said Devan.

Una nodded, her eyes on Ruth. 'Gary told me. I'll go and check on him after our meal.'

'I'll come with you,' Ruth said, her appetite gone.

'He'll be okay, Ruth,' said Una.

'Absolutely,' Devan agreed.

Ruth wished she could be as confident. What if Bobby were to die thinking she didn't care for him. Because she *did* care. Her feelings for Bobby were more powerful and urgent and overwhelming than any she'd experienced before. She was confused because she still loved her fiancé. Yet, her love for Peter felt as if it had been muted, watered down, overshadowed by something stronger.

35

JOE

It was dark and wet and cold. Joe had been out walking for several hours and his raincoat was no longer waterproof. His damp sweater clung to his back. Keeping his head down, Joe turned the final corner and strode towards the pub. He was looking forward to a hot shower. Hopefully Klara would be asleep when he crawled into bed. The last thing he wanted to do was wake her.

Drawing closer, he lifted his head. Someone was standing on the footpath staring at the darkened windows of the pub. 'Hazel?'

She turned to face him, deep rasping breaths coming from her wet, shaking body.

'What on earth?' He took four fast steps towards her and she collapsed into his arms.

'Come on,' said Joe, keeping an arm around her. 'Let's get you inside.' He reached down with his free hand to grab the bag resting beside her and ushered her towards the locked door of the pub.

Fumbling with his keys, he opened the door, led Hazel to a shadowy booth and helped her sit. Hazel clasped her trembling hands on the tabletop and dropped her head to rest on them.

Joe quickly turned on some lights, snatched a bar towel, then hurried back to the booth. 'Here,' he said, wrapping the small towel around Hazel's shoulders. Her entire body was shivering.

'You're freezing,' said Joe, rubbing a hand over her arm. Something was wrong. Seriously wrong. Why was Hazel not speaking? 'I'll be right back, I promise.'

He pounded up the stairs to his and Klara's room and gently shook his wife awake.

Her eyes flew open. 'What is it?' she mumbled.

'I need your help,' he whispered. 'Please.'

He explained the state Hazel was in, and as he shucked off his wet raincoat, Klara pulled on her dressing-gown, then she grabbed some dry clothes and followed him down to the pub.

'Hazel,' Joe said, approaching the booth, 'this is Klara. She's got some clothes for you to put on. We need to get you dry.'

Apart from her shivering, Hazel was like a statue. She stared at the table as if she hadn't heard him.

Klara crouched down and brushed a strand of hair from Hazel's face. 'Hazel, honey, I'm going to help you get this wet top off, okay?'

Joe hovered behind Klara and bit on his thumb to try to suppress the sudden surge of nausea in his stomach.

Klara peeled off Hazel's sweatshirt, then her t-shirt. 'I'm going to put this on you now, okay, Hazel?' She eased a thick cream jumper over Hazel's head.

Blinking, Hazel slid her arms through the sleeves and then hugged herself, the shivering worse than ever.

Klara glanced at Joe. 'I'll go make her a hot drink,' she murmured, moving away.

Joe knelt next to Hazel. 'You're freaking me out here, Hazel. What happened?'

Hazel looked at him, her eyes glazed. 'Were you on one of your walks?' she croaked.

'Sorry?'

'Were you out walking because you couldn't sleep?'

Joe took one of Hazel's hands and rubbed it between his. 'Yes,' he said. 'You remembered?'

Hazel nodded. 'Of course I did.'

'What about you? How are you sleeping? Made up any songs lately?'

Hazel stared at him as if processing what he was saying. 'I don't have my guitar,' she said, her voice a dull monotone.

Klara returned and put a steaming mug in front of Hazel. 'Drink this, honey – it'll help warm you up.'

Hazel looked up. 'Thank you.'

Klara put a hand on Joe's shoulder and glanced down at his hands holding Hazel's. 'I'm going back to bed. Come wake me again if you need to.'

Joe glanced at his wife and nodded. 'Thanks,' he said, knowing she deserved so much more.

The pub was eerily quiet, with only the faint sound of a clock ticking and the hum of the fridges. Hazel didn't move or speak, and Joe continued to rub her hand gently.

'Sorry for turning up like this,' Hazel said at last, giving Joe a tiny half-smile. 'I tried a couple of hotels first but they didn't have a room.'

'I'm glad you came here,' said Joe softly.

'It's just . . .' Hazel gulped loudly. 'I couldn't stay in my flat with him there.'

Joe stopped rubbing Hazel's hand. 'With who there?'

Hazel took a deep breath. 'I was home on my own and my flatmate came home. He was drunk and said he'd had a fight with his girlfriend. I thought he'd go and crash in his room but he came and sat next to me on the couch.'

'Did he make a move on you?' Joe asked, a tremor in his voice.

Hazel nodded once and Joe felt a bolt of pain in his chest. 'He wouldn't get off me,' she whispered. 'I tried pushing him away but he was suffocating me.'

Joe's breathing sped up.

'I bit him on the arm and he got mad and he . . . and he hit me on the side of the head. So I . . . so I kneed him in the balls and then he got off me and threw up on the carpet. I ran to my room and packed my bag and he started yelling about how sorry he was and how he was really drunk and he wouldn't do it again.'

'But you got out of there safely?' Joe growled.

'Yes. I left when he was in the bathroom.'

Joe stood up and covered his face with his hands. He pressed his palms into his eyes and swore softly. Dropping his hands, he did his best to sound calm. 'Shift over, Hazel, so I can sit beside you.'

She looked up at him. 'The seat's wet.'

'I don't care.'

He watched her shuffle further into the booth, then he sat beside her and pointed to the mug on the table. 'You should drink it. Klara makes a good hot chocolate.'

Hazel grasped the mug in a shaking hand and lifted it to her lips. 'You're right — it's good,' she said, setting the mug back down.

Joe could barely look at Hazel without wanting to stand up and punch something. 'There's a room free upstairs,' he said. 'It's yours for as long as you need it, okay?'

Hazel took a long time to speak. 'Are you sure?'

'Yes. And you need to get properly warm. I'll take you up to your room and then run you a bath.'

Hazel leant against Joe and rested her head on his shoulder. 'Thank you,' she whispered.

He kissed her softly on her forehead, his lips hot on her cool skin. 'I'm sorry for what happened, Hazel.'

'It's not your fault.'

'Is your head all right where he hit you?'

Hazel reached up and cautiously pressed above her right ear. 'It's a bit sore but I'll be fine. I'm actually starting to feel pissed off now, which I think is a good sign.'

'Yeah, well, I'm more than pissed off. I want to beat the crap out of the guy.'

Hazel rested a hand on Joe's thigh. 'Well, don't, all right?'

Joe looked down at her hand. 'All right,' he said.

'Besides' — Hazel gave him a fragile smile — 'I'm pretty sure the prick's arm is going to need stitches. I bit him pretty hard.'

Joe placed a palm on Hazel's cheek. 'Of course you did,' he murmured.

36

Townsville, 1941

It was six days before the Australian coastline came within sight of the *Nellore*. Everyone crowded on deck to watch as the land drew close. The days since they'd left Emirau Island had passed peacefully, and the prisoners were feeling well fed and rested. They'd celebrated New Year's Eve in style with much singing, dancing and drinking on deck until the early hours of New Year's Day. Ruth had enjoyed herself, joining in the fun and laughter with her new friends, but she couldn't shake her worry over Bobby, and she wished he could have been there to celebrate too. Bobby's condition hadn't improved, though Una was quick to remind Ruth it hadn't worsened either. Ruth had taken to visiting him every morning after breakfast. She'd sit watching him for a few minutes, before pulling out her book — one of many donated by the Red Cross — and reading a few chapters. When she left, she would kiss him on the forehead and whisper, 'See you tomorrow', careful never to say the word 'goodbye'. Only once did he briefly acknowledge her, smiling vaguely before closing his sunken eyes once more. The delirium and fever were unlike anything the doctor had seen before, and he believed that, along with the sepsis from his infected wound, Bobby was suffering from a tropical disease, most likely malaria.

Ruth stood beside Reverend Kelly at the railing as they sailed into Townsville harbour.

'It's quite a sight,' said the Reverend, grinning at the busy wharf bustling with people. 'I'm certainly ready to spend some time in civilisation again.'

'It's going to feel odd,' Ruth said.

Soon they would be boarding a train to Brisbane, before travelling on to Sydney. Ruth's thoughts flew to Fergus and his sister Rosie. She hoped she would be able to see them again and hear all about their new lives in Australia. Speaking of news, surely there would be letters waiting for her somewhere. Letters from the home that felt so very far away.

'Whatever is that noise?' The Reverend leant forward and Ruth did the same.

On the dock below stood a large crowd cheering and clapping and waving British flags in welcome.

'Good grief,' murmured Ruth.

'It seems we are the talk of the nation,' said Mrs Ellis, coming to stand next to Ruth. 'I believe there's already a reporter on board taking down our stories for the newspapers.'

'Ruth!' Una called, pushing her way towards them. 'I've just been to see Bobby and he's turned the corner! He's talking and eating and drinking, and his fever is almost gone.' Una threw her arms around Ruth. 'Isn't that the best news?'

Ruth tried to reply, but her throat was too choked.

'Well, that's marvellous,' said Mrs Ellis.

'Indeed it is.' Reverend Kelly patted Ruth on the back. 'The boy is a battler.'

Una let Ruth go and laughed at the tears on Ruth's cheeks. 'Darling, you must come and see for yourself. He's asking after you.'

Nodding, Ruth brushed her hand over her wet cheeks. 'Of course.'

She hurried with Una to the hospital and couldn't repress a grin when she spied Bobby sitting up in bed. He smiled back, red splotches on the cheeks of his pale, haggard face. 'Hello, Ruth,' he croaked.

Ruth went to sit on the edge of his bed. 'You gave us quite a scare.'

'So I understand.'

They stared at each other for several seconds. Ruth's heart was pounding; she had a million things bottled up inside that she was bursting to say.

Bobby frowned and reached for Ruth's hand. 'Whatever is running through that head of yours, Ruth?' he asked softly.

'We've reached Australia,' she said quickly. 'A place called Townsville. There's a group of people on the dock cheering our arrival and Mrs Ellis says we're going to be in the newspapers, and –'

'Ruth.' Bobby squeezed her hand.

'Yes?' She risked a quick look at Bobby's calm, kind face.

'You are the bravest, most beautiful young lady I have ever had the pleasure to know.'

'Bobby, you mustn't . . .'

'I know you're engaged to be married. But, darling, war changes people. It has changed me in many ways. Perhaps you are no longer the person you once were?'

Tears welled in Ruth's eyes. He was right. She was not the Ruth who'd left London in search of adventure. She no longer felt restless and eager for her life to change. The frustration and sense she was missing out on something had disappeared. Now all she felt was appreciation for being alive, for having food in her stomach and friends around her. She had no possessions other than her recently acquired clothes and shoes, no money, no idea of what the next day would bring, where she would be, what would occur, and yet she felt complete in a way she'd never felt before.

'You're right,' she whispered. 'I'm someone else entirely.'

37

HAZEL

There was a knock on Hazel's door and she called out, 'Come in.'

Joe's head appeared in the doorway. 'Got a sec?'

Hazel put down her pen and swivelled in her chair to face him. 'Sure,' she said, a little too brightly.

It had been over a week since she'd turned up wet and distraught at the pub. Now she was temporarily staying in a room upstairs which, in other circumstances, she would have loved – it had wood-panelled walls, a wrought-iron bed, an antique desk and gorgeous leadlight windows. As it was, she felt so uncomfortable with the whole situation, she wished she could be anywhere but under the same roof as Joe and his wife, plus the assortment of young Kiwis and Aussies who worked in the pub and boarded upstairs. At least Joe and Klara were on the top floor with their own bathroom and Hazel could avoid bumping into them brushing their teeth in matching pyjamas or some other excruciating scenario.

Joe and his parents had been lovely — which of course only made Hazel feel more embarrassed — and though she'd seen Klara working behind the bar and rushed over to thank her in a long, garbled mess of a speech, they'd both been avoiding one another. Well, Hazel had certainly been avoiding Klara.

In truth, Hazel had been avoiding everyone. She left for work early and came home late, usually having already eaten dinner. Then she'd lie on her carpet and stare at the ceiling until it was time to go to bed. Muffled noise from the pub drifted up the stairs and she found it comforting rather than annoying. Though not quite comforting enough to help her fall asleep.

Joe crossed the room and held out the book Hazel's grandfather had given her to read on the plane. She'd lent it to Joe and forgotten all about it. Her mind had been preoccupied with other things.

'Thanks,' she said, placing the book on her desk.

'I enjoyed it. But . . . well, I don't know about you, but the ending felt off to me.'

'In what way? I thought it was perfect.'

Joe shrugged. 'It just didn't seem to ring true.'

'Are you saying you wanted it to have a different ending?'

'No! Not at all. It just . . .' He paused. 'Never mind. I actually came up here to give you something else.'

He disappeared from the room, reappearing seconds later with a guitar case in his hand. He placed it on the bed and then backed up so he was standing by the door. 'It's for you,' he said. 'My sister has had it sitting at her place unused for years, so I asked if I could have it. I picked it up yesterday.'

'Seriously?' Hazel unzipped the case. 'This is beautiful.' She lifted out a glossy golden-brown guitar. 'Are you sure? I'll return it the second she wants it back.'

Joe shrugged. 'It's yours. Maggie was looking to get rid of it anyway. It probably needs a good tuning.'

Hazel took her time placing the guitar in the case before looking at Joe. They hadn't had a proper conversation apart from 'how are you', 'I'm fine' 'have a good day' since that night. Joe had tried a few times, but Hazel had been quick to shut him down. 'Thanks,' she said, smiling. 'It's really thoughtful of you.'

'Hey, I can't have you pacing about the bar in the middle of the night scaring the shit out of me. I figured this might help.'

Two nights earlier she'd given up on sleep but had been too afraid to go for a walk in the dark. Hence lurking around the darkened pub and giving Joe a fright when he came in from one of his midnight wanderings.

'I'm sorry. I was having trouble sleeping and I thought no-one –'

'It's fine, Hazel. Forget it.'

Hazel sat back in her chair and tucked her hands between her thighs. 'Thanks, Joe. Hopefully the walls are thick enough that Katie won't hear me playing.' Katie was in the room next door. She was nice, in a loud I'm-from-Sydney kind of way.

'They're pretty thick,' said Joe. 'You'll be fine.' He studied the carpet. 'Anyway, I'd better go down.'

'Are you expecting a busy night?'

'Yeah, there's a big football match. Come down if you want to be in a room full of Brits shouting obscenities at the TV.'

'Think I'll pass.'

Joe glanced at the desk. 'You writing a letter?'

Hazel nodded. 'To Gramps. He doesn't have email and I thought it would be nice for him to get a letter in the mail.'

'Have you spoken to him lately?'

'I rang him a couple of days ago.'

'Did you tell him about . . .' Joe trailed off.

'I just said I'd moved to another place. I didn't really want to go into it.'

'Sure.' Joe shoved his hands in his jean pockets and frowned at the desk. 'Are you going somewhere?' he asked.

Hazel followed his gaze to the red folder next to her half-written letter. 'Oh, yes. I booked a ticket.'

'To where?'

'Prague.'

'Sorry?'

'It's on my list of places I want to go. There was a cheap deal on flights.'

'Are you going on your own?'

Hazel nodded. 'I can't wait. I'm already planning what to do. It's not for a few weeks but I wanted something to look forward to. I thought it might help to . . .' Hazel's voice cracked and she didn't try to finish the sentence.

Joe crossed his arms and glared at the red folder. 'I've barely seen you since you moved in here. Are you trying to hide?'

'Yes,' Hazel admitted.

Joe's eyes flicked to her. 'Why?'

'Because I feel weird about this whole situation. I promise I won't be around much longer. I'm looking for another room, and I really do appreciate you letting me stay. Everyone's been really nice and –'

'Why are you hiding from me specifically?'

Hazel sighed and looked at Joe's shoes. 'Because I'm embarrassed about turning up here the other night and being so pathetic.'

'You weren't pathetic.'

'Klara was so lovely, and you were . . . you were lovely too – and I was a mess, Joe. I hated you seeing me that way.'

'Why?'

'Because I just did, okay?'

Joe stepped closer just as Hazel's phone, which was sitting on the end of her bed, began to ring. She got up to retrieve it but not before Joe read the caller ID on the screen. 'It's Matt,' he said quietly. 'Your boyfriend.'

Something Hazel couldn't describe, some kind of indecipherable but important message, passed between them.

'I'll leave you to chat,' Joe said, before walking out and closing the door.

38

Sydney, 1941

The women and children were given first-class sleeping accommo-
dation on their train ride to Sydney. When Ruth and Una entered
their compartment they were delighted to discover packages of
sandwiches, chocolates, cigarettes, flowers and magazines had
been left on their seats.

'Everyone has been so kind,' Una said, immediately devouring
the chocolate.

At every stop on their long trip south, locals gathered to help
feed the hundreds who had been rescued from Emirau Island. At
one station, volunteers managed a delicious breakfast of bacon
and eggs; at another they'd set up a tea party with balloons and
flowers and cakes.

Their arrival in Australia and the various stories of their
adventures were front-page news in all the newspapers, and Ruth
was astounded at the degree of attention they received.

When at last they arrived in Sydney, the platform was crowded with friends and relations of many of the survivors. There were tears of joy as people raced to embrace their loved ones. Stepping from the train, Ruth scanned the congested platform in the hopes of spotting Fergus, but eventually she gave up and was transported with others to the Australia Hotel.

Standing at the threshold to her room, Ruth drew a deep breath. The air was silent and still, the walls solid and comforting. She wasn't rocking about on a boat or looking at the horizon pretending she was admiring the sunset while secretly scanning the ocean for enemy vessels. She was safe here in this empty room. There was no child complaining about a sore tummy; no cramped, uncomfortable sleeping quarters filled with people snoring and shifting about; no smell of unwashed bodies and the permanent taste of salt on her parched lips. Ruth was completely on her own for the first time in a very long while. She was wearing new clothes, new shoes and a new pin in her clean hair.

It was the most foreign feeling in the world.

⁓

The following day a memorial service was held for the passengers from the *Rangitane* who had lost their lives. The cathedral was filled with many of the survivors, and throughout the service, sounds of sobbing filled the air. Ruth sat with Devan, Una and Gary. Bobby had desperately wanted to attend, Gary told Ruth, but the doctors at the hospital to which he'd been transferred on their arrival in Sydney were unwilling to let him go.

Devan kept a stoic look on his face, but Ruth knew from the way his hands shook how hard it must be. She pictured Betty on the *Batory*, leaning over a sick child with a kindly smile and soothing words. Her life had been taken far too soon.

As they exited the cathedral, Ruth heard her name being called and turned to see a boy in a familiar brown cap charging towards her. 'Fergus!' she shouted, as he dodged a group of mourners and threw his arms around her waist. Bending down, she hugged his thin frame. He seemed so much skinnier and younger than she remembered.

'Oh, miss,' he choked. 'I thought you had died.'

'I'm sorry to have given you such a scare, Fergus, but as you can see I am alive and well.'

Fergus sniffed and let her go. 'Did you speak to any Germans?' he asked, his eyes wide.

Ruth nodded. 'The odd one, yes.'

'What were they like?'

Ruth glanced around. 'Where are your' – she'd been about to say 'parents' but stopped herself – 'Australian family?'

Fergus scowled and tapped his cap. 'They didn't want me to come.'

'What do you mean?'

He glared at the ground and Ruth was reminded of the very first time she'd met him. The scared little boy trying to act tough and protect his sister.

'They don't like me, miss. I've tried, honest I have. But they only like Rosie. They –' He broke off.

'Do they know you're here?' Ruth asked softly.

With his head hung low, Fergus shook his head.

Ruth caught Una's eye. 'I'm going for a wee walk with Fergus. I'll meet you back at the hotel.'

Una nodded, glancing at Fergus in concern. 'Take your time,' she said.

Ruth clasped Fergus's hand, and they walked down the street a way, until Ruth spied a small park. She led him to a bench and they sat. 'Now, Fergus, I want you to tell me all about what you've been up to since I left. How is school?'

Fergus stared ahead stonily. 'All right, miss. I don't like the classes much, but we get a long lunchbreak and there's a huge field to play on.'

'And how is Rosie finding school?'

'Oh, she loves it. The teachers adore her, she's got plenty of friends, and —'

Once again, Fergus paused and glared at the ground.

'Did you come here without Mr and Mrs Shirley's permission?'

Fergus gave a barely perceptible nod. 'They'll be right mad at me, but I had to come see you — you've been missing at sea for weeks. And I knew you'd understand about Ma and Da, and how I can't go to an orphanage, miss.' Fergus looked close to tears.

'What are you talking about? What has happened to your mother and father?'

Fergus looked up at Ruth and his lower lip wobbled. 'They were killed last month in one of them night-time bombings.'

Ruth stared at him, trying to comprehend what he had just said. 'Killed?' she whispered. 'Oh, Fergus, I'm so sorry.'

He shrugged helplessly. 'Now they're saying I can't go back after the war cause no-one will have me. My aunty back in Glasgow says she'll keep my baby sister, but she can't afford to take care of anyone else. My big brother Eddie is living with friends but I can't go there. I heard Mrs Shirley say I might have to go to an orphanage because' — his voice trembled — 'because they only want to keep Rosie, not me.'

Ruth couldn't speak. Surely it wasn't true. After everything Fergus had been through they couldn't just send him off to an orphanage. Ruth put her arms around the boy's narrow shoulders and pulled him close. 'Please try not to worry, Fergus. I'll need to speak to some people to work out what's going on, but I won't let anyone send you to an orphanage — you can be sure of that.'

Fergus's shoulders shook as he leant heavily against her and wept. 'I knew you hadn't sunk to the bottom of the ocean, even though people kept telling me I shouldn't keep me hopes up. I heard you, see. I heard your voice in my head and you came back to me, miss.' His voice dropped to a whisper. 'Just like I dreamt you would.'

39

JOE

Monday evenings were always quiet in the pub. Apart from Bertie, who was at his usual seat at the far end of the bar nursing a pint of bitter, the place was deserted. Joe dragged a couple more chairs over to the long table he and Klara had recently finished setting. They'd chatted away happily as they'd placed the knives and forks, wineglasses and napkins. Things were so much easier between them now, as if a barrier between them had finally been removed.

Klara was upstairs getting changed. Joe thought she was fine to stay in her jeans and shirt, but she wanted to put on something nicer for the occasion. Joe went behind the bar, poured himself a small measure of whisky, and swallowed it in one go. He didn't want to admit it, especially to himself, but he was nervous.

The pub door opened and Hazel appeared, her cheeks flushed from the cold and her hair hidden beneath a chunky green woollen beanie. She caught sight of Joe and smiled. He managed what he hoped was a calm, friendly smile in return. 'It's freezing out there,' she said, removing her hat and scarf as she walked towards him. 'I'll have what you're having,' she said, sliding onto a stool and rubbing her hands together. 'I need something to warm the insides.'

Klara had never sat at the bar and asked for a drink. She barely touched alcohol, and if she did it was expensive Sancerre, or more expensive vodka with a splash of soda. Joe poured Hazel a whisky and watched her grimace as she swallowed. 'That's better,' she breathed.

'How was work?' Joe asked, wiping the bar as his pulse pounded in his head.

'Busy. With Paul over in Amsterdam I'm covering his wards too.'

Paul was another pharmacist. He and Hazel seemed to have formed a good friendship, judging by the number of times he was mentioned.

'You haven't forgotten about dinner?' Joe dipped his head towards the long table.

Hazel turned to look and raised her eyebrows. 'Crikey, how many people are you expecting?'

'Just Mum and Dad, Klara, me, you, my sister and her husband, Uncle Sam, Katie, Mark and Susie.'

'What about Erica?'

'She drew the short straw and has to man the bar.'

Hazel bit her lip. 'I was hoping for the support of a fellow Kiwi.'

'Mark's from New Zealand.'

Hazel flashed Joe a withering glare. 'Don't remind me. And please don't let him sit beside me or I'm likely to say something highly inappropriate, like, "Piss off, pretty boy."'

Joe laughed. 'Now *that* I would like to see.'

Normally, Joe interviewed people to work at the pub. He'd hired Susie from Melbourne more than a year ago and she was fantastic: hardworking, friendly, reliable. Erica and Katie were great too. But Mark was the worst employee Joe had ever had the misfortune to work with. He'd come into the bar asking for work while Joe was on his holiday in New Zealand, and Joe's mum must have been desperate, or felt it was some sort of serendipitous moment to have a Kiwi lad asking for work while her son was in New Zealand, so she'd taken him on, much to everyone's regret. Mark didn't know it yet, but his days were numbered. Joe planned to tell him his services were no longer required at a meeting he'd arranged for the following day.

'I've only been here three weeks, Joe, I really don't need the big send-off.' Hazel was now standing and removing her grey coat with the big lapels she'd told Joe made her feel like a regular Sherlock, especially now she was moving into a flat on Baker Street. 'Though I'm sure you'll be pleased to be rid of me.'

She said it jokingly, but Joe didn't feel like laughing. 'Whatever. Are you sure you don't need help moving your stuff tomorrow?'

'Nah, I'll be fine. And I've decided I'll leave the guitar. Actually, I can give it back to Maggie at dinner.'

'Why? It's yours.'

Hazel screwed up her face. 'I feel bad taking it.'

'Well, don't, because no-one else wants it, okay?'

Her eyes were an earthy chestnut colour in the amber light cast by the hanging pendants, though he still noticed flecks of green when she moved her head. Joe hadn't thought it was possible for a person's eye colour to change so dramatically until he'd met Hazel. He grabbed a tea towel and began to dry a tray of glasses. 'I heard you playing the guitar last night.'

'That's embarrassing.'

'What have you got to be embarrassed about? It sounded great. You've got a good voice too. Not that I'm an expert on these things.'

'I hope I didn't wake you. Or anyone else, for that matter.'

'Nah, I'd just got back from a walk and happened to be going past your door. I'm sure everyone was fast asleep.'

'Except us,' said Hazel, meeting his eye.

'Except us,' said Joe, unable to look away.

Hazel scrambled to her feet and gathered up her hat, scarf and coat. 'I should dash up and get changed.'

'Sure.' He watched her climb the stairs and sighed. It was good to see her happy and chatty again after having been so withdrawn and quiet. Joe thought she was brave for putting the dreadful experience with her previous flatmate behind her. Even now, when Joe remembered that night, anger flared in his stomach. His palms ached as he remembered kissing her forehead, his arm around her shoulder, the desire to hold her for as long as it took to ease her pain.

⁓

'When's your trip to Prague, Hazel?' called Joe's mum. The dinner had been a success so far, everyone laughing and talking over each other. Joe's mum was looking so happy and content, sitting at one end of the table, with the dreaded Mark (in his fitted white t-shirt and too-tight jeans) to her right and Maggie's husband to her left. Joe was in the middle of the table, with Klara beside him and Hazel directly opposite.

Joe wanted the night to end right then, at that exact moment, before Klara made the announcement he knew was coming, before he had to witness his mum's bewildered and crestfallen face.

Hazel opened her mouth to reply but was cut off before she started. 'Oh, I've been to Prague,' piped up Mark, puffing out his chest. 'Not a lot going for it, unless you like old bridges and fried pork crackling.'

'I love Prague,' said Maggie, smiling at Hazel. 'You'll have a wonderful time, I'm sure.'

'Thanks,' Hazel said. 'Luckily I'm a big fan of old bridges and pork crackling.' She flicked Mark a scornful stare before smiling at Joe's mum. 'I go next weekend. I'm hoping it might even snow.' Her eyes were wide and glimmering with excitement, and Joe concentrated on slicing the roast lamb on his plate, dipping it in gravy and placing it in his mouth. He felt Klara's hand on his thigh and turned.

'Now?' she whispered.

Joe's heart thudded loudly as he gave her a tiny nod and a weak smile. He swallowed his mouthful and felt it lodge in his throat.

Klara pushed back her chair and stood. 'Joe and I have some news,' she said loudly.

Joe looked at his lap.

'We're moving to Sweden,' she said. 'Hopefully by Christmas.'

There was a long heavy pause before anyone spoke.

'That's great,' boomed Joe's dad from the other end of the table.

'Yes, wonderful,' said Joe's mum, her voice hesitant. 'It will be lovely for you to be home, Klara.'

Klara rested a hand on Joe's shoulder. 'Yes, it will be.'

Maggie cleared her throat. 'Well, I imagine it's not been an easy decision, but I'm sure Joe will relish a chance to learn another language.'

Joe lifted his head at last to roll his eyes at his sister. 'Thanks, Maggie.' Ever since he'd tried to speak French on the family's one and only trip to Paris, his sister liked to tease him.

Maggie gave him a hard stare and he knew she was wondering where on earth his decision to move to Sweden had come from. Especially given he'd told her a couple of weeks ago how difficult he was finding it, trying to make their marriage work.

Uncle Sam, who was sitting on Joe's other side, slapped him on the back and congratulated them both as others around the table joined in. Joe didn't look at Hazel but he listened for her voice, wondering when she would speak. She didn't say a word.

Klara sat down and placed a hand on top of Joe's. He interlaced his fingers with hers and smiled, desperately wishing he was happy and knowing with instant heart-sinking clarity that he was not.

40

Sydney, 1941

Bobby's shoulder brushed against Ruth's as they walked along the Sydney waterfront. 'Isn't this marvellous?' he said, raising his face to the late afternoon sun.

'Are you sure you're up for a walk? I imagine you're exhausted after yesterday.'

They'd had a wonderful time at the zoo with Fergus and Rosie, and though Bobby hadn't said anything, Ruth had noticed him grow pale, quiet and slower-paced as the day wore on. Bobby had been out of hospital for almost a week and they'd spent much of that time together either drinking tea in the hotel lobby, going to a cafe or the cinema, or strolling in the nearby gardens. Mostly, Ruth was relaxed and happy around Bobby, but occasionally he'd look at her a certain way, or their hands would touch, and she'd find herself both elated and miserable at the same time.

'I've more energy now than I've had in a long time,' he said, flicking her a smile.

Ruth smiled back, her stomach giving a strange flutter. She quickly looked away and pointed to a kiosk. 'Fancy stopping for an ice cream?'

'Love one.'

They sat on a park bench in the shade to eat.

'Any word from CORB regarding Fergus?' Bobby asked.

Ruth shook her head. 'Not a thing.'

'I still can't understand why the Shirleys would adopt Rosie and not Fergus,' he said. 'How could anyone separate siblings in such a way?'

Ruth sighed as she recalled her meeting with Mrs Shirley a couple of days earlier. Rosie had looked so happy in her new home with her soon-to-be parents and sister. She'd chatted to Ruth excitedly about school and her friends, and it was very clear there was a loving connection between her and her adoptive family.

Fergus had sat hunched and subdued on the low armchair in the corner of the room. Ruth had tried hard to engage him in their conversation, but he'd refused to join in.

When Mrs Shirley went into the kitchen to make some tea, Ruth followed, hoping to have a quiet word. 'I was very sorry to hear about the children's parents,' she began.

Mrs Shirley glanced at Ruth, her expression neutral. 'Yes, it was very upsetting for them both, but they're aware of the burdens war places on us all.'

Ruth wondered as to the extent of the burdens Mrs Shirley was bearing. 'Rosie looks the happiest I've seen her, which is a credit to you.'

Mrs Shirley smiled as she poured water into the teapot. 'She is an absolute delight. If only the same could be said for Fergus.'

Anger flared hot and acidic in Ruth's stomach. 'I'm surprised to hear that. Fergus was a little reserved to begin with, but he became a most wonderful companion on our sea voyage out here.'

Mrs Shirley crossed her arms and fixed a stern eye on Ruth. 'Before you say any more, let me tell you a few truths. Mr Shirley and I tried extremely hard with Fergus. We helped him with his schoolwork, bought him a bicycle when he asked us for one. We encouraged his manners but were careful to never yell or mistreat him. Mr Shirley took him to the beach, played cricket with him in the backyard. We treated Fergus as we would a son. But he resisted it all. When we speak to him, he pretends not to hear. The principal at his school has called us in four times, as he is concerned about Fergus's inability to settle to his tasks. At the dinner table, Fergus fidgets and never sits still. He disappears and doesn't tell us where he's going. We had no idea he had caught the train to the quay to see you, and when he returned that night there was no apology. None. He simply shut himself in his room and sulked.'

'Do you know why he is acting out in such a way?' Ruth asked, hoping she sounded calm and level-headed. It was clear to her the boy was suffering and needed someone to provide love and support.

'Sorry?'

'Have you sat down and talked to Fergus? Listened to his worries and concerns?'

Mrs Shirley's cheeks flushed red. 'Are you trying to tell us we don't know how to raise a child?'

'Not at all. I'm merely suggesting —'

'Out of the goodness of our hearts, we have taken in two children from the other side of the world. We have done our very best to love these children as if they were our own, and I believe we've succeeded with Rosie. She is every bit our daughter. But Fergus has made it crystal clear he doesn't want to be our son. I would be glad if they could continue to live under the same roof. They're brother and sister; they should be together. I wish the situation were different, but it isn't, and I'd appreciate it if you weren't so quick to pass judgement.' Mrs Shirley took a deep breath and wiped at the tears in her eyes. 'Feel free to adopt Fergus yourself, if you would like.'

Fergus chose that moment to enter the kitchen. He stared at Ruth, his eyes wide and hopeful. 'You want to adopt me?'

Ruth willed the ground to open up and swallow her whole. She couldn't possibly adopt Fergus, no matter how much she cared for him.

'Oh, Fergus.' Ruth crouched before him. 'I must return to England soon and you need to say here in Australia, where it is safe.'

'I want to be with you,' he insisted.

Pain spread across Ruth's chest. What was she to say? Fergus had been made to travel to other side of the world. To leave his parents and home would have been hard enough, but then to lose them, to have nowhere to call home — it was unbearable.

'I promise I'll work something out for you, Fergus. I will do everything I can to make sure you are happy and cared for.'

'Just not by you,' Fergus said, narrowing his eyes. Then he turned and left the room.

Bobby put an arm around Ruth's shoulder. 'You're doing all you can.'

She rested against him. 'But it isn't enough, is it? CORB say unless a family member or approved couple is willing to adopt Fergus, they have no choice but to send him to the orphanage. If Fergus was a baby, there'd be couples crying out to adopt him, but he's a troubled boy.'

'He's a fine lad,' said Bobby. 'Actually, he reminds me of myself as a kid. I always wanted to be running around on the farm, not stuck in the classroom.'

'I agree. He's not the only boy struggling to *be good*, as Mrs Shirley would say.'

Bobby cleared his throat. 'I wrote to my sister Anne last week and mentioned . . . well, I wasn't going to say anything until I'd heard back, but she could be interested in adopting Fergus.'

Ruth leant away and stared at him, open-mouthed. 'What?' she breathed.

Bobby turned to face her. 'Please don't get your hopes up just yet, Ruth. Anne has been married for four years to a wonderful chap, Bill. She would dearly love to be a mother but the doctors believe it may not be possible. I know Anne is looking into adoption, and she has such a generous heart I believe she'll want to help Fergus in any way she can.'

'Oh, Bobby, that would be wonderful. Only, it would take him so far away from his sister, and we can't assume CORB would agree to the idea.'

'Well, let's wait to hear from Anne first. I hope to hell I'm not setting you up for further disappointment.'

'No, Bobby, it has given me some hope at last.' She leant in and kissed him on the cheek. 'Thank you.'

They sat in silence, finishing their ice creams.

'What about us?' Bobby asked eventually.

Ruth closed her eyes briefly. She knew this moment had to come, but she wasn't ready to face it.

'I received a telegram from my mother this morning. She . . .' Ruth swallowed. 'Peter, my fiancé, has been injured. I need to go home to see him and I promised my mother I'd return.' Ruth stopped. How could she explain the agony she was going through? She had to go back to England. It was the right thing to do and she had to make sure Peter was okay. She had been about to post him a letter calling off their engagement when the telegram arrived, and it would be too unkind, too cruel, to send the letter now. Her mother needed her, and she was desperate to see her brother and Florrie. Ruth's life, her identity, was in England. Yet to leave Bobby and Fergus . . . To walk away from two people she cared so greatly for . . . Every cell in her body seemed to cry out that it was wrong. Wrong to leave, and wrong to stay.

'I have a passage booked back to Auckland next Friday,' Bobby said, his face wooden.

'Next week!' Ruth swayed in her seat. This couldn't be happening so soon.

'The New Zealand government has told us we must abide by our word – at least for now.'

Bobby and the other male prisoners had been forced by the Germans to sign a document stating they would not fight the enemy. The assumption was that such a hollow declaration would be ignored. Instead, the New Zealand government had decided a man's word must be honoured, even when given under duress.

'I'm sorry.' Ruth would never tell Bobby how secretly relieved she was. How the thought of him risking his life on the front line made her nauseous.

Bobby grasped Ruth's hand and held it to his chest. 'Don't go back to England, Ruth,' he implored. 'Come to New Zealand with me instead. You must see how much I love and respect you. I know it's wrong to ask when you're engaged to another man, but what we have is special. I can't leave without at least asking.'

'Bobby, I . . . I love you too.' The words were out of her mouth before she realised what she had said. *It's true*, she thought, acceptance sweeping through her. She'd been so determined to ignore her feelings for Bobby, but she loved this man beside her. All the same, she refused to turn her back on her life in England, the way her father had so carelessly done. 'Bobby, I want to be with you but . . .'

'But you can't,' Bobby said, pain and resignation in his eyes. He let go of Ruth's hand and stood. 'I'm afraid I need to go. Will you be all right finding your way back to the hotel?'

Ruth's pulse pounded in her ears. Light-headed, she saw black spots in her vision. 'Bobby, please don't go.'

He faced her, his jaw clenched. 'I'll let you know if I hear from Anne.'

Ruth stumbled to her feet. 'Bobby —'

'You've just told me you love me, Ruth, and yet you're going to throw it away — for what? For Peter, for your mother, for whatever it is you see as right and proper?' His voice rose. 'Why can't you be honest with yourself, take a risk, take a chance on us? Because what we have is real love, Ruth: it's right here in front of your eyes and you're determined to reject it.' He breathed in and out heavily, his eyes glittering with anger.

Ruth felt herself grow numb. Once again she was outside of her body looking down, a witness standing at a safe distance. She needed to speak, to do something, but she couldn't.

'Goodbye, Ruth,' growled Bobby.

Ruth stood motionless, wordless, as he spun around and strode away.

$\sim$

'Ruth, open up!' Una pounded on the door. 'I have news!'

Ruth blinked and her eyes came back into focus. She'd been sitting on the edge of her bed in a daze since returning from the waterfront. Had it really only been an hour since Bobby had said goodbye? How many more hours would she have to go through, knowing she might never see him again?

Staggering to her feet, Ruth opened the door and Una burst in.

'Gary proposed!' she shrieked. 'Oh, Ruth, can you believe it? I hoped he might but you never can tell, and he's been a little distant lately – but it turns out he was nervous about proposing and that's why he wasn't himself. I was worrying for nothing.' Una took a breath and frowned. 'Are you all right? I thought you'd be a tad more excited for me!'

Ruth tried to absorb her words. 'I'm thrilled for you, Una.' Her tongue moved awkwardly in her mouth. 'Congratulations.'

She hugged her friend and tried to muster some enthusiasm. 'Tell me everything.'

Una threw herself onto Ruth's bed. 'It was ever so romantic. He'd booked a table at this delightful tearoom with a view over the water, and we'd only just sat down when he suddenly got down on one knee and asked me to be his wife. I was so overcome I burst into tears, and of course I said yes, and then all the other diners clapped and cheered.'

Ruth smiled, knowing how much Una would have enjoyed being the centre of attention in that moment. She briefly recalled Peter's more subdued yet equally romantic proposal in Stratford-upon-Avon. They'd toured through Shakespeare's house then walked down a quiet lane, stopping to admire the spring flowers, when Peter had taken Ruth's hand and quietly asked if she would do him the honour of being his wife. She'd been so sure of her answer.

'We've decided to wait till after this blasted war before we get married,' Una went on. 'You'll be invited, of course — we plan to have the wedding in Brighton. My sister lives there, and my parents aren't far away. The big decision is where we'll live. Gary's happy to live in England to begin with, but he wants us to move to New Zealand once our children are old enough to start school.'

'Goodness, you've discussed everything.' Ruth wished she could sound more cheerful. It wasn't fair to put a dampener on Una's special moment.

Una's face fell. 'I expect you think it's a little rushed.'

'Oh no, not at all. I can see how happy you make one another. Honestly, if you can survive the events of the last couple of months together you can surely be confident of your relationship.' Ruth tried not to think of Bobby and failed. If she hadn't been engaged to Peter, would she have agreed to go to New Zealand with Bobby? Maybe. Maybe they would have taken Fergus with them. Maybe she'd be as happy as Una was right now, instead of miserable.

Una leapt off the bed and gripped Ruth by the shoulders. 'Whatever is the matter, Ruth? You appear quite out of sorts. Has something happened? Has there been news from home?'

Ruth shook her head and raised her chin. 'I'm sorry, Una – I really am thrilled for you. I'm just suffering from a silly bout of homesickness, that's all.'

'Well, I have good news on that front. I bumped into Mrs Ellis in the foyer earlier today and she tells me we're booked on a passage home. The boat leaves in less than two weeks.'

'Two weeks!' Ruth repeated, aghast. Soon she would return home, leaving Fergus and Bobby behind. Once again she would have to spend weeks at sea, living in constant fear of a German attack.

Stop this, Ruth told herself. Her personal struggles were of little importance when the world was at war. It was time to put her emotions aside and face what came next with resolve and maturity. She'd left London because she'd wanted to do something important for the war effort and, she might as well admit it, she'd wanted an adventure. Well, she'd helped children to safety (though she feared she had let Fergus down), and she'd had adventures – far more than she would have liked. But there'd been more to it than that. When Ruth had signed up to be a CORB escort, she'd been restless, looking for something she couldn't put into words. Something she may have found, only to lose it again . . .

⁓

Everything happened too fast. The next day Bobby left a message for Ruth at her hotel informing her that his sister had replied saying she would take Fergus. Anne had suggested Fergus could live with her and her husband for a year and then, all going well, they would look to adopt him. Ruth was relieved and confused and despondent at the news. In order to cope, she threw herself into helping CORB with the paperwork and assisting the Child Welfare Department in New Zealand. The department insisted on conducting a home visit to inspect Anne's house and asked both Anne and Ruth a great many questions before they would give their approval. Then, once confirmation finally came through, there was a further scramble to find Fergus a berth on the same ship as Bobby; Ruth was adamant that Fergus shouldn't travel to New Zealand with a stranger. Bobby would be able to look after him on the trip, introduce him to Anne, and help him settle into his new home.

When at last the plans were in place, Ruth asked Mrs Shirley if she could be the one to tell Fergus. She sat down beside Fergus on the couch in Mrs Shirley's lounge room and took the boy's hand. 'Fergus, I'm sorry for everything you have been through. It has been a difficult time for you and you've been a very brave, strong young man.'

Fergus narrowed his eyes, as if suspicious of where their conversation was going. 'Thank you, miss.'

Ruth took a deep breath and let it out. 'Fergus, Bobby has a sister. Her name is Anne, and she lives with her husband in New Zealand on a lovely big farm. They have no children, even though they would dearly love to.'

Fergus's eyes were slits now.

'Anne has offered to take you in, Fergus. If things work out, which I'm sure they will, then she and her husband would be interested in adopting you. They have two dogs and plenty of sheep, and there's a small school down the road.'

Fergus gave no sign he was registering Ruth's words. He sat immobile and held his breath. She squeezed his hand, lying limp and sweaty in hers. 'It's a wonderful offer, Fergus, and while I know it will be awfully hard to leave your sister here in Australia, New Zealand isn't too far away. You'll be able to write, and you'll visit one another in the future, I'm sure, and she is happy – you will have the comfort of knowing she is happy here with Mr and Mrs Shirley.' Ruth knew she was rambling but she didn't want to stop talking. She knew silence would bring to the surface her guilt and despair. 'It is another big adjustment for you, Fergus, and I know it must be unsettling, but here is an opportunity for you to finally feel safe and . . . and for you to belong.'

Fergus's eyes widened at this. 'How can I belong to people I haven't even met in a country I've never been to?' he said loudly.

Ruth winced at the anger in his voice. 'You *will* come to belong, I'm sure of it, Fergus. All I want is for you to be happy, to have people care for you the way you deserve.'

Fergus's expression softened. 'I know, miss,' he muttered.

'So will you go? Will you be brave once more?'

'It's not like I have a choice, miss,' he said. 'But I'll go, and I'll try hard so they will like me.'

'They will love you, Fergus, because you are a special boy. And Bobby . . .' Ruth hesitated. 'Bobby will visit you often, and he's promised to take you to the beach and teach you how to play rugby, if you would like, and of course you can carry on with your boxing lessons.'

Fergus pulled his hand out of Ruth's and stood up. He looked at her with tears in his eyes. 'Am I leaving now, miss?' he asked. 'Can I say goodbye to Rosie first?'

Ruth stood too, knowing she would never again feel as wretched as she did in that moment. 'You leave the day after tomorrow, Fergus; there's plenty of time for goodbyes.'

Ruth ran along the wharf, scanning the crowd of people walking up the gangway and milling on the wharf waiting to embark. Suddenly she spied them: Bobby with a suitcase in each hand and Fergus beside him, his head bowed.

'Fergus!' Ruth called. 'Bobby!' She hurried up to them, panting. 'I'm so sorry I'm late.'

Bobby gave Ruth a small smile. 'I was just telling Fergus I was sure you would turn up to say goodbye.'

Ruth smiled and tears welled in her eyes. 'I'm not saying goodbye. I'm coming with you.' Waving the ticket she clutched in her hand, Ruth looked from one stunned face to another.

Bobby slowly placed the suitcases down. 'Say that again?' he said quietly.

'I'm going with you!' she yelled. 'It's crazy, I know, and I have no idea what will happen and what I'll do, but I belong with you, Bobby – you and Fergus. If you'll have me?'

Fergus let out a high-pitched yelp and launched himself at Ruth. She picked him up and swung him around then hugged him tightly. 'I'm so sorry, Fergus. I should never have put you through this, and there is nothing I want more in the world than to adopt you.'

'Really?' he said, tears streaming down his precious little face.

'Yes, if you'll agree.'

'Of course, I agree!'

Ruth lowered Fergus to the ground and faced Bobby, who was staring at her, dumbfounded. She reached for his hands. 'Bobby, I'm going to call off my engagement. I can't marry Peter. Not now. I want to be with you. I know we'll make each other happy. The three of us: you, me and Fergus.'

'Are you sure?' Bobby asked, his voice cracking.

'I've never been more sure of anything in my life.'

As Bobby pulled her into his arms, Ruth knew that whatever lay in her future, she could face it. With Bobby and Fergus by her side, she could take on the world.

41

HAZEL

The bar was packed with people in smart outfits having after-work drinks and Hazel wished she'd chosen a different spot to meet Joe. The last time Hazel had been to this bar had been for a midweek staff lunch and it had been a quiet oasis compared to the bustling street outside.

Hazel still experienced a thrill every time she remembered that she was actually living in London. The day before a tourist had stopped her to ask directions, and they'd really believed she was just an ordinary Londoner. They hadn't even picked up on her accent. Hazel felt she would never get over the buzz of being in this vibrant city where anything and everything felt possible.

Of course, her life wasn't perfect. It was still awkward at work after Hazel had finally had to tell Paul she wasn't interested in him romantically, and her new flatmate was useless when it came to doing dishes or putting things away. But these were small things, easy for her to overlook. What she couldn't overlook, and tried hard not to think about, was the fact that Joe was about to move to Sweden.

Hazel hadn't seen Joe for well over a month; not since the day she'd moved to her new flat. She'd wanted to call him a few times – okay, all the time – but she also knew it was better if she didn't speak to him. She was getting on with her life and so was he. If she was honest, the only reason she'd phoned him a few days earlier was because she'd had a couple of glasses of wine on the couch while she finished re-reading the book Gramps had given her. She'd remembered what Joe had said about the ending, and she'd had a desperate urge to talk to him about it.

'Hi, Hazel.'

Hazel started, and turned to see Joe standing behind her with a pint of beer. 'Hi, I didn't see you come in,' she said, heat rushing to her cheeks. He looked different somehow, not as relaxed and dishevelled as she remembered. Maybe it was the haircut and smart shirt that made him look older and more uptight.

Joe sat opposite. 'I'm not surprised; this place is heaving.'

'Sorry,' said Hazel. 'Should we go somewhere else?'

Joe placed his beer on the coaster, leant back and crossed his arms. 'This is fine.'

Hazel wondered if he had agreed to catch up with her out of a sense of obligation rather than because he actually wanted to see her again. 'It's been a while,' she said. 'How's it all going?'

His expression was flat. 'Fine. You?'

Hazel gulped down a mouthful of wine. 'Good. Actually, I wanted to talk to you about the book – *Oceans Apart*. Remember when you said you felt the ending was off? Well, I kept mulling it over, and you're right, it didn't make sense, so I asked Gramps.'

Joe uncrossed his arms and leant forward to grasp his beer. 'What did he say?'

'He said our instincts were right: none of the last chapter was true.'

Joe frowned into his glass. 'So someone invented a whole different ending? Why? And what really happened?'

Hazel shrugged. 'Gramps wouldn't tell me – but I'm going to find out.'

'How?'

'By asking Florrie and Una.'

'What?!' Beer sloshed over the side of Joe's glass.

Hazel nodded. 'Gramps told me Florrie is still alive. She sends him a card every year. He had her address, and from that I managed to track down her phone number. When I rang her, she said she'd love to meet me and suggested Una join us too.' Hazel pressed her palms onto her thighs. 'I'm going to see them in Wimbledon tomorrow.' She knew she shouldn't ask him the question, even as it started to form on her lips. 'Do you want to come with me?'

Joe was silent for several loud thumps of Hazel's heart.

'Sure,' he said at last. The word was spoken with so little emotion, Hazel instantly regretted the impulse to invite him.

'Oh, I'm sorry – I shouldn't have asked. You're probably frantically busy organising the move to Sweden. The last thing you need is to go and listen to some old women talk about people you don't even –'

'Hazel, I'd like to come with you, and I'm not busy with the move to Sweden because . . .' Joe rubbed a hand over his face. 'Klara moved back to Sweden a couple of weeks ago. We've decided to . . . I mean it's been on the cards for a while but . . . we're splitting up. Separating.'

Hazel clasped her hands together. 'Oh, Joe, I'm sorry.' She wished she could see the expression on his downturned face. 'I – I hope I didn't contribute in any way.'

Joe lifted his head, his eyes bright. 'It's nothing to do with you.'

'Right,' Hazel said quickly. 'Sorry.'

Joe groaned and ran a hand through his hair. 'Hazel, that didn't come out the way I meant it to.'

Hazel pushed back her chair. 'I should go,' she said.

Joe stood. 'Stay a bit longer, please.'

'If you still want to come with me to see Florrie and Una, I'm planning to catch the ten o'clock train from Waterloo,' Hazel said to his shoes. 'I don't care either way.'

'Hazel . . .'

'Bye, Joe.' She pushed her way through the throngs of people and stumbled out onto the street.

⌐

Joe was waiting at Waterloo when Hazel arrived, two tickets to Wimbledon in his hand. She tried to act composed but was sure Joe must have noticed the tremor in her voice when she said hello. They talked about mundane, unthreatening topics on the train: the weather, their plans for Christmas, Hazel's recent trip to Prague.

Exiting the train, neither of them spoke until they reached a wide street lined with attractive white-stone buildings fronted by immaculately trimmed hedges and elaborately carved gates.

'How's Matt?' Joe asked, watching the footpath ahead.

Hazel glanced at him quickly. 'I haven't spoken to him for a while. We agreed a long-distance relationship wasn't going to work.'

'Right.'

Hazel stopped abruptly. 'This is it,' she said, pointing.

Joe whistled. 'Crikey.'

'It's pretty swanky, all right.'

They approached the tall black wrought-iron fence and peered through at a majestic white three-storey building. It had a curved balcony extending off the second level and wide black-and-white tiled steps leading up to an enormous wooden door.

The house was grander than any Hazel had ever set foot in before, and she wished she'd worn a dress instead of jeans.

'Come on,' said Joe, opening the gate. He waited for her to step through, climb the stairs and press the polished brass buzzer.

When Joe came to stand beside her, Hazel had to stop herself from reaching out to take his hand.

The door swung open and a glamorous middle-aged woman in an elegant two-piece with blonde hair swept into a French roll flashed them a welcoming smile. Giant pearl earrings swung from her ears. 'You must be Hazel,' she said in a plummy British accent. 'Delighted to meet you. I'm Betty, Una's daughter.'

'Hello, Betty, it's incredible to meet you. This is my friend Joe. He was sitting beside me on the plane over from New Zealand when I starting reading the book Gramps gave me, and he's read it too and –' Hazel stopped abruptly. 'Did you say Betty? It's just that there's an escort in the book called Betty, who died when the *Rangitane* was attacked – which was awful, by the way – and I was wondering if –' Hazel felt a hand on her shoulder and turned to look at Joe.

'Take a breath, Hazel. It's all right.'

'Oh! I'm sorry,' she said, turning back to Betty. 'I talk too much when I'm nervous.'

Betty laughed. 'Oh, my darling, wait until you meet Mother and Florrie – they are going to love you. And yes, I am named after Betty. Now come inside out of the cold. Florrie is upstairs and said to say she will be down soon, and Mother can't be too far away.'

'I was thrilled when Gramps told me they were both still alive,' said Hazel, stepping through the door.

'And I'm not dying anytime soon, if I can help it,' came a voice.

Turning, Hazel saw an elderly woman in a red coat and black beret coming through the gate. Her grey hair hung in a plait over one shoulder, and she could have passed for a woman in her seventies rather than one nearing ninety.

'You must be Una!' Hazel hurried back down the stairs and threw her arms around the woman. 'I feel as if I know you, though it's silly, because we haven't met. You were so *brave*, really you were.'

Una laughed. 'Oh, Hazel, I can see a bit of Fergus's spirit in you already.'

Joe introduced himself, and with Una clutching Hazel's hand, they entered a vast entrance hall with marble tiles on the floor, a lavish crystal chandelier hanging from the ceiling and a beautiful curved staircase. 'Wow,' said Hazel, stopping to take it in.

Betty smiled. 'Aunty Flo asked me to organise tea in the living room.' She walked briskly into a nearby room and waved her hand at an elegant powder-blue velvet couch. 'Please, take a seat.'

Hazel perched on the edge of the couch, Joe beside her, while Una sank into an armchair beside the fire. 'Ah,' Una said with a sigh. 'That's much better.'

'This is a lovely house,' said Joe politely.

'Yes, it's very grand,' said Una. 'Far too big for Florrie, but she insists on staying.'

'I heard that,' said a frail-looking woman at the door.

Hazel jumped to her feet. 'Florrie,' she exclaimed. 'I'm so happy to meet you. I'm Hazel, Fergus's granddaughter, and I know I'm a complete stranger to you and I should stop talking, but please tell me that you married Frank!' Hazel heard Joe chuckle behind her.

Florrie shuffled towards them in a pair of tailored linen pants and a soft fluffy blue top, her grey hair cut in an immaculate bob. 'It's wonderful to meet you, Hazel.' She hugged Hazel and shook hands with Joe before settling into the armchair on the other side of the fireplace. 'Well, Una,' she said, 'this is a turn-up for the books, isn't it?'

As they nodded at one another, a knowing look passed between them.

'Now,' said Una, turning to Betty. 'How about that cup of tea, my darling?'

'Coming right up.' Betty left the room and Hazel shuffled back on the couch, her leg bumping against Joe's. They glanced at one another and smiled.

'Right,' said Una, sitting up straighter. 'First things first, I'm pleased to say that Florrie and Frank did get married.'

Hazel clapped. 'Fantastic news.'

'It was a very grand affair,' continued Una. 'The ceremony was at Westminster Abbey.'

'Really?' said Joe, incredulous.

'You did say you wanted a wedding with all the trimmings,' Hazel recalled, remembering the moment in the book when Florrie got engaged.

'That I did,' Florrie confirmed. 'Frank and I were wonderfully happy together for fifty-three years, until the silly man died of heart failure.'

'I'm sorry,' said Hazel.

Florrie sniffed. 'I wouldn't change a thing,' she said, as Una reached out to clasp her hand. 'We were both very lucky.'

'What about you, Una? Did you marry Gary?' blurted Hazel.

'Yes indeed. We were married in Brighton and spent our honeymoon in New Zealand visiting Gary's family. We talked about one day moving there, but it never quite happened.'

'Is Gary still . . .' Hazel hesitated.

'He's in a nursing home. A couple of years ago he developed Alzheimer's; some days he remembers me and some days he doesn't, but he seems content, which is the main thing.'

Betty arrived carrying a silver tray and proceeded to pour cups of tea for everyone. Then she handed around biscuits and took a seat next to Joe.

'Thank you, dear,' said Florrie fondly.

'What did I miss?' Betty asked.

'We were filling Hazel and Joe in on our husbands.'

Hazel sipped her tea and carefully placed her cup on her saucer. 'I've been wondering, how did you meet one another?'

They looked confused for a moment, then Florrie laughed. 'Why, we met the second Ruth and Una stepped off the boat. I was on the docks waiting to greet Ruth and she came walking down the gangway, arm in arm with some woman I'd never laid eyes on before.'

'I thought Florrie was extremely glamorous and of course we hit it off straight away with our love of fashion,' said Una.

'Oh yes, we've had some wonderful shopping trips to Paris and Milan,' said Florrie.

Una closed her eyes for a moment and took a rasping breath, reminding Hazel of Gramps. 'And of course later we . . . we were a support for each other.'

'Yes,' murmured Florrie.

There was a long stretch of silence as Hazel tried to work out what they were talking about. 'Hang on,' she said. 'Ruth came back to London with you, Una? You mean she didn't go to New Zealand with Bobby and Fergus?'

Una, who had a faraway look in her eye, didn't answer.

It was Florrie who finally responded. Fixing her eyes on Hazel, she said, 'I think it's high time you and your grandfather learnt the full story, don't you?'

42

London, 1941

The front door flew open while Ruth was still pacing about on the footpath. 'Ruthie, where have you been?' exclaimed Florrie, hurrying out and pulling Ruth into a tight hug. 'I was getting worried.'

Ruth did her best to smile. 'Sorry, I ended up walking the entire way and there were several detours. This city is such a mess, Florrie – how can you stand it?'

'Because I must.' Florrie studied Ruth's face. 'You look tired. Still having trouble sleeping?'

Ruth shrugged. 'About the same.'

It had been over four weeks since Ruth had arrived back in England. She'd stepped off the ship into the depths of a bleak British winter and hadn't felt properly warm since. She hadn't been able to sleep either. It was a combination of her overactive mind, the constant doubts over her decision to return home and a panicky fear that set her heart racing and had her sitting up in bed to catch her breath.

Ruth didn't understand how she could be so calm during the day then so unsettled at night. Anxiety would build like a storm cloud as the night wore on. It was similar to the fear she'd been unable to shake during her return journey from Sydney to a bomb-stricken Southampton. Every night she'd retired to her cabin and imagined waking to the sound of gunfire. It kept her lying awake until the early hours of the morning. Both Una and Mrs Ellis, who had also been on board, tried their best to help Ruth relax but with little success.

But now Ruth was on dry land, and the number of air raids had reduced, and up until a few days ago she'd been living with her mother and aunt in rural Dorset, a place so quiet and peaceful it was extremely unlikely Hitler had any interest in the area at all.

'How is dear Mrs Best?' Florrie asked, hooking her arm through Ruth's and leading her inside. 'Still berating you for your harebrained adventure?'

They entered Florrie's apartment and headed to the two armchairs by the tall window in search of some warmth from the weak sunlight coming through the glass.

'You'd think it was all my fault that I was silly enough to be taken prisoner,' said Ruth, rubbing her arms to try to warm up.

'She's not going to forgive you for a long time yet, Ruthie. And neither will I. We were beside ourselves when the *Rangitane* went missing. It was bad enough with Frank and Peter in France, but when you . . . well, it was a dreadful time, make no mistake.' The haunted look on Florrie's face disappeared and she smiled. 'But you're with us now.'

'It's good to be back in London,' Ruth said, 'though I must say my bedsit is very dreary having been empty for so long. I couldn't have lasted another day in Dorset, though. I love Mother, but living under the same roof as her is a serious threat to my sanity.'

Florrie laughed. 'Hats off to you, Ruthie; there's no way I would ever consider living with my own mother, even with a war on.' She clapped her hands and stood. 'I'll make tea and then you can tell me all your news.'

As Florrie disappeared into the kitchen, Ruth leant back in her seat and closed her eyes, wondering yet again if there would be any mail waiting for her when she returned to her bedsit. She'd written to Fergus almost every day since arriving back in England and so far had heard nothing. Her letters to him had been deliberately cheerful and she'd done her best not to reveal how miserable she felt at leaving. Missing him was a permanent ache in her ribs; an ache without a cure. As for Bobby – Ruth hadn't written to him at all. She didn't know how to write, or what to say, after she had rejected him in such a way.

Ruth's heart began to race as she thought of the two envelopes she had sealed and placed on her desk before she left to come to Florrie's.

'What time is Una due?' she called out, her eyes still closed.

Florrie poked her head around the kitchen doorway. 'Her train should have arrived ten minutes ago. She won't be far off.'

While Ruth had been keeping her mother company in Dorset, Una and Florrie had been catching up whenever they weren't busy driving ambulances or working in the hospital.

'She must be exhausted,' said Ruth.

Florrie returned with a tray and placed it on the low table between them. 'Una does work long hours, and I understand the conditions in the hospital are rather grim, but she manages to keep smiling. I suspect her engagement has something to do with it.'

Ruth nodded, her thoughts briefly turning to Betty. 'It takes a special type of person to be a nurse.'

'That it does.' Florrie poured the tea and settled into her chair. 'Now, tell me what you've been up to while stuck in that dull little village.'

Ruth laughed. 'You are a city girl through and through, Florrie.'

'Indeed I am.' Florrie settled back in her chair, cup in hand.

'Well, as you know, I've been teaching part-time in the local school, which has been pleasant.' Ruth didn't add that it was also a welcome distraction from her thoughts. 'And I've been doing some writing.' She stared into her cup of tea. 'About my recent adventures.'

'What a jolly good idea,' Florrie enthused. 'Will you try to have your story published?'

Ruth looked up in alarm. 'It hasn't crossed my mind. I simply had a strange compulsion to write it all down. I can't imagine other people wanting to read about my silly exploits.' Ruth didn't fully understand why she'd felt so drawn to write. Perhaps it had been what she needed to do in order to decide on her future.

'Nonsense,' Florrie said. 'You've had more adventures than most women will have in their lifetime. Yours is an important story to tell, Ruth. People should know this war isn't just about the men out there fighting. Women are doing bold, courageous things too.'

Ruth took a sip of tea, wondering if now was the time to tell Florrie about Fergus and Bobby. She'd mentioned both of them in passing, but had been unable to reveal to anyone how much of her heart she'd left thousands of miles away in New Zealand.

Florrie sat forward, frowning. 'Ruth, what's going on? There's something you're not telling me.'

Tears pricked Ruth's eyes. 'Maybe,' she whispered.

'Oh, Ruthie.' Florrie placed her cup on the table and put her hand on Ruth's leg. 'Tell me what is going on inside that head – or should I say heart? Maybe I can help.'

Ruth swallowed. 'Florrie, you know me so well. I've decided on something and I'm nervous about telling you – but I must, even though I suspect you'll say I'm being ridiculously impulsive.'

Florrie snorted. 'I'm not your fiancé, you know.'

At the mention of Peter, Ruth sucked in a breath. 'I went to visit him this morning,' she said in a rush. 'He's recovering very well – so well he'll be discharged in a couple of days. He's going to convalesce at his parents' house in Kent.'

'That's good,' said Florrie, eyeing Ruth cautiously. 'And?'

'And I called off the engagement,' burst out Ruth. 'I couldn't marry him, Florrie. We don't fit anymore; I'm not even sure we were ever a good fit. And also . . . well, I couldn't marry him when I have feelings for another man. It wouldn't be right; it simply wouldn't.'

'I agree.'

Ruth froze and stared at her friend. 'You do?'

'Of course I do. To be perfectly frank, I wasn't sure about the two of you getting married in the first place.'

'Florence Wright! You never said a thing.' Ruth exclaimed.

'I'm sure you had genuine affection for him, Ruth. Maybe you loved him.'

'I did. I still do . . . in some way.'

'But not the right way,' said Florrie softly.

'No,' said Ruth.

'And this other man? Is it to do with this Bobby you hardly mention? Una told me about him. She said you tried your best to hide your affection for him but did a fairly average job of it.'

Ruth allowed herself a smile, thinking again of the two letters waiting to be posted. The first was addressed to Bobby, telling him she had called off her engagement and that she hoped to travel to New Zealand as soon as the war was over. She begged for his forgiveness, telling him she loved him and asking for him to wait for her. The second letter was to Fergus, explaining she had made a dreadful mistake and was returning to New Zealand. She promised that she would never abandon him again. If only she'd had time to post the letters before she'd left. As soon as she'd finished lunch, she would go home to get them. With luck, she would be in time to catch the evening post.

Ruth was just opening her mouth to tell Florrie what she'd decided when the doorbell rang.

'That will be Una,' said Florrie, leaping to her feet. 'Don't go anywhere, Ruth. We've got so much to discuss.'

By the time Florrie returned with Una, Ruth had made a decision. She'd keep the contents of the letters to herself until she heard back from Bobby and Fergus. There was no rush. She was finally sure of herself, of her future, of the person she wanted to be and the people she wanted to share her life with.

Smiling, Ruth rose to greet her friend.

43

JOE

'So Ruth did plan to go back to them,' Hazel said, as Joe took a sip of his lukewarm tea.

'That was her plan,' said Una.

'But Ruth never posted the letters because' – Florrie sighed – 'because she was killed that evening. We hadn't had an air raid for several days, so when the siren sounded a short while after Ruth left my apartment I thought it was nothing to worry about. But the bombings started almost immediately and they were vicious, relentless attacks that didn't let up until dawn.' Florrie stopped talking; her eyes glazed over with tears.

Joe felt a tremor coming from Hazel's body and he put a hand on her back. She gave him a weak smile.

Betty went to Florrie and put an arm around her shoulders. 'Aunty Flo, are you all right?'

Florrie blinked as she was drawn back to the present. She straightened and glared at the flames flickering in the fireplace beside her before continuing. 'Una had spent the night sheltering with me in our basement, and the next morning we decided to walk over to Ruth's bedsit to check on her. We were nearly at her place when we saw the butcher, Mr Hamble. He was standing a few yards down the street from his shop, surrounded by a pile of rubble, and he was crying. There was a group of men shifting these big lumps of brick and I knew the moment he caught my eye.' Florrie took a deep shuddering breath. 'I knew before I saw her body. Una . . . she . . . I tried to stop her from going to look, but I couldn't hold her back.'

Hazel gave a faint strangled sound and Joe rubbed her back soothingly.

Florrie sighed. 'It was awful. The worst day of that blasted war. Mrs Best, Ruth's mother, she didn't cope well after her daughter's death. It sent her to bed for months. We sent a telegram to Ruth's father in New Zealand, but it was too difficult for him to come with a war raging. Frank managed to get leave and he' – Florrie paused and shook her head – 'he was a wonderful help. He came with us to sort through Ruth's belongings, and he was the one who found the letters she'd written to Fergus and Bobby. He cried when he read them. And we did too, didn't we, Una?'

Her friend nodded wordlessly.

'Would Ruth have gone, do you think?' Hazel asked hoarsely. 'To New Zealand, I mean.'

Florrie snorted. 'Of course! I wouldn't have been at all surprised if she'd gone within a month. There's no way that girl was going to wait until the war ended. Not once she'd made up her mind. But she wouldn't have found Bobby there.' Her voice grew sombre once more. 'He ended up rejoining the Fleet Air Arm after the New Zealand government had a change of heart. He died on his first mission off the coast of Italy. Even if Ruth had sent the letter, he most likely wouldn't have received it.'

'What about Gramps? Did he know about Ruth's letter? Did he know she was planning to go back?'

Florrie frowned. 'We discussed it, and in the end we decided it was probably worse for Fergus to know, so no – we never told him about the letter. Sometimes I wonder if we made the right decision.'

'Tell us about your grandfather,' said Una. 'Do you think he was happy in New Zealand?'

'I think so,' said Hazel, clasping her hands on her lap. 'He's a bit of a gruff old man these days, but he's said Anne and Bill were wonderful parents. He loved being in the countryside, tramping and going to the beach. When my brothers and I were little he used to take us camping and we'd play cricket on the sand and play games in the bush. Gramps loved swimming in the sea and he never found the water too cold.'

'Well, when you've spent time in Glasgow,' said Una, 'I suspect nothing's cold after.'

Hazel nodded. 'He said his clearest memory of his childhood in Scotland was the grey skies. He'd always tell us how lucky we were to be surrounded by so much green and blue. He told me when I spoke to him last night that his older brother passed away several years ago, but his youngest sister, Lily, is still alive. She was only three years old when he left Glasgow and they've not seen each other since, but they write to one another occasionally. I might try to visit her if I ever get up that way.'

'What a lovely idea,' Una said. 'And whatever happened to dear little Rosie?'

'She grew up in Sydney, got married and had five children. She visited Gramps a few times, and he said he went to visit her once but the house was, in his words, too loud and boisterous for his liking.'

Una laughed. 'Did you ever meet her, Hazel?'

'No – I didn't even know she existed till I read your book. Gramps said Rosie died of a stroke when I was a toddler.'

'Oh, how sad,' Betty murmured. 'She must have been young.'

'Only sixty-something, I believe,' said Hazel.

'And he became a farmer, your grandfather?' Florrie said.

'Yes, he did. My dad runs the farm now, and Gramps claims he doesn't miss it, but I think he probably does. He once said he reckoned he had at least forty years of sleep-ins to make up for.'

Joe smiled. He wished he could go back to New Zealand to meet Hazel's grandfather. She spoke of him with so much love and warmth.

'I was wondering,' said Joe, reluctantly removing his hand from Hazel's back, 'how you came to write the book?'

'Ah,' said Florrie. 'That's where it gets interesting. Una found Ruth's journal under her pillow a week after the funeral. Ruth had told me she'd been writing about her journey as an escort, but I thought it must have been only a few pages. Instead, the dear girl had filled that journal from cover to cover.'

Una nodded. 'For the first time we understood why Ruth was desperate to go back to Fergus and Bobby. How hard it must have been for her to leave.'

'They went through so much together,' said Hazel softly.

'They certainly did.' Florrie was slumped in her chair, and Joe could tell from her wavering voice that she was getting tired. 'Una came to visit me one Sunday morning around a year before the war ended. She had Ruth's journal with her and she said we should turn it into a proper story. One that might be published. I still missed Ruth so very much, and with Gary and Frank away fighting, it gave us both a focus and helped to bring Ruth closer to us again. Of course, by writing from Ruth's point of view we couldn't be one hundred per cent sure we'd got it right, but her notes were extremely detailed.'

'Why didn't you publish it as a memoir?' Hazel asked.

Florrie considered Hazel's question for a long time. 'Because what we'd written wasn't all true,' she said.

Joe sighed. 'The ending.'

'Why did you make it up?' Hazel asked. 'Why not stick to the truth, however sad?'

Florrie lifted one eyebrow. 'Why do you think?'

'Because you wanted to give her the ending she deserved,' Hazel whispered.

'We did,' said Una. 'Very much.'

Joe felt sadness swell and fill the room. He wanted to drag Hazel away, tell her it didn't have to always end this way. 'Did Ruth regret signing up to be an escort?' Joe asked, suddenly anxious for an answer to his own conflicted emotions. 'Did she wish she'd stayed in London?'

Florrie shook her head. 'Ruth never wrote anything to that effect, and I don't believe she regretted a thing. Ruth loved an adventure. She left in search of something and I believe she found it with those children she helped to safety, with Fergus, and with Bobby. Remember her Christmas Eve on Emirau Island?'

'Yes,' Joe and Hazel said together.

'Have you looked up the island on a map? It is in the middle of nowhere. Most of the world have never heard of it and will certainly never go there. Think of the remarkable journey Ruth took to end up in that place at that time. It almost defies possibility. In her journal, Ruth described how she felt that night on the island and her words have stayed with me all these years. She wrote: *As I stood singing Christmas carols next to Bobby and Una on the beach, our voices drifting out over the dark moonlit sea, I felt content. I knew if I were to die the next day, it would be with gratitude and joy. I was no longer searching for anything. I was complete.'*

Joe pressed his hand into the couch beside Hazel and she put her hand on top of his.

'I think you're right, Florrie,' said Hazel. 'Ruth wouldn't have regretted going, even after everything she went through. How could she, when she gained so much?'

Florrie tipped her head to one side and smiled. 'You remind me of her, Hazel. I see the same sparkle in your eye. The desire for adventure, for something you can't quite reach.'

'Is that a bad thing?'

Florrie laughed. 'Not at all. It makes you special. Go after it, Hazel; go after it bravely, the way Ruth did.' She glanced at Joe. 'You too, young man. Life's too short to let possibilities pass you by.'

Betty had been sitting quietly beside Joe, but now she stood. 'It's time you had a rest, Aunty Flo. Perhaps you could see Hazel and Joe again soon?'

Hazel and Joe got to their feet at once. 'Yes, of course,' said Joe. 'We'd like that. Thank you for having us over, and for telling us what happened.'

'It was a pleasure.' Florrie shuffled forward in her chair.

'Don't get up.' Hazel hurried to her side. 'We can say goodbye here.'

Hazel gave her a hug then Joe leant down to give Florrie a quick kiss on the cheek.

As they started to move away, Florrie grasped Hazel's hand. 'I regret it now,' she said, agitated. 'I should have sent Fergus the letter Ruth wrote him. At the time I thought it would have made matters worse for the boy, but now I wonder if he might have found some comfort knowing she'd planned to go back.'

'I don't know whether it would have helped or not,' said Hazel.

'Will you send it to him?' Florrie asked.

'The letter?'

'Yes.' Florrie looked over at Una and gave her a watery smile. 'We've held on to it long enough.'

44

HAZEL

'Can't sleep?' Joe said. He sounded different over the phone tonight. More like the no-point-in-rushing Joe she'd met on the plane. Even the way he spoke was slower, more relaxed.

Hazel tucked her phone between her pillow and her ear. 'Nope. You either?'

'Hmm.'

They'd been speaking to each other fairly regularly since their visit with Florrie and Una. Hazel had reached a point where she felt an absence, a sense of things not being quite right, if they went more than a few days without talking. She'd wanted to suggest they meet up, maybe visit a museum together, but the words lodged in her throat. It was easier to talk on the phone, to not have him so close.

'I hope you don't mind me ringing so late,' said Hazel, tucking her feet under the blanket on her bed to keep warm.

'It's only midnight. And I was still tidying up downstairs.'

'Busy night?'

'Yeah, for a Wednesday. There was a big group of tourists from South Africa. They got pretty rowdy. One guy even threw a punch.'

'At you?' Hazel sat up. If she'd been there, she would have . . . well, she wasn't sure what she would have done.

'Nah, at one of his mates. I told them to go home because the bar was closed — to them, anyway.'

There was a lull in conversation, not uncomfortable, but odd. Hazel felt an energy, a heightening of her senses. She stared out of her window at the two stars she could just make out in the sky above the building across the road. 'At least it's stopped raining,' she said.

'Hazel, there's no pressure, but Mum wanted me to invite you to come here for Christmas lunch next week. I told her you had plans, but she said walking around the centre of London on your own to look at Christmas lights was not a good enough reason to say no.'

Hazel laughed. 'I won't be on my own.'

She heard Joe suck in his breath.

'The new girl from work, Sophie, is joining me,' she said quickly.

'Well, why don't you bring her too? Erica and Katie will be here.'

Hazel wanted to accept, but she was worried everyone would catch her looking at Joe and she'd give herself away. 'I'm not sure.'

'Please, Hazel, I'd like you to come.'

'Okay,' she said finally.

'Good.'

Again there was a weighted pause.

'All set for your trip to Dublin tomorrow?' asked Joe.

'Yeah, I can't wait. It's like my life is finally on track, which I know sounds melodramatic, but I finally feel like I'm where I'm meant to be.'

She heard him laugh softly. 'Your enthusiasm must be contagious,' he said.

'How?'

'Well, I kind of wish I was going to Dublin too. To see what all the fuss is about. Actually, since meeting you I've realised that I've spent most of my life not really considering the possibilities out there. I think I was afraid to try anything or even think about doing something in case I failed. And now, well, I want to try new things: travel, study, maybe . . .' His voice trailed off. 'I'm rambling, sorry.'

'No, you're not. I love that you can talk to me about it – and I am constantly failing, Joe. I swear I make more mistakes than anyone I know.'

Joe laughed and Hazel grinned, picturing his gorgeous, smiling face.

That was it. She had to do something. Sitting up, Hazel swung her feet off the bed. 'I'm going to go and see her,' she said firmly.

'Who?'

'Ruth.'

'Now?'

'Yes.'

'You're going to a graveyard in the middle of the night?'

'Yes.'

She waited for him to tell her it was a reckless, stupid idea.

'Okay,' he said. 'I'll come too.'

'Really?'

'I'll pick you up in twenty minutes.' He hung up before she could argue. Not that she wanted to argue. Hazel put down her phone and looked back out the window at the stars.

$\sim$

Their breaths formed white puffs in the air every time they breathed out. It was a freezing night but Hazel was sweltering in her coat, hat and gloves. Her heart pounded and her cheeks felt flushed and warm to touch.

Having Joe walking beside her probably had something to do with it. She was so aware of his every movement. Every time his hand moved close to hers, her stomach flipped. 'I was sure you'd tell me it was a crazy idea,' she said, their footsteps echoing down the empty street.

'It is crazy,' said Joe. 'But I like crazy when it comes to you.' He spoke without breaking stride, his eyes trained on the foot-path ahead.

Hazel's heart beat even faster. 'Is that a compliment?'

Joe didn't answer. Instead he pointed at a wrought-iron archway. 'This is it.'

He pulled a torch from his pocket and flicked it on.

'Clever thinking,' said Hazel.

'I'm not just a pretty face.'

She met his eye briefly and looked away. 'Florrie said Ruth is near the back, on the right.'

Joe swung the torch across the gravestones and Hazel shuddered. Why hadn't she waited to come to visit Ruth during the day, like a normal person?

'This way,' said Joe, aiming the torchlight onto a narrow brick path.

They walked slowly, their shoulders brushing together.

'I saw a ghost once,' whispered Joe.

'Really?'

'Well, I thought I did. Turns out it was my dad sneaking out of my room after replacing the tooth under my pillow with a coin. I saw this dark shape float out of the room and I swear to this day it wasn't Dad. Whatever I saw had long, flowing hair and a billowing dress.'

Hazel smiled in the darkness. 'It could have been a ghost.'

'You're being nice.'

They reached the end of the path and veered right, Joe shining the torch on each headstone so they could silently read the names.

At the fifth headstone, they both stopped. 'Here she is,' whispered Hazel.

'Ruth Elizabeth Best, 1918–1941,' Joe read. 'Beloved daughter, sister and friend.'

Hazel swallowed over the lump in her throat and slipped her hand into her pocket. She felt the cool disc and pulled it out. Holding her palm out flat, she could just make out the words *Fergus McKenzie* in the dim silvery light.

'Hi, Ruth,' murmured Hazel, speaking to the shadowed headstone. 'My grandfather wanted you to have this. He wanted me to say . . .' Hazel gulped. 'He wanted me to tell you that he never forgot about you and he was . . . he was lucky to have met you.'

Hazel felt Joe's arm slide around her shoulders. She leant against him, and rested her cheek against his chest.

Joe cleared his throat. 'The ground's frozen,' he said softly.

Hazel lifted her head. 'What?'

'Fergus wanted you to bury his CORB tag with Ruth, but the ground's frozen. We won't be able to dig a hole.'

'Oh.' Hazel bit her lip as Joe brushed a strand of her hair off her face.

Then he let her go and walked up close to the headstone. He moved the torch beam back and forth. 'There,' he said. 'You could slide it into that crack.'

Hazel stepped closer and peered at the split in the concrete near the bottom of the stone. She knelt down and carefully pressed the tag inside. Then she straightened and faced Joe.

He placed the torch on the ground and reached up to run a hand past her ear, his fingers gliding through her hair. 'Hazel,' he breathed. 'On the phone earlier, I told you how I was afraid of failing, but the truth is . . .' He took a deep breath. 'Mostly I'm afraid of failing you.'

'Me?' Hazel leant so close her lips were millimetres from his. 'I'd like to see you try.'

⌒

'Merry Christmas!' shouted Katie. She rushed up to Hazel and hugged her with a squeal. 'Our first white Christmas – isn't it exciting?'

Hazel squeezed inside and shut the pub door. 'I hate to point out the obvious, Katie, but it's not snowing.'

Katie grinned. 'But it did snow for a minute. I saw snowflakes, so I'm claiming a white Christmas and no-one is going to talk me out of it. I've already phoned my family in Sydney to tell them.'

Hazel laughed as she shrugged off her coat. The pub was crowded, the fire ablaze, and the Christmas lights strung around the dark wooden beams looked wonderfully festive.

'Merry Christmas, Hazel,' called Joe's dad from behind the bar. 'The lad has just whipped himself upstairs to get changed.' He winked and she smiled back nervously before walking over to the table by the window.

'Merry Christmas, everyone,' she said.

'Hazel!' Joe's sister Maggie rose to her feet. 'You look radiant. Bea! Lily! Here she is – come and say hello to Hazel.'

Two cute little girls in matching red corduroy pinafores and colourful tights leapt from their chairs and came so close one of them stood on Hazel's foot.

'Are you from New Zealand?' one of them asked, clutching Hazel's skirt.

'Yes I am.'

'Is it really summer over there now?' asked the other.

Hazel nodded, feeling more than a little intimidated.

'Okay, girls, let's not scare Hazel off before she's even sat down,' said Joe's mum, appearing at Hazel's side. 'I'm glad you could make it, dear,' she said, squeezing Hazel's arm.

'Thank you for inviting me.'

'Where's your friend, Sophie?'

'Oh, she ended up going to visit her aunty in Cornwall.'

'Well, what can I get you to drink? Fancy trying our world-famous eggnog?'

'Sounds great – yes, please.'

'Hazel.'

Turning, Hazel spied Joe heading towards her with his wide grin. 'Merry Christmas,' he said.

Hazel burst out laughing. 'Oh, Joe,' she said. 'You didn't.'

'What?' Joe said, looking down at his pale blue t-shirt with *Los Angeles Lakers* printed across the front. 'It's my favourite.'

'Really?'

He slipped his arms around her waist. 'Absolutely.'

For a moment they just looked at each other, then Joe ducked his head quickly and his lips brushed hers. Taking her hand, he led her to her seat.

Hazel greeted Maggie's husband and the others sitting around the table. Everyone was so welcoming and friendly, she immediately relaxed. Joe was right: she'd bought into the stereotype of the British being reserved when they were nothing of the sort. Glancing around the pub, she observed families and friends sitting around tables laughing and eating and drinking, their cheeks flushed and their eyes bright. She thought of her own family – her grandfather in particular. He would be asleep now, Christmas Day already behind him. She'd spoken to him that morning and he'd sounded happy. He was at the farm with her dad and brothers. They'd had a barbecue lunch on the deck then driven to the coast for a swim. Gramps had said the water was warm and Hazel could hear her brothers in the background yelling, 'It was freezing!'

Hazel didn't wish to be back in New Zealand, even though she felt a million miles away. As Joe draped an arm over her shoulders, she turned to look at him. She was exactly where she wanted to be.

AUTHOR'S NOTE

Twelve years ago I stumbled across a slim book in my local library titled *Shipwrecks Around New Zealand*. I wasn't searching for the book, it wasn't even the type of book I would normally pick up, but somehow the book found me. I opened it at random, and as I read of the remarkable events surrounding the sinking of the MS *Rangitane* during World War II, my heart began to race. I remember thinking, *One day I am going to write about this*. And here, finally, after much trial and error and gnashing of teeth, I have.

In the early hours of 27 November 1940, less than forty-eight hours after leaving Auckland harbour, the *Rangitane* was attacked by German raiders. Several passengers and crew were killed and the rest were taken as prisoners before the Germans sent a torpedo through the *Rangitane*, sinking it quickly.

Just prior to the attack, Captain Upton had transmitted a warning message to the New Zealand and Australian coastguards:

suspicious vessels had been sighted. Unfortunately, by the time aircraft reached the coordinates transmitted by the now-destroyed *Rangitane* radio, all that remained were some floating pounds of butter and an oil slick.

No-one knew of the fate of the passengers and crew on board the *Rangitane* until Christmas Day, when remarkable news travelled around the world that survivors from the *Rangitane* were alive and awaiting rescue from a small, remote island in the Pacific Ocean. Among them was a group of women who had been returning to England after escorting children to Australia and New Zealand as part of the short-lived, contentious Children's Overseas Reception Board (CORB) evacuation scheme.

While I have drawn on many resources during my research for *The Girl from London*, two in particular have been invaluable. I am eternally grateful to the musical maestro Meta Maclean for writing *The Singing Ship*, a fascinating chronicle of her experience as a CORB escort aboard the *Batory*. And I suspect *The Girl from London* would never have seen the light of day were it not for the serendipitous finding in a rare bookshop of the incredible memoir *Prison Life on a Pacific Raider*, written by two brave, adventurous CORB nurses, Betsy Sandbach and Geraldine Edge.

As a parent, I have tried to imagine how difficult it would have been to send my children to the other side of the world, not knowing when or if I would see them again. I wonder how the children (some as young as five!) must have felt on leaving their homes and their families and sailing across dangerous waters to live in a foreign country with strangers. It's impossible to fathom.

So often when we think of war we reflect on the pain and sacrifice of men fighting bravely for their country. Yet, in writing this story, I'm reminded that women and children suffered, fought bravely and made sacrifices too.

ACKNOWLEDGEMENTS

A massive thank you to my publisher (and extraordinary editor), Kate Stephenson, for believing in this story. I am grateful for your guidance, spot-on editing advice and general awesomeness. To all the wonderful team at Hachette Aotearoa New Zealand – Mel Winder, Suzy Maddox, Tania Mackenzie-Cooke, Sacha Beguely, Dom Visini, Alison Shucksmith, Maiko Lenting-Lu, Sam Barge, Sharon Galey, Ellie Kyrke-Smith and Cyanne Alwanger – thank you for everything you have done to bring my novel to life (and into readers' hands). I feel so lucky to be able to work with such a fantastic group of people. On that note, thanks to the Mighty Moas! I'm thrilled to be in for the ride with you guys.

Special shout-out to my amazing copyeditor, Ali Lavau. I am truly in awe of your skills. Thank you for your insights and thoroughness! And thank you to Christa Moffitt for a stunning cover design – it is more beautiful than I could have imagined.

Humungous thanks go to my family and friends who have supported me in my writing successes, failures, and the many peaks and troughs in between. I was going to name you all, but then I panicked because I didn't want to accidentally leave anyone out. Just know I mean YOU.

To Brea, Rachel and Laura at The Booklover Bookshop — thanks for loving books as much as I do, and for giving me a boost (and time off) when I needed it. And epic thanks to the sales reps, customers, authors and other bookish types who I've been lucky enough to meet. I am so lucky and proud to own an independent bookstore, and I couldn't imagine a better job or a better bunch of book-loving people to hang out with.

To Mike, I'm getting emotional thinking of all the many big and small ways you have helped me with my writing journey. Thanks for your constant love and support, and for refraining from giving me advice, even though I know you wanted to!

Finally, to my children, Grace, Sophie and George. Thank goodness I never had to go through the agony of deciding whether or not to send you to live on the other side of the world in order to escape a war. I don't think I could have done it. You are not only the best company, you're also the best three people I know. Thank you for being outrageously kind, fun, talented, imaginative, thoughtful, helpful humans. Thank you for giving me time and space, and for doing all the jobs around the house! Is it weird that I like hanging out with three teenagers this much? I hope you will see this book as proof that any dream is possible. It might just take awhile. xx

The Girl from London is Olivia's first historical fiction novel. She is the author of two contemporary novels, *A Way Back to Happy* and *A Bumpy Year*. Olivia lives with her family in Auckland, New Zealand, and runs her own business, The Booklover Bookshop, an independent bookstore in the seaside suburb of Milford. To find out more about Olivia and for book club notes, go to oliviaspooner.com